What merrier way to say Seasons Greetings than with this heartwarming collection of holiday love stories by three of your favorite authors—

Janet Dailey, Jennifer Greene and Patricia Gardner Evans

And as a special treat, the authors share their favorite holiday recipes and personal stories about their most cherished gifts and the meaning of Christmas at their houses.

Happy Holidays, from *our* house,

The staff of Silhouette Books,

Janet Dailey, Jennifer Greene and Patricia Gardner Evans on their most cherished Christmas gifts

Janet Dailey

When I was a child, I received a teddy bear for Christmas. I promptly named him Toby. He soon became one of my most treasured possessions. In fact, Toby was the inspiration for the very first story I ever wrote back in grade school. It was called "Toby, the Bad Teddy Bear." From that day on, I was hooked on writing. Today, my ragged and worn Toby sits proudly on the bookshelves in my office.

Jennifer Greene

My husband and I have a farm in southwestern Michigan, and in the summer of 1980 we were hit with a tornado. Our children were tiny then—Jennifer was only a year old, and Ryan just three. For months after this traumatic storm, we were so busy rebuilding that we barely had time to lift our heads. When Christmas rolled around…well, it just wasn't a year we could afford generous presents, but I can still remember the exact moment we turned on the tree lights. It hit me stronger than tears. We were all right. We had each other. No matter how devastating that tornado, we hadn't lost anything that mattered. In fact, no one could have given me a richer or more precious gift than what I had— my family, safe and sound, and the joy of being together with those I love most.

Patricia Gardner Evans

Once I found an interesting tree knot while picnicking with my grandparents. When we got home, I was disappointed to learn that my grandfather had tossed it out, not knowing I wanted it. The knot reappeared at Christmas, transformed by him into a lamp. My grandparents had forgotten my other presents, but my invariably graceless tongue for once found the right thing to say, telling him that it didn't matter. I had the lamp. Almost forty years later, I still have the lamp and remember a wonderful man every time I look at it.

Santa's Little Helpers

Janet Dailey

Jennifer Greene

Patricia Gardner Evans

Silhouette Books

Published by Silhouette Books
America's Publisher of Contemporary Romance

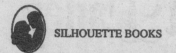 SILHOUETTE BOOKS

SANTA'S LITTLE HELPERS

Copyright © 1995 by Harlequin Books S.A.

ISBN 0-373-48311-2

The publisher acknowledges the copyright holders of the individual works as follows:
THE HEALING TOUCH
Copyright © 1995 by Janet Dailey
TWELFTH NIGHT
Copyright © 1995 by Jennifer Greene
COMFORT AND JOY
Copyright © 1995 by Patricia Gardner Evans

CONTENTS

THE HEALING TOUCH
Janet Dailey

Christmas at Janet Dailey's house:

Christmas is my favorite time of year. I love everything about it—the strings of twinkling lights and acres of garlands, the mobs at the malls and the stores, the cookies and candy and fudge, the presents under the tree, and the Christmas cards from friends you haven't seen in years, the old Christmas songs and the new, the parties and the family gatherings, the smiles and the bah-humbugs.

Christmas starts early at our house. The first part of November we haul the decorations out of storage. (We have tons of them.) Believe it or not, it takes almost three weeks to get all of them up, both inside and out. You can't turn around without bumping into Christmas at our house. Every room gets the Christmas treatment.

At the center of all our decorations is a modest collection of crèches, or Nativity scenes, that Bill and I have acquired during out travels over the years. In fact, it is the only thing we collect. I think it's the perfect way to remember the true reason for the season—the birth of our Savior Jesus Christ.

May this Christmas and all your holidays be blessed with the fullness of God's love.

Janet Dailey

Chapter One

"I'm sorry to bother you at this time of night, Dr. Barclay. But we have an emergency here at Casa Colina." The male voice on the phone had a gentle Irish brogue, but not gentle enough to soften the blow. Rebecca Barclay groaned as the words sank into her half-asleep brain. *No...no more emergencies tonight, please!* Rolling over in bed, she peered at the clock on her nightstand. Three o'clock in the morning.

"What seems to be the problem, Mr. O'Brien?" she asked, hoping it would be something simple. Normally, Rebecca would have been pleased to hear from Neil O'Brien, one of her favorite people. He was quite proficient at animal husbandry himself, and Rebecca knew he would never call her unless he truly needed her services. She just didn't want to be needed...at least not for the rest of the night.

"I've got myself a fine little nanny goat here who's tryin' to deliver her first kid," the Irishman replied. "But surely, somethin's amiss. She's been at it for hours, and she's made no headway at all."

A birthing. A *goat* birthing. Rebecca groaned again. Something simple, huh? Wishful, but naive thinking on her part. It was some sort of cruel cosmic rule that no call was ever simple at three o'clock in the morning.

With an effort she forced a note of cheer into her voice. False, perhaps, but cheerful all the same. "I'd be glad to come out, Mr. O'Brien. I'll be there as quickly as I can."

There's no rest for the weary, Rebecca thought as she hung up the phone and heaved her aching body out of bed. She had only been asleep for an hour. One lousy hour since the last emergency.

At midnight she had been wakened by a frantic phone call—a distraught cat owner who lived across town and far out in the country. As she had tried to find her way in the darkness, Rebecca had decided that the area was so rural it could be considered a suburb of the boondocks.

Weighing in at almost thirty pounds, sleek and shiny black, the feline named Butch had more closely resembled a panther than a common house cat. Her next two hours had been spent reassembling the tomcat's mangled ears. Having lost a skirmish with an even bigger and meaner male, Butch had been in a foul mood. Rebecca's hands and arms still stung from his scratches, and her left thumb bore several holes where he had sunk his cute little fangs into her flesh.

Unfortunately, Rebecca was the only veterinarian in the small town of San Carlos who was willing to do house calls. As a result, she could count on being hauled out of bed several times a week . . . at least.

Exactly why did I want to be a vet? she asked herself as she pulled on her jeans and a plaid flannel shirt that she had only recently draped over a chair nearby. *Wasn't it something about helping animals . . . relieving suffering, healing the wounded?*

Ugh! Altruistic reasons aside, right now she didn't want to see another furry face for at least a month.

Grabbing a favorite old woolen sweater and her case full of pharmaceuticals and surgical instruments, she hurried out to her ancient, battered pickup.

For a brief moment she allowed herself the luxury of pausing to breathe in the sweet smell of the California night. The delicate scent of the star jasmine planted beside her door blended with the heady perfume of the orange blossoms in a nearby grove.

The night air was silent and unusually cool for summer. Her breath frosted, white puffs in the moonlight, as she pulled the sweater more tightly around her and climbed into the truck.

Not a single headlight shone on the highway that ran in front of her house. The town of San Carlos was asleep . . . except for her and Neil O'Brien . . . and, of course, that poor little nanny who was struggling to deliver her first baby.

"I'll be right there, sweetie," Rebecca whispered as she pulled the old jalopy out of her driveway, grinding a gear or two in the process. "Just hang on. Help is on the way."

Ten minutes later, Rebecca arrived at Casa Colina, a lavish estate on the northern edge of town. The enormous house gleamed blue-white in the moonlight, an old-fashioned Spanish hacienda with a red-tiled roof and graceful arches covered with climbing roses.

Rebecca knew the place well. As a child, she had spent many happy hours playing on the estate, exploring the nooks and crannies of the old house, the gardens, barns and orchards. The Flores family had five daughters and she had been friends with them all.

But over the years, the girls had grown up, gone to college, established careers and gotten married. Finally, even the youngest, Gabriella, had left home. Last winter, feeling lost and alone on such a large property, Jose and Rosa Flores had sold Casa Colina and moved to an apartment in town.

Rebecca had been told that the new owners were private people, but she had heard little else about them. Even the standard town gossips seemed in the dark and hungry for tidbits of information about their reclusive neighbors.

She had been pleased to hear that they had chosen to keep Neil O'Brien as their caretaker, and his wife, Bridget, as their housekeeper. After working for the Flores family for twenty years, Neil and Bridget knew more about running Casa Colina than anyone. Rebecca felt a great deal of affection for the couple and enjoyed their company. She admired Neil's skill and compassion with the animals in his care, and he always seemed to have a big smile and a corny joke for everyone he met. Bridget was equally friendly, graciously offering a cup of Irish breakfast tea and queen cakes, as she called her special cupcakes, to visitors at Casa Colina.

Having paid many social calls to the property, Rebecca was intimately familiar with its layout. She didn't bother to go to the house first; Neil would be in the barn with the goat and Bridget would probably be sleeping. So she drove around the front of the house and toward a series of outbuildings in the back.

With her bag in hand, she climbed out of the truck and headed for the stables, where a light shone from one dusty-paned window, throwing a golden glow across the lawns. She rushed inside, hoping she wasn't too late.

O'Brien was kneeling beside a small white nanny goat, who lay on her side in a pile of straw. She was a Nubian, Rebecca's favorite breed of goat, known for its friendly, playful disposition and long, floppy ears. The animal was panting hard, straining with the contractions. But, in spite of her efforts, there was no sign of a new arrival.

With her attention focused on her patient, Rebecca didn't notice the little girl who sat huddled in the corner of a stall. She was hugging her knees, which were drawn up to her chest, her big blue eyes filled with tears.

"How long has she been in hard labor?" Rebecca asked. Kneeling beside the goat, she ran her hand over its bloated belly. She could feel the animal shivering with fear and fatigue; the goat couldn't take much more. But Rebecca felt something else, which gave her hope—the movement of the kid inside. There was still a chance of a positive outcome for both mother and baby.

"She's been at it since yesterday morning," Neil replied, pulling a red kerchief from the pocket of his coveralls. He wiped his brow, which was wet with sweat, despite the coolness of the night. "As you can see for yourself, nothing's happened. I'm thinkin' that somethin' must be tangled up in there."

Rebecca opened her bag and pulled out a tube of antiseptic, lubricating cream. "I believe you're right."

"Since I called you, she's been goin' downhill fast," Neil said, his ruddy, freckled face registering his concern. He looked exhausted, and for the first time, the thought occurred to Rebecca that Neil O'Brien was growing older. When had those lines appeared on his face? When had he lost his youthful vigor? He brushed back a lock of his curly red hair from his forehead—red that was mixed with more silver than Rebecca remembered. "Hilda's a nice little goat," he added, stroking the Nubian's long silky ears. "I'd hate to lose her."

Rebecca heard a sob from the far corner of the barn. Turning around, she peered into the shadows and saw the girl for the first time.

"Hilda's going to die…isn't she, Doctor?" the child asked, tears rolling down her cheeks. "I knew something awful was going to happen. And I was right, it is."

Rebecca walked over to the girl and dropped to one knee beside her in the pile of straw. "My name is Rebecca," she told her. "What's yours?"

"Katie," she said with a sniff.

"Well, Katie, I don't think you need to worry so much about Hilda," Rebecca said, reaching out and gently touching one of the girl's shining black curls, which lay on her shoulder. "I run into this sort of problem all the time. It usually works out just fine."

"Really?" The girl choked back her sobs. "You do it all the time?"

"Ten times yesterday," Rebecca replied with a teasing smile.

The child laughed through her tears. "I don't think it happens *that* much," she said.

"I think you're right. But I think Hilda's going to be fine. You'll see."

Having comforted the child, Rebecca returned to Neil and the goat. She rolled up her sleeves and smeared the antiseptic cream from her fingertips to her elbows. Then she pulled on a pair of long, surgical gloves.

"I'll check and see what's going on in there," she said. "We need to know what we're dealing with."

As Rebecca examined her patient, the animal lay still, too weak to resist. After only a couple of minutes, she had her answer.

"Well, we have twins," she said. "And the first one is a big fellow. He's the one who's holding up the works."

"What are you going to do?" Neil asked.

"I'm going to turn him a bit to get him in the proper position. Then I can ease him out."

As gently as she could, Rebecca performed her task. Hilda seemed to sense that something had changed and, encouraged, she began to bear down again and push with a vengeance.

In only a few minutes, Rebecca delivered the first kid. As she had predicted, he was huge with an especially large head. But he didn't seem any the worse for having gone through his ordeal. He snorted his disapproval as Rebecca aspirated his nose and mouth and wiped his face with a towel.

Grabbing a handful of straw, Neil began to give the youngster a brisk rubdown. Hilda bleated and craned her neck around to get a better look at her newly arrived offspring.

From the corner of her eye, Rebecca watched as Katie slowly left her spot by the wall and inched toward them.

"Is it a boy or a girl?" the child asked. Her tears had evaporated, but her blue eyes were still big and round with wonder.

"It's a billy," Rebecca said. "A fine, strapping fellow. I certainly won't want to fool around with him in another year or so."

Katie looked disappointed. "Oh . . . I was hoping for a girl."

Neil laughed as he pushed the kid toward his mother's face. She sniffed him curiously, then began to give him his first tongue bath. "Poor Katie," he said, "I promised her she could have one of the kids for a pet if it was a nanny."

"Well, there's one more left in there," Rebecca said. "And we'll know soon whether it's your nanny or this billy's brother."

Katie lost her shyness as she scrambled to Rebecca's side and knelt on the straw. Reaching out her small hand, she stroked the goat's belly. "You're okay, Hilda," she said in a soft, soothing voice. "The nice doctor is going to take care of you."

"Yes," said a deep voice from behind them, "it looks like everything is under control."

Rebecca glanced over her shoulder and caught her breath. The man who stood in the doorway was the most knock-down-dead gorgeous guy she had ever seen. With his shining black hair and blue eyes, it was obvious that he was Katie's father. He almost filled the doorway with his broad shoulders, and the room seemed to vibrate with his presence.

But Rebecca didn't have time to think about a handsome man at the moment. As attractive as he was, she had work to do. With its oversize brother no longer an obstruction, the second kid was on its way into the world.

She felt a pang of concern when she saw the baby. It was much smaller than the first, and it seemed limp and lifeless as she eased it out and onto the straw.

Quickly she cleared its nose and mouth, then began to rub its body with the towel. Neil understood the urgency and did the same to its legs.

"Come on, little one," she whispered. "Let's get you going. Breathe for me . . . come on . . ."

She noticed that it was a female and her heart sank. Katie would be crushed if she didn't live.

Just when Rebecca was about to give her CPR, the tiny animal shuddered. She gasped for air, and kicked her hind legs.

"There she goes," Neil said, his face splitting with a wide grin. "You did it, Doc!" Jumping to his feet, he grabbed Katie, lifted her and gave her a bear hug.

"And it's a girl!" Katie said when he set her back on her feet. "It's a little nanny... for *me!*"

"That's right, Katie," Neil said. "A bonny nanny for a bonny lassie."

Hilda bleated and sniffed the second kid as Rebecca presented it to her. The mother wore a relieved and contented expression on her face, her long Nubian ears flopping as she bathed her twins.

Finally, both kids snuggled close to their mother, nuzzling her, seeking her warm milk.

Rebecca sat down in the straw and enjoyed the scene. Moments like this one made it all worthwhile. She had done her job well. Hilda was relieved of her burden. The kids were safe and cozy. Katie and Neil were thrilled with the new arrivals. And Katie's father...

Rebecca turned to see if he was enjoying this warm scene as much as they were, but, to her surprise, he wore a frown on his handsome face.

He took a couple of steps closer to them, studying the second nanny. "That goat is obviously a runt," he said. "I don't think it will make an appropriate pet for a child."

"She is too an appropra...approp...a good pet. I want her!" Katie said. She glared up at her father, her blue eyes angry, but pleading. "And she's *not* a *runt*... whatever that is. If it's bad, she's not one!"

Rebecca had to fight to control her temper. What was wrong with this man? Didn't he have a heart? How could he ruin such a beautiful, happy moment?

"A runt is an animal that is born small and un-healthy," he told his daughter. "They often have things wrong with them, and they're hard to care for. And you don't even know if she'll live."

Rebecca couldn't stay quiet any longer. "Excuse me, Mr.—"

"Stafford," he said. "Michael Stafford."

"Mr. Stafford...I understand your concern about having a healthy pet for your child. But even though this nanny is a bit small, there's no reason to assume she won't live."

"Oh, really?" His blue eyes were cold and angry as he stared down at her. Apparently, he resented her of-fering her opinion without being asked. "And can you guarantee that, Doctor?" he snapped.

Rebecca couldn't understand the bitter tone of his voice. Why was he reacting this way? "Of course I can't guarantee the animal will stay healthy, Mr. Stafford," she said. "Life doesn't offer guarantees like that."

"It certainly doesn't," he said.

Again Rebecca heard the anger in his voice. What had happened to this man to make him so cold?

Looking down at Katie, Rebecca could see the same pain mirrored in her blue eyes. It seemed to run in the family.

"Mr. Stafford," she said, trying again to sound more patient and understanding than she felt. "I truly believe this goat is healthy, in spite of her small size. If you'll let Katie have her as a pet, I promise to help all I can. I'll teach your daughter how to take care of the goat. If anything goes wrong, all you have to do is call me, and I'll be here right away."

"Please, Daddy?" Katie pleaded. She ran to her father and, grabbing his hand in both of hers, she said, "Dr. Rebecca thinks it's okay. Let me have her. Please, please, please."

Michael Stafford said nothing for a long time as he looked down at his daughter, who was tugging at his hand. Rebecca couldn't understand how he could resist those big blue eyes. *She* certainly couldn't.

He couldn't either. Gently, he pulled his hand away from hers and turned toward the door. "Well," he said as he walked away, "if the good doctor thinks it's okay, it must be okay. I'm sure she knows more about these things than I do. I only hope she's right this time."

Rebecca wished he hadn't sounded so sarcastic, but as long as he had given his permission and Katie had her baby goat, that was all that counted.

Neil helped her as she gathered her things and placed them in her bag. Her work here was finished. At least, for the moment.

Having said her goodbyes, she turned to leave, but paused at the door to take one more look at Hilda and her kids, Katie and Neil. Katie had her arms around the baby nanny's neck and was saying sweet things in her ear.

Yes, Rebecca thought, *I knew there was some reason why I became a vet. And this is it.*

The moment Rebecca stepped through the door of the Hair Affair beauty salon, she was accosted by a furry missile named Twinkle. Twinkle had been white the last time Rebecca had visited, but this morning the dog's coat was a strange shade of lavender.

Rebecca had seen a lot of animals in her career, but she had never seen a purple Pekinese. She had her first clue as to what might have caused the mysterious skin irritation that Twinkle's mistress had described earlier on the telephone.

"Oh, Twink," Rebecca said as she dropped to one knee and stroked the dog's ears, "what has Betty Sue done to you now?"

The dog simply whined in reply and rolled her eyes pitifully.

"I know, I know..." Rebecca accepted the wet kiss on her cheek. "I've tried, Twink, but you know how Betty Sue is. By the way, where is your mistress?" she added, looking around the empty salon.

A door in the back of the salon swung open and a young woman in a hot-pink uniform entered, bringing with her the smell of permanent wave solution and nail polish. For some reason, Rebecca wasn't surprised to see that Betty Sue had dyed her own bleached, platinum blond hair the same shade of lavender. Nothing about Betty Sue shocked Rebecca anymore. But Betty had been born and raised in the heart of Hollywood, so Rebecca tried to take that into consideration. The poor girl probably couldn't help herself.

"Hi there, sweet thing," she exclaimed, hurrying over to give Rebecca a warm hug. "It's our very favorite doctor, huh, Twinkle Toes...."

"Don't give me that 'favorite doctor' bull," Rebecca said, shaking her head in mock disgust. "You're just trying to butter me up because you know I'm upset with you."

"Upset?" Betty Sue batted her false lashes. "You're upset with me? Whatever for?"

"You didn't hear a thing I said when I was here last time."

"Why, that's not true. Of course I heard you. I—"

"Then you didn't listen. I told you to stop doing weird things to this poor innocent creature."

"But... but I..." she stammered. "I'd never do anything to Twinkle Toes that I wouldn't do to myself."

Rebecca looked Betty Sue up and down, taking in the multiprocessed hair, the porcelain nails, the pounds of trowel-applied makeup. Betty wasn't what you'd call a natural beauty. That list of things she "wouldn't do" to herself or her long-suffering pet must be pretty short.

"Betty Sue, you have to stop this nonsense. I'm tired of coming over here to treat problems that *you* have caused. You airbrushed this dog's toenails and—"

"But she liked that. She was having fun."

"She was *high*, Betty Sue. Twinkle was buzzing on the fumes! And remember when you gave her corn-rows down her back with those beads and feathers?"

"Well, I thought—"

"I had to cut them out. I had to shave the poor little thing. She ran around looking like a scalped rat for an entire winter."

"But I knitted her a little sweater to wear."

"You didn't finish it until spring."

"My heart was in the right place."

Rebecca stifled a smile. "Then maybe you'd better start thinking with your head." She bent down and picked up the dog. Running her hand backward over her fur, Rebecca exposed the red, irritated skin. "Look at that! It's a reaction to that stupid purple dye you used."

"I did a patch test first, just like it said in the in-structions!" Betty whined, refusing to meet Rebecca's eyes. "I really did, and it turned out fine."

"Those instructions were for a *person*, Betty Sue, not a Pekinese. I'm not kidding, you have to *stop* doing this, or I'm going to turn you in for cruelty to ani-mals."

Betty Sue's chin began to quiver slightly, and her lower lip protruded in a pout. Rebecca felt a wave of relief; finally, she might have gotten through to her.

"I'll give you some shampoo that's medicated. It'll help stop the itching and keep the skin from getting infected. She won't smell very nice afterward, but—"

"Don't worry," Betty interjected, "I won't put perfume on her. No matter how much I want to. I'll resist."

"Attagirl."

As Rebecca took the medication from her bag and wrote her instructions on the label, Betty Sue held Twinkle and cooed into her ear.

"Does her love her mommy?" she asked the dog in a nauseatingly sweet tone. "Yes, yes, her does. Her knows Mommy was just trying to make her look beautiful. Twinkle Toes lo-o-o-oves her mommy."

Betty Sue set the dog on the floor and took the bottle from Rebecca. "By the way," she said, a smile on her perfectly outlined, carefully blotted crimson lips, "I heard something... but I don't know if it's true."

"What's that?" Rebecca asked, trying to look uninterested as she snapped her bag shut. Betty Sue was a hopeless gossip, and like most people, Rebecca found the idea of gossip appalling and the reality fascinating.

"I heard you've been spending a lot of time at Casa Colina lately... with that hunk widower, Michael Stafford."

"Then you heard wrong," Rebecca said, trying to stifle her irritation. Gossip that was about *her* wasn't nearly so fascinating. "I was out there *one* night, and it was business, not pleasure. Believe me. I had my hand in a goat's rear end, up to my elbow. That's not what I call a good time.''

"Oh . . . I . . . oh.''

Rebecca was pleased to see that she had finally managed to shock even Betty Sue Wilcox. She considered it quite an accomplishment to shock someone from Hollywood.

"But, you *did* meet Michael Stafford, didn't you?'' Betty was still trying to squeeze something juicy from the rather dry story.

"Yes, I met him. I saw him with my own two eyes. I gazed, spellbound, upon his handsome face for . . . heck . . . probably all of three or four minutes.''

Betty Sue brightened. "And is it true, what they say? Is he really that good-looking?''

"He's stunning, he's breathtakingly gorgeous.'' She picked up her bag and slung it under her arm. "He's also very cranky, and, personally, I didn't like him . . . not one little bit.''

Without another word, Rebecca spun around on her heel and marched out the door, leaving Betty Sue with her mouth hanging open.

But Betty soon recovered and scooped Twinkle up. "I just don't think I believes her, does you?'' she asked in a singsong, baby voice. "Mommy thinks Dr. Rebecca likes Mr. Michael more than she's letting on. Don't you think so, too, Twinkle? Yes . . . Mommy knows true love when she sees it.''

Betty Sue watched until the decrepit pickup had disappeared around the corner. "There, there, she's all gone. Now, let's go try out that new tooth-whitener stuff Mommy bought at the drugstore. Your little choppers have been looking pretty yellow lately. Yes, they have. And we can't have that, can we, sweetie pie? No, sirree. It worked really great on Mommy's teeth. See...."

Chapter Two

For the next week, Rebecca couldn't stop thinking about Katie, her father and the baby goat. Finally, she gave in to her worries and dropped by Casa Colina.

The warm sun made her feel lazy as she got out of her pickup and walked up to the house. It was the perfect morning to just sit in the sun and sip ice tea.

She sighed to herself. No such luck. The busy life of a vet didn't offer her much time to be lazy.

She found Katie and the kid romping in the backyard. Playing a game of tag, they seemed to be enjoying each other's company.

"Hi, Dr. Rebecca!" Katie shouted as she ran toward her.

"Hello, Katie." Rebecca reached down to pet the goat. It lowered its tiny head and butted against her fist. "I see you've been teaching her bad habits," Rebecca teased.

"I didn't have to teach her that," Katie said with a giggle. "She seemed to know it all by herself."

"Yes, goats are little rascals. You have to teach them to behave. How is she doing?"

"Oh, fine," Katie said. "I named her Rosebud. But I call her Rosie."

"Rosie...um..." Rebecca said thoughtfully. She studied the little goat, its silky white coat, its long floppy ears, blue eyes and pink nose. "Rosebud. Yes, I like that name. It's perfect for her."

Katie beamed at the praise. "I'm out of school now for the summer," she said. "We play all the time. She's my best friend."

Rebecca looked around for any sign of another human being. In the distance, Neil was digging in the garden, and his wife, Bridget, stood in the kitchen window.

But Katie's father was nowhere in sight. And Rebecca was sorry to see that Katie had no other children to play with.

"So, it's just you and Rosie?" she asked the girl. "No people friends to play with?"

The girl looked sad for a moment, then shook her head. Her black curls bounced and shone in the sunlight. "Nope. Just me and Rosie. I don't have any other friends."

"Don't you ever invite the girls from school to come over?" Rebecca asked. She thought of all the wonderful times she had shared with the Flores girls here at the Casa.

"I used to have friends over to play," Katie said. She wouldn't look up at Rebecca as she bent to scratch behind Rosie's ear. "But that was before. You know... when we lived in Los Angeles and my mommy was still alive."

An unexpectedly sharp pain shot through Rebecca. The pain of loss that was always so close to her heart.

About the time she dared to hope the wound might have healed a bit, something pricked it, and the pain returned as deep and searing as ever.

"I'm sorry, Katie," she said. She stroked the girl's shining hair. "It's hard to lose someone you love. Believe me, I know."

Katie looked up at her with curious eyes. "Really? Did someone you love die, too?"

Closing her eyes for a moment against the memories, Rebecca found them there, playing on the screen of her mind. The emergency call in the middle of the night—a dog at the Humane Society, hit by a car, in need of immediate attention. Tim volunteering to go. "You've had a tough day, Becky. I'll take care of it. Just go back to sleep." Hours later, the other call—from the Highway Patrol.

"Yes," she said, opening her eyes. "I lost my husband. He was a veterinarian, too. We had a practice together. We'd only been married two years."

"Was he sick for a long time?" Katie asked.

So, Rebecca thought, *that's how her mother died. A long illness.*

"No," she said. "He was in a car accident."

"Oh..." Katie nodded in understanding. "That must have been awful. You didn't even get to say goodbye."

"No, I didn't," Rebecca agreed. "I think that was the worst part."

Katie looked away, as though remembering. "My daddy told me to tell my mommy goodbye," she said. "But I cried, and I wouldn't do it. I was just a dumb seven-year-old. Now I'm eight, and I'm a lot more grown-up."

"Yes, I can see that," Rebecca said with a smile. "But you shouldn't blame yourself. Everyone finds it hard to tell someone they love goodbye. I don't think you were a dumb seven-year-old. I think you were just really scared, that's all."

Katie's eyes brimmed with tears, but she smiled up at Rebecca. "That's nice," she said. "Maybe that's all it was."

"I'm sure of it."

"Want to see something really neat?" Katie asked, suddenly lighthearted.

"Sure, what is it?" Rebecca said, happy to change the subject.

"Just wait until you see this. It's really funny."

The girl ran away to a nearby plum tree and picked a piece of the fruit. Rebecca had a feeling she knew what the "something" was. But she didn't say so.

"Watch this!" Katie said as she held out the plum to Rosebud.

Rebecca had seen goats eat peaches and plums before. She knew what was coming.

The goat took the fruit and rolled it around in her mouth for a couple of seconds. Then she spat out the seed...perfectly clean. As the pit sailed through the air, Katie cackled with glee.

"Did you see that?" she said. "She gets *all* the plum off the seed and spits it really far!"

"Most impressive," Rebecca agreed. "A lot of boys I know would love to be able to spit like that."

Katie giggled again, and Rebecca thought what a beautiful child she was. Why didn't her father take more of an interest in her?

"So, has your dad seen this?" Rebecca asked.

Katie's smile disappeared. "No. He's almost never around. He works a lot at his car place in Los Angeles."

"Car place?"

"Yeah. He sells really expensive cars that he gets from Europe." Katie looked away, as though remembering again. "He used to be home a lot. He used to play with me and Mommy and make us pancakes in the morning. But now he just works all the time."

Rebecca recalled the months after her husband's accident, the long hours of trying to escape into her job. It hadn't worked. Sooner or later, she had to stop working and go to bed. Alone. And then she couldn't help remembering.

"I miss my mom," Katie said. "But I miss my dad, too. I wish he was around more."

Rebecca felt a rush of anger toward the man who could neglect this child. When Tim had died, she had been so lonely. If Tim had only left her with a beautiful reminder of himself...like Katie, she certainly wouldn't have deserted the child, no matter how much pain she had suffered.

"Have you told your father how you feel?" Rebecca asked.

"No." Katie shrugged her small shoulders. "I don't want to make him feel bad. He's sad enough already."

"Maybe you should tell him," Rebecca said gently. "Perhaps he doesn't know that you're feeling sad, too. It always helps if you have someone to feel sad with."

Katie considered her words for a moment. Then she shook her head. "No. I'll just talk to Rosebud. She doesn't have as much to worry about as my dad does."

Rebecca glanced at her watch. She had another call to make. "I have to go now, Katie. But I'll come by again soon to check on you two."

Katie seemed disappointed, but she nodded. "Okay. Thanks for coming over." She blushed and stared down at her purple and pink sneakers. "I mean...Rosie likes you and she was glad to see you."

"I like her, too," Rebecca replied. "Very much."

Rebecca said her goodbyes and walked around to the front of the house. Just as she was about to step into her pickup, a late-model, dark green Jaguar XJ12 pulled into the drive.

Michael Stafford climbed out, looking as striking as he had the other night. He wore a charcoal designer suit and a white silk shirt. His dark hair was combed back. But one lock had escaped and hung boyishly over his forehead.

The look in his blue eyes was anything but boyish. He gave her a curt nod of his head, but no smile of greeting.

"Good morning, Mr. Stafford," Rebecca said. Her tone was much more friendly than she felt.

"What's wrong?" he asked. "Has something happened to the goat?"

"No, not at all," she assured him. "I was just dropping by to say hello to Katie."

He looked relieved, but still angry. "I haven't changed my mind, Dr. Barclay. I believe it was a mistake to let her keep that mangy goat," he said. "My daughter is obsessed with the thing. If it were to get sick or..."

"Yes?" she asked, her temper rising.

"Or die, she would be crushed. And I can tell you now, Doctor, I'll blame you if it happens."

That did it. Rebecca could no longer control her tongue. She knew she was about to say things she would regret later.

"Mr. Stafford," she said, gritting her teeth, "your daughter needs a living being to love. Maybe she wouldn't be so obsessed with a goat if her father spent a little time with her."

She turned and stomped back to her truck. "And by the way," she added as she climbed in and slammed the door behind her, "Rosie isn't mangy. *None* of *my* patients have mange, thank you!"

"And *I*, Dr. Barclay..." he shouted back "...am not *cranky!*"

Oh, Lord, she thought, *someone told him what I said!* She only hoped they hadn't told him the rest. The last thing she wanted was for him to think she found him at all attractive. She'd get Betty Sue for this.

Tires squealing, she pulled away. In her rearview mirror she could see him standing in a cloud of dust...*her* dust, his mouth hanging open.

"So there, Mr. Stafford!" she said, still embarrassed, but satisfied with her dramatic exit. "Just put *that* in your pipe and smoke it!"

Michael slammed his desk drawer closed, caught the end of his thumb in the handle and yelled out a curse. Instantly, there was silence in the showroom, the conversation between his secretary and a salesman coming to an abrupt halt.

A second later, Mrs. Abernathy peeked around the corner into his office, a look of concern on her face. "Have you hurt yourself...again, Michael?" she asked in a soft, grandmotherly voice. Usually, he would have been flattered by the attention, but her words had a distinctly sarcastic undertone. And, judging by the ever-so-slight smirk she was wearing, she must have been thinking he was a child who had just injured himself while throwing a temper tantrum.

Where the hell would she have gotten an idea like that?

"I'm fine, Mrs. Abernathy," he replied with equally saccharine sweetness. "I just flattened the better part of my thumb. I had two major deals fall through before noon. My pastrami on rye was soggy and dripping with Dijon mustard. I hate Dijon mustard. And I just had the pleasure of informing Mr. Hillman that we can't find the parts we need to repair the brakes on his Silver

Ghost. He intends to sue us. But, other than that, I'm having a perfectly *wonderful* day. Thank you for asking."

Instead of turning around and leaving, as he was hoping she would, she walked into his office and sat on one of the overstuffed chairs beside his desk. She adjusted her glasses, cleared her throat and folded her hands demurely in her lap—the picture of feminine grace.

How deceiving, he thought. *Here it comes. She's going to give it to me with both barrels.*

Mrs. Abernathy had worked for Michael for the past five years, and he knew all of her maneuvers. Not that the knowledge did him any good. With Mrs. Abernathy, forewarned wasn't necessarily forearmed. She always initiated, directed and won these little debates of theirs. Sometimes he wondered who worked for whom.

"Okay, what's the matter with you?" she asked, peering at him over the top of her wire frames.

"Excuse me?"

"Don't give me that. You know exactly what I'm talking about. All day you've been acting like a cantankerous grizzly bear, hibernating here in your cave and growling at anybody who gets within ten yards of you. I'm not surprised your deals fell through, you smashed your thumb and alienated Mr. Hillman. I'd sue you, too, if I were him."

He stared at her for a moment, his mouth working up and down as he searched for a suitable retort. "And I suppose the sandwich was my fault, too?"

She shrugged. "Hey, it's karma. You're sending all that negativity out into the universe and—"

"Oh, give me a break. Do you really think that the great cosmos cares if I yell at a few people? Do you really think that some yokel at the deli smearing Dijon mustard on my sandwich is an act of divine retribution? Get real."

She shook her head sadly. "See what I mean? Negative vibes. You're radiating all this hostility and—"

"I'm tired," he snapped. "And...and maybe I'm sick. I'm just having a bad day, okay?"

"Well, I'm tired and sick, too. Sick and tired of you being so grouchy. And, thanks to you, *everyone* here at Le Concours d'Excellence is having a bad day. Enough already."

Her authoritative tone didn't leave much room for argument. It was all he could do not to duck his head and blubber, "Yes, ma'am, sorry, ma'am."

Instead, he assumed a semiapologetic look and said, "Okay, point taken. I'll work on it."

Her face softened. "Thanks," she said. Leaning across the desk, she rested one hand on his forearm. "Come on, Mike, what is it? What's wrong...really?"

Warming to the genuine concern in her voice, he found himself opening up a bit. She was a feisty old broad, but she was also a sweetheart and a good listener. During his wife's sickness, and afterward, she had been there for him. Every day and some long, dark nights. She was truly a good friend.

"I had a run-in with this veterinarian yesterday," he said. "The one I told you about before."

"The woman who delivered your goats? The one you said filled out her jeans nicely but was difficult?"

"Yeah, that's the one."

Had he really told Abernathy that bit about the jeans? He didn't think so. He could recall saying it to one of his mechanics. Maybe she had been eavesdropping. Wouldn't be the first time.

"So, what were you two fighting about yesterday?" she asked.

"She just said some things that she had no right to say. Stuff about Katie and me...and..."

"And?"

"And about how I don't spend enough time with her."

"Mmm-mmm." She nodded solemnly.

For once, Mrs. Abernathy seemed noncommittal in her response. Michael wasn't sure what to make of it. Usually, she was disturbingly forthright with her opinion.

"She said that Katie was obsessed with the little goat because she needs a living being to love. Can you believe that? She thinks my child's life is so empty that she's got to look to some scrawny little goat for affection."

"And what do you think, Mike?" Mrs. Abernathy said softly as she stared down at her hands, which were still folded demurely in her lap.

"I think that vet's got a big mouth," he replied without thinking.

Mrs. Abernathy said nothing, and her silence was far more telling than any of her lectures.

"And what she said is really bothering me," he added, although the admission cost him dearly, "because... I'm afraid... I'm afraid she's right."

Mrs. Abernathy patted his hand, then squeezed it. "I know you're afraid, Mike. I know what you've been through that made you that way. And I know how much you love Katie. You have a battle going on inside, fear versus love. I'm sure your love for your little girl will win in the end."

Michael was thankful that she had the sensitivity to rise from her seat and walk over to the door. He didn't want her to see the moisture in his eyes, and she knew it. Good ol' Abernathy. She knew when to make a graceful exit.

"Abby," he said, "I hope you're right. Thanks."

"No problem." She paused at the door, bared her teeth, and growled at him. "Don't come out until you're in a better mood," she said.

He nodded.

Sitting alone, staring at the picture of his beautiful daughter in its silver frame on his desk, Michael allowed the emotions to wash over him: the fear, the guilt, the love. She looked so much like her mother. So much.

He reached out and with one finger traced the soft line of her cheek. "Oh, Katie," he whispered. "I need you, too, sweetheart."

But the moment he uttered the words, the anxiety rose in him, building until he felt it would squeeze his throat and suffocate him.

He needed her. That was the problem. After losing her mother, he was so afraid. He needed her far too much. That was why he had to guard his heart. Michael Stafford knew his own limitations all too well. And he knew he could never stand to love and lose like that again... *never* again.

Autumn arrived in its usual California fashion. Except for the dry Santa Ana winds, the occasional brushfire and the calendar on her wall, Rebecca couldn't tell it was fall. The month of September and the Christmas holidays were the only times of the year when she wished she lived somewhere other than Southern California. In September she found herself longing for a New England autumn, the brightly colored foliage and the smell of burning leaves scenting the crisp air. At Christmas she wished she could see the elaborate decorations on Fifth Avenue in New York City and skate at the foot of the giant tree in Rockefeller Center.

But most of the time, she was perfectly content with her lot in life and the quaint little oceanside town of San Carlos. It felt like home.

One community tradition that she particularly enjoyed was the county fair. As the local vet, she was always asked to judge the dog, cat and rabbit shows.

Handing out the blue ribbons was the high point of her year.

She arrived at the fair early on Saturday morning and stood in the center of the hustling, bustling activity, soaking in the unique ambiance. Sheep, cows, pigs and goats protested loudly with grunts, groans and bleats as children herded them down gangways and into their pens. Women scurried from tent to tent, carrying prize flowers, cakes and pies and needlework of all kinds, many bearing ribbons of distinction.

In the Quonset hut, some of the local men displayed their woodworking and leather crafts, miniature train sets, and homegrown vegetables of outrageous proportions.

Seeing dozens of familiar faces, Rebecca greeted almost everyone she met. In a town as small and intimate as San Carlos, most of the citizens knew one another—by reputation, if not by name. The gossip grapevine kept everyone informed.

Just as Rebecca was nearing the livestock area, she spotted a particularly endearing and familiar face. Katie Stafford was clinging to the end of a small, white, leather bridle. At the other end was a transformed Rosebud. The little nanny was decked out with pink ribbons, silver bells and pale blue bows in her tail and around her neck. The goat was behaving quite well—for a goat—as she pranced proudly along behind her mistress.

But most surprising of all, Rebecca saw Michael Stafford walking beside his daughter and her pet, looking almost as proud as they did. Wearing a broad, carefree smile, he appeared more relaxed and at peace with himself than Rebecca had ever seen him.

"Hey, Dr. Rebecca! Doctor, over here!" Katie shouted across the way as she bounced up and down and waved her free arm enthusiastically. She turned to her father. "Look, Daddy, over there! It's Dr. Rebecca!"

"So it is," Michael said. He gave Rebecca a dazzling smile that nearly stopped her heart. "How are you today, Doctor?"

"Ah . . . fine, thank you," Rebecca replied, feeling suddenly, inexplicably, shy and awkward.

"See what we won!" Katie said as she held up a bright red ribbon and waved it under Rebecca's nose. "See! See! Rosie won second place!"

"A red ribbon! Good for you, Katie." Rebecca leaned down and scratched the top of the nanny's head. Many animals seemed to be embarrassed when their masters and mistresses "dressed them up" in ribbons and fluff. But Rosie appeared to love being the center of attention. "You deserve a red ribbon," she told Katie. "Rosebud looks *beautiful* today! You did a wonderful job of grooming her."

"Daddy helped." Katie beamed up at her father. "She wouldn't hold still when I was giving her a bath. So he helped me chase her around. She got more water and soap on *us* than we did on *her*. But it was fun."

Rebecca turned to Michael and their eyes met over the top of Katie's head.

For a moment he seemed embarrassed, then he shrugged. "A red ribbon isn't too bad," he said with a silly half grin, "for a mangy runt. Huh, Doc?"

"Not bad at all," Rebecca replied.

Michael looked down at Katie and patted her shoulder. "Why don't you and Rosebud go on ahead without me," he said. "I want to talk to Dr. Barclay for a minute. I'll be right there."

Katie looked from her father to Rebecca and back. A smirk played across her face. "Sure, Dad. No problem," she said knowingly.

As soon as Katie and the goat were gone, Michael seemed even more nervous than before.

"I…ah…" he began. He paused to clear his throat.

She leaned closer to him. "Yes, Mr. Stafford?"

"I wanted to thank you for what you said the other day," he blurted, as though afraid to lose his momentum and courage. "I don't mind telling you, I was furious with you then. But I thought about it, and I decided you were right. I *have* been neglecting Katie."

He drew a deep breath, and Rebecca could see the pain in his eyes. This man was no coward, but he had been deeply hurt. That much was obvious, in his face, his voice, even his body language. Usually, he stood with his arms crossed over his chest, as though guarding his heart.

It was ineffectual armor, Rebecca knew. Unfortunately, there was no way to shield the soul from life's cruelest arrows. She remembered Tim and how she had felt the first year after he died. Yes, she knew all about having your heart pierced when you least expected it. A wound like that took a long, long time to heal, if it ever totally did.

"I was married once," she said, "and I lost my husband, too. I've felt some of what you're going through, and I know it's a really tough time for you."

"Yes, it is. But that doesn't excuse the way I acted about the little goat." He stared down at the ground, unable to meet her eyes. "I don't know why I said what I did and . . ."

His voice trailed away, and Rebecca could see the depth of his guilt on his handsome face. Who would have thought that a face that looked so strong could reflect so much doubt? So much self-condemnation?

"I was afraid for Katie," he admitted, "because I truly thought the goat was unhealthy. I didn't want her to lose something else she loved . . . not so soon after . . ." He paused to gather the rest of his thoughts. "I know I overreacted, but the poor kid has already lost so much."

"I understand." Rebecca stood there, wondering if she should say what was on her mind. She would risk making him angry again, but she felt she should be honest with him.

"Mr. Stafford," she said. "I don't claim to know everything you're feeling, everything you've experienced. But if you overreacted, I think it's only because you love your daughter so much."

"Yes, I do," he said. "And her mother's death was very hard for her."

Rebecca nodded. "I know you're afraid of her suffering another loss, and you don't want her to love something else that could die."

"That's true," he said, obviously touched that she understood. "Living things are just so…so…fragile."

"I know they are. Believe me, in my line of work I know that all too well. But Katie can't close her heart, not even to protect it. She has far too much love to give. And so do you," she added quietly.

He said nothing, but stared down at the sawdust on the ground.

She continued, "To love a living being is to risk getting hurt, because we all die, sooner or later. But there is one thing that's worse than losing someone you love. It's not having anyone to love in the first place."

She couldn't tell how her words had affected him, because he continued to look down at the toes of his boots.

"I know you're afraid to feel your love for Katie," she ventured, knowing she was going too far. But if she was going to upset him, she might as well go all the way. "You know, Michael, there are lots of ways to lose someone…besides death, that is. We can lose someone we love, even though we see them every day…if we allow our fear to get in the way."

He cleared his throat and nodded curtly. "Yes. Of course you're right, Dr. Barclay. But I have to get going. Katie needs help loading Rosebud into the trailer."

Before she could reply, he was gone.

"Way to go, Rebecca," she muttered. "You sure have a great way with people. The true gift of gab. Maybe, in the future, you'd better confine your conversation to fuzzy faced critters who can't talk."

Chapter Three

"Would you like another cup of tea, dear?" Bridget took the cobalt blue china teapot from under its knitted cozy and offered it to Rebecca. "Why don't you finish this one off and I'll brew another."

The offer was too tempting to resist. Bridget made the finest cup of tea in town—claimed it was a special County Kerry blend—and Rebecca had managed only three hours of sleep the night before. A little caffeine was exactly what she needed to get her over the midafternoon slump, and sipping tea here in Bridget's homey kitchen was a great way to infuse.

Besides, Rebecca had never been able to deny Bridget anything. Something about those bright green eyes, the translucent skin and the open, friendly smile made her irresistible. Twenty years ago, when Rebecca first met her, Bridget had been young and beautiful. In spite of the passage of two decades, she was still youthful in spirit and more beautiful than ever.

"Oh, okay," Rebecca said, twisting her own arm behind her back. "If I must, I must."

Bridget placed a plate, which was covered with an ornate silver lid, in the middle of the table. With elegance and flourish, she swept the lid aside, revealing a dozen or so of her famous queen cakes. Rebecca remembered the first time she had ever eaten this particular delicacy. She had been ten years old, visiting the Flores girls, and Bridget had treated them all to a formal afternoon tea.

Dressed in old-fashioned clothes garnered from the attic trunks, the six girls had glided into the dining room, nearly falling off their oversize high heels, tripping on the long hems, dripping with costume jewelry. On their heads they wore an assortment of wide-brimmed bonnets, sporting plumed feathers, silk flowers, satin ribbons and, in Rebecca's case, a rhinestone brooch.

Apparently, Bridget was remembering too. She wiped her hands on her snowy apron, sat across the table from Rebecca and helped herself to the plate of goodies. "You girls always loved my queen cakes," she said. "You were so cute all decked out in those fine old clothes. I miss havin' you around."

"But now you have Katie." Rebecca bit into the cake, which looked like a simple cupcake without frosting, but tasted divine. One bite and you could tell that Bridget didn't spare the butter, fresh eggs or cream. Rebecca tried not to think about the fact that she could almost hear her arteries hardening with every swallow.

"Yes, I have little Katie, and a darlin' child she is, too," Bridget said, a smile softening the lines that had begun to develop around her eyes and mouth. "Have you ever seen eyes so blue...outside of ol' Ireland, that is?"

"No, I haven't. Her eyes are a beautiful color, but I see a lot of sadness in them, too."

Bridget nodded and took a sip of her tea. "Aye, 'tis true. She still grieves so for that dear mother of hers— may she rest in the arms of the angels," she added, crossing herself.

"Did you know Mrs. Stafford?" Rebecca felt a bit guilty for trying to get information out of Bridget. If she wanted to know details, she should probably just ask Michael. But the few encounters she'd had with him had proved that they were neither one particularly good at communicating with the other.

"No, I never laid eyes upon the departed lady," Bridget said, "but I'm sure she must have been a saint, considering the love her husband and daughter still have for her."

"Yes, I'm sure." Rebecca felt a tiny stab of jealousy toward the woman for having been adored by such a wonderful child as Katie and a man like . . .

No, that didn't bear thinking about. She pushed the thoughts aside, feeling horribly guilty for entertaining them even for a moment.

"When does Katie get home from school?" Rebecca asked, glancing up at the cuckoo clock on the wall.

"Any minute now. I'd say your timing was just about right," Bridget said with a knowing grin. "Unless you dropped by to see Mr. Michael. I don't expect to see him for hours yet."

Blushing violently, Rebecca searched her mind for an appropriately adamant denial. Nothing came, so she found herself stammering like an idiot. "Ah...no... I...I never wanted...I don't even...no!"

"Oh, I see." Bridget raised one eyebrow and patted her every-hair-in-place blond French roll. "You haven't taken a fancy to him then?"

"Certainly not."

"Hmmm...now I would have thought...oh well, never mind."

The squeak and whoosh of school bus brakes outside relieved the tension of the moment, and Rebecca silently blessed its arrival.

"Why, there's the darlin' lass now," Bridget said as they both watched through the kitchen window while Katie climbed down from the bus.

"She doesn't look very happy," Rebecca commented, noting how slowly Katie was walking and how her shoulders slumped.

"No, 'tis a terrible shame." Bridget clucked her tongue and shook her head sadly. "A wee thing like that should have someone to play with after school. I try to give her as much attention as I can, but I have my other duties and..."

"You know," Rebecca said, thinking aloud, "I'm not all that busy this afternoon. Do you think she'd enjoy going down to our old swimming hole? The weather's pretty warm."

"Oh, aye! I'm sure she would. What a lovely idea, dear. She's very fond of you. I know she'd be pleased to spend some time with you."

"Do you think it would be okay with Mr. Stafford?" Rebecca was reluctant to mention his name, for fear of more teasing, but he seemed so definite about certain things. She didn't want to find herself locking horns again with him any time soon.

"Well, I don't see why not," Bridget said thoughtfully. "You're a trustworthy adult. And you'll be right here on the property. I think he'd be grateful that you paid attention to her."

The back door opened, and Katie shuffled in. Without looking up, she tossed her books on the counter and placed her Beauty and the Beast lunch pail in the sink.

"Hi, Mrs. Bridget," she said listlessly.

"Welcome home, love," Bridget replied. "Look who's here."

The instant Katie saw Rebecca, she was transformed into a bouncy, animated eight-year-old, a bright smile lighting her face. "Dr. Rebecca!" she shouted, running across the room to the table where Rebecca sat.

For a moment Rebecca thought she was going to receive a hug, but at the last moment, shyness seemed to intervene. Katie stopped abruptly a few feet away and stood with her hands behind her back, awkward but happy.

"Hi, Katie. It's nice to see you again."

Katie blushed and shuffled her scuffed lavender and pink sneakers. Then a look of horror crossed her face. "Oh, no, you're not here because of Rosie, are you? Is she okay? Are Hilda and Pepe all right?"

"The goats are just fine," she said. Reaching out, she placed her hand on the girl's shoulder. "I came to see you."

"Really?" She looked relieved and happy, but a tad dubious.

"Really, really." Rebecca waited as the hint of a frown melted. "But who's Pepe?"

"He's Hilda's other baby... the boy. You know, Rosebud's brother. He's a *lot* bigger than Rosie. Mr. Neil won't let me play with him. He says Pepe's too rough."

"I'm sure he's right." Rebecca donned a business-like face. "What I'd like to know is this—do you have plans for the next couple of hours? Because if you don't..."

"Wow, this is really neat!"

Rebecca could tell by the glow on Katie's face and the enthusiasm in her voice that the secret swimming hole was a success.

"The Flores girls and I spent hours here," Rebecca said as she led Katie through the narrow gap between two rocky cliffs toward the natural pool that lay nestled in the tiny arroyo. "On a hot afternoon, it's the perfect place to cool off."

Large smooth rocks surrounded the basin, which collected the meager runoff from nearby hills. In recent drought years, the water level had dropped considerably, but the pool still contained enough clear, clean water to splash around. Old oak trees spread their gnarled limbs over the far end, shading the deepest part of the water.

Various species of water bugs danced along the surface, causing tiny, rippling rings. A dragonfly buzzed among some reeds, its wings nature's most delicate filigree, its body teal blue luminance in the sunshine.

In the distance they could hear the cawing of a crow and nearby the rustling of other smaller birds in the surrounding scrub brush. The air smelled of dust and earth and growing things, a scent that evoked a hundred fond memories for Rebecca.

"We used to bring along a picnic lunch," she told Katie. "Usually peanut butter and jelly sandwiches that we made ourselves...or some of Bridget's queen cakes, like today." She held up the brown paper sack that Bridget had packed for their little excursion. Fortunately for them, the Irishwoman lived in constant dread that someone, somewhere might faint from lack of nourishment. And she believed it was her mission in life to make certain that such an awful thing never happened to anyone she knew.

"Are there fish or creepy things in there?" Katie asked as she climbed up onto one of the rocks and peered down into the water.

"One great white shark, two Loch Ness monsters, three electric eels and four stingrays," Rebecca answered promptly. "That's all."

Katie gave her a dubious look. "No partridge in a pear tree?"

"Nope, afraid not."

They both giggled. Rebecca set the sack of goodies on top of one of the boulders and slipped off her socks and sneakers, then removed her denim shirt. Wearing only her T-shirt and shorts, she slid down the rock and into the water with a clumsy splash.

"That was a lot easier when I was your age," she called up to Katie as she shook the water from her hair. Droplets flew, bits of glittering crystal in the sunshine. The pool was fairly shallow, just deep enough for her to tread water.

Katie laughed as she watched her. "Is it cold?"

"Of course it's cold. This is no sissy, heated whirlpool, kiddo. This here is the real thing. So, the question is, are you woman enough to jump in here, too?"

Katie's smile faded and she fumbled with one of her shoelaces. "I...uh...I can't."

"You can't what?"

"I can't swim."

Rebecca was shocked. She had never known anyone who couldn't swim. The child lived in Southern California, for heaven's sake.

"Didn't one of your parents teach you?" she asked.

"My mom was going to, that summer, but she got sick. And after she...left us...my dad was afraid for me to go near the water. I think he was scared that I'd die, too."

Rebecca bit back the sarcastic comments that rushed to her tongue. She found it terribly sad that Michael Stafford was so consumed by fear, but it was even worse that he had passed that anxiety on to his daughter. In

Katie's eyes, Rebecca could see the uncertainty, the lack of self-confidence as she stood on the edge of the rock and stared down into the water.

"I can understand why your dad might have been worried about you learning to swim," Rebecca said, choosing her words carefully. The last thing this child needed was to have someone speak ill of her father. "Water is something we have to respect. It can be wonderful, but it can be very dangerous if we aren't careful."

Katie crept a bit closer to the edge. "I wish I knew how to swim...just a little...so that the kids at school wouldn't laugh at me."

"They laugh at you? How do they know that you don't swim?"

"I was invited to a beach party. One of my friends was having her birthday there. My dad wouldn't let me go, 'cause he was afraid I'd try to go in the water and drown. He said, 'The water near the beach has a severe undertow.' I didn't know what that meant, but it sounded awful. It's okay." She shrugged. "I didn't really want to go anyway."

One look at that slightly protruding lower lip and the moisture welling up in those beautiful blue eyes told Rebecca that Katie wasn't being honest with herself. Being excluded for any reason from a friend's birthday party was an emotional trauma for a girl her age.

"Well, you don't have to worry about undertows here in the swimming hole," she said, trying to change the subject. "I can absolutely guarantee you that there's never been a single undertow in this pond."

"Since the beginning of time?" Katie asked with a grin.

"Since *before* the beginning of time."

The girl mulled that information over for a while, looking wistfully down at the water.

"Katie, do you really want to learn how to swim?" Rebecca asked gently.

"Well, yes, but... I don't think my dad would let me."

Good point, she thought. She certainly didn't want to go against any parent's wishes where their child was concerned. Especially Michael Stafford. But, on the other hand, the girl really needed to know how to swim and was still young enough to learn quickly.

"Did your father ever tell you that you *couldn't* take lessons or try to learn in any way?" she asked.

"Umm-m-m-m... I don't think he said I couldn't learn. He just said he didn't want to teach me and he wouldn't let me go to the beach party."

Rebecca decided to take the chance. The child had enough to fear in her life, without having to be afraid of water.

"Then, why don't I give you a little, bitty swimming lesson. This pool isn't very deep at all, and it's nice and still. I promise I won't let you drown, no matter what."

For several long moments, Rebecca watched as the girl tried to decide. Her pretty face registered her internal battle: her nervousness versus her trust in the woman who had saved Rosebud's life.

Finally, the trusting side of her nature won, and she reached down to remove her sneakers.

"So, it's pretty cold, huh?" she asked as she neatly folded her socks and tucked them into her shoes. "Do you suppose there are any polar bears around?"

"Nope, no polar bears," Rebecca replied, reaching her arms up to ease the child off the rock and into the shallowest part of the pool.

"Are you sure?" As Katie slipped into the water she shivered with excitement.

"Absolutely positive." Rebecca tried to remember back to those days at the YWCA where she had learned. What came first? "Relax, kiddo, there are no polar bears in Southern California. I guarantee it. They all hang out up in the San Francisco Bay area."

When Michael turned his Jaguar XJ12 down the gravel driveway to his home and saw the battered and distinctive pickup parked in front of his house, he felt a flash of pleasure, quickly eclipsed by a bigger rush of irritation. What now? Why was *she* here?

For a second, he entertained the dark thought that something might have happened to one of the goats. But as he drove around the side of the house and into the garage he could see all three of them, romping around in their pen, the picture of health and exuberance.

So, *she* had better have a darned good reason for coming around uninvited and unannounced. That was the problem with a small town, people took liberties with your privacy, just dropping by for no good reason any time of the day or night.

As he crawled out of the car, he quickly checked his reflection in the window. His hair looked like hell. Great. He ran his fingers through the unruly mess but, as always, it had a mind of its own and refused to lie in any sort of order.

She could have at least waited until he had jumped into the shower and changed clothes to inflict her presence on him.

"Where is she?" he demanded as he trudged through the back door and into the kitchen.

Bridget stood at the sink, peeling potatoes for the evening meal. She turned to him with too wide, too innocent eyes. "And whoever might you be speakin' of?" she asked.

"You know who." He walked over to the refrigerator and grabbed himself a beer. "That pesky vet."

"Oh, it's Rebecca you mean." Bridget tossed the peeled potatoes into a colander and rinsed them at the faucet. "She offered to entertain your Katie for me, while I got some extra work done around here."

"Entertain Katie?" He didn't really like the sound of that. "What are you talking about? How is she entertaining her?"

"Took her out on a hike, she did. Meant to show her a bit of your property that she hasn't seen before."

"You mean they're just roaming around, God knows where?" His irritation and anxiety levels were rising by the minute. Not only had she dropped by uninvited, but she had absconded with his kid, too. The nerve of that woman!

"Ah...I wouldn't be worryin' if I were you, Mr. Michael," Bridget said, wiping her hands on a kitchen towel, embroidered with violets and daisies. "Rebecca used to come here all the time when she was a wee lass. Knows the place like the back of her own hand, she does. I'm sure they won't lose their way."

"Did you give your permission for this...excursion?" he asked.

She turned and flashed him one of her famous smiles. "I did, indeed. Thought it was the very thing for the little miss. She needs a friend or two, she does, to do things with."

"Well...I..." He didn't know exactly what to say, so he tilted his beer bottle and chugalugged the first third. Common sense told him that he was overreacting. Bridget was right. Katie did need a friend. And Rebecca was a responsible adult; at least, she appeared to be. So he probably had nothing at all to worry about.

He just wasn't comfortable not knowing exactly where his child was and what she was doing. Anything could happen to her, and he wouldn't know.

"In the future," he said, "I'd like for Katie to stay at home when I'm away, unless I've given my permission."

Bridget looked surprised and a bit hurt, but she nodded agreeably. "I beg your forgiveness, Mr. Michael," she said. "But I thought, as long as she was here on your property, with Rebecca to watch over her, it would be—"

"Yes, yes," he said, holding up one hand. "I understand. I'm not angry with you. I just wanted to make my wishes clear."

"Oh, they are, sir. Very clear, indeed."

Michael heard halting footsteps on the back porch and the sound of voices. Katie's and Rebecca's.

"See there," Bridget said. "Back, safe and sound, the both of them."

Michael crossed the kitchen to open the door for them. But when he looked outside, he saw something that made his heart nearly stop.

His Katie wasn't safe and sound after all. Rebecca was carrying the girl in her arms, and there was blood all over them both.

He threw open the door, rushed out onto the porch and grabbed Katie away from Rebecca. "What the hell did you do to her?" he shouted as he searched his daughter for the source of the blood. She felt cold and her clothing was wet, but she wasn't crying and didn't appear to be particularly upset.

"She's all right, Mr. Stafford," Rebecca replied. "It looks much worse than it is. She has a small cut on her foot, and it bled quite a bit at first. But it's stopped now and it isn't serious."

"Where my daughter is concerned, I'll be the judge of what's serious or not." Michael didn't like the woman's nonchalance. So everything was fine, huh? Easy for her to say; it wasn't her kid who had blood smeared all over her.

"I'm okay, Daddy," Katie said, wrapping her arms around his neck. "I stepped on a sharp rock and cut myself, but Dr. Rebecca wrapped my socks around it and carried me all the way back so that I wouldn't get dirt in the ow-wwie."

Michael looked down at the bloody sock wrapped around his daughter's foot and felt a sick, dizzying sensation of being out of control. Good God, anything could have happened and he wouldn't have been there.

Turning around, he carried Katie into the house, nearly colliding with Bridget, who looked equally distressed.

"Poor little lass," she murmured. "Lay her on the sofa, Mr. Michael, and I'll fetch a cold compress right away."

"No, we're not going to waste time with that," he snapped. "I'll take her straight to the hospital."

Rebecca caught up with him at the front door. "Mr. Stafford, if you want to take her to a doctor, that's certainly your choice. But I assure you that the wound isn't that serious. It isn't even big enough to require a stitch. I had intended to bring her back, clean the cut and close it with a butterfly bandage. I'd still be glad to do that, if you like."

"Let her do it, Daddy," Katie said, holding her foot up to Rebecca. "Please, let Dr. Rebecca take care of me. I don't want to go to the hospital. I don't like hospitals."

Michael didn't have to ask his daughter why. They had both spent too many heartbreaking hours in hospitals. He decided it wasn't fair to force her to return if it wasn't necessary.

"All right. If that's what you want." He turned to Rebecca, reluctant to ask her for assistance. Just on principle, he was still angry with her for taking off with his daughter without permission. And, even worse, getting her hurt. "Go ahead, Dr. Barclay," he said, his voice sounding brusque even to his own ears.

"Thank you," she replied with a softness that made him feel like a bigger jerk than ever.

"Bridget, if you would, please, my bag is in my truck cab...."

"I'll fetch it straightaway," she said, heading for the door.

Rebecca sat on the end of the sofa at Katie's feet and pulled the injured foot onto her lap. "Let's see what we have here," she said as she carefully unwound the bloody sock. "Ah... just as I thought... you're developing a pretty serious case of creeping cruditis."

Katie's eyebrows pulled together over her pert nose. "The creeping what? What's that? It sounds awful."

"Oh, it is. That's why we have to use some very special treatments to make sure it doesn't turn into *acute* creeping cruditis."

"What kind of treatments?"

Michael could tell by the half grin on Katie's face that she knew she was being teased. He also noticed that Rebecca's chatter was keeping Katie's mind off the fact that she was examining the cut. Okay, so she was good with kids. So what?

"The special treatment," Rebecca said thoughtfully. "Well, let me see.... Oh, yes, I remember now. We have to make a poultice for it. Do you know what that is?"

"Isn't it a name for chickens and turkeys and geese and stuff like that?"

Rebecca laughed, and so did Michael, in spite of himself.

"No," she said, "that's poultry, not poultice. A poultice is a mixture of stuff that you make and spread it on a wound to help it heal."

"What kind of stuff?"

At that moment Bridget entered the living room, Rebecca's medical bag in hand. "Here you go, dear," she said, handing it to Rebecca.

"Tell me, Bridget—" Rebecca reached into the bag and pulled out cotton, antiseptic, gauze and tape "—do you have onions in the kitchen?"

Bridget looked puzzled. "Yes, of course I do, but—"

"And hot mustard?"

Again Bridget nodded. "Why do you—"

"We need to throw this stuff in the blender and then smear it on Katie's foot. How about garlic and chili peppers?"

Bridget grinned. "Aye, we've got lots of those."

"How about raw liver?"

Katie's self-control reached the end of its tether. "No! Yuck, no liver! I don't want slippery, slimy liver on my foot!"

"And, of course, you have to wear it to school, every day for a month."

By the time Katie had recovered from the shock of wearing such a disgusting and smelly poultice to school, Rebecca had disinfected and bandaged the small cut.

"There you go, kiddo," she said, gently patting the child's foot. "Good as new. Almost."

Michael felt a stab of jealousy when he saw the look of adoration in his daughter's eyes as she gazed at the vet, spellbound and brimming with affection. Besides, he was the only one who called her "kiddo."

In a small corner of his brain, he knew he was being petty, but the rest of him didn't care. This woman was trying to usurp his position with his daughter and he didn't like it one bit.

Rebecca looked up and their eyes met. He could tell that she was angry with him, too. But, probably out of consideration for the child, she wasn't saying so.

She was pretty, in a down-homey sort of way. No makeup, but then she didn't really need it. She wore her chestnut hair in a simple, no-nonsense cut—shoulder length and blunt. Her slightly damp T-shirt and shorts were covered by a plain denim shirt. Not exactly a fashion plate, but then, businesslike attire wouldn't have been practical for her line of work.

Too bad she wasn't more pleasant.

"Thank you, Dr. Barclay," he said, rising from his chair. "I appreciate what you did. May I see you out now?"

There. That had been pretty blunt. Surely she would get the idea that he wanted her gone.

"No, thank you," she said, standing up and collecting her things into the bag. "I can find my way out alone."

"But I insist," he replied, following after her as she headed for the door.

"Goodbye, Katie." She bent over the girl and placed a quick kiss on her forehead. "I'm sorry you got hurt, but you did a wonderful job with your swimming lesson. I'll drop by to give you another one soon."

She nodded a goodbye to Bridget, then headed out the door. He followed at her heels.

"Just a minute, Dr. Barclay," he called to her as she was about to climb into her pickup. "I'd like to have a word with you."

"Well, *I* don't think that *I* want to have a word with *you*. Unless, of course, you're going to offer me an apology for your rudeness."

"Not on your life! What do you mean 'apology'? You're the one who took off with my kid without asking me first. You're the one who got her hurt. And what's this about you teaching her to swim? You've got a hell of a nerve, Doctor. But you'd just better back off when it comes to my daughter."

"Mr. Stafford..." She drew a deep breath. "*You* are acting like a first-rate jerk. I haven't known you very long, so I can't tell if it's because you *are* a first-rate jerk, or maybe it's just a temporary lapse in your social skills due to indigestion, a painful hangnail or constipation. For Katie's sake, I'm going to assume the latter."

She spun on her heel and climbed into the pickup. He tried to think of some great, smart-aleck retort, but he was so mad that his mind was blank.

"I suggest," she said, "that you take a big healthy dose of castor oil and sleep with a coat hanger in your mouth. Maybe you'll wake up tomorrow morning with a load off your mind and a smile on your face."

He sputtered. He fumed. He thought of a perfect rebuttal. Scathing, insulting, crude... almost vile. Absolutely perfect.

But, unfortunately, by then Dr. Rebecca Barclay was five miles down the road and long out of sight.

Chapter Four

"Are you mad at me, kiddo?" Michael studied his daughter's bent head as they helped themselves to the last two pieces of Double, Double, Cheese and Trouble pizza on the platter.

He had taken Katie to her favorite eatery in an effort to cheer her up, but so far it wasn't working. She had been unnaturally quiet during the meal and had turned down an offer to play video games with him in the adjoining arcade.

Something had to be wrong. And Michael had a sinking feeling that he knew what it was.

"Well, are you?" he asked again when she didn't answer.

He reached across the table and tweaked a lock of her hair.

"No," she said, so softly he could hardly hear her.

Her tone was anything but convincing.

"I think you are. It's okay, Katie. We can talk about whatever is bothering you."

She looked up at him with those beautiful blue eyes that constantly broke his heart, and he could see that she was much more than just angry; she was deeply hurt.

"Is it about what happened this afternoon?"

She nodded.

"What did I do wrong?" he asked, dreading the answer. Why were the members of the male gender forever messing up with the females in their lives? If a man wasn't disappointing his mother, it was his girlfriend, sister, wife or daughter. A guy just couldn't win with a woman, no matter what age.

"You were mean to Dr. Rebecca," she said, her lower lip quivering.

He reached out and touched it with his fingertip. For the thousandth time he reflected on the fact that she was so soft, so sweet, and that he was so lucky to have her in his life.

"Do you really think I was mean?" he asked.

Again, she nodded.

"I guess I came down on her pretty hard, but I was worried about you. I was mad that she took you without asking me. I was upset that she let you get hurt."

"But that wasn't her fault. We didn't see the rock through the water. And it wasn't a big deal anyway. It hardly hurt at all. Dr. Rebecca was being nice to me, and we were having a really good time until . . ."

"Until I messed it up?"

"Yeah," Katie admitted, hanging her head again. "I was looking forward to coming home and telling you how good I did on the swimming stuff. But then . . ."

"So, tell me now. How did you do?"

Her eyes brightened and she wriggled in her seat with excitement. "I did *great!* Dr. Rebecca said I was very brave. First I did the mouth part—you know, sticking my mouth under the water and blowing bubbles. Then I did my nose, then I floated on my back and did my ears. That was really weird and it sorta tickled. And *then*...and *then*...I did *the eyes!* I stuck my *whole* head under the water! All the way! I did it three times, and the last time I even opened my eyes. Right there, under the water, I opened them and looked around. I could see Dr. Rebecca. She was under the water, too, making a funny face and waving to me!''

Michael's heart warmed to see her so excited. She truly had enjoyed the afternoon, thanks to Rebecca Barclay. And the experience had obviously been worth a little cut on the foot.

He *had* been a first-rate jerk.

''I'm sorry, kiddo. Really, I am.''

''Thanks, Dad. But you shouldn't tell *me*,'' she said. ''Dr. Rebecca is the one you yelled at.''

His stomach tied into a ball at the mere thought of approaching that woman and offering an apology. But what was a guy to do? He was wrong. His daughter knew he was wrong. They both knew he owed the doctor a heartfelt apology. Maybe he should kiss her ring and oil her feet while he was at it.

''Okay, okay, I'll tell her I'm sorry, but—''

''When?''

''When...ah, yes, well...''

''Tomorrow.''

''Tomorrow? I have a lot of things to do tomorrow, and I don't think I'll have a chance to...''

Thick, dark lashes batted over brilliant blue eyes; the rosebud mouth began to tremble again.

"All right, all right. Tomorrow."

Katie grinned, satisfied, and licked the last bit of sauce from her fingers. "You know," she added slyly, "you *could* ask her out on a date—a nice romantic dinner, a movie, a little mo-oo-onlight dancing."

He growled and tossed a piece of crust at her. "Watch it, kiddo. You *could* have to weed that flower bed beside the driveway."

"The one with all the dandelions and crabgrass?"

"That's the one."

She considered for a moment, then said, "Okay, just buy her a double-decker ice cream cone, and we'll call it even."

"I've been instructed to buy you ice cream. A lot of it."

Startled, Rebecca looked up from her examining table where she was clipping the right wing feathers of a parrot named Frederick. Michael Stafford was standing in her doorway. He wore an off-white linen shirt, just-right-tight jeans and a smile on his face that reminded her of the grins worn by a few sheep she had treated in her career.

Fred squawked and flapped, obviously irritated by her hesitation.

"What?" she asked, unable to believe what she had heard.

"I said . . ." He hesitated. "I'd like to buy you some ice cream, as a way of saying that you were right and I was a jerk. Or so I've been told by my eight-year-old daughter."

"I see." She paused to comfort Frederick, who had decided that the examination and feather clipping had gone on long enough. Fortunately, she was nearly finished, close enough to agree with him.

Stroking the bird's head and tickling the back of his neck, she coaxed him into his portable cage. His owner, Marge, would be by to get him soon.

She walked over to the sink and washed her hands, trying to decide how to react to this less than enthusiastic invitation. Half of her wanted to accept—okay, more than half—but the rest wanted to stomp across the room and slap him silly.

"Katie thinks you were a jerk, huh?" she asked as she turned toward him and stood with arms crossed over her chest and a defiant look on her face. "So do I. But the important thing, Mr. Stafford, is what *you* think."

He sighed and walked into the room. Looking weary and frustrated, he sat on one of the stools beside the examining table. "First, please stop calling me Mr. Stafford. People only call me that when they're mad at me or trying to sell me something. Just call me Michael."

"I'm not trying to *sell* you anything, Mr. Stafford," she said.

"Secondly," he continued, ignoring her subtext, "I agree with my daughter—and with you—or I wouldn't be here. I might buy ice cream on command, but I only apologize when it's from the heart.''

He took a deep breath and looked her square in the eyes, causing her pulse to pound hard enough to lower her cholesterol level for six months.

"I was unfair to you yesterday," he said. "I was rude, insensitive and stubborn. I don't blame you for being mad at me. I'm mad at me, too, possibly more than you and Katie combined. To be honest, I was feeling guilty that *I* hadn't taken the time to teach her to swim, that *I* hadn't shown her the swimming hole, that *I* hadn't been there when she was hurt. And I took it out on you. I'm truly sorry. Will you forgive me?''

For a moment she saw that same beguiling expression in his eyes that she had seen in Katie's. And, as with the daughter, she couldn't resist it.

"Yes, all forgiven, all forgotten," she said. "You don't even have to buy me ice cream if you don't want to.''

"Oh, no, I *have* to do the ice cream bit or Katie will go on strike and not clean that grungy room of hers for two weeks. How do you feel about banana splits?''

After eating the first third of her ice cream and spending twenty minutes in conversation with Michael Stafford, Rebecca decided that she loved banana splits. Funny, she couldn't recall one tasting this good before.

The ice cream parlor was one of the most charming food establishments in town. Its stained glass lamps gave the dining room a cozy glow. In traditional, turn-of-the-century style, the tables and chairs were ornate filigree of white wrought iron with marble tops. A miniature train circled the room on a narrow shelf just below the copper tiled ceiling, puffing smoke and whistling when it passed the front door.

"This was a good idea," she said, dipping into a bit of whipped cream stained pink from the maraschino cherry juice. "Tell Katie I like it when she takes charge of her father."

"No way. The kid's got me under her control too much already. There's no point in encouraging tyranny."

Rebecca couldn't help noticing, not for the first time, that Michael Stafford had a breathtaking smile. And she couldn't deny the way she felt when he flashed it in her direction. Did he know the effect he had on women? More specifically, on her?

Probably, she decided. Most gorgeous men were all too aware of their attractiveness. Rebecca had never found herself drawn to that type—at least, not for more than a few minutes. She found their vanity diluted their overall appeal.

But Michael didn't seem vain. Guarded, maybe a bit sarcastic at times, deeply hurt, but not conceited.

"Tell me about your business," she said, fishing for an impersonal line of conversation. Her heart seemed to be leading her mind down paths that were best left unexplored.

"We import specialty automobiles from Europe," he said, seeming pleased that she would ask. "Usually, we have an interested customer first, then we use our contacts to locate what they want and bring it in for them. I've been in business for seven years, and I make a pretty decent living at it. What else would you like to know?"

"What do you like best about what you do?" she asked, hoping the answer would tell her something new about this man who kept himself so closed off from the rest of the world.

He thought for a moment before answering. "The challenge, I suppose, of finding exactly the right car, of being able to fulfill a lifelong dream for someone. Many of these people have been saving for years in hopes of owning that one special car. Besides, most of our cars are vintage classics, and some are in really bad condition when we get them. It's wonderful to rescue an old Rolls-Royce Silver Ghost from a scrap pile in Britain and bring it back to life."

"You like to take something old and worn-out and make it young again," she observed. "I wish I could do that for some of my patients. What do you like least?"

"Sometimes I'm not fulfilling a lifetime dream. Some customers are just spoiled and the car is nothing but another expensive toy to them. I still get paid, but it isn't as satisfying."

Silently, Rebecca digested this information. She had thought him a materialistic workaholic, spending long hours in search of the almighty buck. But he didn't seem to care that much about money. So why did he work so hard?

She didn't have to think too long about that one. He threw himself into his work because he was a man running scared. Scared of his own emotions, scared of loving, scared of losing and hurting.

She knew the feeling.

When they had finished their splits, he ordered a cup of coffee for each of them, then settled back to drink it. "Tell me about your work," he said. "What do you like and what do you hate?"

"I suppose it sounds pretty sappy, but I really do love the animals. I enjoy helping them, relieving their pain when I can, preventing it sometimes."

She looked into his eyes to see if he found her silly or overly sentimental. But she saw something unexpected in those blue depths—respect.

"You have that special gift, Dr. Rebecca," he said. "I've always admired someone who has the healing touch. Being a healer, of man or beast, must be a wonderful way to spend your life."

Rebecca started to reply but was interrupted by a buzzing vibration against her ribs. She sighed as she reached down and unsnapped her pager from her belt.

"This," she said as she pressed the button to display the telephone number, "is what I *don't* enjoy about being a vet. I seldom get to eat or sleep without being interrupted at least once."

When she saw the number and the 911 suffix, her heart sank. Instantly, she knew who was calling and why.

"Is something wrong?" Michael asked.

"Yes, I'm afraid so. It's the Rileys, an old couple with an ancient golden retriever named Midas. He hasn't been doing very well lately." She replaced the pager on her belt and grabbed her purse. "They live only a few blocks away. Would you mind terribly dropping me off there? They'll give me a ride home."

"Of course." He tossed some bills onto the table and followed her to the door. "But when I take a lady out— even for ice cream—I also take her home. I'll give you a lift there, but I'll wait while you do your doctoring thing."

"Thank you," she said, grateful for his company. But as they walked across the restaurant parking lot to the Jaguar, she recalled the details of Midas's condition and had some misgivings. "I appreciate your offer, but I don't know if you'll want to be along on this one, Michael. Not all of a vet's stories have happy endings."

He thought for a moment, then nodded solemnly. "I understand. But if it's going to be a difficult call, wouldn't it be easier to have a friend along?"

"Yes," she said, not caring what the implication might be, what a comforting, male presence might mean, how the events of this afternoon might complicate her life. Against her will, she thought of Tim and how much she missed having someone go with her on these difficult calls. "It would make it a lot easier," she heard herself saying. "Thank you, Michael."

Beatrice and Jack Riley had each other, pretty good health for their seventy-plus years, a small house with a rainproof roof, a 1956 Chevrolet that they had bought new and Midas.

In dog years, the golden retriever was older than either of them, and Rebecca had been called out several times in the past few months to address his various aches and ills.

But the last time she had been to the little house on Cleveland Avenue, she had suspected that Midas wasn't long for this world.

Her suspicion was confirmed the moment she stepped through their doorway and saw him lying on his blanket in front of the fireplace. No matter how sick he had been before, he had always rushed to the door to greet her. But now, he simply lay there, the only sign of life his chest barely rising and falling.

Beatrice Riley ushered Rebecca and Michael inside and closed the door behind them. Rebecca briefly introduced Michael to her, then turned her full attention to the dog.

"He seemed kind of under the weather last night," Beatrice said. "More than usual, that is. And this morning, he couldn't get up. He hasn't moved or eaten all day and he's been whimpering constantly. I know he's in pain. That's why I called you."

"Yes, of course, Bea," Rebecca replied. "Don't worry. You did the right thing."

The retriever was lying on his left side, his nose pointed toward the fire. As she knelt beside him on the floor, his tail gave a faint thump of recognition.

"Yes, Midas, it's me," she said, stroking the once beautiful golden coat that had lost its luster. "It's that mean woman who sticks needles and thermometers in you and makes you take rotten-tasting medicines."

Gently, Rebecca ran her hand along his spine, searching for the growth that she had discovered on her last visit. There it was, next to the vertebrae, at least twice the size it had been only a few weeks before.

The dog whined more loudly as she palpated the area around the lump. "I'm sorry, Midas," she said, stroking his ears instead. "I didn't mean to hurt you anymore, old boy. Is it pretty bad? Yes... I thought so."

Looking up at Beatrice, Rebecca saw the anxiety, the sorrow in her eyes. Michael stood behind her, wearing a similar expression. They both knew. Rebecca had only to speak the words, but they were the most difficult words she had to utter in the course of her work.

"The tumor has invaded his spine, Bea," she said softly. "That's the reason for his paralysis. There's nothing we can do about that. As I told you before, it's too involved for surgery."

Beatrice said nothing but nodded, her eyes filling with tears.

"Where is Jack?" Rebecca asked, looking around, hoping Bea wouldn't have to endure this experience alone.

"He's gone to Orange County, to visit his sister. She hasn't been feeling well either."

Rebecca wished she could wait for Jack's return, but Midas deserved better than that. "Well, I wish I didn't have to tell you this, but you were right, Midas is in a lot of pain. We have to think about what's best for him. I don't think it's fair to let him go on suffering when we can help him."

"You mean . . . put him down? Now?"

"Yes, that's what I mean. You've given him a wonderful life, he's sixteen years old, and I believe he's finished and ready to leave. We'll just be easing him on his way. It's a very gentle passing, I promise."

Rebecca watched as the fear rose in the woman's eyes. In her years as a veterinarian, Rebecca had found a pet's owner far more afraid of death than the animal.

"I can't," Beatrice said, backing away. "I mean, I'll let you do it, if you think it's best, but I can't watch." She burst into tears. "I'm sorry. I feel like a traitor, but I just can't help you do it."

Rebecca rose, walked over to the woman and put her arms around her. "Please don't feel guilty, Beatrice. Many owners can't watch their pets be put to sleep. There's no reason to put yourself through it if you'd rather not. I'll take care of it all."

"Will you . . . will you talk to him and pet him when you . . . ?"

"Of course I will."

Michael stepped forward and placed a hand on Beatrice's forearm. "Mrs. Riley, why don't you let me take you out into your backyard. Some fresh air will do you good."

He turned to Rebecca and lowered his voice. "I'll be back in a minute or two to help you."

"Thank you, but I'll be fine. You just take care of Bea for me," she replied, silently blessing him for his compassion.

She waited until she heard the back door close, then she returned to her patient.

Sitting beside him, she slowly, carefully lifted his head into her lap and began to stroke his ears. The big, brown eyes opened for a moment, and she knew, despite the pain, he was enjoying the attention.

She pulled her bag toward her and reached into it for the syringe and necessary medication. Laying her supplies aside, she petted him again, speaking soft, soothing words. "There, there, Midas. It's going to stop hurting very soon. You've been such a good dog, guarding the house all these years, chasing those pesky mailmen and meter readers. You put up with Bea's bunko parties, and Jack's snoring and those noisy grandkids. You fetched all those sticks and took Jack for all those walks. But now your work is done and you get to rest."

Quickly and efficiently, Rebecca administered the necessary dosage. The dog barely even flinched when her needle found the vein. He truly was tired and ready to leave.

Relief came within seconds; Rebecca felt him relax in her arms and his tail thumped once more. She continued to stroke his ears and speak to him until she felt the essence that had been Midas Riley leave the worn-out body.

* * *

"How can you stand it?" Michael asked as he turned the Jaguar onto the main highway that led back to Rebecca's home. "How can you deal with that sort of sadness on a regular basis? I wouldn't be able to take it."

He wasn't the first to ask that question; Rebecca had asked her own heart the same thing many times. So she gave him the answer that she had always received.

"Sadness isn't necessarily a bad thing," she said, watching as the landscape swept by her window. "It's just part of the fabric of life. So is death. Souls come into the world, souls leave."

"Are you telling me that Midas is in heaven now?" he asked with a half-sarcastic smirk.

"I don't think he's sitting on a cloud somewhere, sprouting wings and a halo and playing a harp, if that's what you mean. But I've held enough living creatures in my arms at the moment of their deaths, and I do know one thing . . . they leave, they don't just stop."

He was silent for a long time, and she could feel the impact that her words had on him. She wasn't sure why.

Pulling off the highway, he guided the car up the drive to her house. He parked in front and turned off the ignition.

"I wish I could believe you," he said softly, staring straight ahead . . . and into the past.

Rebecca said nothing but waited, knowing that he needed to continue.

"I wasn't there when my wife died." His expression and the tone of his voice suggested that he was making a confession of the most difficult kind. "I left the hospital twenty minutes before..."

She noticed that he was gripping the seat with fingers that trembled. Reaching down, she covered his hand with hers. "If you'd known, you would have stayed," she said. "Your wife knew your heart. I'm sure she understood."

"I hope so. Were you there, with your husband when he...?"

"No. He was killed instantly in the accident."

"Does it feel strange to you that you weren't there, that you didn't share something so important with your mate after going through so many other things together?"

"Yes, very strange."

Neither of them spoke as he waited for the flood of emotion to subside. Finally, he said, "How long does it take, Dr. Rebecca, for a heart to heal? At least enough that you can stand the pain?"

"I suppose that depends on the person and the circumstances. But for me, the hurt began to fade when I began to let go of it."

He turned to her, puzzled. "What do you mean? Why would anyone hang on to a pain that hurts so much?"

She shrugged and gave his hand a squeeze. "Maybe to punish themselves because of some sort of misplaced guilt."

Rebecca knew that her words had struck home by the way he winced, then pulled his hand away from hers.

"Thanks for having ice cream with me, Dr. Rebecca," he said, making it clear that he considered the social amenities over. "I'll walk you to your door."

His abrupt dismissal surprised and hurt her. One moment they seemed close, almost friends, but the next instant the intimacy was broken. She felt as though she had reached out to him and he had pushed her away.

"You don't need to escort me," she said as she opened the car door. "It's still daylight. I can find my own way."

"Rebecca, wait," he said, reaching for her. His hand closed around her forearm, his touch imparting his warmth and particular male vitality. "Thank you for what you said. You're right. But I have to think about it before I can . . . you know . . ."

"Yes, of course. I understand."

As Rebecca watched him drive away, she realized that she understood him much better than she wanted to. His heart had suffered a blow from which he would probably never fully recover. So had hers. He was afraid to love that deeply again, to risk losing again. So was she.

And, judging by the look in his eyes when he had told her goodbye, he was terrified that continued contact with her might cause his heart to open up again, might make him vulnerable to loving and maybe losing.

Oh, yes, Rebecca understood all too well. She was terrified, too.

It was always so much easier to see what someone else needed to do, to give advice and expect them to accept it gracefully. But it was quite another to take your own words to heart, she decided as she walked into her house, which seemed more empty, more silent than before.

In spite of all the wonderful things in her life, Rebecca knew there was an emptiness, a void in her heart. It had been there since Tim's death.

The silence . . . the heavy, oppressive silence was always there to remind her of all she had lost.

Her heart didn't seem to be speaking to her much anymore.

Or, maybe, somewhere along the line, she had simply stopped listening.

Chapter Five

"Well, how did it go? What happened, Daddy? Huh? What did you do? Where did you take her?" Katie bounced up and down on the front porch, unable to wait until her father had entered the house.

"For heaven's sake, kiddo, let me get my foot in the door before you interrogate me."

Katie gave him one of those female know-all-and-see-all looks. Damn, she was good at that and she was only eight. He pitied the poor guy who was to be his son-in-law someday. She propped her hands on her waist and planted her tiny sneakers apart, blocking his entrance.

"Did you guys have another fight?" she demanded. "You did! You were rude to her again, weren't you?"

He slipped his hands under her arms, lifted her and set her aside, out of his way. "No, we didn't have a fight. Good grief, you make it sound like we're heavyweights, going fifteen rounds. I don't *fight* women."

"Were you mean to Dr. Rebecca?" She followed him inside, slamming the door behind her. "Did you yell at her again?"

He reached the living room and collapsed into his favorite easy chair, suddenly exhausted. Patting his knee, he invited his daughter to sit on his lap. He knew he was in trouble when she shook her head. Having always been an affectionate child, Katie never refused the opportunity to cuddle.

"I'll stand, thank you," she said with cool formality and dignity far beyond her years.

He stifled a chuckle. "Katie, I did *not* yell at your dear Dr. Rebecca. I was not rude to her. You will be pleased to hear that I even refrained from chewing my nails, scratching my armpits and picking my nose in front of Dr. Rebecca."

"No burping?" she asked without cracking a smile, hands still on her hips.

"No burping. No bodily expulsions of *any* kind."

She continued to give him the deadpan stare. "I'm so very proud of you," she replied flatly.

"Thank you."

Dropping the indignant act, she climbed happily onto his lap and gave him a hug and a peck on the cheek.

"So, tell me all about it," she said. "I want to know everything. Did you kiss her?"

He drew back and stared at her, eyebrows raised in shock. "Katherine Stafford! How could you suggest such a thing? I'm a gentleman!"

"Nah," she said, pinching his cheek, "just because you didn't burp or pick your nose doesn't make you *that* much of a gentleman. Did you kiss her or not?"

"Not! I took her out for a banana split, and I *didn't* kiss her, didn't serenade her, didn't tango with her in the moonlight, didn't—"

"Okay, okay. Then tell me one more thing, but it has to be the truth. You can't fib at all, promise?"

"Yeah, I guess so. I promise."

"You didn't kiss her, huh?"

"Katie!"

She leaned forward until the tip of her nose was touching his, her blue eyes filling his vision. "Did you *want* to?"

Did he want to?

Hell, yes, he had wanted to. It was all Michael could think about as he sat at his desk the next day, pretending to be working, pretending to be doing anything except fantasizing about Rebecca Barclay.

She had looked so cute, sitting there across from him in the ice cream parlor, a couple of yellow and blue fluffs of feather in her hair, compliments of Frederick the parrot. And later, the kindness she had shown the old dog and his owner had touched Michael's heart, whether he had wanted it to or not.

"Michael, I'm going home now. Michael..."

The soft voice reached into his reverie, pulling him back to the present. Mrs. Abernathy stood in his office doorway, purse and keys in hand.

"Oh, yes, good night. See you tomorrow."

She gave him a crooked smile and shook her head. "I don't think so."

"Why? Are you taking the day off? Did I forget your dentist appointment again?"

"No, Michael," she said, "I'm not going to the dentist, because he's taking the day off tomorrow, too. The whole country is taking off. It's Thanksgiving, you nit-wit."

Briefly, Michael wondered how he had ever hired an employee who would call him a nitwit to his face. Then he realized she was right. How could he have forgotten Thanksgiving?

"Oh, well sure. I knew that."

She laughed and shook her head. "I assume this means that you and Katie don't have plans for dinner."

"Ah... not solid plans."

Her face softened. "I'm sorry, Michael. I'd love to have you come to my house, but I'm not cooking this year. I'm going to visit my daughter in the valley."

"No problem, Abernathy, really. We'll be fine. See you on Monday."

After a couple more apologies, Mrs. Abernathy left, and Michael decided to do the same. Without her there, and with the salesmen and mechanics gone, the place seemed too quiet. Tonight he wasn't in the mood for quiet. Aware now that it was the day before Thanksgiving, he felt more lonely than ever.

Each holiday since his wife's death, he had tried to celebrate with Katie, but it was difficult. Beverly had always done the decorating, the cooking, the shopping, and he had taken her efforts for granted. He didn't seem to have that knack for making occasions special for Katie. Or for himself, either.

A multitude of plans raced through his head as he walked through the elegant showroom with its restored classics, turning lights off and alarms on. Bridget and

Neil would be leaving at sunrise tomorrow morning to go to her mother's home in San Francisco. Weeks ago, they had asked for the days off and he had gladly granted them. He had assured Bridget that he would make Thanksgiving dinner plans on his own, that she didn't need to leave a full meal in the refrigerator.

Which left him with a dilemma: What should he do for Katie?

He could take her out to a restaurant, try to cook a bird himself—fat chance he could pull that one off—or get a bucket of chicken somewhere and pretend it was turkey. Maybe he could fake her out with some of those deluxe microwave dinners.

No, she was a little too sharp for that. He could see it now, Katie hauling the empty boxes out of the garbage and shoving them under his nose.

A restaurant was probably the best bet. He wondered what might be open. In this small, family-oriented community, most businesses closed on the holidays.

When he stepped outside the back door, locking it behind him, he heard a strange sound that interrupted his frantic planning session. A tiny, high-pitched whimper, coming from the garage area.

Curious, he took a flashlight from his trunk and followed the sound, trying to find its source. It didn't take long.

There, shivering beneath the Dumpster, was a tiny black puppy. The pup yelped with fright as Michael reached down and picked it up.

"Hey, what are you doing under there? Where's Mom and the other kids?"

Michael looked around but saw no sign of any more dogs. He called out and whistled, but the alley was silent except for the puppy's snuffling against his chest.

"Here you go," he said, tucking the dog inside his jacket. The pup nuzzled its cold nose against him. Its paws and belly were also chilled. Michael realized that if he hadn't found it when he had, the pup would have died. Eyes barely open, it was much too young to be weaned from its mother.

Michael took the puppy to his Jaguar, climbed inside and turned on the heater and the overhead dome lamp.

"Let's take a look at you," he said, pulling the puppy out and examining it. The dog was male and appeared to be a mixed breed, but mostly Labrador. A mutt, perhaps, but handsome, nevertheless. Considering the size of his paws, he was going to grow up to be a big boy, a fine pet and watchdog for someone.

Finding Michael's little finger, the pup latched on to the end, sucking hard in hopes of finding milk.

"Sorry, Bruiser," he said, "but you're barking up the wrong tree."

He had to feed him . . . soon. But what? How?

Michael didn't have a clue. But he did know who would, and all he needed was an excuse—any excuse—to see her again.

Whether he could kiss her or not.

* * *

Rebecca answered the door, expecting some terrible calamity. Usually, when they came directly to her door, it was an emergency, often an accident with a vehicle.

In the past few years she had grown to hate cars and what they did to innocent animals unfortunate enough to come under their wheels. Those were, by far, the worst cases she had to handle, traumatic for her, the animals and the owners.

But when she had pulled her robe around her and opened the door she found, not some poor mangled cat or dog, but Michael Stafford. He was standing there, whole and handsome, with a giant grin on his face.

"Oh, hi," she mumbled. "I . . . I wasn't expecting you." She tied the robe more tightly, suddenly feeling very underdressed. Beneath the terry cloth, she was wearing only a thin T-shirt and panties, her usual sleeping garb. If she had known he was coming over, she would have put on something more appropriate. Like a satin robe and matching chemise.

Stop that, she thought. *A chemise, indeed.*

"I'm sorry for just dropping by like this," he said. "I suppose I should have called first, but I have a new patient for you."

She glanced down at the ground to see if he were leading something on a leash. "A patient? Where? I don't see anything."

At that moment she heard the distinct whimper of a young puppy, coming from somewhere inside Michael's jacket.

"I've got him in here," he said, pointing to his chest. "He was cold."

"Mmm-hmm . . . I see. You'd better bring him in—sounds serious. I've heard of a hot dog, but a cold pup?"

He groaned. "That was awful, Dr. Rebecca."

"Well, Mr. Stafford," she said, pulling him into the house, "call next time and let me know you're on your way. I'll have someone write me some better material."

Half an hour later, Michael sat on the end of Rebecca's sofa, holding the puppy in his lap, a tiny baby bottle stuck into its puckered mouth. "He's slobbering all over my hand," he said. "It's running down on to my leg."

Rebecca sat at the other end, watching, laughing at Michael's clumsiness. The puppy didn't seem to mind at all as he slurped hungrily at the rubber nipple.

"What am I going to do with him?" he said, dabbing the milk off the pup's face with the soft white towel that Rebecca had given him. "I can't take him home. Katie will claim him right away."

Rebecca shrugged. "Let her have him."

"I'd like to, but she has enough responsibility right now, caring for Rosebud. Rosie is her first pet. I don't want to overload her with too much too fast."

"I understand, but that does leave you with a problem. He's going to need a lot of care, especially for the next few weeks. Middle-of-the-night feedings, all that."

"Not interested in having a dog, are you?" He gave her a beguiling smile and held the puppy out to her. "Here, I'll give him to you for a birthday present. Happy birthday, Rebecca! Don't ever say I never gave you anything."

She laughed and shook her head. "Nice try, but my birthday was four months ago."

"Happy Thanksgiving? Merry Christmas, maybe?"

The puppy was cute and the offer tempting. But Rebecca had learned long ago that she couldn't adopt every cute, four-legged creature that needed a home. "Nope," she said. "You found him. *You* are responsible for him. I'm sure you'll find him an excellent home."

"But how? I'm new in town. I don't know anyone."

"Gee, what a great opportunity to meet your neighbors!"

He scowled at her and raised one eyebrow. "I'm learning something about you, Rebecca Barclay. You are not a nice lady."

"I'm a very nice lady. But I'm not going to puppy-sit for you."

Rebecca enjoyed watching the wheels turning in his head. He was in a difficult position, to be sure, but she didn't intend to help him out of it. So many times she had witnessed the power of a small, whimpery fur ball to melt a heart encased in ice. Nothing broke down the barriers faster than the disarming innocence and charm of a puppy or kitten.

Michael Stafford needed this pup more than the dog needed him, whether he knew it or not. Even if only for a few hours.

"Take him home with you, hide him in your room so that Katie doesn't see him, and by tomorrow morning you'll probably have a great plan."

Michael sighed and tucked the dog back inside his jacket. "Yeah, sure. Tomorrow is Thanksgiving Day. Unless I can truss him up like a turkey, no one is going to be interested."

She stood, handed him a bag full of puppy formula and ushered him to the door.

"Hey, wait a minute! I know what you can do!" she said brightly.

He perked up instantly, gullible and hopeful. "What? What can I do?"

"He's already black. Just stick a white collar on him and pass him off as a pilgrim."

Chapter Six

Michael hung up the telephone and flopped back on his bed, exhausted. Beneath the covers he could feel a soft wet nose, sniffing at his ankle. The tiny lump under the blanket slowly moved up his pajama leg to his knee.

"Don't tell me...you're hungry again?" He reached between the sheets and pulled the pup out by the loose scruff of his neck. He held the animal up to his face and looked him in the eye. "I just fed you at seven, and six, and five, and four, and...no wonder I'm tired. I don't remember Katie being this much trouble when we first brought her home."

Michael had to admit that she might have been this difficult, but he wouldn't have known. Those were the old days when he and a lot of other men believed that parenting young children was a pastime only for women. Beverly had been the one to roll out of bed at all hours of the day and night for feedings, changings, fanny pattings and lullabies.

Now, looking back, Michael wasn't particularly proud of his record. He could have helped a bit more. Who was he kidding? He could have helped a *lot* more.

Reaching for the miniature baby bottle, which he had wrapped in a heating pad to keep it warm, he wondered if that had been such a great idea. Last night it had seemed brilliant, but he had been half-asleep. This morning the concept seemed dubious, maybe even dangerous.

"Here you go, Bruiser," he said, popping the nipple into the dog's mouth. "Chugalug. At least *somebody* will get to eat today."

He had spent the past hour on the phone, calling around for a reservation at a restaurant for Thanksgiving dinner. But he had found only three establishments that were open and serving, and they were all booked solid. Even thinly veiled bribes to the maître d' had done no good.

Grocery stores were closed, even the convenience stores. So much for the fancy microwave dinners bit. He was in trouble. Katie wasn't going to take this well at all.

A knock on the door startled him. "Daddy, can I talk to you?"

He pulled the bottle from the puppy's mouth and tucked both it and the dog under the blankets again. "Sure, come on in."

The door opened and Katie appeared, wearing her pajamas, her beautiful black curls tousled. "Whatcha doin'?" she asked, her voice still bed-drowsy.

"Doing? Ah...nothing. Why do you ask?"

She gave him a suspicious once-over. "No reason," she said slowly. "I was just making conversation. But now that you mention it, what *are* you doing? You look guilty."

"Guilty? Why would I look guilty?"

The puppy, unhappy about having had his breakfast interrupted, let out a loud squeak. The blanket did little to muffle the protest. Katie's eyes widened, and she was instantly alert.

"What was that?" she said, hurrying to the side of his bed.

"What was what?"

"That noise. It sounded like . . . like . . ."

"I coughed, okay? It came out wrong."

"No way. Not even you can make a sound like that. It's something little. Something cute. I can tell."

She got down on her hands and knees and searched under the bed. Michael used the opportunity to peek beneath the covers and find the pup. Hoping to appease it, he stuck the tip of his finger into its mouth. But the dog had quickly learned the difference between a nipple that would give milk and a finger that wouldn't. He promptly spit it out and began to squeak again.

This time Katie had no problem identifying the source. Michael grabbed her hand just before she yanked back the covers.

"Now, you have to understand, Katie, that we're only baby-sitting. We can't keep this for our own, so don't even think about it. Okay?"

"Okay," she replied, straining to see under the blanket.

"Katie, I mean it. You already have a pet and—"

"Ooo-ooh, it's ado-o-rable!" She lifted the pup gently and kissed the top of his head. "You got me a puppy for Thanksgiving! Thank you, Daddy!"

"No, that's not it at all! I discovered him in the alley behind the showroom last night. I'm going to find a home for him, a really good home, today."

Her face fell, her smile evaporated. "Oh."

He felt like an ogre, the worst father on the face of the earth. But what could he do? With Rosebud, Katie really didn't need a dog. She was too young to take responsibility for both animals, and he was far too busy.

"So," she said, "are we going to take him to his new home before or after we eat our turkey dinner?"

"Turkey dinner...ah...well..."

"We *are* going to have turkey, aren't we, Daddy? And pumpkin pie? We *always* have pumpkin pie. It's my favorite."

"Don't worry, kiddo," he said with far more assurance than he felt. "I have something special planned."

She cocked her head and gave him a scrutinizing look that made him want to crawl under the covers. "Do you really?" she said. "Or did you just forget all about Thanksgiving?"

"Forget? Do you really think I'd forget Thanksgiving?"

She nodded.

"Well," he replied indignantly. "Now I know what you think of *me*. Forget all about Thanksgiving, really...." He reached for the dog and popped the bottle into its perpetually hungry mouth. "Boy, are you going to feel bad when you see what I have planned! Forget, indeed."

She gave him another probing look, then turned and slowly left the room.

Michael groaned. "Bruiser, ol' pal, we've certainly stepped in it this time."

Michael could have sworn the dog gave him a look that was very similar to the one on Katie's face.

"All right, all right," he said with a sigh. "You had nothing to do with it. I'm in there all by myself."

Since the other vets in town had families, Rebecca always offered to be the one on call when a holiday rolled around. Holidays were just like any other day to her, she had decided, and there was no point in depriving others of the opportunity to be with their spouses and children.

Somebody had to be available. Unfortunately, accidents and illnesses didn't take time off just because someone had declared a national holiday.

"Just another day," she whispered as she stood at her living room window, wearing her terry-cloth robe and slippers, and holding her coffee cup.

It would be so easy to simply sit at home, missing Tim, and feeling sorry for herself. But she had learned long ago that handling the situation in that way wasn't to her advantage. If she did, it took her days to crawl up out of her depression. Trial and error had taught her that it was better to avoid slipping down into that emotional mire in the first place.

With a pager, she wasn't confined to the house, but as always, she faced the dilemma of where to go. Stores and amusement facilities were closed. Her friends were visiting with their own families. Tim's relatives and her own lived on the East Coast, too far away to consider dropping by for a turkey drumstick.

"What to do, where to go?" she whispered.

Suddenly, she thought of Michael Stafford and his new charge. How were they getting along? Had they made it through the night?

Of course, they had. But she decided she had to go out to Casa Colina and check on them. After all, it was the only neighborly thing to do.

"Chinese food, for Thanksgiving? *This* is your special surprise? Oh, Daddy, you really blew it this time."

Katie stared down at her chicken chow mein and sweet and sour chicken, both of which Michael had tried in vain to convince her were turkey. The kid had pretty sensitive taste buds and wasn't that easily fooled.

In fact, he didn't believe he had fooled her about anything today. She knew exactly what had happened, and his pretending otherwise had only made the situation worse.

"Come on, kiddo," he said, reaching across the table for her small hand. "It isn't what we eat, is it? Thanksgiving is supposed to be a day when we count our blessings. We can do that whether we're eating turkey, or hamburgers, or chow mein. Right?"

She nodded.

"Then let's think of some things we're thankful for."

"I'm thankful for Rosie, and Mrs. Bridget and Mr. Neil, and you, of course, and Dr. Rebecca."

Michael named off his list which included Katie and all of her favorite people as well as Mrs. Abernathy.

The ritual took less than five minutes, and with the traditional stuff out of the way, Michael was at a loss as to how to proceed with the festivities. Katie was obviously still upset with him, and he wasn't naive enough to think it had anything to do with the lack of pumpkin pie on the table.

Inside his jacket, which he had refused to remove, Bruiser had wakened from his nap and was beginning to wriggle around. Michael certainly hadn't wanted to bring a puppy into a restaurant, but what else could he do? The little guy was too young to be left at home for that long, and the weather had turned chilly, so he couldn't leave him in the car.

Glancing around at the red, black and gold decor, and the tables—all empty, except theirs—Michael felt another rush of shame. He loved his daughter so much. Why hadn't he arranged a traditional Thanksgiving for her? All in all, he considered himself a responsible sort. He never forgot a shipment or delivery date at work. Never. So how could he overlook something like this?

"Daddy," Katie said, "can I ask you something?"

"Sure, kiddo." He braced himself because he could tell by the sadness in her eyes that it was something painful.

"Now that Mom's gone..." She paused and swallowed hard. "I guess we're not like a real family anymore, right?"

Braced or not, he was thrown for an emotional loop by her question. He couldn't blame her for asking such a thing, but her words still stung.

"Sure we are, Katie," he replied. "I mean, we aren't the all-American family with a mom and dad, three kids and a dog. But we live together, we love each other, we try to do what's best for each other. I think that makes us a family, even if there's only two of us."

When she didn't reply, he nudged her under the table with his foot. "What do *you* think?"

After a long hesitation, she said, "I don't think we really are, 'cause we don't do the things that a real family does together."

"Like what? Besides eating turkey on Thanksgiving, that is."

"Like going on vacations, going to Disneyland, playing games at home on Saturday night, camping out, you know...stuff like that."

"Stuff like we used to do before Mom got sick, right?"

She nodded. "You don't even make your pineapple pancakes on Sunday morning anymore. I really liked those."

Tears welled up in her eyes and seemed to spill over into his. The chow mein was suddenly difficult to swallow.

Pineapple pancakes. He had made them for Beverly on their first weekend together and had won her heart forever. They were a Sunday treat every week for as long as they had been together. Until she had gone to the hospital that last time. He hadn't even thought of them since.

"Katie, I'm so sorry. I can see I have some explaining to do." He thought for a moment, then continued, "What would you do if you found yourself face-to-face with something that really, really frightened you?"

"Something really scary?"

"Well, let's just say it's something that scares *you.*"

She bit her lower lip, concentrating, trying to come up with the right answer. "I guess I'd either hide or try to run away."

"Me, too," Michael replied. "When you were born, I thought I was always going to have a wife to help me raise you. I was really worried that I wouldn't be a good dad. But your mom helped me learn, and after a while, I relaxed and began to really enjoy being a father. But then she got sick, and she died, and I was really scared."

"Of what? Of me?"

He laughed softly. "No, sweetheart, not of you. I was afraid I wouldn't do a good job of raising you, of providing a good home for you, of making a real family with you. I love you so much, and I was afraid I would blow it."

"Really?" Her blue eyes showed that she was astonished at this revelation of her father: He was afraid of something, something having to do with her.

"Yes, Katie. I was scared then, and I'm still scared now. I'm afraid I won't do it right, so sometimes I try to hide from it, or run from it. Not very courageous, I'll admit. But...do you understand any of this?"

She nodded thoughtfully. "I guess it's like when I was scared to go bowling with Sandra and her friends. I was afraid that I'd do it bad and they'd laugh at me. Is it kinda like that?"

"Kinda, but I care a lot more what you think of me than you do what Sandra thinks of you. Whether or not I do a good job with you is the most important thing in my life. I suppose that's why it's so scary for me."

A small, shy smile brightened Katie's eyes and a corner of his heart. "I don't think you need to be so scared, Daddy," she said. "You're a really good dad. Turkey and pie aren't all that big a deal. I just wanted to know that...you know."

"That I love you?"

She nodded and bent her head, staring down at her still full plate.

He reached across the table and cupped her chin in his palm, causing her to look up at him. "Katie Stafford, I couldn't possibly love you more," he said, feeling her chin quiver against his fingers. "But I could be a heck of a lot better at showing it."

At that moment, the restaurant owner appeared, bearing a pot of fresh jasmine tea. With no one else eating in the restaurant, he had apparently sent his staff home and was running the show himself.

"You like food?" he asked, pointing to their plates, which had hardly been touched. "Something wrong?"

"No, nothing's wrong," Katie piped up. "Me and my dad have just been talking about important family stuff."

"I see." He nodded politely as he poured her another cup. "And you, you like food?" he asked Michael.

Michael opened his mouth to answer, but all anyone heard was a distinct and plaintive howl from inside his coat.

He cleared his throat, trying to cover the sound. But the puppy had decided that he had been ignored and imprisoned long enough. With another piteous yowl he demanded to see the warden.

The restaurant owner nearly dropped the teapot. "What that?" he asked, glaring at Michael. "What make that sound?"

"Nothing, nothing important," Michael said, mentally searching for some reasonable excuse. He had never been skilled at making up lies under pressure. Inevitably, the truth always came blurting out before he could think of anything good enough to use.

The dog howled again, even louder than before. Katie gasped and clapped her hand over her mouth to stifle a giggle.

"Animal!" the restaurant owner shouted, his face turning dark with anger. "You have animal in coat!"

"Just one little bitty dog," Michael began, reaching into his jacket. "He isn't hurting anything, he's just—"

"No! No animal! No dog in restaurant! Inspector see dirty dog, take license!" He reached over and snatched both of their chopsticks out of their hands. "Out! You, out of Lee's restaurant with dog!"

Michael's temper soared. "Wait a minute, buddy! We haven't even finished eating yet!"

"You lucky. You no pay. Out!"

A moment later, Michael, Katie and the offending canine stood outside the restaurant as Lee slammed and locked the door behind them.

"I can't believe this," Michael said, shaking his head, "eighty-sixed from a Chinese restaurant. What a Thanksgiving this has turned out to be!"

He looked down, expecting to see Katie's woebegone little face. But, instead, she was snickering, still holding her hand over her mouth.

"Well," she said through her laughter, "it's one we won't forget. Not *ever!*"

Rebecca thought she recognized Michael's car as she turned down Cleveland Avenue. How many dark green Jaguar XJ12s could there be in town?

But why was he heading in that direction, the exact opposite of his home or office?

She decided to follow him and try to get his attention. Soon her question was answered as the Jaguar came to a stop in front of Beatrice and Jack Riley's house.

Of course, she thought as she watched Michael and Katie walk, hand in hand, up to the door. She should have thought of it herself. The Rileys were the perfect couple to adopt the new pup. The dog would do as much to heal their hearts as they would do for him.

"Good choice, Michael," she whispered as she turned her pickup down a side street.

Michael and Katie were doing a kind and generous deed on Thanksgiving Day... together... and this just wasn't the time to intrude.

Yuletide had arrived in Southern California. But, once again, Rebecca had to rely on the calendar and shop window displays to tell her so, not the weather. Houses strung with colored lights reflected their owners' personalities. Some had been carefully hung with every bulb lit and pointing in the same direction, while others had been tossed haphazardly and with gay abandon on any exterior surface of the house.

A strange weather pattern seemed to have dumped several feet of "real" snow on the rear parking lot of the local mall. Rebecca thought of the massive snows in upstate New York where she had been raised. Gladly, she would have imported a foot or so from her past to the present so that California kids could know what it was like to build an honest-to-goodness snowman.

Four days before Christmas, she was strolling down the center of the mall, looking for those last few gifts.

Every year a plethora of goodies arrived on her doorstep from her patients and their grateful owners—everything from chocolates to bubble bath to eight-by-twelve "autographed" photos of various furry and feathered creatures. Rebecca tried to give something in return, even if it was only a new squeaky toy for a dog, a sack of catnip for a feline or a mirror for a parakeet's cage.

She had done well and was considering calling it a day. As she left the mall and walked into the parking lot where a gaggle of children were pelting one another with snowballs, she spotted Beatrice Riley, standing on the sidelines, cheering on her favorites. At her feet on the end of a bright red leash sat the black Labrador puppy. Several of the smaller children had gathered around him and were taking turns petting his glossy head.

"Dr. Rebecca," Beatrice called, waving to her. "Merry Christmas!"

"To you, too," Rebecca replied as she crossed the lot to join her. "My goodness, how that dog has grown in only a few weeks."

"I know. I think that Mr. Stafford of yours lied to me when he said it was a puppy. I'm beginning to think it's a colt! You wouldn't believe how much he eats!"

"He isn't exactly *my* Mr. Stafford," Rebecca said. "He's just a friend."

"Hmm, he certainly thinks a lot of you. Talked about you the whole time he was there . . . the day he gave us the puppy, that is."

Rebecca bent down to pet the dog, trying not to look interested. "Really? What did he say?"

Beatrice's sly smile showed that she hadn't bought the nonchalance routine. "He said you had taught him a lot about letting go after a loss and moving ahead."

"He said that?"

Beatrice nodded. "I didn't want the puppy at first. I didn't want to go through having to put another animal down. That was so hard with Midas."

"I know. He was a member of your family."

"Yes, he was. And I told Mr. Stafford that no one could take Midas's place. But he told me that the puppy wouldn't be a replacement for Midas. He was a new little someone who needed me. Nothing could ever fill the void that Midas had left, but Mr. Stafford showed me that I had enough love in my heart to care for another dog, even if it would mean losing him, too, someday."

"I'm so glad, Beatrice," Rebecca said, patting the woman's back. "Michael was right. This little guy couldn't have found a better home."

After they had, once again, exchanged the season's greetings, Rebecca walked back to the pickup, a lightness in her step that was more than just holiday cheer.

Michael had listened to her after all. And he had heard—with his heart as well as his ears.

People could learn, grow and change. In a season of hope and love, it seemed that miracles were still happening.

* * *

"Oh, no! Katie, what have you done to your goat?" Rebecca stood behind Casa Colina, staring at the vision before her: a Nubian nanny goat with something that resembled a small, badly pruned tree tied to her head. Her pink nose had been transformed into a red monstrosity, smeared with crimson lipstick. Around her scrawny neck hung a plastic holly wreath.

Katie stood by, grinning broadly, extremely proud of herself. "It's Christmas Eve," she explained, "and I thought Rosie would make a great reindeer. Daddy helped me make the antlers. Aren't they great?"

Rebecca gulped. "Ah...yes...wonderful!"

Rosie seemed equally delighted with her new persona. She pranced from one end of the yard to the other, tail wagging, head high.

"Rosie the Reindeer. Now I've seen everything." Rebecca turned her attention back to Katie. "It looks like you are definitely in the Christmas spirit."

"Oh, yeah. Me and Daddy—whoops, my father and I—went out the other night to one of those places where you get to cut down your own Christmas tree. And we found the ornaments and lights and stuff in the garage and put them all on it." She rattled on breathlessly. "Then we went out and bought a new box of really pretty balls, four of them, and I got to pick them. They're pink and purple. And Daddy said we could buy some new ones every year because every Christmas is new and special."

Rebecca smiled. "Your father is a very wise man."

"And we're going to have turkey tomorrow, and dressing and pumpkin pie. Mrs. Bridget gave Daddy lessons on how to make it because she's going to leave tonight to go see her mom."

"Sounds great!" She glanced around, hoping to see some sign of Michael, but his Jaguar was gone. "Is your dad around?" She tried not to sound too eager.

"Nope, he had to go get a can of cranberry sauce. He forgot it the other day. And when he gets back, we're going to go down and listen to the carolers in the park, you know, the ones that hold candles and walk around like this...."

She gave a good impression of one of the dignified and somber chorale members who performed in the candlelight service every Christmas Eve in a small park downtown.

"Are you going to go, Dr. Rebecca? Are you? It's really neat."

"Yes, I had planned to. I know a lot of the people in the choir and I really enjoy hearing the old carols."

"Then maybe we could go together."

A Christmas Eve candlelight service, together, the three of them. Part of Rebecca's heart leapt at the thought, but the other part seized up, paralyzed by fear.

She couldn't do something like that. Never.

Although, at the moment she couldn't recall exactly why.

"I don't think so, Katie," she said, "but thank you for the offer. Here—" She reached into her purse and pulled out a small gift. "I just dropped by to give you something. Actually, it's for Rosie."

"For Rosie? Really?" Her eyes brightened as she unwrapped the bright gold and red paper to find a tiny silver bell.

"It's to go on her collar. All of her relatives back in Switzerland wear them, so I thought she should have one, too."

"Thank you, Dr. Rebecca," the girl said as she rang the bell and delighted in its delicate, silvery tones. "It's bea-uuu-tiful. Come here, Rosie, and see what the doctor brought for you."

A minute later, Rosie pranced by again, prouder than ever, with the tiny bell dangling from her thick, leather collar, tinkling with every step.

"I have to go now, Katie." Rebecca stooped to give her a hug. "Merry Christmas to you and your dad. I'll be thinking of you tomorrow."

"Me, too. I wish you could come over for dinner."

"Thank you, but I'd better stick around the house, in case somebody's dog decides to eat their Christmas tree."

"Ah, you're just teasing. That doesn't really happen."

"You'd be surprised, Katie Stafford. At this time of year, *anything* could happen."

Chapter Seven

Rebecca saw them that night at the candlelight vigil. Michael and Katie stood almost directly across from her as the carolers filed down the road that bisected the park and led to the old mission up the hill. Katie waved furiously, hopping up and down with excitement. Michael simply smiled and mouthed the words, "Merry Christmas."

Lifting her hand, Rebecca gave a quick wave in return, but even that was a tremendous effort.

She knew she should have been touched by the attention. She should have responded with genuine warmth, rather than forced civility, affection rather than fear. What was wrong with her?

Don't do it, her heart told her. *Don't get too close. You know what will happen.*

Yeah, so what's going to happen? she silently asked herself. *You might get to truly know and love a great guy and a fantastic kid. Wouldn't that be a tragedy?*

Yes, her heart replied. *It could be. It was before.*

Rebecca turned and disappeared into the crowd. For the moment, she had enjoyed as much of the holiday season and its beauty, peace and love as she could stand.

* * *

Rebecca lay in bed, dreaming that she could hear a ship's horn echoing across a foggy sea. One, two, three deep-throated blasts. Then she realized the sound wasn't that deep. In fact, it was annoyingly shrill.

It wasn't a ship at all. It was the darned telephone.

Another call in the middle of the night.

"Maybe it's Santa," she muttered as she fumbled for the phone, "and his reindeer won't fly. Yes?" she asked, trying to mentally shake herself awake.

"Rebecca, this is Michael Stafford. I know it's Christmas Eve, and I hated to call you, but I'm afraid it can't wait."

She sat up in bed, instantly alert. Even in her half-asleep state she realized that he had called her by her first name without "Doctor" preceding it. And from the worried tone of his voice, she knew that something was very wrong.

"That's okay, Michael," she said. "What's going on?"

"Rosebud is sick. I don't know what's wrong with her, but I think it's bad. Neil and Bridget left this evening for the holidays, and Katie...well...Katie is terribly upset."

"I'll be right there."

As Rebecca jumped out of bed and threw on her clothes, dread—icy and paralyzing—rose in her chest. With an effort, she pushed it down. This wasn't the time to panic.

"Not Rosie, not on Christmas Eve," she whispered as she hurried out the door and climbed into her truck. "Please, not Rosie. Katie really needs her."

The child had lost too much already. Even a heart as buoyant as hers would have a difficult time bouncing back from another tragedy so soon after the last. Rebecca was determined to do everything she could to make certain that didn't happen.

She only prayed her efforts would be enough.

The moment Rebecca entered the stable, she saw that Rosebud was even worse than she had expected. She lay on her side, bleating pitifully, Rebecca's bell still attached to her collar, smudges of lipstick still staining her nose.

As she knelt beside Michael in the straw and examined her patient, Rebecca's heart sank. The little goat's stomach was badly swollen and she was obviously in a lot of pain.

"What's wrong with her?" Katie said, as tears ran down her cheeks. "Is she going to die?"

Rebecca wanted to tell her everything was going to be fine, as she had before, but she wouldn't lie to the child. This time she wasn't sure at all. She didn't even know what was wrong.

She asked the usual questions, and Katie and Michael supplied the appropriate answers, but none of those replies gave her the information she needed.

Quickly Rebecca ran the symptoms through her head, trying to match them with an illness or injury that she had studied.

"Wait a minute," she said at last. "Do you still have avocado trees on the property? Back there behind the grape arbor?"

Katie and Michael looked at each other and nodded in unison.

"Could Rosebud have eaten any of the leaves today after I was here?" Rebecca asked Katie.

"Well...when we went to the park to hear the choir, I left her in the backyard. I guess she could have eaten some then."

"I need to know for sure," Rebecca said.

Michael jumped to his feet. "I'll check," he said.

A moment later he returned, holding a half-eaten avocado and some munched leaves. "I'm afraid you were right," he said. "Is that bad?"

Rebecca couldn't bring herself to tell them that she had lost several horses this way. Avocado leaves were deadly for animals. She felt sick with guilt. Why hadn't she warned Katie before about the avocados?

"The problem is—Rosie can't digest the leaves," she told them. "They say a goat can eat anything, and that's true...almost. But even a goat's stomach can't handle avocado leaves."

"What can we do?" Michael asked.

"We have to help her get rid of them," Rebecca said, "even if it takes all night."

"How do we do that?" Katie asked.

Rebecca smiled down at the girl. "You may think this is silly," she said, "but the old-fashioned way is the best. Do you guys have a turkey baster?"

"A *turkey baster?*" Michael asked. "Yes, Bridget just showed me how to use it the other day."

"Good, that's what I need."

"I'll go get it."

Rebecca rolled up her sleeves, then reached down to touch the little red nose as she waited for Michael to return. "Poor baby," she said. "I guess Santa will have to make his run without Rosie the Reindeer tonight."

"Do you really think this is going to help?" Michael asked as he watched Rebecca fill the baster again with a mixture of mineral oil and milk of magnesia. Gently he held the nanny's mouth open as Rebecca squeezed it in. Rosie swallowed weakly, then began to cry again.

For the past five hours they had been taking turns giving her the medicine. But so far, there had been no results.

"I don't know yet," Rebecca said, laying the baster aside and sitting in the straw beside the goat. "If we can just get enough into her, it may all work out...in the end," she added, pointing to Rosie's tail.

"A bad pun, Dr. Rebecca," Michael said with a tired smile as he sank onto the hay next to her.

"Hey, at six o'clock in the morning that's as good as it gets."

Rebecca looked over at Katie, who was sleeping in the corner, curled into a ball in the straw. Michael's leather jacket was draped over her small shoulders.

"She finally gave it up, huh?" Rebecca said.

"Yes, and I'm glad," Michael replied. "There was no reason for her to be up all night worrying. A hell of a way for a kid to spend Christmas Eve."

He gazed at the child for a long time, then he turned back to Rebecca. "You were right. I am afraid I'm going to lose her, too. I wake up in the middle of the night, sweating, worrying about it."

Rebecca nodded. "I'm not surprised, considering all that's happened to you. I felt the same way after Tim's accident, but as time passed it got easier. It will for you, too."

"Do you think so?" He looked at her with a light of hope in his blue eyes that were so much like his daughter's.

"Yes, I promise. The first two years are the worst. Then it gets easier."

Michael ran his hand over the kid's swollen belly. Rebecca noticed that his fingers were shaking slightly, and her heart went out to him. She wondered how she could ever have considered him cold and uncaring.

"When I think of Beverly," he said, "I only remember her death...the fact that I wasn't there. I remember the last time I saw her. She was so sick and helpless—she didn't even know me. Beverly was always a strong, proud woman. She wouldn't want me to remember her that way. *I* don't want to think of her that way."

"Time will help you with that, too," Rebecca said, laying a comforting hand on his broad shoulder. "The day will come when you'll remember her life—the happy times, her strength, her laughter, her beauty— more than the sad circumstances of her death."

To her surprise, he reached out, grabbed her by the shoulders and pulled her to him. For a long time, he held her tightly against his chest, his face buried in her hair, saying nothing.

Her arms went around his waist, and she allowed herself the wonderful luxury of melting into another human being. The embrace was the first intimate contact she had experienced since before Tim's death. And she couldn't believe how much she needed it or how good it felt to hold someone and to be held in return.

Finally, he released her and she was shocked to see the depth of emotion in his eyes. What she saw there was a mirror image of what she was feeling.

"You've done so much for us, Rebecca, for *me,*" he said as his hand slipped lightly down her cheek. His fingertips were so warm, so gentle as he brushed a stray curl away from her temple. "In the time I've known you, you've shown me how important it is to reach out to others."

After a quick glance at his sleeping daughter, he leaned toward her and tenderly kissed her cheek. The sensations of acute desire and equally sharp fear shot through her at the contact. Suddenly, she felt as though she couldn't breathe, couldn't speak.

"I want to reach out to you, Rebecca," he said. His fingers twined in the hair at the nape of her neck, sending shivers of pleasures down her back. "If I do... if I find the courage to reach out... will you be there?"

A hundred replies raced through Rebecca's mind as she sat there in the straw, looking into the eyes of a man she could easily love. A man she already loved. Her heart could only allow her to give one reply, "Michael... I—"

Her words were cut off by a loud bleat as Rosie began to thrash around, struggling to stand.

"Hey, hey," Rebecca said, setting issues of romance aside for the moment, "this looks promising."

"Here," he said, rising from his seat on the straw, "let me help her up."

Carefully, he lifted the nanny, his arms under her belly and supported her for a minute or so. When he released her, she stood on wobbly legs, but, shaky or not, she *was* standing. And that was what mattered at the moment.

"Now we wait again," Rebecca said. "She seems to be ready to do something."

A few minutes later, the medicine had finally worked, and the little animal had rid herself of most of her burden. She wasn't crying any longer, and her tiny tail had even begun to wag a bit.

"What a good girl!" Rebecca said. She dropped to her knees and hugged the goat around the neck. "Your mistress will be so proud of you when she wakes up."

"Should I tell her?" Michael said, nodding toward Katie.

"I wouldn't yet," Rebecca said. "In another hour or two, Rosie will be feeling even better and ready to celebrate Christmas. Why don't you let Katie sleep until then."

Michael walked over to his daughter and tucked the jacket more snugly around her shoulders and neck. "You were right about something else," he said. "Even if I lose Katie someday, I wouldn't have missed having her in my life. She's given me so much joy."

"I can imagine," Rebecca said.

"I was so afraid to love her the way I had her mother," he said. "But just look at her. How could I help it?"

Rebecca smiled. "I know what you mean. She has a beautiful spirit. I fell in love with her right away."

"Well, that feeling seems to be mutual," he said. "All the way around."

His eyes met hers and the affection she saw there went straight to her heart, bringing a rush of happiness, quickly followed by the ever-present wave of anxiety.

It never went away completely... the fear of loving... of losing.

But something in his eyes gave her the courage to push it away. At least for the moment. She stood and looked out the window at the sun, which was rising in a cloudless sky. "Merry Christmas, Michael," she said.

"Merry Chr—" He gasped. "Oh, no! Santa hasn't come! And he's spent the past month shopping and buying decorations and food to try to make up for the Thanksgiving Day Massacre."

She laughed and waved a hand toward the door. "Go, see to it that Santa takes care of business. We're fine here."

"Gee, thanks for reminding me." He hurried to the door. "Boy, if I'd blown this one, I'd have been on Katie's bad side for the next ten years."

"Katie?" a small voice piped up from the corner. "Somebody call me?"

Michael groaned. "Too late. I'm dead."

Katie sprang up from her bed in the straw, looking sleepy and tired, but delighted. "Rosebud!" she shouted. "You're standing! You're not crying anymore!"

She threw her father's jacket aside and ran to her pet. The goat's tail began to wag as she nuzzled her mistress.

"You made her well!" the child cried as she hugged the animal. "Dr. Rebecca, you fixed her! Thank you! Thank you *so* much!"

"You're welcome, Katie," Rebecca replied. "But I couldn't have done it alone. I had a lot of help." She nodded toward Michael.

Katie glowed with pride as she looked at her father. Clearly he had risen to the status of "Hero Extraordinaire" in her eyes. She bounded over to him and threw her arms around his waist. "Thanks, Daddy," she said. "This is the *best* Christmas present in the world!"

"You're welcome, kiddo." He returned her hug, then tugged on one of her curls. "But, speaking of Christmas..." He paused to clear his throat. "You see, Katie, I've been so busy with Rosebud, that I...I didn't... I haven't had the chance to..."

"Let me guess," she said, rolling her eyes heavenward, "the guy with the beard hasn't shown up, right?"

"Uh...I haven't been in the house yet, but I strongly suspect you're right."

Katie's eyes softened as she looked up at her father, then at Rosebud, who was becoming more like her frisky self by the moment.

"It isn't important, Daddy," she said. "Rosie's all that really matters. You made her better, and that's what I care about." She paused. "Rosie and pumpkin pie, that is."

Michael laughed and kissed the top of his daughter's head. "Katie, I'll have you know there are *three* pumpkin pies in that refrigerator and gobs of whipped cream to go on them. There's a great big turkey—which I'd better get into the oven—dressing, cranberry sauce, the works. You can eat and eat to your voracious little stomach's delight."

"You won't want to overdo it," Rebecca warned, "or you'll end up like Rosebud and we'll have to chase you around with a turkey baster full of mineral oil."

"Oo-ooo, yuck."

"I have a better suggestion," Michael said, walking over to the corner to retrieve his jacket. "I was just about to ask Rebecca if she wants to have pancakes with us this morning."

"Really?" Katie's smile grew even wider. "Your special pancakes?"

"With pineapple and pecans and maple syrup," he said, looking at Rebecca. "Then, of course, you're invited to hang around for my first, experimental Christmas dinner. No guarantees."

"Sounds great!" she agreed. "I accept."

Katie hurried over to Rebecca and motioned for her to lean down. Placing her lips against her ear, the girl whispered, "He doesn't make his special pancakes for just anybody. I think he really likes you."

"Hmm...that's nice," was all Rebecca could say. She felt the blood rushing to her cheeks, turning them nearly as red as the lipstick on Rosie's nose.

"What are you two whispering about?" Michael asked.

"Nothing." Katie giggled and gave Rosebud a hug. "I'll go put the syrup in the microwave," she told Rebecca. "That's *my* job when he makes pancakes."

She bounded away and out the door, running and skipping toward the house.

"Thanks for making me look good with the kid," he said when Katie was out of earshot.

"No problem," she replied. "But I do charge more for that. It'll be on my bill."

"So, I'll owe you, huh, Doc?" He lifted one eyebrow.

"Big time."

He held his hand out to her, a look of affection and apprehension in his eyes. She knew what the gesture symbolized.

"I'm here, Michael," she said, giving him her heart's answer. She took his hand and squeezed it. "Right here."

A second later she was in his arms again, but this time it wasn't a hug between friends; it was a lovers' embrace.

His kiss was warm, soft and gentle, but it conveyed a depth of passion that surprised and thrilled her. Feelings, long dormant, rose and spread deliciously through her body, reminding her that she was still very much a woman.

He gave her another, and then another. She didn't even think of resisting. Why should she, when it felt so natural, so right?

Finally, when both of them were breathless, he led her and Rosebud out of the stable and over to the goat's pen. "Considering the size of my debt," he said, carefully securing the gate, "I might have to pay you off in pancakes."

Again, he took her hand and escorted her toward the house.

"Pineapple pancakes…huh?" She bit her bottom lip, contemplating the offer.

"Maybe every Sunday morning for the rest of your life ... if you like pancakes that much."

She held on to his hand, afraid that she was going to fall off this whirling carousel of happiness any moment. "I like pancakes," she said. "Actually, I love them."

He paused in the middle of the lawn to give her another kiss.

"What about Katie?" she asked, nodding toward the house with its many windows.

"She's going to figure it out pretty quick anyway," he said before he gave her another one that made her weak in the knees.

"Okay," she said, struggling for breath, "the pancakes sound great. Let's call it a down payment."

* * * * *

THUMB PRINT COOKIES

¹/4 cup brown sugar
¹/2 cup butter or margarine
1 egg, separated
1 cup flour
¹/2 cup chopped nuts—pecans or walnuts

Combine brown sugar, butter, egg yolk and flour. Mix well. Shape dough into small balls. Beat egg white. Roll each ball in egg white, then in chopped nuts and place on ungreased cookie sheet. Preheat oven to 400°F and bake for 2 minutes. Remove from oven and push thumb in each ball, then bake approximately 2 more minutes.

Garnish

icing
maraschino cherries
chocolate kisses

After cookie cools, a dab of icing, half a maraschino cherry or a chocolate kiss can be placed in hollow left by thumbprint. Makes approximately 3 dozen cookies.

—Janet Dailey

TWELFTH NIGHT

Jennifer Greene

Christmas at Jennifer Greene's house:

Like Laura, my heroine in *Twelfth Night,* my house is a disaster at Christmas. I don't believe in making a mess halfway. Our Christmas tree always sags from the weight of decorations; we love mounds of presents and endless lights and Christmas smells in every room.

Because we live in the country, our extended family usually descends on us on Christmas Eve—and camps out here for several days, which adds to the mess, and suits us all fine. Adults open their presents on Christmas Eve, but the little ones, of course, have to wait for Santa. We spend all morning playing with the children and their presents...then inevitably play with the boxes, which always seems to be more fun. Eventually, we get around to stuffing ourselves at a massive Christmas dinner.

By Christmas night, my house looks as if a herd of elephants trampled through every room. But that evening, I confess, is my favorite time. We're all beat, but it's so rare that our family has a chance to be together. All we do is talk. But the love and sharing spirit of the holiday always make that evening precious—a memory to cherish and savor, no matter how many miles we live from each other or what different directions our lives have taken. Christmas is the glue that knits us all together.

I hope it is the same for all of you.

Enclosing a huge hug for each of you—and wishing you the most special of holiday seasons,

Jennifer Greene

Chapter One

Laura Stanley was drying her hands on a kitchen towel when she heard the muffled sound of a knock. Only burglars would consider this a respectable hour to call—it was past eleven—but prowlers wouldn't knock. So she flew through the hall in her stocking feet to yank open the front door. When she saw the man standing in the shadows, her hand flew to her heart.

"Santa! What are you doing out on the streets? It's Christmas Eve, for heaven's sake. You're supposed to be delivering presents!"

"I am. This is one of my more critical pit stops."

Laura cocked her head and once-overed her visitor with suspicious brown eyes. "I don't know if I should let you in. You have any credentials that you're the real Santa? You look like the riffraff kind to me, and I don't see any reindeer out there—"

She looked past his shoulder. The satin-black sports car parked in her drive definitely had nothing in common with a sleigh and reindeer. And although her intruder wore an authentic red Santa hat with a white fluff tassel—and was carrying an unwieldy size bag over his shoulder—she sensed a hoax. The leather jacket was hardly standard Claus attire, and even in the porch shadows she could see the fella was built lean, mean, and elegant. There was no rotund tummy, no plump cheeks, no white beard. His hair, in fact, just touched his neck and was jet black. Instead of innocent blue eyes, his were as midnight dark as the Wisconsin sky and just as fathomless.

"I don't know..." she said warily.

"Geesh, are you a hard sell. I have presents." The intruder jostled the bag on his shoulder, creating rustling, jingling, enticing sounds. "But you have to let me in to get them."

"You think you can bribe me with presents?"

"No. God, no. But if you want credentials, I have to put the presents down to show you. And I don't want to put the presents down in the snow. So if you'd let me inside, just for a second or two—"

Laura hated to be suckered in for such an obvious con job, but a bitter wind had been gusting fistfuls of snow for hours now. Madison, Wisconsin, invariably had snow for the Christmas season, but the weather gods had been outdoing themselves this year. White mounds weighed down the huge blue spruce in her front yard; artistic swirls and minimountains blanketed her steps and porch, and though the snowy landscape was magical, the air was spanking cold. Her conscience would never survive if he froze his tush, so she crossed her arms across her chest and let him in.

He pushed off his cordovan loafers at the door, stomped past her and plopped his bag of presents on the overstuffed chintz chair—acting, amazingly, as if he were familiar with the place.

She closed the door and bolted it, her eyes on him. In three seconds flat, he yanked off the Santa hat and stripped off his leather jacket. Still, as fast as he'd jettisoned those items on the back of the chintz chair, he no longer seemed in a hurry. Rolling his shoulders, he took a long, meandering glance around.

The only illumination in the squinch-size living room came from candles and Christmas tree lights. The tree branches were perilously sagging with mismatched bulbs and carnival strands of flashing lights. Floppy-bowed presents nested under the tree. Candles danced the length of the fireplace mantel, smoking the room with their cinnamon and bayberry scents. There was no conceivable place to set a glass or a pair of gloves. The spangle and glitter of Christmas decorations crowded every surface, and the splashes of reds and greens noticeably clashed with the original blue decor.

The wildly cluttered room didn't seem to bother him. For certain, he'd never seen her house decked out for Christmas before, yet he shook his head as if the mess and confusion were exactly, precisely, what he'd expected. Ambling around, he straightened the wilting angel at the treetop, peered in the windows of the gum-drop-roofed gingerbread house, then touched a ceramic Santa—the one with the chipped paint and the garish red cheeks.

She had no reason to think he even noticed the mistletoe greenery hanging from the brass chandelier in the hall, until he wandered in that direction and parked himself directly under it. When his eyes met hers, her heart thumped harder than a puppy's tail. He crooked his finger. "C'mere."

She pointed to her chest. "You mean, me?"

"Are there any other curly haired brunettes in the house by the name of Laura Stanley? Weight, about one hundred twenty pounds? Brown eyes?"

"Nope. Just me . . . although I probably weigh closer to one twenty-five—"

He crooked his finger again. "Close enough. You'll do. C'mere and I'll give you all those credentials you were asking for."

She walked toward him, but her step was deliberately cautious and wary. He didn't look like anyone who belonged in her house—or her life. She probably still had flour on her nose—she'd been baking all evening for Christmas dinner the next day. Her red sweatshirt, old jeans and Mickey Mouse socks could have come from a rummage sale special.

She was clearly meat loaf, where he was unmistakably rare prime rib. His starched white shirt was expensive linen and the watch glinting on his wrist probably cost the moon, but it was more than money that made him an intimidating kahuna. Even standing still, his whip-lean frame radiated power and tension and a vital, virile male energy. His face was carved with sharp cheekbones and a strong jaw. His rough, unruly mane of dark hair contrasted to stark white skin, and his black eyes cut, snapping with awareness of everything around him. He didn't have a single soft edge and he certainly wasn't pretty, although Laura grudgingly gave him credit for being unforgettably striking...at least to a woman who was attracted to lightning.

Personally, Laura had always been attracted by safer, gentler types. Never mind those sexy black eyes—at thirty-one, she was far too mature to be swayed by anything as inconsequential as a mountain of sheer male chemistry. She'd have to be crazy to take an emotional risk with a guy who was way, way out of her price range.

She wasn't crazy. When she reached his side, her arms were still protectively crossed over her chest. At least for a second or two.

He brushed his knuckles under her chin, coaxing her face to tilt up, and then his mouth came down on hers.

The first kiss was cold. Shivery cold. His lips were as icy as the snow-dipped landscape outside, as chill as the bitter, lonely blizzard wind. Still, his mouth was amazingly soft compared to all those strong, harsh lines in his face. Just like a Christmas present, the layer of wrapping concealed unguessable surprises. Anticipation surged through her pulse, rich and heady and achingly intoxicating.

His lips warmed up fast. So did he.

When her hands slowly climbed his shoulders, she could feel the stress and tension gradually seep out of his muscles. Will Montana rarely lost that alertness—he always seemed prepared to defend himself against an alleyful of thugs. There were no thugs in her house, no life battles or business wars to be fought of any kind, but it always took him some time to notice that.

Tonight, he noticed fairly quickly. Very quickly. With frightening speed, his black eyes took on fire, the flame of emotion that burned from the inside. He stole a second kiss, a sinking-deep kiss this time, his mouth homing on hers as if the taste of her was the only thing that had gone right for him all day.

She worried that might be true. Six months ago, when Will had stopped to help her change a flat tire, she'd been charmed by the chivalrous gesture—and him—but certainly she'd never expected to see him again. For a long time she couldn't fathom why Will wanted *her* when they were as unalike as chicken soup and caviar. They had nothing in common from economics to emotional temperament...but this wasn't the first time he'd kissed her as if she were the only thing standing between him and the insanity of life. Will was driven to work, to excel, to achieve—and he was wonderful at all three—but terrible, downright terrible, at relaxing and letting go.

He never let down his guard... until he touched her. He was always one scary, powerful stranger...until she had him in her arms.

Her fingers sieved into the coarse, thick hair of his nape. A damp, wet kiss turned darker, deeper, softer. Her whole body swayed, snuggling against him, until her breasts flattened against his hard, angular chest and a dizzying rush of sensations whooshed through her bloodstream.

At times she was desperately unsure of him, and painfully aware that Will never mentioned marriage or a future or babies—everything that mattered to her. But falling in love with him had been hopelessly easy, and the reasons were as elemental as rain. He made her feel sky-high as a woman. He made her feel more needed than air, water, shelter. She'd never experienced the ache of longing or this fire of wanting, not with any other man, and she sensed from her feminine soul that there would never be anyone like Will Montana. Not for her.

She pulled back, only because her lungs were starved for oxygen, and touched his whiskery cheek. Desire simmered between them like a stew dying to boil. The heat in his eyes was as intimate and vulnerable as his kisses, although she suspected Will would laugh at the idea of his being vulnerable. "Well, I'll be damned," she murmured. "It's you. Not Santa at all."

"You had to kiss me to figure that out? You kiss every guy who walks in your door, to check out his identity?"

"Not *every* guy. Just the ones who walk in wearing Santa hats. It was an incredibly effective disguise. For a minute there, you had me completely fooled."

It used to take such work to make Will smile. And at first she'd been shy about teasing him; he'd seemed so forbiddingly serious, such an unlikely man to enjoy a woman's brand of nonsense...but she'd been wrong. It was nonsense that brought out his slow, crooked grins and the wicked light of laughter in his eyes.

He captured the slim hand that had been accidentally wandering down his chest. "You're in trouble, Laura Stanley."

"That's hardly headline news. I knew that the instant I let you in the door." He may have handcuffed her one hand, but she had another one free.

"If you can't keep your hands off my body, you're not going to get to open your presents for a long, long time." His tone turned low and rough.

She bet he scared a lot of people with that harsh baritone. But she'd heard it before. And reveled in her feminine power to put him on that edge. "I don't need other presents. I'm perfectly happy with the one I'm holding right now."

"You don't get that one until last." He noosed her other hand. "I can't wait for you to open your stuff."

"Christmas isn't until tomorrow," she objected, but Will was insistent, tugging on her hands as he pulled her into the living room.

Once she was installed on the carpet by the tree, he upended the stack of presents from his Santa bag. A lump filled her throat. She could have guessed Will would want to do Christmas privately with her. She'd had to bully him into agreeing to coming over tomorrow for Christmas dinner at all—when it was no big thing, just her dad joining them, the only family she had since her sister had moved across the country. But Will had grown up alone, an orphan shuffled around the foster care system, and he was uncomfortable around the holidays and family traditions.

She understood his wanting to share a private Christmas, but his generosity—and pleasure in springing extravagant surprises—went beyond all boundaries she knew how to cope with. The first foil-wrapped package held a slinky, satin, white nightgown. The next, a bundle of classic old movies for her VCR. There was a year's supply of Mickey Mouse socks, a box of decadent Godiva chocolates, a scarlet bath towel bigger than a blanket, and an Italian cashmere sweater.

Her discomfort grew with each package. She'd always been happier giving than receiving, so she was doomed to suffering some awkwardness and uneasiness and not-knowing-what-to-say. But he was having fun, and she didn't want to burst his joy-of-giving bubble, and she was okay—or almost okay—until he handed her the last present. It was a tiny, black-velvet box, and inside was a sapphire heart pendant so precious that it stole her breath.

"Will," she said thickly, "you can't do this."

"We can take back anything you don't like."

"It's not about liking or not liking. It's about your giving me too many gifts and spending too much money. And I just can't take something like this," she said helplessly. She was afraid to touch it. The gold chain was impossibly delicate, and the sapphires seemed alive from within, shooting tiny, prism-blue lights into every dark corner of the room.

"Why?"

"Why? Because I have no possible way to give you presents back like this." Boxes and ribbons were strewn all around him, too. She'd chosen gloves and a muffler, because the witless man ran around in the dead of winter without any protection from the cold. And he'd draped the hand-knit muffler around his neck the instant he'd opened the package, crowing like she'd given him gold—but it wasn't gold, and her gifts were never anything like what he gave her.

"Laura, I never had a cent to call my own when I was growing up. I've got money to burn now, and there isn't a reason in hell I can't have a good time spending it. I love surprising you. What's the harm?"

It wasn't the first time she'd tried to discuss the problem of his extravagance, but it was like arguing with a man who'd been raised by the wolves. Will didn't respect any of the civilized rules. "Surprises are fine. Surprises are wonderful, but accepting a necklace like this is just . . . different. It's too expensive. And I don't want you thinking that your money matters to me."

He stretched back on his elbows, his eyes glinting with lazy amusement. "Well, if *that's* the only problem . . . I already know how you feel about my money. You'd have let me put a new roof on this place if you weren't so allergic to a little help. Or you'd have let me replace that screaming, squeaking washing machine of yours. You took my head off when I had the brakes fixed on your car, remember? Good Lord, what a hullabaloo about nothing. I thought you were going to strangle me with your bare hands."

"I can have my own car brakes fixed."

"I know you can, Ms. Independence. But you were waiting for a paycheck on Friday, and those brakes were shaky on Tuesday. It was a question of safety, not money."

"You're trying to distract me." She waggled a finger in front of his nose. "This is not about brakes. It's about sapphire necklaces."

"You can throw it out if you don't want it," he offered helpfully.

"Over my dead body. My God, you could drive a woman to violence. I'm trying to tell you that you don't *need* to be extravagant with me. I'd be perfectly happy with a key chain, for Pete's sake—"

"You need a new key chain?"

That did it. She launched herself at him with a low, dark, feminine growl of frustration. God knew, Will Montana was unpredictable enough to hit the streets shopping for key chains even at this insane hour—if she let him. There had to be some way to distract the beast and get his mind on something else.

There was.

The scoundrel would have her believe that a single kiss from her was power-packed with a narcotic. She kissed him good—but not that good. She kissed him spanking-hard—because, damnation, he was aggravating!—but she hardly had the physical strength to level a two-hundred-pound man.

Amazingly he collapsed, falling back on the bed of crinkling ribbons and bows and crumpled paper. Just as amazingly, his arms happened to be around her when he crashed, so that she toppled straight on top of him.

Any other time she'd have given him a good scolding for being such a manipulative son of a gun. She just wasn't in a scolding mood right then. She was far too busy kissing him.

Tongues found each other in the dark privacy of that kiss. He tasted like hunger, and his hands roamed down her body like a blind man defining treasure through the sense of touch. She could feel his body tightening, tensing, already hard and hot, and she hadn't even given him any real trouble yet.

She tore free of the kiss while she still had an ounce of sanity left. "I'm not taking that necklace," she warned him.

"Let's fight about that," he said, "just a little later." He rolled her beneath him. Faster than a thief, he discovered she wasn't wearing a bra under her sweatshirt. It was a dangerous mistake, not wearing a bra around Will, and she knew better than to wave a red flag in front of a bull. She knew, but it was so damned much fun to tempt him.

He needed tempting, she thought fiercely. There were a hundred worrisome, troubling things she didn't understand about the mysterious and complex man she'd fallen in love with. But she knew he had no last name. He'd chosen the tag of Montana because it was the state he was born in, and he had no other tie to anything or anyone. Maybe he loved with such abandon because he'd been abandoned. Maybe he gave so completely because it was the only way he knew to express emotion.

She was unsure of all those maybes, unsure of him in a dozen ways... but not unsure of her feelings for him.

His belt fought her like a snake, but eventually she pulled it loose and then tugged his crisp, expensive linen shirt free. She wanted her hands on him, and she wanted that now... but he wasn't helping at all. He'd already lanced her sweatshirt somewhere across the room, and then dipped down to the shadow between her breasts. His cheeks were rough, tickling rough, erotic rough, especially compared to the tracing-soft path of his tongue. Will, drat him, had always known more about her body than she did. And because he was an unprincipled rogue, he took great pleasure in driving her out of her mind.

Eventually she won the battle with his shirt buttons. Eventually—with a little help—he lost his shirt altogether. When she had his chest bare, her hands splayed, slithering, shivering, through the thatch of bristly hair on his ribs. The tempo in her blood slowed to soft time. As much as she loved that wild blood rush, there was a time and place when soft and slow and silky were simply better. Will had no patience for being treasured, but sometimes—sometimes—she could force him to suffer through it.

Candlelight flickered on his face, capturing the lonely darkness in his eyes. The tree lights flashed colors on his bare, broad shoulders. She suspected he'd forgotten the tree, the candlelight, all the signs and symbols of Christmas all around them.

She hadn't. A dozen memories spun in her mind. He'd chartered a plane to fly her to the mountains one weekend. Another time he'd shown up on a Tuesday night driving a limo, wearing a tux—and carrying a take-out bag of fast food. From the very beginning he'd made her reel with his unpredictable romantic whims, his wicked sense of humor, his lovemaking, and the so-unexpected wild streak he only let loose when they were alone.

Still, it had never been the extravagant and wildly romantic lover who'd captured her heart...but the lonely man who hungered for family. He never brought up families or children or a future together. But there had to be a reason he hung around a meat loaf-maker and a baby lover and a woman who cluttered up an entire house until it was a home. Surely he'd found her, came apart for her and with her, partly because of the sense of belonging and family she gave to him.

Anxiety suddenly thrummed through her pulse, a discordant note on a night pure with music before. Her whole relationship with Will had been a dream—a romantic dream she'd never thought would or could happen to an ordinary woman like her. Possibly she was caught up in want-to-believe. Possibly her mysterious rogue knight avoided subjects like babies and families because he had no interest in either, never had, and, oh, God, maybe never would.

"What's wrong, love?" he murmured.

"Nothing," she said fiercely, and kissed him clumsily and and wildly and hard, wanting to banish all those anxieties and fears. Given his background, it was probably natural he was uneasy about commitments. He knew nothing about the joy of families, and Will wasn't a man to be pushed. It was just that the more deeply they became involved, the more she had the increasingly frightening sensation of tiptoeing on the edge of a cliff. Her heart had never been so vulnerable. She'd never taken such huge emotional risks.

She'd never been this crazy in love with anyone.

Not like she was crazy in love with him.

"Laura—"

"Shh." She was going to love him until he couldn't see straight, and damn the risks. She simply didn't know how to make any other choice. Not with him.

"Laura, love—"

"Sssshhhh." He sensed when she was distracted, always had. It was extremely annoying, having a compelling, demanding lover who was so damned sensitive to her body—and her moods—that she couldn't get away with anything. Men never knew when a woman was faking it. How come she got landed with a rascal who could sense the first offbeat note for her?

Besides.

She was back in the mood.

Her hand stole down to the zipper on his pants. He was breathing hard. His eyes, in fact, had a whiskey glaze, though he hadn't had a lick to drink, and he could have melted all two feet of snow outside with the heat radiating from his body—yet the devil suddenly grabbed her wrist. "Laura, there's someone at the door."

"Hmm?"

"There's someone knocking," he informed her.

There couldn't be. She'd just heard the cuckoo clock in the kitchen peal out twelve bells. It was Christmas, on the button. The only Santa with any relevance to her life was already installed in-house, and no one else could conceivably be calling at this hour.

And then she heard it—the impatient, frantic, thunderous rap on her front door—and stared at Will in confusion.

"There *can't* be anyone here."

"Well, there is. I'll take care of it." But he had to leave her to do that. He twisted away, grabbed his shirt and stumbled to his feet.

She pushed a hand through her tumbled mass of curly hair. For some appalling reason, she seemed to be lying there sockless and topless on a wanton mattress of ribbons and bows and crumpled paper. It was one thing for Will to see her that way—and quite another to face unexpected company. Lurching to her feet, she searched wildly for her sweatshirt. She yanked it on and tried to finger-comb some order into her hair as she hustled toward the front door.

At the first moment when Will opened it, his broad shoulders blocked her view. A battering blizzard wind blasted through the opening, though, hurling pockets of fat, stinging snowflakes. "Who—" she started to say, and then stepped beside Will, and saw.

She hadn't seen her younger sister in a year and, especially during this holiday season, she'd been painfully lonesome for Deb. Laura had never liked or trusted the fast-talking charmer her sister had married three years before, but the pair had moved to Oregon—which seemed like the other side of the world—and the best the sisters could do was keep up via Ma Bell. Which they had. As Deb was going through her first pregnancy this past year, Laura's long-distance bill had to rival the national debt—but she hadn't cared.

Perhaps the reason babies had dominated her mind so much this Christmas season was knowing that she had a newborn nephew. More than that, Laura had simply been worried about her sister, who hadn't sounded like herself for months now. Pregnancy was known for emotional ups and downs, and Deb had told her, over and over, that everything was fine and she couldn't be happier.

There was no rational reason why Laura had sensed her sister was lying and covering up some kind of trouble.

But she hadn't realized, until that instant, what an incredibly skilled liar her sister was.

Deb had no hat, and her worn wool jacket was unbuttoned and gaping. She'd lost twenty pounds since Laura saw her last, and her kid sister had never had spare weight to throw away. Deb was the beauty in the family, yet now her cheeks were gaunt, her hair hanging straggly and unkempt. And her eyes, her wonderful, full-of-life-and-sparkle eyes, were damned near haunted with fear.

"Laura!" Deb shot one bewildered glance at Will, but then her gaze connected with Laura. Her whole face seemed to crumple. Tears brimmed in her eyes, then almost immediately turned into huge, exhausted, uncontrollable sobs.

Shock momentarily stunned Laura's vocal cords—but neither shock nor the marines nor anything as minor as an avalanche could have repressed her instinctive response. She bolted toward her sister with raised arms.

A little belatedly she realized that Deb wasn't the only one wailing at top volume.

The baby in her sister's arms was trundled and bundled up tighter than a fat papoose—and screaming like a banshee.

Chapter Two

"I just need you to take Archie for a while. I swear it won't be for that long, Laura. I just have to get settled somewhere, and right now I have no idea where we're going to end up. Roger—he doesn't want the baby. But he wants me, and until I find a place to hide out where we can both be safe—"

"Will you stop running around for thirty seconds? You *know* I'll take the baby. You *know* I'll help any way I can—you're a nitwit if you thought you ever needed to ask. Damn it, why didn't you tell me you were in trouble?"

"Because."

"Because? What kind of answer is *because?* Oh, God, did that creep put that bruise on your neck?"

"I'm fine, Laura."

"You're *not* fine. And I don't want you going anywhere. You and Archie can both stay right here with me—"

"No."

No was not a word Laura wanted to hear, but her sister had flown out to the rusty blue car again. Deb kept carting in baby debris—diapers, diaper bags, formula, a suitcase of clothes, a collapsible playpen, a baby carrier, a plastic laundry basket filled with baby toys and stuffed animals. Each time Deb jogged back outside, her gaze scanned the street as if she'd fully expected to be followed. Each time she came back in, her face looked more white, her eyes more frantic.

"You're not going anywhere," Laura repeated, louder this time, as if an increase in volume might force her sister to listen. But Deb was an unbudgeable as rock.

"I can't stay. I refuse to have you or Dad involved in this, and family would be the first place Roger would look for me. I have to worry about Archie, too, but I honestly believe Roger won't show up here—not for the baby. That was when everything really went to hell—when I got pregnant. He really *doesn't* want the baby, and he can hardly chase after me if he's bogged down with an infant. Oh, Lord, I *have* to believe Archie will be safe here—"

"You can forget that worry right now. The baby will be perfectly safe with me. I'd boil anyone in oil who even tries to lay a finger on my nephew—"

A hollow smile from Deb. Then a brief, bone-crunching hug. "I always loved that violent, blood-thirsty streak in you. You can't imagine how much I've missed you! And I'm so sorry to land this trouble at your door—"

"It's not *trouble*. You're my sister and I love you, you doofus. Let me give you some real help, for Pete's sake. We'll get the police and a lawyer—"

Deb shook her head. "I've been to the police. I've been to lawyers. Divorce papers have been filed, and a restraining order is already on the books. It's all just paper to Roger. You can't stop a man with a temper out of control with a few pieces of paper. Believe me, I know."

"Deb—"

"Just love Archie for me. Love him like I do, okay, because I couldn't stand it if he missed me. I'll be back for him, I promise, as soon as I possibly can."

"Deb—"

But Deb left faster than the spin of a dime, long before Laura could finish arguing with her. Once the door was closed, the hall was suddenly completely silent, and Laura found herself staring at the mounds and boxes of baby paraphernalia as if they'd come from outer space. She just couldn't seem to take it all in. Her sister had been abused. Was, in fact, so scared of the jerk she'd married that she was living on the run and hiding. Laura tried to absorb the information, believe it, but it seemed as unreal as a nightmare.

This couldn't be happening. The Stanley women had never lived melodramatic lives. Deb was more than just beautiful. She was sweet and giving and kind to everyone around her. No one would hurt her. How could anyone possibly hurt someone so good? Laura pushed a shaky hand through her hair, suddenly aware of all the questions she hadn't asked. She had no way to contact Deb. No way to know where she was going, or even if her sister had enough money to live on.

"Laura?" She looked up in a daze, to find Will wrapping her hands around a glass. "I heated some brandy. I know you're not fond of it, but I want you to drink some. Just a little—''

She gulped a sip. It hit her throat like a streak of fire, but it didn't help. "Will...I couldn't stop her. I couldn't even get her to slow down."

"I know you couldn't. I don't think a mountain could have made your sister listen to reason, not tonight."

"But she was scared."

"I know she was scared."

"I didn't know that Roger was that kind of rat. But I'd guessed something was wrong. We talked on the phone all the time, and I knew she wasn't sounding like herself. I should have done something!"

"Now, you know better than that. There's no way to help anyone until they're willing to admit to a problem."

Laura gestured wildly, making the brandy slosh and splash in the glass. "I'm going to kill him. Maybe with my bare hands. If that creep dares shows up here... My Lord, I can't stand it, not knowing where she's going or if she's safe or where that jerk is—"

"We'll get those answers." Will's voice was deep, quiet, calming. "You're not going to argue with me about money, not on this, are you? Because there are all kinds of things we can do for your sister. We can track down what legal help she's had so far, and we can trace where this guy is. If she's traveling on credit cards, we can use a private detective to find her, too, and then there are ways to protect her. Legal and financial ways, as well as hiring some direct security.''

She met his eyes. At some point during that emotional cyclone of a visit, Will had tried to talk with her sister, too, but there'd come a point where he'd fallen silent. Maybe he'd intuited that her sister was incapable of listening to a stranger, much less a man right then. So typical of Will, he hadn't intruded, but he'd missed nothing. He wasn't the kind of man to run away from problems—he *loved* problems, the more challenging, the better—and his concrete suggestions were exactly what she needed to reassure her.

"Let me do this, Laura," he said quietly. "I don't want to hear about your pride about money, not with a problem like this—"

"You won't. This is for my sister, not for me. Oh, God, Will, could we hire a dozen thugs?"

"Truthfully, I hadn't considered...thugs. How about if you take another sip of that brandy? I know it's hard to think rationally when you're so upset, but if you just try to calm down a little—"

"I don't want to calm down. I don't want to think rationally. I want thugs, and damnation, I've never even met a thug, much less have any idea how to go about hiring one. We need a dozen. Maybe two dozen. Enough to make sure that jerk can't get to her or the baby—"

The baby. She'd forgotten completely about the baby. Laura's eyes widened, and then she pushed the brandy glass into Will's hands and took off for the living room faster than a catapult.

Archibald Merle Gerard Thompson was lying on the floor by the Christmas tree, still swaddled in pounds of outdoor gear. Although her heart was racing, she knelt down slowly, feeling suddenly engulfed with huge, overwhelming and alien emotions.

It was such a big, unwieldy name for a little tyke. Deb always had had a back door sense of humor, but humor had nothing to do with her crazy choice of names, Laura knew. Deb had been determined to give the baby a sense of roots, so she'd taken a blend of great-grandfathers' names and packaged them together.

But the baby didn't look like an Archie. He didn't look like anyone in the family—or anyone in the universe. He just looked like... himself. His tiny face was red with heat, but he'd long quit crying and seemed entranced with all the flashing lights on the Christmas tree.

A lump filled her throat. She had never been around a newborn and didn't have the first clue what to do— how to feed or change him, what he wanted, what he needed. But loving him... oh, God, loving him was going to be no problem at all.

Clumsily she unzipped him from the blanket snowsuit bag and untied the nest of strings at his throat. His face turned toward her. Blue eyes. That dipped blue that was softer than sky and as pure as innocence. His miniature body was sturdy and plump, and, like a miracle, he fit right in the curve of her arm, the weight of him feeling as welcome and natural as her own heartbeat.

For a moment she was so engrossed in the feel and look of the baby that she didn't realize Will had come in and was standing just behind her.

When she glanced at him, his eyes flashed from her to the baby and then away. "There's some kind of playpen thing in the hall," he said swiftly. "You want it set up here? And the rest of the baby stuff put in the den?"

"Thanks, that'd be terrific," she murmured, yet a charge of anxiety suddenly shivered down her spine. It was just like Will to take over and offer practical help, and there was nothing in his face to indicate he was upset or unsettled by anything that had happened.

Yet he *had* to feel unsettled, she thought. Even in the darkest, wildest heat of passion, Will never forgot birth control—he'd never expressed a single desire to have a baby, much less to have a stranger's child suddenly forced into his life.

Instinctively Laura's arms tightened around the little one. She hadn't hesitated, even for a second, to leap in and help her sister. Will not only hadn't objected, but everything he'd done and said implied that he understood she had no choice; Deb was in trouble and Deb was family.

But the freedom and privacy their relationship had thrived on was about to disappear. Neither could have anticipated this happening, and the circumstances were only temporary. Yet her lover, for sure, had never volunteered for a complete change in their relationship like this.

And Laura wasn't at all certain how he was going to cope with it.

"Merry Christmas, Daniel!" Because Laura was busy in the kitchen, Will played host and answered the door. Laura's father was red-cheeked and smiling, but he suffered from rheumatoid arthritis and had trouble walking even on his best days. Will knew exactly where Laura had inherited an excessive dose of pride—there was no way the older man would ever ask for help—but Will swiftly took the cumbersome present from Daniel's hands and ushered him in.

"Merry Christmas to you, too! Good to see you, Will." Daniel tossed his hat on the hall tree. "I don't have to ask where Laura is." The men exchanged a wry glance. "Is the turkey big enough for the neighborhood?"

"And a battalion of the Marines, too." He took the older man's coat. "I'd better warn you now. She threatened dire harm to anyone going near the kitchen."

Daniel chuckled. "I've told that girl a hundred times not to fuss, but might as well be talking to a wall. She loves Christmas and all the rigmarole that goes with it. Where's my new grandson?"

"Sleeping right by the Christmas tree." Will watched the older man adjust his cane and beeline straight for a look at the sleeping urchin. He stayed in the doorway, rubbing the back of his neck.

Laura had telephoned her father early that morning, so Daniel knew about the baby—she had decided to tell her dad a creative version of the circumstances. Daniel had only been told that Deb was getting a divorce and moving, and that Laura had volunteered to baby-sit until her sister was resettled.

Will didn't like the fib. He understood Laura's reasoning—because of her dad's precarious health, she wanted to protect him from whatever stress she could. But Daniel was still a man, and neither weak in mind nor character just because he was physically frail. He had a right to know his daughter was being abused, a right to act. Still, Will hadn't argued with Laura. There had been no time to argue—or talk—or do anything at all last night except cope with a baby, in a household where neither had a tip sheet or rule book on anything to do with newborns.

"Daniel, can I get you a drink?"

"I wouldn't mind a little nip of sherry," Daniel admitted, and then sighed. "No, don't get it for me. She'll raise Cain if I ask for anything alcoholic. Might as well be on my head. And I need to give her a Merry Christmas kiss besides."

Will lingered behind when Daniel headed for the kitchen, but the sound of voices and laughter reached him. Typically, he heard greetings, hugs, Laura scolding her dad, his cajoling her. Family talk. He'd never felt comfortable joining in. Daniel had always welcomed him in Laura's life; he'd never asked any emotionally loaded or awkward questions...but Will could never shake the feeling that he might not be accepted.

The baby let out a howl.

Will jerked his head, first toward the kid, then toward the kitchen—assuming either Laura or Daniel would immediately come hustling in. But neither of them seemed to have heard the baby.

Jamming his hands into his pockets, he edged closer to the playpen. Archie. What a confounded, ridiculous name to give a wrinkled, red-faced alien creature with strange blue eyes that seemed murky and unfocused...except now. The baby turned its head and stared right at him...and let out another howl.

The bugger didn't like him.

Will hadn't laid a finger on the squirt last night, so he wasn't quite sure how the two of them had drawn battle lines. But they had. When Will came in sight, the baby cried. Maybe the squirt guessed that Will had some ambivalent, uneasy feelings about babies. His own mother had thrown him away when he was around this half-pint's size. That past history had nothing to do with Archie, but being anywhere near a baby reminded him of all those years when he'd felt unwanted, a misfit who belonged nowhere and to no one.

The little piker started revving up the volume, but Laura still didn't appear from the kitchen. Neither did Daniel.

Hesitantly he bent down and awkwardly patted the tyke's stomach—and earned another high-pitched wail for his trouble. The kid couldn't possibly be hungry;

Laura had fed it less than an hour ago. And at a glance, Will could see the doofus had kicked off the blankets and used some form of locomotion to wedge himself into the corner of the playpen—but Will had seen him do that a couple of times the night before; it hadn't made him cry then, so that wasn't likely the problem.

He supposed he could pick the baby up and take him to Laura. There was no way to hurt the monster by just picking him up, was there? And then she could figure it out. Every time the devil cried last night, Laura had somehow figured out what it wanted.

Gingerly he scooped up the baby—and immediately discovered it was wet. Real wet. He couldn't hold the monster out at arm's length because Laura had said something about needing to support the "darling's head." So he supported the kid's head, but he aimed for the kitchen at the speed of an Olympic track spring. Archie quit crying as soon as he started running. In fact, the infant kind of... chortled.

The moment Will reached the doorway, his mouth framed Laura's name. Instead of bellowing out an SOS, though, he hesitated. It just wasn't that simple. The whole kitchen was a scene of noise and confusion. Laura was chattering to her dad. Pots on the stove were bubbling frantically. Daniel had his hands full, taking out plastic-wrapped bowls and plates from the refrigerator. Steam was rising from the oven, where Laura was bent over, poking the golden-brown turkey.

It seemed damn selfish to interrupt them when they were both so busy. Only, how the hell was he supposed to know what to do with the kid?

His gaze automatically honed, then lingered, on Laura. Her cheeks were flushed from the heat and a swelter of unruly curls clung damply to her forehead. Her hair often looked that wild after they'd made love. She'd abandoned her shoes somewhere, and was racing around the kitchen in stocking feet. Her outfit was Christmas-red, a short skirt and long tunic top in some fuzzy material. The soft texture was no surprise; Laura was a die-hard sensualist straight to the bone.

Her throat was bare. She hadn't worn the sapphire necklace, although he noticed the tiny gold earrings winking in her ears. He'd given her those, but he suspected dryly that she wore them willingly only because he'd lied and told her they were fake, not real gold. The lady had a pit-bull stubbornness about money that he just couldn't dent. If she'd let him, he'd have showered her in jewels, but the confounded woman had an allergy to anything that cost more than a dime store sale.

His body was still on fire for her. An unappeased, frustrated fire, left over from their interrupted lovemaking last night. He understood she'd never expected the family crisis; he knew her fierce loyalty and protectiveness for both her sister and dad, and there was no question about what her priorities needed to be the night before. It was just that watching her bent down, that soft skirt cupped so alluringly to her plump fanny and sweet, warm curves....

Archie, baby-fashion, smacked him in the face. The action couldn't be deliberate. The small arm had simply flailed out blindly and happened to connect—directly with Will's nose.

It smarted. It also reminded him that he really didn't want to stand around forever with a soaking wet baby. With a baleful glance at the urchin, he trekked down the hall and turned into the den. There wasn't a room in the whole bungalow that was big enough to breathe in, but the den was really pinch-size—no space for anything but a TV, desk, and an old, worn couch in deep burgundy. They'd made love for the first time on that lumpy couch, but Will couldn't even see the material at the moment. Baby "stuff" was piled everywhere.

Archie squalled again. Will set him down on a teddy bear blanket as he hurriedly scanned the clutter for diapers and clothes. Archie wailed louder—and this time the little rat sounded mean.

"Now don't get your liver in an uproar. Have a little trust. I can do this. How hard can it be? You have to have something else to put on, though.... Well, you want to wear this white sissy thing with the clowns, or the green pajamas with the nice, macho football?"

The tyke showed absolutely no potential for making such management decisions. In fact, he started blowing a pile of bubbles. Gooey saliva bubbles. Alarmed, Will started stripping the wet pajama thing off him. The urchin quit fussing as soon as he was half naked. Gingerly, Will peeled off the diaper straps, lifted the soaker—and then didn't have a clue what to do with it.

God, this was complicated.

"You *could* be a little help here," he muttered to Archie. "This diaper business isn't news to you, and it's not like your mom sent a manual for the rest of us. I suppose we need to get you clean somehow, right? And then just put on another diaper. That general program sound okay by you?"

Bubbles. The only way the kid wanted to communicate was with bubbles. Will felt sweat forming on his brow. Science had been his ticket out of poverty; he was at home around labs and computers and formulas, no sweat. But this was so different. It seemed to take him an hour to find a receptacle for the wet diaper, track down a package of wipes and gather up the tiny clothes and a bunch of newborn-size diapers.

When he was finally ready, the kid wasn't. The baby had kicked up its legs and quit that infernal crying as soon as it was naked, but the darn fool urchin was somehow managing to suck on a toe.

Perplexed, Will crouched down on his knees and waited. Who knew? Maybe interrupting this toe-sucking ritual could somehow permanently scar the child's development. Guardians and parents were blamed for everything. Twenty years from now, Will could just picture a psychiatrist telling the kid, "Well, now we know why you're a terrorist, because that jerk stopped you from sucking your toes."

But waiting wasn't accomplishing anything, either. The kid seemed prepared to suck his toe indefinitely.

Seeking a compromise, Will straightened and started dabbing with the sticky little wipe thingie.

Momentarily he was distracted by the infant's miniature anatomy. Male anatomy was hardly unfamiliar; it was just interesting to see it in this shrunk-in-form size. Actually, the little devil seemed overendowed compared to the rest of him. Will's jaw suddenly dropped. Holy kamoly, the baby got an erection. An *erection*. At *his* age.

"I'm just gonna give you a little advice," Will muttered. "If you don't have your hormones under control at six weeks, you're headed for a lot of trouble in this life. Sexual responsibility is in, fella. And speaking for myself, I think people should take a *lot* more care not to bring babies in the world that they just want to throw away. It's hell on the baby. Trust me, I know. So when you're old enough to wear a zipper, you just keep it zipped unless you really care about the lady. You hear me?"

It was a pretty good lecture, Will thought. And amazingly, the baby actually seemed to be listening, because he released that tight gum grip on its toe and was gravely staring at him. The tyke was balder than Telly Savalas, no hair, no looks, but there just *might* be a mind between those two itsy-bitsy ears. "You ready for the diaper now?" Will asked gruffly.

He never saw it coming. Never once anticipated the method the kid would choose to answer him. He was crouched over the baby, reaching for one of those palm-size diapers, when the little monster squirted him—a full bladder load—right in the face.

Chapter Three

"The little darling's finally asleep." Laura stumbled into the living room and aimed straight for Will. "I don't know what I'd have done without you today."

"I didn't do anything."

"You made five feet of dishes disappear. You call that nothing? I don't know why you're wasting time in the lab, doing all that brilliant scientist stuff, when you could be making a real living as a magician."

He chuckled, and motioned her beside him. He didn't have to ask twice. She crashed on the couch, pretzeling her legs and fitting next to him closer than a puzzle piece. He'd drawn the drapes and turned the lights off, she noticed. A dying fire hissed in the hearth, the coals glowing like amber jewels. For the first time all day, the house was quiet, peaceful, still. She snuggled closer. It was exactly the kind of private evening they both relished. "You're always so great with my father."

"I like your dad."

"I happen to love him to death myself, but he always yells at me for making too much fuss. What would Christmas be without a fuss? And a new baby in the family made the holiday even more special...but I just had no idea how much time and energy a little one would take."

"I know. A baby is one hell of an overwhelming change to suddenly drop in your life, even if the circumstances are only temporary."

She tilted her face to look at him. All day she'd tried to read his feelings and reactions to the baby, but he hadn't sent out any clear-cut clues. Hours earlier she'd heard the shocked yelp coming from the spare room and gone running. Will had taken the urchin's squirting him as funny—they'd all laughed about it. But as much as he'd helped her with the holiday chores, she could hardly miss noticing that he steered a careful distance to avoid contact with Archie.

Lots of men were scared of small infants. And there was no rational reason for Will to form the instant, heart-clutching attachment for the baby that she had. But she'd hoped he might. Neither had asked for this sudden surprise in their lives, but if Will just had the chance to be around a baby, she'd hoped some of his wariness about children and families might naturally disappear.

He threaded a finger around a lock of her hair. "Have you thought about your job? What you're going to do about the baby on Monday morning?"

"Some, but not much. There just hasn't been time to think about my job or plans or anything else. This all happened so fast." Tiredness was wrapping around her tighter than a lasso. She'd barely slept the night before, then raced all day because of the holiday. She'd had no way to be prepared for the sudden advent of a baby in her life. Her job was only one of the overwhelming problems looming on the horizon. "I think I'm going to have to try taking him with me to work, at least until I can make other arrangements. I can't just give up my job."

"Sure you can. If you want to."

"Will, don't you dare offer to support me while I sit home and play mom. It's out of the question. My mother didn't raise her daughters to be princesses in ivory towers, singing 'Rescue Me' to every passing guy."

"I'm not a 'passing guy.'" He yanked that curl of hair, just a little. "And it isn't a crime to need some temporary financial help. Your whole world just turned upside down, for Pete's sake."

"But that's just it. Archie is only temporarily here. It took me six years to climb to this job and pay scale at Creighton's. It wouldn't make logical sense to give it up, especially when I really need that salary to support him . . . and to help my sister if I can."

"So . . . you're thinking along the lines of a baby-sitter or a nanny. Are you going to threaten violence if I offer some help with that? You need someone fast. Seems pretty damn silly not to let me open doors and get that moving, when it's something I could easily do for you."

She lifted her head. "You calling me silly, Montana?"

"I think you could knock off ten pounds of pride, and still have more than any ten people I ever met."

"My Lord. Is that *another* insult?" She twisted in his lap and murmured an ominous warning. "You're turning me on."

"I know." Even in the semidarkness, he had no trouble finding her mouth. She tasted like the only present he'd wanted this whole holiday. "You love being called names. I've never understood it, but I'm sure as hell willing to take advantage of whatever works."

She kissed him back. Once and ardently. To pay him back for the tortuously teasing kiss he'd put her through. "Don't you think that attitude is disgustingly... manipulative?"

"Well... yeah. But as I'm pretty sure you know by now, I can take it as well as dish it out." The glint in his eyes was playful. Until he really got his arms around her. "Come here, love. Manipulate me."

Since he insisted... she obliged. Weariness slipped away. She hadn't been alone with him all day. She'd barely seen him alone for a minute since her sister had shown up last night. She hadn't realized, until that instant, what a long-suffering dearth of time twenty-four hours could be.

Her tongue found his. Her hands kneaded, clutched, roamed the playground of his back. One abandoned kiss fed into another. His mouth was wet silk, hers warm satin. Need lapped at all the dark shadows, nothing so minor as carnal need, but the fiery lick of excitement and anticipation. He knew, intimately, what she could give him. She knew there was no limit to what she could take.

No man had ever touched her soul like Will. And no small mountain of a problem, she thought fiercely, was going to change anything between them. She'd make sure of it. Will never had anyone in his life he could count on. He'd been through every life battle alone, but he hungered to trust . . . as deeply as she hungered to be there for him.

She heard a vague sound in the background. And ignored it. When she was with Will, the strength of her lungs was always a source of fascination. Occasionally, of course, she had to come up for air . . . but amazingly rarely. Her lungs just didn't seem to need much plain old ordinary air, not when exposed to the rarified oxygen she breathed in through Will's touch, his scent, the sound of his breath turning hoarse and rough.

The discordant background sound echoed again. A cry. Then a muted wail. Then an amplified version of a ticked-off, complaining howl.

Archie.

Will froze at the same time she did. A bath in the Arctic couldn't have cooled her mood faster. The only mother the baby had right now was her.

He never objected when she scrambled off his lap. The baby needed her—which Will surely understood.

"So . . . what was your reason for leaving your last place of employment, Mr. Redling?"

"We needed to move. My father was ill, he was in an accident, and we're all the family he has. Madison was my hometown, and I just hoped I'd find a job here."

Laura nodded at the fresh-faced, earnest young man. "You're aware we're not offering the salary you were making in Chicago?"

"I understand that. But it won't cost us as much to live in a smaller town. And I need the job."

Laura knew he needed the job. The poor guy's face was sweating so profusely that he could barely keep his glasses up. His willingness was obviously sincere, but Creighton's had had too much turnover in the comptroller's office. She just wasn't sure if Mr. Redling would settle for long on the salary she could offer him. Judging character was a critical part of her job as employment manager. She was supposed to be good at it. "Mr. Redling..."

He waited for her to finish the question, but the thought had completely vanished from her mind. She patted Archie, who was starting to fuss, and swung out of her office chair so she could pace with the baby.

Her cubicle of an office, unfortunately, only allowed about six steps of pacing. Mr. Redling squinched back so she'd have more room, but truthfully the intrusion of a baby in his private job interview seemed to completely bewilder him. Her telephone rang—which was about the fiftieth interruption in the last half hour—and then June's head appeared around the door. "Don't forget you've got that workmen's comp meeting in ten minutes."

"Thanks, June. I know." Another fib to add to the week's full quota of them. She'd forgotten the workmen's comp meeting. She'd forgotten the Human Relations staff meeting, too. She'd forgotten whatever she'd been planning to ask Mr. Redling, and if pressed to the wall, she wasn't positive she remembered her own name. The office, she'd discovered over the past week, was just no place to bring a baby.

Answers were in the mill. It wasn't as if she'd sat on the baby-sitter problem. But her boss, James Simaker, was fast running out of patience, and she couldn't keep running a hundred miles an hour much longer, and damn... Mr. Redling was still sitting there with that hopeful expression, and her mind was shooting nothing but murky blanks.

She shifted the baby to her other shoulder, and smoothly offered a hand to the applicant. "I've really enjoyed talking with you. I'm impressed with your qualifications and I think you'd fit in well with the comptroller team. How about if we both take a couple of days to think about it? And I'll connect with you on Monday by telephone."

Mr. Redling looked startled, but hardly unhappy, that the interview was over. Laura felt relieved that she'd pulled off a reasonably professional and businesslike demeanor...until the baby suddenly chose to throw up on her white blouse. She could handle it, she told herself. And did. But it was a track race to get rid of Mr. Redling, get her blouse cleaned up, the baby changed, a bottle warmed in the lunchroom microwave, and still make the workmen's comp meeting.

By three o'clock she was back in her office with her head in her hands. Archie was cheerfully napping in his baby carrier, making snoozy little baby snores.

She'd read three baby books cover-to-cover over the last week. They all claimed newborns napped all the time. They all lied. This was the first snooze Archie had indulged in all day, and she was hopelessly envious. If she didn't catch a full night's sleep soon, she was going to lose her mind, and a murderous headache was pounding in her temples when June buzzed an incoming call. She grabbed the phone and crisped out a greeting.

"I'm trying to locate the sexiest woman in Madison, Wisconsin."

She closed her eyes, leaned back in her office chair, and savored the first easy grin she'd had all day. "You've got her, Montana. And I sure hope your day is going better than mine."

"You sound tired."

"Nah. Just an extra busy day. I'm doing great." She touched her nose, wondering if the Pinocchio gods were going to catch her for that blockbuster lie—and she'd never fibbed to Will before. The problem was that he'd been as solid as a brick this last week.

He'd not only been good. He was scaring her, he'd been so damn wonderful. She'd dragged him crib shopping—he hadn't complained. She'd invited him to dinner, then never managed to get anything prepared because she got busy with the baby—he'd ended up doing all the KP, but he hadn't said a word. And three times they'd been partially stripped and roller-coasting toward some deliciously wicked, wanton oblivion— when Archie woke up and cried.

Will was an understanding man, but it wasn't *human* to be that good. She hadn't heard a single impatient word. She hadn't heard one complaint. The Lord knew, she appreciated his understanding—how could she have guessed that one small baby could cause so much upheaval? But she sensed, in every feminine bone in her body, that Will could feel shunted as a priority in her life unless she was damn careful.

She refused to neglect Will. She simply refused. How they handled this problem together could make all the difference in their future. So far, by running at the speed of sound, she'd managed to keep up with everything she had to do. Only marginally managing, but who was handing out report cards?

"Actually, I'm calling for a pretty serious reason," Will admitted.

"Oh, Lord, did you find out anything new about my sister?"

"No, love." She could hear him switching the phone to the other ear. "She must be traveling on cash instead of credit cards, because so far our team hasn't picked up any trail. But you can easily take that as good news, Laura. If we're having trouble finding her, she's hiding just as well from the jerk. And I've got a lawyer looking into her rights, but that's going to take him some time. There isn't anything this instant we could do for her, not until we get more complete answers."

Laura rubbed her temples. "I don't know how you've put all this in motion so fast, but thanks. I wouldn't have known how to begin finding this lawyer and security people...and it's not just finding them, but knowing what questions to ask and everything else."

"You learn a different set of rules when you grow up on the wrong side of the tracks. We'll get your sister out of trouble, not to worry... but on another subject—I found a couple of nannies for you. Excellent references, already checked out. They could come over tonight if you want a look at them—"

She hesitated. She couldn't appreciate more the way Will had leapt in to help. He'd taken charge with the thoroughness of a bulldozer. It was just that he occasionally forgot—she had the same take-charge nature, too. "Well, that would be fine...except that I'm afraid I already set up someone coming over to the house to interview tonight."

He fell silent for a moment. "Well, that's great that you found someone, too, of course. But, Laura, I know how you feel about money, and if you were afraid to look at the qualifications of baby-sitters that were outside something you could afford—"

"No. This lady just plain sounded wonderful, honestly. Money had nothing to do with it."

"Okay. But having three to interview at one shot would give you more to compare with, right? And hopefully you'll hit gold with one of them." He switched gears. "I'll pick you up from work tonight."

"You don't have to. And I have my car—"

"I'll take care of your car. And I think our temporary mama has had enough pressure on her plate lately and could probably use a break. This is a surprise. You can't say no to a surprise."

She never could say no to Will about anything, but she shook her head when she saw the gleaming white limo parked outside the office at 5:05.

It wasn't the first time Will had thrown away money on a rented limo for her—or the first time she'd been startled by his outrageous and impulsive spending habits. She still remembered walking into his apartment, and shaking her head then, too. Will had every toy known to man. A scale that talked. An electric rack to warm his bath towels. A stereo that made the New York Philharmonic sound live. And a toy train that ran around the circumference of his living room, flashing lights and chugging through miniature mountains.

He'd never had toys, Laura understood, and for sure Will Montana had never expected to grow up and have money. A teacher in a rough inner-city school had realized Will's brilliance for science. He'd copped enough scholarships to earn his way through college, then started with a private, scientific research firm. That hadn't lasted long. It was never money that motivated Will, but a thirst for impossible challenges. When he started patenting some of his discoveries, the money poured in faster than rushing water. And still did. Will just kept getting ideas that were worth gold.

He'd earned that money. He had every right to enjoy it. But from the start his spending habits with her went beyond the indulgent or generous. Laura worried that he had some mixed-up feelings about money and security. But she'd also seen him at work—he had his own lab now, and was supposed to be spending his time managing a staff of employees. More often than not he could be found, sleeves rolled up, cold coffee at his side, bent over a microscope with no idea that he was two hours late for a date.

Money wasn't as important to Will as he thought it was. But, damn, when he had his mind on spending it, an avalanche wasn't likely to stop him.

"You like the chariot for the baby?" He took everything she was lugging from the office—except the baby—from her arms.

"I think you're out of your mind." But there was no scold in her voice. His eyes were full of dance and darkness. He loved to pull off a surprise.

"There's a crab bisque dinner inside. And champagne. A little Tchaikovsky for mood music. That was all easy...." Will opened the door, and ushered her into the plush, white interior. "Customizing a mini crib where we could strap the squirt in was a little tougher."

She saw the customized car seat/crib. And the five choices of pacifiers for the baby—all colors. And the just opened champagne sitting in a sterling-silver icer, resting on a bed of ice diamonds. The inside of the car was already heated. Will urged her to slip off her coat and shoes and just relax.

Once Archie was strapped in, she pushed off her coat and sank into the smooth leather seat...but relaxing came a little harder. No one had ever pampered her like Will. She'd never even been exposed to these kinds of luxuries, and she'd have to be holier than a saint not to love being spoiled.

She was no saint. She loved it fine. It was just when Will went cockamamy crazy and indulged her like this, she felt tongue-tied and awkward. How could this possibly be happening to *her?* It was as scary as a dream, where Will played the part of a rich, handsome, dark stranger that she couldn't possibly know.

But she did, of course, know him. And he wasn't the tall, dark, rich stranger out of some Cinderella fairy tale, but just him. Just her Will. Who was as easy to talk to as he'd always been.

"You give her a hard time today, fella?" Will directed the comment to Archie, who blew him a frothy bubble in response. "Yeah, I figured you did. You're about as predictable as dynamite, aren't you, doofus?"

Laura chuckled. "He was good."

Will raised a humorously skeptical eyebrow. "The day it rains cats, this little hell-raiser'll be *good*. But, thank God, he likes anything in motion. We just might be able to con him into letting us have a dinner in peace." He poured two flutes of champagne, then settled at her side while the driver sped off. "We've only got a couple of hours to goof off. I know we have to have you back to interview those nannies. But it sure felt like a good day to escape from everything for a little stretch."

"Did you have a rough day in the lab?"

"Blistering. Power failure in the middle of an experiment. Two men out sick. The phone ringing every time I got settled down to concentrate on something serious. It wasn't just one of those days when Murphy's Law was operating big time, but like Murphy was right there, trying to kick me every time I turned around."

"Well, I'd give you sympathy, because it sure sounds like you deserve it—" she tugged on his tie "—except that I know darn well, that's your favorite kind of day."

"How come I can't fool you anymore?"

"It's not *my* fault you're one of those weird people who love putting out fires, Montana. You had a blast today, so don't waste your breath denying it. You're flying high—the devil's still in your eyes."

"It's possible that I get a little bored when everything's running smooth—"

"It's possible you can't stand it worth spit," she said demurely.

He gave her a dark look. "You know, I have an entire lab full of employees who are intimidated by me. How come you're the only person in my entire life who gives me grief?"

"Because you're so easy to tease?"

"I think it's because you're one of those dangerous women who go looking for trouble...and, hey, what's this?" His fingertips stroked her nape.

"What's what?"

"This nasty, tight muscle on your neck. It feels like you've got steel wires knotted in there." He stole the fluted glass out of her hand, and leaned over to stash it in the well holder.

"I'm fine. Honestly."

"Turn around and bend your head down."

"Now, Will. Honestly I'm fine, and there's no room in here to—"

"Sure there is." The back seat had ample space for her to swing her legs around. Faster than she could protest, he had her nestled between his thighs with her head drooping on her knees. His fingers were long, strong... and mean.

She'd known her muscles were knotted up. She'd known the stress and exhaustion of the past week had been building up and taking a toll, no matter how hard she was trying to deny it. But she didn't know how incredibly whip-tired she was... until his palms and fingers started rubbing and kneading. "I'll give you a back rub after," she offered.

"Good."

"Good isn't the word for this. You're gonna turn me into putty. In fact... I'm starting to worry how you learned to be so terrific at this particular talent. How many women did you practice back rubs on before me?"

"Are you kidding? I never touched a woman before you," Will assured her.

"Uh-huh."

"It's true. All those years I was saving myself, a virgin with all my virtue and honor intact—just waiting for the right woman to come along."

"Montana?"

"Hmm?"

"You're full of bologna."

The baby had dropped off for a snooze. The warm interior and tinted windows blocked out any hint of the blustery gray winter landscape. A neon wincing-bright day suddenly turned quieter than a whisper. Her bones were begging to turn liquid.

Laura had never understood how he did it—make her feel like nothing was real before him. Maybe it was dangerous, believing that the two of them made a complete world together. But she felt safe with Will. Reality never disappeared: she was desperately worried about her sister, her heart had developed an umbilical cord attachment to the small infant sleeping in the corner, and tomorrow was likely to present even more problems than today. But when she was with Will, she felt as if there was no mountain too tall to climb as long as they were together.

Her eyelids drooped. The pressure and tension of the day seeped away. Will's palms rolled and kneaded her shoulders, then stroked a lazy, slow path down her shoulder blades and spine.

This was exactly what they'd been missing this week, she mused. It wasn't the back rub that mattered, but the time, just being together, savoring the attention they counted on from each other. Everything had been so hectic, so confoundedly busy. She needed to talk with Will, to check in and find out what his feelings were on all the sudden changes in their lives. To let that kind of communication go was dangerous, she knew, and especially with Will, who tended to bury his feelings.

She wanted to talk with him. She *needed* to talk with him.

But she hadn't slept a full night in more than a week. Her body couldn't be more tuned to Will, but she seemed to have lost control over the specific channel. A whoosh of a sigh escaped her. She could feel herself slipping, like a smooth, warm dive into the bottomless depths of a lake. There was so much sensuality in the warmth of his hands, so much tenderness in the texture of his touch.

Her eyelids drooped farther, then fell, heavier than lead. And that was the last thing she remembered.

Chapter Four

Finally, Will thought. Over the past week, he'd
doubted that he would ever have Laura alone again.

He'd been with her. Just not exactly *with* her.

The evening in the limo, she'd zonked out in the
middle of a back rub. And two nights in a row, she'd
crashed on the couch right after dinner. Will wasn't
complaining. Laura desperately needed rest, he knew,
but thankfully the unprincipled little banshee had slept
through for three nights now. She had finally had a
chance to catch up on sleep. More relevant, tonight the
urchin was with the baby-sitter. At her place. Fifteen
nice, distant, *long* miles from here.

The restaurant was called Joe's, implying a casual
eatery. It wasn't. The secluded place overlooked a lake
and private golf course; from their window view, the
landscape looked like a whipped-cream sponge cake
with a frosting of night-lights. Inside were white table-
cloths and black-tuxed waiters. An orchid centerpiece
sat on their table, along with a half-finished bottle of
Pinot Noir.

In the far corner a pianist with gentle fingers was
making the ivory keys whisper a range of love songs.
The pianist was a woman, dressed in low-cut black

crepe, with a long train of silky red hair and an upper deck guaranteed to appeal to a man's fantasies.

Will noticed her. But the woman sitting across from him was the only fantasy he wanted.

Desire coiled through him, as primed as a rattler ready to strike. That fierce hormonal response was worrisome—considering that Laura was only wearing a simple, round-necked, long-sleeved dress in a nun-demure cream color. She'd pushed cloisonné combs in her hair, undoubtedly to con all those wild, mink-brown curls into behaving. Typically they'd slipped the noose and were tumbling free. Her cheeks had a splash of blush and she'd darkened her lashes, but if she wore any other makeup, he could never see or tell it.

She could sell ads for wholesome. There was nothing in her appearance to make a man feel dangerous . . . but he did, around her. Beneath the dress, he guessed she was wearing red silk because she had a secret vice for wild underwear. He worried that other men had discovered that. He worried that other men had discovered that those soft, honest, brown eyes could glaze in passion. He worried how many other men had figured out that that naked, pink mouth could tempt a man into losing all sense of place, time and control, because they were right in the middle of dinner and he was in danger of losing all three.

"I think it's been a while since you had prime rib," he murmured.

"Did you reach that conclusion just because I fell on it like a starving wolf?" She grinned. "No man—or woman—should have to live on low-fat forever. God, I love being bad. And to give in to sin like this is all the more tempting, because it feels like I haven't had an uninterrupted meal in a hundred years. Or at least two weeks. I can't understand how the baby knows every time I pick up a fork."

"Archie doesn't like your attention diverted from anything but him," Will said. On that issue, he thought wryly, he was definitely on a wavelength with the squirt. "Thankfully, this is one night you don't have to worry about him."

"Will?"

"Hmm?" He watched the waiter discreetly set a plate of chocolate mousse in front of her. God knew where she was going to put it after leveling a five-course dinner, but he was more than willing to watch her try.

She waited until the waiter was out of sight and then picked up her fork—but her eyes were on him. "It bothered me—that your feelings might have been hurt about the baby-sitter I chose. You went to a lot of trouble to set up interviews with those nannies. And they were wonderful. Terrific qualifications, just like you said."

"There's no problem," he said swiftly. "Obviously you had to choose someone you trusted and felt comfortable with."

She nodded. "Exactly. And what I really wanted was my mom."

"Your mother?"

She nodded again. "I know that must sound a little nuts. It's been ten years since I lost my mom, and you never had a chance to know her, Will. But she would have been crazy about a new baby in the family. She'd have doted and spoiled him half to death. And Mrs. Apple is a grandma herself. She even talks the way my mom used to—if there's a baby to rock, the housework can go hang. And no matter how qualified those professional nannies were, Archie would just have been a *job* to them."

"Laura, you don't have to explain anything to me. I was fine with whatever you wanted to do...the ice cream on your mousse is melting."

She glanced down. "So it is." Her tone turned morose. "But I shouldn't. I really shouldn't. You know this is going to fly straight to my thighs, don't you?"

Will cupped his chin in a palm, and watched her rapturously inhale the mousse the same way she'd inhaled two servings of prime rib, baby asparagus tips, her salad, part of his salad, and a marine-size serving of mint-glazed potatoes. The whole time he wondered how she sensed the baby-sitter thing had gnawed on him. Technically it shouldn't have bothered him who she chose as a caregiver. But it had.

It was just...he'd wanted to help her, and she hadn't needed him. People, his entire life, had needed or wanted something from Will. He knew what to do, how to respond and react, in those scenarios. He felt comfortable. But Laura wouldn't take a dime from him, and trying to do something—*anything*—for her was harder than pulling teeth.

Neither of his parents had wanted or needed him. Will had picked up the back-street rule of life a long time ago—unless you fulfilled some function in life, people split on you. No one had any reason to stick around.

Her choice of baby-sitter didn't specifically *matter.* It was just that everything about the Christmas advent of a baby in their lives had made him less sure of her.

She put down her fork with a hedonist's heavy sigh. "That was beyond-belief good."

Will lifted his head to spot the waiter, ready to order another mousse for her. But Laura clutched his wrist before he could lift a hand.

"Don't you dare. In fact, if you allow me any more calories tonight, I'll strangle you with my bare hands."

He twisted his palm so their fingers bridged together. "Well, now you have me scared. When you start with the violent threats, I always start shaking in my boots."

"Sure you do, Montana." She motioned toward the postage-size dance floor. "You willing to risk your life with me out there? But I'm warning you. This is a test of your courage. I have two left feet."

"I sense a dare." He stood. "When a guy's gotta prove his manhood, a guy's gotta prove his manhood. And I can't believe you'd doubt I'd risk my life for you. I thought you knew long before this that I was a tough, macho kind of guy." He paused. "Who's leading, by the way?"

She was laughing when he pulled her into his arms. Only two other couples were taking advantage of the dance floor. One pair looked like they were celebrating an anniversary, and the other were just young kids in their twenties, too wrapped up each other to notice anyone else. It was the same as no one there.

Will didn't know the love song, never had learned any formal dance steps. That didn't matter, either. It was cobweb dim in the quiet corner, the lighting as blurred and hazy as smoke. Her eyes were smoky, too, as she tilted her head to look at him. She started to say something, then didn't.

Her head dropped on his shoulder, and she wrapped both arms around his neck. He caught her scent, the vague drift of something spicy and mysteriously female, and it hit him like a shot of whiskey. Like a moth to a flame, her breasts nuzzled teasingly against his chest. Their thighs were already glued. She couldn't miss feeling how easily, how intimately, he was turned on.

They swayed to the music, her hair tickling his chin, cocooned in a private world of two. She'd never had the nerve to tease him when they'd first met. He'd had no idea that making love with her would unleash a tigress—but he loved paying the price. Now she had the guts to dare a bear, and revel in the frustration she caused him.

He reveled in her. The rhythm of the music was the song of foreplay, the beat of two hearts tuning, tensing, catching the unison of desire.

The pianist changed songs.

They didn't.

Relief rushed through his bloodstream. Stress eased from his mind that he hadn't known was troubling him. It was just...that baby. He'd watched her attach to Archie like a magnet pulled to its natural pole. That she had an abundance of perceptive, caring instincts was no shock, but she'd never mentioned wanting a baby—nor had she ever mentioned marriage. Laura had never pushed him about anything.

Will knew his own character flaws. Anyone pushed him, and he locked in his heels. But it wasn't that he'd spent twenty years blocking the subject of babies and families from his mind. It wasn't like he was *afraid*.

It was just that he'd never risked losing anyone before. He'd never expected to find someone who meant the sun and the moon to him—and what he had with Laura was terrifyingly perfect. Right now, she was free to be with him, with no one intruding on their intimate, private time together. He loved romancing her, loved the freedom of being able to seduce her in unexpected places at unexpected times.

To get married and risk ruining all that?

Will snuggled her even closer, where that wild, whispery scent of hers was even more potent. Her body was warm. His was becoming hot enough to combustibly melt.

They'd make love tonight, he thought. At his place. He'd unplug the phones and lock the doors, and like always, they'd come together like fire and smoke. At a gut level, Will sensed an emotional distance between them that had never existed before Archie. Tonight they'd make that distance disappear. All they needed was some private time together. It was all they'd ever needed.

"Ms. Laura Stanley?"

Will heard the apologetic, hesitant tenor behind them. Laura lifted her head at the same time he spun her around.

The black-tuxed waiter was holding a cellular phone. "Are you Ms. Laura Stanley?"

"Yes," she said swiftly. "Good heavens. What's wrong?"

"I don't know that anything's wrong, ma'am. There's just a phone call for you."

She took it. He watched her dreamy eyes come alert, her lazy smile disappear, her relaxed posture stiffen. "It's Mrs. Apple," she told him. "We have to go home. Right away! Archie's running a fever and he won't quit crying!"

"You and I need to discuss some reasonable terms, bugger. So you got a little ear infection. You heard the doc. Squirts your size are real prone to ear infections. And that's tough, kid, one of those real unfair crapola things in life. But you scared Laura half to death, for

God's sake. You hear me? I don't want you doing it again.''

Will turned his head to make sure the kid was listening. Archie looked right at him from the depths of his infant seat—and spit out his pacifier. The thing bounced on the kitchen counter and landed on the floor, requiring a washing—*another* washing—before he could use it as a mouth plug again.

Will automatically picked it up, washed, dried and replugged—he knew *that* routine by rote—and then went back to unpacking the brown bag of groceries. Caviar, Russian, none of that idiotic domestic stuff. Crackers. A cluster of purple grapes. Brie. A bottle of dark, rich burgundy with a twenty-year-old vintage label. And a dark chocolate cake with marshmallow frosting—the look of which made him grin. He knew damn well Laura would dive straight for the chocolate and skip the wine.

''Will? Are you two getting along okay?'' Laura called from the bathroom.

''Are you kidding? No sweat. You just relax. We're getting on like a houseafire,'' Will called back, and then lowered his voice with a baleful glance at the infant. ''She doesn't think I can handle you, slugger. As if handling a fifteen-pound little twerp were even a challenge.''

He dried his hands on a towel, then scooped up the infant seat and headed for the living room. Creating a bed for Señor Trouble was the next chore on the agenda. His condo definitely didn't come crib-equipped. Two chairs pushed tight against the couch should make a safe, makeshift baby bed, but the couch material was white. He needed some kind of spit-and-diaper protector. Five pounds of impenetrable plastic?

From the corner of his eye, he saw the pacifier fly—at least five feet from its source. Will gave the kid credit for remarkable wind power, but once the pacifier had been expelled, the baby's face suddenly screwed up.

"Damn it, don't *do* that. If she hears you cry, she'll get all upset again." Faster than lightning, Will un-strapped the kid from the seat and settled the squirm-er's belly on his shoulder. "We didn't finish that talk about your learning to be reasonable. You need a lot of time. I get that. It has to be frustrating as hell to be so helpless. I get that, too. But the whole world can't re-volve around you. She has to be able to eat. She has to be able to sleep. And you're not giving her even a min-ute to catch her breath. I'm telling you right now—it's got to stop."

A belch erupted out of the infant that would have made an adolescent boy proud. Will thunked his back again. Maybe getting a Ph.D. in burping techniques had never been on his educational agenda, but he was cramming it into his lesson plan now.

Laura was in the bathtub. Actually it was a ten-thousand-buck malachite whirlpool. He'd loaded it with almond bath salts, piped in a CD of Ravel's *Bo-lero* from the stereo, and lit scented candles for light-ing. It wasn't a bath she should be enjoying alone.

In fact, thinking about her in there, naked and alone, was having a life-threatening effect on his blood pressure. But, damnation. His lover hadn't had a moment to herself since Archie had arrived. She had the plump-cheeked Mrs. Apple, but she also had a job, the house, and a life full of nuisance chores just like everyone else. The advent of the baby had just plain run her ragged.

Will clearly needed to take charge of the situation. And at home, in his own condo, he figured he had all the controls.

The baby let out a squawk. Alarmed, Will thumped harder. "Now, don't you start with me, buster. She's getting a bath, and I'm talking free time where *nothing* is gonna interrupt her—and that includes you."

Bending down, he switched on the miniature electric train that ran around his living room. Noise. The kid liked noise. Vacuum cleaners, loud stereos, choo-choo trains. But not garbage disposals—turning on one of *those* with Archie in the same universe was *not* a mistake Will would make again.

Archie squirmed, drawing up his legs and inhaling a lungful of air—then out it came. An eardrum-piercing caterwaul.

"Will?"

"He's fine, just fine," Will called cheerfully. But alone in the living room, he patted the kid on the back and picked up his pace to a jog. "I know you don't like me. You took one look and decided you couldn't stand me, but this is truce time, fella. You're not wet. You're not hungry. Damned if I can see how you could be bored. What do you *want?*"

Apparently the kid wanted to...run. Back and forth, around the couches, in between the coffee table, down the hall, back. That easily, the urchin seemed to forget his bad temper and tears. The bitsy body relaxed, sinking into the niche of Will's shoulder as if nesting there. The baby suddenly made a strange gurgling sound—almost a chortling giggle—that did the strangest thing to Will's insides. He wasn't admitting to *liking* the kid or anything as insanely impossible as that. But...the baby seemed happy. Those chortling sounds seemed a clear indication that the monkey felt secure and safe and just plain happy. With *him.*

On the eleventh lap around the condo, Will had to stop to catch his breath.

Archie let out an immediate ear-shattering bellow.

Will closed his eyes, opened them, and then started running again.

Laura flicked the faucet for the drain and shut off the bubbling jets. She reached for a thick, emerald, bath towel and stood, feeling like a new woman. How she'd needed a few minutes of no-care, no-thinking, no-worry time!

The silky warm water had been so soothing that she'd almost fallen asleep at first. But as the tension and stress seeped out of her limbs, she'd found herself smiling in the candlelit darkness...and then humming along to the wicked rhythm of *Bolero.*

Will had manipulatively set her up in that mini hedonistic paradise, she mused darkly. Her poor, naive lover undoubtedly believed he'd never have to pay the consequences for his actions. He was dead wrong.

She thumbed on the overhead light and bent over to snuff out the candles. Vanilla and almond scents overpowered the misty room. Thanks to the bath salts, her skin felt as soft and slippery as satin. She glanced at her face through the steamy mirror. Her hair was a disaster of wild curls, which would normally have depressed her—bad hair days were bad enough, but she seemed to be having an entire bad-hair life. But Will liked those curls. And her skin had a natural rose flush from that indulgent bath, and her eyes.... She leaned closer in the mirror. Personally, she'd always thought she had plain old ordinary brown eyes, but they definitely had the promise of hell in them at the moment.

Montana was never gonna know what hit him.

She fluffed, patted, dried and then hung up the towel. On the sink counter, neatly folded, was a spaghetti strap nightie. Black as sin and slinky. She lifted it over her head and let it slide down her body in a whispery whoosh.

The baby, of course, needed to be asleep before she executed any of the plans she had in mind. And Archie, much as she adored him, wasn't much for sleep—but that was okay. Parading such flagrant, flaunting attire in front of Will would do for starters. He wasn't escaping trouble tonight. No way.

He'd been asking for it—being there for her, coming through from every direction, never losing his patience, supporting her way beyond a marine's call of duty. And, man, tonight, he was gonna get it.

Cool air rushed over her skin when she opened the bathroom door. Even as she shivered, her mouth curled in an irrepressible grin. There wasn't a sound in the place—except for the toot-tooting of the Lionel toy train running around the living room. Archie wasn't crying or fussing. They were getting *along*. If Will just had time alone with the baby, she knew they'd form a bond—at least, she'd fervently hoped they would.

"Will?"

She adjusted her posture, sucking in her stomach and pushing out her breasts . . . and then forgot about looking seductive as she padded barefoot toward the kitchen. Heaven knew, there were a thousand and one gadgets around the ivy-and-white kitchen, but no live bodies.

She turned the corner in the hall and peeked in the living room. At first she saw no one there, either. Absently she bent to flick the off switch on the toy train, her gaze roaming around the room. His place had always made her uneasy; the room was all wrong for Will—all sterile whites and chrome, harsh blinds instead of curtains, an electronic paradise of entertainment "stuff" from stereos to speakers to a body-size TV. Everything in it cost the moon, but there wasn't one confounded thing that had any warmth or personal meaning. Will loved it, she knew; he'd been like an excited puppy when he'd first shown her around. But his actions told her a different truth, because they were almost never here—from the very beginning he'd always chosen to hang out at her place.

She straightened, and spun around to aim for the master bedroom—where her two lost darlings must have wandered—when she heard a breathy sigh.

She leaned over the back of the couch...and there they were. Will was lying on his back, no pillow, squished between the back couch cushions and the two chairs he'd pushed tight so the baby couldn't fall off the edge. The baby wasn't likely to fall off anything. Archie was snoozing, tummy flat on Will's chest, secure as a bug in a rug with Will's arms protectively wrapped around him.

Neither of her men showed any signs of opening their eyes. Leaning on her elbows, she cocked her chin in her palms, in no hurry to stop looking at her loved ones. True, she'd had a slightly different plan for the rest of the evening. Also true, she deeply wanted and needed some private time with that man.

But this *was* the Will she'd fallen in love with. So many times she'd been troubled by their difference in values. On the surface, Will lived for today, couldn't seem to accumulate enough *things,* and was gut-positive that money deeply mattered to him.

But this was *her* Will...the man who'd seduced her heart from the start. Even zonked out in a dead sleep, his arms protectively secured the baby. He couldn't know he was doing that. Will never seemed to know that his deepest instinct was to keep safe and care for. He so stubbornly wanted to believe he was a self-sufficient island. He *needed* to care for. He needed to love.

And be loved, she thought fiercely.

The two of them would catch a chill without a blanket. Laura turned away and hustled off to fetch one, but for the first time since Archie had barreled into their lives, she felt reassured. Everything was going to be all right. The baby may have thrown them a curveball, but there couldn't possibly be a better chance for Will to experience the joy of what family life was really like.

Chapter Five

Mrs. Apple met him at the door, wringing her hands on a ragged-edged dish towel. "I hope you don't mind my calling you," she said swiftly.

"You did exactly the right thing," Will assured her. In the background he could hear the baby wailing, and somewhere, music blaring over the sound of rushing water. In two shakes he stomped the snow from his shoes and yanked off his jacket.

"I don't want Ms. Stanley to be angry with me. She's my employer, after all, and I didn't like the idea of calling you and going behind her back. It was just—"

"Laura's not going to be mad at you, because neither one of us is going to mention that call. It's strictly an accidental surprise that I stopped by this afternoon—and we'll both just stick to that story, okay?" He winked at his fellow conspirator to reassure her. At the same time he smoothly stole the kitchen towel from her hands and reached for the older woman's wool coat from the hall tree.

"I could stay," she offered guiltily. "There's no reason I can't still take care of the baby. It was just her I was worried about. And I hate to leave you with both of them to take care of—"

"I'm a tough guy. Trust me. Don't you worry about a thing—I can handle those two in my sleep." A rash and unfounded claim, Will knew, but if he had to argue with Laura, he didn't want spectators. Once he had the plump Mrs. Apple stuffed in her wool coat, he steered her gently toward the door.

"I made her some chicken soup—"

"That was real thoughtful. Thanks."

"And I fresh-squeezed some orange juice—"

"That was real kind, too. You have a good day now, Mrs. Apple, and I'll give you a call tonight to let you know what's going on." He smiled, then firmly closed the door in her face and let a bellow whoosh of a sigh escape his lungs.

Daniel probably felt this way just before the Romans locked the door with him on the wrong side of the lions' den.

Will pushed off his shoes, then rapidly padded toward the source of the baby noise, his gaze taking in the status of the house along the way. Laura had always been a clutter bug, but the house, today, gave new meaning to the word shambles.

The Christmas tree in the living room had been taken down two weeks ago. Technically, with the tree and a ton of holiday debris long gone, there should have been room to walk around. Instead, mounds of laundry that no one had had time to fold were heaped on the couch. Baby toys and shoes were scattered everywhere, as were blankets and bibs and God knew what else.

The kitchen was worse. He only took a peek. The baby bottles had their usual pristine-clean niche, but the dishwasher gaped open—nobody'd had time to empty it. The sink counter was a beach of crumbs, and lunch food sat abandoned at the table, as if nobody'd had time to eat, much less clean up.

He hustled down the hall and found his two in the bathroom. Archie was happily chortling up a storm—naturally, the kid was stark naked—but Will didn't waste more than a swift glance at the bath-splashing baby.

The lady he loved was a mess. Curls flying. Bruise-colored shadows under her eyes. Skin whiter than a ghost. Her face was strained with exhaustion and nerves, and not that Laura could be tricky to handle, but he just had the sneaky feeling he'd have better luck juggling a lit stick of dynamite—particularly when she whipped her head around and saw him. There were times she looked at him with the glow and anticipation of passion.

This wasn't one of them.

He cautiously cleared his throat. "Hi, there."

"Will!"

"I didn't mean to startle you." He tried his best boyish grin. "I was just getting nowhere in the lab this afternoon, said to hell with it, and decided to drop by. Got lucky, huh? You got off from work early?"

"Dabbit, Will! Did Mrs. Abble tattletale to you that I cabe home sick?"

Any *normal* woman who looked like death warmed over should have been easier to con. Still, he feigned a look of surprise. "Sick? Right before she left, Mrs. Apple may have mentioned you were a little under the weather, and I can hear you have a little head cold . . ."

"I'b not sick! I don't hab *time* to be sick! I refuse to be sick! And I'b not run down from trying to do too much. Anybody and his mubber could catch a little head cold—"

Since Mrs. Apple had apparently already delivered the lecture about her doing too much—and it had gone in one of Laura's ears and out the other—Will couldn't see pushing a dead horse.

"Of course they can," he said soothingly, and leaned over to kiss her hello. His lips deliberately connected with her forehead, and rather than risk being socked in the jaw, he just laid his cheek against hers for a second. Damn it, she was burning up, and under that cobweb pallor, her cheeks were flushed darker than a scald.

"I'b *fine*," she asserted, her scowl as ornery as a bulldog's.

Will had the brief sensation that this must be what it was like to tiptoe through a bed of porcupine quills. Barefoot. "I can see you're fine—and looking beautiful," he said cheerfully. "But I don't suppose I could bribe you into letting me take over with Archie? So far, I haven't had the chance to give the little . . . darling . . . a bath. Of course, maybe you'd be afraid I'd risk drowning him . . ."

The stubborn-crab temper immediately disappeared from her expression. "Do you want to?" she asked hesitantly. Her gaze searched his. For reasons he'd never understand in a thousand years, any hint that he wanted to be around the baby worked on his lady like a potent aphrodisiac. Never mind how rotten she was feeling. Her eyes instantly settled on his like a blanket of sensual warmth. "Archie gets awfully enthusiastic around water. I'b afraid you'd get all wet—"

That was precisely the reason he'd offered to help. She wasn't just wet. She was about soaked. And although normally he'd be more inclined to notice the enticing, delectable, damn-near-mesmerizing outline of her breasts in the damp shirt, temporarily he was more worried about her catching pneumonia. "I don't mind. I've got a sweatshirt around here I could put on later. Of course, if you don't trust me to do it right—"

"Oh, Will, of course I trust you! And it really is fun, because he lubs his bath."

Will didn't know about "fun." But the miniature monster *did* behave like a charm in a bathtub—which Will discovered a number of times over the next three days. He wasn't sure if there was some danger in water-logging a baby. But the tyke quit fussing right off and went into the chortling, blowing-bubble routine.

Will wasn't about to argue with success. In fact, if they were stuck with the kid much longer, he was considering soliciting bids on an indoor swimming pool.

"I think you're a genetic throwback to the dolphin era," he told Archie on Thursday afternoon. By then, he knew every grout and tile crack in Laura's red bathroom. He had the routine down to a science by now. Four towels handy—minimum. Support the baby's head, because, man, the kid was slippery when wet. Keep a washcloth over the devil's favorite weapon...and another washcloth free to dribble water over the urchin's chest, because the kid was a hopeless sucker for the tickling dribble of water.

"You're going to take a nap after this, right? Now, don't give me that look. I already know there's no purpose in trying to reason with you. Let's talk bribes. If you sleep good, I'll give you some of that icky rice cereal in your formula when you wake up. How's that sound? Is that a bribe or what?"

From the other room, Will heard the telephone ring. He guessed Laura would answer it, but he would have ignored the call regardless. No way he could take his eyes off the kid for even a millisecond, not when Archie was in the water. God knew how new moms coped with this baby-caretaking business, but his IQ, imagination and determination had sure been challenged over the past few days.

KP should have been nothing for a couple of adults. And it wasn't—for *just* the adults. But the amount of bottles and itsy dishes a *baby* could accumulate in a matter of hours astonished Will. And then there was the wash. The proportion seemed to be one load for the adults, six for the kid. Where was the logic? The kid was smaller than a ham. It seemed to go through about fifty of those itsy-sized sleepers in about as many minutes, and then there were the fitted crib sheets. They wouldn't fold. Stomp a stocking foot on the damn things, and they still wouldn't fold. Will was a scientist, for God's sake. He had the brain and the mind to conquer serious things, *real* things, like exploring the genetic link to viruses. How the patooties could it be so hard to get those idiotic fitted sheets to lay flat?

Never mind if he'd been a tad frustrated, he told himself. Never mind that he'd never in this life expected to have dishpan hands. And never mind if his work and life had been put on entire hold this week.

He felt good.

Blisteringly, exhilaratingly good.

For the first time since the problem of Archie had descended on them, he'd been able to do something for Laura. Help. In a concrete way that mattered. And there was no question that Laura had really needed him.

"Will?"

He heard her voice from the doorway, and responded instinctively to the odd catch in her tone. "What's wrong? Who was on the phone?"

"My sister."

He couldn't look up—not until he'd safely scooped the slippery eel out of the water and pinned the wiggleworm in a bed of scarlet towels. But his gaze zoomed on her then.

Unlike three days ago, she had color in her face. The fever glaze in her eyes was gone, and so was the shrewish temper. She looked like his Laura again—dressed in an oversize Mickey Mouse sweatshirt and tight black leggings, her hair in a fresh-washed nimbus framing her face, eyes a man could beg to drown in. But something was wrong. He knew how anxiously she'd been awaiting a call from her sister, and he saw the first layer of a smile. There was relief in that brilliant smile, but she had her hands clasped so tight they were knuckle-white.

"Deb's okay?" he asked her.

"Fine. Safe, living in a women's shelter. She didn't want to give me the phone number and address. I guess...it isn't done there. Security rules or something." It obviously hurt, that her sister hadn't broken the damn rules and chosen to confide in her, but Laura pushed past it. "I had the chance to tell her that Archie was okay and doing great."

These days, Will could dry, diaper and thread the baby into a sleeper blindfolded. He didn't have to take his eyes off Laura. She was relieved to hear from her sister, no question about that, but something in her face kept ringing the red phone in his personal White House. She was shook up. He just couldn't exactly pin down why. "Deb should have called you before this. She had to know how worried you were."

"Yeah...well." Laura pushed a hand through a windfall of curls. "I told her about the lawyer you hired, his phone number and address, all the legal stuff you've done. She sounded ready to deal with it, Will. When we saw her at Christmas, she scared me to death. I thought she was going to break apart. But now she sounded so good, so strong... Oh! She said to give you a million thank-yous, and as soon as she possibly can she'll pay you back—''

"No, she won't. I didn't volunteer help because I expected a return, and the bills'll all be hidden way too deep for either of you to ever find them." He scooped up the baby in a football hold—the kid's favorite mode of transportation—and carted him into the spare room with Laura trailing just behind.

"I told her to forget it, that she'd just be wasting good energy ever trying to argue with you about money. But when she gets on her feet, I know she'll try to pay you something, Will. Deb has a lot of pride."

"Now, there's a shock. Coming from your family." He rolled Archie onto his tummy in the crib, and then both adults waited. Assuming Arch decided to buy into this nap plan, he'd either go for his thumb or want a pacifier. It was the thumb this time, and plugged right in. Laura snuggled a blanket over him, and Will switched out the light. "So she finally called. And she sounded like she was doing okay. Basically all good news. So what's bothering you?"

"Did I say something was bothering me?"

"You didn't have to. You're gonna knit your hands into a sweater, you're that strung tight. Come on. Something else is obviously on your mind." Laura, perhaps, wasn't conscious of being steered toward her bedroom. It was part of the routine he'd set up while she was sick—once the tyke was down for a nap, concoaxing her into lying down herself for at least a few minutes.

"I just don't understand how my sister got into this mess." Laura flopped down on the pansy-purple comforter and bunched a pillow behind her head. "Deb has a soft heart, but she was never a wimp. The boyfriends she picked in high school were all steady, nice guys. I just don't get it—how she could have fallen prey to a jerk like that."

"I wouldn't guess he came across as a jerk in the beginning. I think, by the stats, that abusers have a gift for looking real good at the start of a relationship." There was a mound of pillows stacked against the brass headboard. All of them were the same sissy pansy-purple color as everything else in the crowded bedroom. He confiscated a couple and stretched out next to her.

She immediately turned toward him. "Well, that's really the truth. In the beginning, he was really sweet to her. Hung on her every word like it was gold. Made out like everything she did was important to him—what she wore, where she went, what she thought." She sighed. "She couldn't choose a pair of shoes without his offering advice. I tried to tell her once that he seemed to be clinging tighter than a noose. She told me I was crazy."

"And you're still," Will said gently, "feeling guilty as hell."

"Guilty?"

Her window had one of those frilly curtains that bunched and swagged and, most unpractically, blocked the view. Even so, enough winter-watery sunlight sneaked through for him to see, clearly, the expression on her face. Whisper-light, he used the pad of his thumb to trace the frown on her forehead. "You've got a guilty sign imbedded pretty deep right here. You just can't get it off your mind, can you? You think you could have—should have—done something to get your sister out of that situation."

She didn't move away from his touch. In fact, for a second there, she seemed to quit breathing. "You make me real uneasy, Montana, when you can read my mind."

"It'd make me a lot happier if I could do it more often." He had no desire to talk about *that* frustration. "I don't know what went wrong with your sister, tiger. And I don't have answers about why she was sucked into that jerk's web. But I do know that when she was ready to ask for help, she showed up on your doorstep. She trusts you. She knew you'd be there for her. Her actions should be telling you something about the strength of the relationship you two have. If she didn't reach out before that, it wasn't because of you."

She seemed to need to think that over, and Laura never liked to think anything over too fast. It took a while before that frown gradually and completely disappeared...and then the pad of *her* thumb reached up, whisper-light, to stroke his cheek. "Montana?"

"What?"

"How is it that you persist in making me feel better? Even when I'm lower than a pit?"

"I do that, huh?"

"Yeah, you do that. And another thing. I don't know why you didn't drown me over the last few days. Some people might object to being murdered, but I'd have understood. My family always runs for cover when I'm sick. Everyone knows I turn into a cranky, unreasonable crab."

"You've sure got that right. You've been as much fun to live with as a two-headed monster," he fervently agreed.

She grinned. And then she leaned over and kissed him.

He'd almost forgotten how much she loved being insulted. He remembered now. He also remembered every broken spring and lump in the couch he'd been sleeping on for the past three nights. Laura hadn't kicked him out of her bed, but he knew she was weak as a kitten and needed serious rest. And though it seemed a distant fog of memory, he also remembered now—explicitly—that Laura lacked a certain patience for chastity.

Eventually she freed up his lungs to intake a little oxygen, but her mouth didn't move very far from his. "Take off that sweatshirt, Montana."

"I'm not so sure you're ready for the Olympics. You still had a fever last night—"

"You want me to rip it off?"

Faced with such a terrorizing threat, he promptly obeyed. But once the shirt had been hurled onto the floor—just in case she was still feeling tired—he helped participate in the sudden, violent assault on his body. He peeled off her tight black leggings, for instance, in case she was still too weak to do it. And he warmed her skin real good underneath the Mickey Mouse sweat-shirt, because he certainly didn't want her chilled when he stripped it off.

"This isn't working," she said suddenly. "At all."

"No?" He checked. She'd come up for air after that last kiss with a damp, rose-red mouth and a cloudy sheen in her eyes. His clothes were gone. So were hers, except for a bra strap and sweatshirt sleeve dangling vaguely from her right arm. As far as he could tell, it was going just fine.

"It's obvious you haven't figured this out. This is *my* seduction, Montana. Not yours. Now you just wrap your hands around the bedposts and keep 'em up there."

"Mercy," he murmured.

"Don't even bother begging. There'll be no mercy for you," she warned, and then swooped down again. Her lips took his, claimed his, like a huntress with unerring radar for her prey. At the same time, with amazing strength, she pulled his hands above his head and wrapped his fingers around the cold brass poles.

He indulged her "amazing strength," because he'd always wanted her to explore every fantasy she ever had, freely, with him. But this was different, even if he'd bite a bullet before letting her know it. It was just a small, uncomfortable secret he'd kept from her, that he couldn't stand feeling helpless, not in bed or out of it, not ever. When he was a child, Will had had too many indelible experiences at being powerless.

But she was loving this game of playing the no-mercy and no-quarter seductress. Her hands were climbing all over his body, her touch shy, then wickedly bold, her eyes checking in with his every so often—probably to make sure she was making him good and miserable.

She could have made a career as a torturer. And made CEO with no competition. Outside the skies had darkened to muddy gray. Only bleak winter light shone through the window; the pansy-purple bedroom was cluttered with debris—there was nothing in the setting to spur a romantic mood. Except her. The dim light glowed on her hair, on the flush gradually rosying her bare skin. She stopped once, vaguely searched the room, and then grabbed a white canister of baby powder from her bedside stand.

Sitting, straddling him, she liberally shook the baby powder into her palms. Lots of it. So much it went everywhere. The scent he associated with babies, not romance. But it made her hands slippery and soft. Unbearably slippery. And die-for-her soft. And her eyes met his, luminous as moonbeams, as she deliberately made a white powder road down his chest, past his belly. She took her own good time before touching the most vulnerable part of him. And she took a year caressing between his legs with a silver touch and all those satin promises in her eyes.

His knuckles had a fist grip on the bedposts—he was trying *that* hard to cater to her—but a man could only endure so much. His hands sprang free. She was all done with this game. In a small, private corner of his mind he was vaguely aware that he'd totally forgotten his intolerance of being helpless. That tiny revelation hit him with the slam of emotion. Somehow with her, only with her, he didn't mind being vulnerable. Possibly because Laura offered her own vulnerability to him with such complete honesty and trust.

He took a minute to gift wrap what she was asking for. And then he took her mouth and swept her beneath him. Laura, by nature, had a need to give. But so did he.

Making love had little in common with giving her a Christmas present, a surprise, but there were certain similar elements. Anticipation, so huge he couldn't stand it. Wonder, rising from the richness of longing and belonging. And sentiment, as if they'd had seasons of tradition loving each other, stoking deep, hot fires that burned straight to the heart of a man's soul.

Only with her. He'd only felt that with her. His whole life he'd fought needing anyone else. He'd never wanted to feel helpless or powerless again, never dependent on others for his happiness or shelter or welfare. But it wasn't like that, not with her. Need, with her, was its own power. Something to be shared, not held back.

The baby powder stuck to flesh suddenly slick and hot. The evening light had dimmed to a dusky charcoal, as dark and private as secrets. Pillows sailed and were strewn around the floor, and the covers bunched and tangled, because neither of them had taken the time to get to the sheets. To even find the sheets. He didn't give a damn about the silly fool sheets.

His hands were framing her face when she cried out, riding the powerful crest of a tidal wave. Her limbs tensed as she sailed through that ride, her eyes glazed as they met his; her hands clenched his back. "I love you, Will," she said fiercely. "Love you, love you . . ."

The anger in her voice was silk-soft, her whisper so pure female that it tipped his last prayer for control. For a second he had the oddest fear that he was lost. So lost, so out of control, that he'd never find his way again. But that crazy, inexplicable emotion sparked for only a second.

She was right there. With him. Two people couldn't get closer if they were inseparably glued.

It was a slow ride back to earth. Hearts slammed against each other for a long time. Her forehead was damp, her eyes closed, a hint of a less-than-saintly smile on her mouth. Will would have laughed—maybe roared from sheer male ego—if he'd had the energy. He didn't.

So he just held her close until they were both breathing normally again. Eventually they both collapsed, side by side, arms still tucked around each other and hands still stroking, but easy now. Languorously. Intimately. Her eyes drifted closed. Then his did, too.

From the other room, abruptly, came the wail of the banshee.

And Archie sounded more than a little ticked off.

Chapter Six

The chicken was burning. Wearing only jeans and two hot pads—Will hadn't had time to put on anything else since the baby woke up—he took the sizzling pan from the oven and set it on the burners with a clatter.

He glanced around the kitchen. The salad was done but he hadn't gotten around to starting the beans yet. He had the sneaky suspicion that he should have. The end result was going to be a reasonably nutritious dinner, but the odds were dim—okay, okay, downright dismal—that the hot foods were going to be ready at the same time. Potatoes seemed to take a whole hour. Who could have guessed? Did women come out of the womb just *knowing* those confounded tricks about timing?

"Will, are you doing okay? I can help you in there in just a few minutes," Laura called.

"Hey, you're busy with Arch. Don't sweat it. I'm doing fine—just be a few more minutes until the whole dinner's ready." Possibly that promise was a tad optimistic. Will scratched an itch on his bare chest with the hot pad, vaguely aware that he seemed to have forgotten some other critical stuff. Like setting the table. Plates, forks, butter, nonsense like that.

He hustled around the kitchen, absently whistling an off-key version of "Satisfaction." The golden oldie was way before his time, but the wicked beat suited his mood. He couldn't remember the last time he'd whistled doing anything, which momentarily startled him. Briefly he considered whether he'd missed his lab, his work, his condo—his life—over the past few days.

It relieved his mind to realize he had. He hungered for his lab, for a stretch of solid, challenging work hours. He'd dropped everything while Laura was sick, no hesitation, but it'd have been damn scary if baby-sitting and KP duty had obliterated everything that mattered to him. He missed the mind-driving, demanding concentration of his work, but when he thought about going back to his condo, he suddenly felt . . . flat. Edgy. Lonely.

Impatiently he buried that odd feeling. Obviously he needed to go home and resume his regular life again. Laura didn't need him anymore. He'd been pushing it by even staying today—and this afternoon, no question, Laura had proved beyond all sanity that she was back to her normal, dangerous energy level.

Remembering their love play that afternoon, he started whistling again. After tearing off a couple of paper towels for napkins, he flicked the beans on high, shook off the hot pads and leaned a shoulder, just for a moment, in the kitchen doorway.

Abruptly the tune disappeared from his mind. His cocky grin faded just as fast. His exuberant mood didn't slam-die so much as change, turn into something more sober and thoughtful.

The living room was only lit by a single lamp, its shade blue, so that the pool of color around it was muted and soft. That pastel light fell on Laura as she fed the baby a bottle.

After they'd made love, he'd tended the impatient baby so she could take a quick shower. She'd pulled on an ivory robe, but her feet were still bare. Her toes were keeping the cherrywood rocker in motion; her hair had dried in a fuzzy halo around her face, and her arms were around the baby like she had a hold on the Timur ruby.

Will rubbed the back of his neck. The two of them could have been done in oil: *Madonna and Baby.* For a millisecond, the image flashed through his mind of a different baby. His and hers. *Their* baby. She'd be even worse about cherishing one of her own, he mused, undoubtedly spoil it dumbfoundingly rotten and wear herself completely out, leaping for its every beck and call.

Considering how long he'd been scared witless of babies, Will wasn't sure why that image lingered as warm and enticing as a warm fire on a cold night. But his smile suddenly faded, replaced by a ripple of uneasiness snaking down his spine.

Archie *wasn't* their baby—and had absolutely nothing to do with questions buried in the back of Will's mind about the future of his relationship with Laura. Right now he had an excellent excuse for burying those questions and feelings yet again. It wasn't the time. Not while his lover was grappling with a heavyweight problem of her own.

And Laura *did* have a problem. She was holding Archie...as if the child were hers. For sure, Will had seen that look before, seen from the start how fiercely and completely she took to the tyke. He'd never said anything—hell, how would he know how a naturally loving woman responded to a baby? But now he remembered her level of anxiety after the phone call from her sister, the sick, sad look in her eyes, the way she'd laced her fingers into knots.

Laura looked up and saw him. And smiled. "Almost done here. The little darling's really having a greed attack."

"I can see that." Will glanced back at the kitchen, swore, then galloped across the room to turn down his roiling beans. But he returned to the doorway in a minute's turnaround to study her again.

"Something on your mind?" she asked humorously.

"Yeah, kind of. I forgot to ask you... After you talked with your sister, did she happen to say when she was coming back for Archie?"

Her arms suddenly tightened so protectively around the baby that the urchin's sleepy eyes popped open. Will saw that. But he wasn't sure if Laura had a clue how instinctively she clung to the baby.

"No," she said shortly. "All Deb said was 'soon.' As soon as she possibly can. She misses him terribly."

Will nodded. "The baby's only on loan, tiger," he reminded her gently.

Her chin shot up. "I know that."

"If you get too attached, make that baby everything to you, it's only going to hurt more when your sister comes back."

She quit rocking. "I'm not too attached."

"No?"

"For heaven's sake, Will. He was separated from his mom, the only security he ever had. He needs to be loved. He needs all the attention and love I can possibly give him. Whether I get attached or not has nothing to do with it—his needs are the only things that count."

Will hesitated, feeling like his stocking feet were suddenly ankle-deep in quicksand. Nothing she said was untrue or unreasonable in itself, but her tone was sharp and don't-mess-with-me defensive. She'd been ornery when she was sick, but that was fever and flu blues. She was mad at feeling bad. She wasn't mad at *him*.

He couldn't remember her ever being angry with him. They'd had a few dicey discussions about his money, but nothing that ever escalated to a serious fight. He'd never done anything—at least to his knowledge—to make her aggravated with him. But it was damn clear that she didn't like being questioned, not about this, because she responded faster and meaner than a cornered cat.

He tried a more cautious back door. "I understand how responsible you feel for Arch. But you've been investing a lot of time—"

"Time I haven't given you?" she quipped.

Hell. "Laura, I didn't say that—"

She slapped the bottle down on a table, shifted the baby to her shoulder and thumped him good. It was absolutely true that the kid needed a good thump to bring up a burp, but Will just had the sneaky intuition that she wouldn't mind thumping *him* good. "It's bothered you, hasn't it? I know—you never said you wanted children. And suddenly you were stuck, discovering exactly how much time a baby takes. But sooner or later, this was all bound to come out in the wash, Will. I can't do it forever. Pretend that wanting children and a family doesn't matter to me—"

"I always knew that family mattered to you."

She wildly shook her head and stood, still thumping Archie, but obviously too anxious and agitated to sit still in that rocker. "No. I don't think you did. I think we've both had a great time being selfish, wrapped up in each other as if nothing else in life existed. But that's playing at love. And I don't think either one of us could have gone on that way forever."

The floorboards weren't shifting, but the sensation was the same—as if the bottom was dropping out and he couldn't find a secure foothold. She hadn't exactly put it in blood—either put kids and rings in the picture, or it was over between them. But he'd have to be a brainless fool not to realize what she meant.

All the uneasy feelings he had about children and marriage—he was getting ready to deal with them. Sooner or later. Eventually. It was just so much easier to keep a dead horse buried than drag it up again. He came from never-give-a-damn parents who couldn't define commitment or love with a big-print dictionary. As a scientist, he fully intellectually understood that there was more to a man than his gene stock. Understanding that in an emotional realm was just trickier. He had some fierce feelings about children. He'd just always been afraid to bring a kid into this world until he had a notarized guarantee that he wasn't flawed in the same way as his parents. Possibly, no one in life got those notarized guarantees. Possibly, it was past time he dug up those old painful feelings and took another look at them. But at this precise moment, he'd rather chew rats.

"Laura, we weren't talking about *us*. We were talking about you and Archie, and whether or not you've got your heart so attached to that kid that you're going to be hurt—"

The baby interrupted with a loud-volume belch. It didn't divert her for even a second. "I'm going to be hurt, Will, if I keep on falling deeper and deeper in love with you, and playing at love is all you ever had in mind."

That bit. Sharper than a barbed-wire arrow. Playing at love was all his parents had ever done. "I never *played* with you. Never in a manipulative sense, or as in playing some mind game—"

"I don't think you *meant* to...but if we're being honest, I was always uneasy at your attitude about money." Again, she lifted her chin, with her eyes lanced straight on his face. "I was never sure how much of that *was* playing. You did so many romantic and wonderful and generous things, but, Will, I was always afraid you were trying to buy my affection—or that you were just willing to invest *things,* instead of emotions."

Hell, how had this deteriorated so fast? One unreasonable thing after another was coming out of her mouth. Suddenly they were on money? "I was never trying to buy your affection, for God's sake—"

"Are you sure of that? In your heart?"

He was unsure of anything, except that he couldn't remember the last time he'd been this rattled. Maybe when he was ten? No problem or challenge in life had shaken him in years. He never let it, but damn if he wasn't good and shaken now. "Look, this is just no time to be having this discussion. The baby is wide awake—"

"The baby is doing fine."

Well, he wasn't. Having the baby in the room changed everything. If he *had* to have this out with her, Will wanted it to be one-on-one alone, where he could touch and hold her, where he could make her see reason by showing her how strong, how real, how *right* certain things were between them. None of that could happen with Archie bobbing and blowing bubbles on her shoulder. With the baby right there, he couldn't even *think.* "Dinner is probably burning up in the kitchen—it's got to be ready," he said abruptly.

"So we can turn it off. I'm not hungry."

"Well, you need to eat and get your strength back." He'd lost his appetite, too. And he didn't want to hear any more. He clipped toward the hall, pushed on his shoes and grabbed his jacket. "I was going to have to leave right after dinner, anyway. It's been days since I was back at my place. You're feeling okay now, and I have a mountain of work that I can't keep neglecting—"

"Montana," she said furiously, "you're running."

There wasn't a soul in the building at seven o'clock at night. The labs were all dark. The only light in the place shone from his office.

For three days he'd worked harder than a plow horse, but somehow found himself staying late at night rather than going home. Slouched in his desk chair, feet cocked on his battered mahogany desk, he considered how many women had chased him over the years.

There'd been lots. Dozens. Most of them had been far more physically beautiful than Laura. None of them had given him constant grief about his money—in fact, a few had chased him solely because of his bank account—but all of them had been *reasonable* women. Not inclined to argue. Easy company, no challenges, no surprises, no hassles.

He could call any number of those women up, he told himself. Any time. Laura's accusing him of running away had been laughable. He'd never run from anything tough in his entire life. He just didn't appreciate being pushed against a wall. He'd been pushed against a wall too many times as a kid, forced to live by others' whims, so starved for security that he'd towed any line handed him. He had security now. He had money up the wazoo. Nobody—no way, no how—was ever going to push him again.

Abruptly his stomach grumbled and rumbled, and he thought, *Damn it. Not again.*

He'd lost his cookies after both breakfast and lunch. Usually he had a cast-iron stomach, but this problem could have been anticipated. There was a perfectly obvious reason why he was having trouble keeping food down.

He'd caught Laura's flu.

It had nothing to do with anxiety about losing her.

This time, slowly, his stomach quit pitching those sharp acid pains and settled back down. He was fine again. Completely fine. It just miraculously happened that he had a shorter-lived flu than Laura'd had.

The overhead cast a glaring light on the slab of his mahogany desk. The desk was beat up, as were the file cabinets and the old red leather couch that he sometimes slept on when he was working too late to go home. His labs were spotless and had the best technological equipment that money could buy. He always meant to get around to doing something about his office. It looked as whipped-around as he felt. And it was too damn silent.

Silken-soft snowflakes were falling outside, silver against the blackening night. Like magic, the crystal flakes splashing on the window had extraordinary beauty—but they were gone in a blink, changed to nothing more than mini rivulets of water. Some things in life didn't last, Will mused, no different than those pricelessly beautiful snowflakes.

He knew that fact of life, had known it since he was knee high. You couldn't count on anything lasting. You enjoyed whatever good or joy you could glean from life, but you never counted on anyone being there for the long haul. A man could fall into a well so bottomless he could never climb out if he were unrealistic. Will had molded himself into a hard-core realist. He had never allowed himself to expect snowflakes to stay in their crystal state forever.

He'd find someone else, he told himself.

The logical, scientific part of his mind easily defined some specific criteria. She'd be a blonde or a redhead, definitely nothing near the entire brown or brunette realm. She'd have blue eyes or green, anything but that dark, sweet-tea brown color. She'd be comfortably greedy—at least greedy enough so he could spoil her all he wanted without her raising Cain—and since the entire natural world was overloaded with greedy people, that criteria should be finger-snap-easy to fill. She'd like jewels, not Mickey Mouse sweatshirts. And she'd be someone, for damn sure, who had more brains than to unreasonably push a man.

He slouched deeper in his creaking office chair and closed his eyes, determined to picture this imaginary woman.

He waited, but no imaginary woman came into his mind. Only a real one did. Only *her.* In that most unwilling and unwanted mental picture, she was wearing floppy socks, and those tight leggings that cupped her fanny, and her nut-brown hair was a soft frizz fest of untamable curls. Her mouth was tipped in one of those smiles that could drive a man clear out of his mind—no way she had mercy or morals, not when she was feeling full of pepper. In that mental image she had her heart in her eyes, just like when he'd left her... And Will knew damn well he was right about her being dangerously, vulnerably overattached to the baby—but cows would fly before he could get that woman to listen.

He loved her, Will thought morosely.

She was always going to have her unreasonable moments. There were always going to be times when she wouldn't listen, when she threw him for a loop, and no way was she ever going to cut him any slack in the honesty department.

How terrifying to realize that he knew her flaws. And damnation, he even loved her for those, too.

It wouldn't do a lick of good to find someone else. Laura was the one clawing at his stomach, stuck like a needle in his heart. Hell, he missed her so much he felt like a corner of his soul had been ripped off and torn jagged. And nothing was making that pit-empty awful feeling go away.

Laura half expected the lab's front doors to be locked, but she gained entry with no problem. Her upset stomach wasn't so easy to resolve. She stepped inside the dark lobby with a hand on her abdomen, afraid she was going to be sick any minute.

Will's car was in the lot; the lone light from his office shone in the dark snowy night, and he'd have turned on the extensive security systems before leaving. So he was here. And since he hadn't answered the telephone in his condo for days, she figured her best chance of tracking him down was here.

She wanted to track him down.

It was just, temporarily, she was a little short on guts.

Mrs. Apple was lined up to have an all-night pajama party with the baby, so Laura didn't have to worry about time. She dropped her jacket on a chair in the lobby, took a breath, stuck her hands in her jeans' pockets, and—ignoring the drunk butterflies in her stomach—forged ahead.

A dim lighting system came on automatically after dark, so neither the receptionist's office nor the labs were ever pitch black. The halls, though, were ghostly, eerily dark and haunted with shadows, but Laura could hardly use that as an excuse to slow down. She knew the way. It was hardly the first time she'd tracked Will down to his spare office in the back. But all those other times, she'd known for positive that he'd wanted to see her.

A yellow rectangle of light spilled from his open door. She saw it, but she couldn't hear a single sound coming from within. Without making a sound herself, she fluffed up her hair, straightened her red cashmere sweater—the one he'd given her—and then told herself to put on a smile.

It was probably a sick-with-nerves smile, but she plastered it on her face before forcing herself into that naked pool of yellow light.

He didn't see her. Not immediately. But she saw him, and suddenly she forgot about all those nerves and nausea and anxiety.

He was slouched in that mammoth office desk chair like he'd lost his best friend. At some point he'd taken off his lab coat and tossed it over a chair arm, but it looked as if he'd been sleeping in that blue chambray shirt for a week. His chin had a three-day growth of whiskers; his hair was rumpled and disheveled; and his eyes had huge, dark shadows. Energy. She'd never seen Will when he wasn't packing a full pistol of vital, virile—exhausting—male energy. Not now. Right now he looked more whipped than a heart-sore puppy.

"Will?"

He'd been staring blankly out the window, but his head instantly swiveled toward the sound of her voice. She'd been so afraid he wouldn't want to see her, afraid that he had been so angry or fed up that he'd written her off. In his shoes, she'd be damned fed up. But his eyes scored on hers, seared on hers, like a man with a thirst that no drink of water was going to quench.

"You've been harder to catch up with than an Olympic track runner. I didn't want to bother you at work, but I kept calling the condo and couldn't seem to catch you at home—" She stopped abruptly, thinking, No, starting out with that lightweight level of chitchat is all wrong. Pride was the problem. It had never been easy for her to lay herself bare, even when she wanted to. Even when she needed to. She took a long breath and started again. "Will . . . you have every right to be madder than a hornet with me."

"I'm not mad at you." The words came out quiet, with a too-much-coffee hoarseness and as if his throat were acrid dry.

"Well, you should be. I'm sorry. You did so much for me—helping when I was sick, never complaining—and then I jumped all over you. It was the wrong time to have any kind of serious talk, just like you said—"

"Maybe I was running. Like *you* said." His eyes hadn't left her face yet. "I won't do that again—run out on you. If you want to talk, I'm listening."

Maybe he was willing to listen, but she suddenly lost all interest in talking. For darn sure, she was going to die from misery trying to communicate *anything* from the five-mile distance across the room. His hands lifted when he saw her take the first step. His arms were wide open by the time she launched herself in an awkward tumble on his lap. Damn it, she seemed to be trembling from head to toe.

"I didn't like quarreling with you, Montana. At all. For God's sake, don't ever let me do it again."

"It may be just a little unrealistic, love, to think we'll never have another fight—"

"Forget that. I don't want to hear about being realistic. Not right now." She framed his face in her hands and kissed him. There was no way a bunch of stupid words was ever going to express how terrified she'd been at losing him. She told him. She just told him from the medium of her heart. She was curled up in his lap as awkwardly as a folded-up accordion, probably killing off his circulation in a dozen places, but that first fierce kiss desperately needed to be said.

One kiss couldn't begin to explain everything, so she poured her heart into a second one. His beard scraped her cheek. And his mouth, she discovered with her tongue, was as painfully dry as she'd guessed. But his lips were softer than butter, and man. He responded with all the wildness of relief, as if combustible emotions had been trapped inside him for days. She wasn't the only one who'd stored up a mountain of feelings.

His hands stole under her red sweater faster than heat lightning, but there was nothing sexual in that first contact. It was as if he were seeking the texture of skin, the warmth of flesh, the surety of knowing she was really there.

She was there. Groping blindly to loosen the buttons on his shirt, and struggling to change positions and straddle him in that big chair without permanently injuring him in the process.

"Laura—"

She heard the huskiness in his voice, but she also felt that sandpaper whisper against the pulse of her throat. Heat pooled low in her belly, an instinctive response that she simply couldn't help.

"Shh." She shouldn't have pushed him. It was a mistake she'd never make again. He mattered more to her than the sun and the moon. She had no idea how their future was going to be resolved—and she didn't care. She'd take every moment in life she could savor with Will. Nothing was right without him. Nothing was the same.

She could have survived if she'd lost him, because, damnation, a woman could survive anything she had to. But to throw away love that felt this right was crazy. Crazy and unbearably wrong.

He tore loose from her mouth, but only to brand a series of grazing kisses down her throat, into her hair. "I think we may kill ourselves in this chair."

"We'll have to cope." She wasn't taking her hands off him. His shirt was finally open, his skin warm, and his heart beating, beating, under her hands.

"There's a couch right there—"

"Hmm." The relevance of the couch momentarily escaped her. She simply had another, more serious problem requiring her immediate attention. Loving him. At some instinctive level she sensed Will had never shaken the memories of being abandoned. He'd never really trusted words of love, no matter how often she said them, no matter how much she meant them. It was something they needed to get straight, she thought. Right now. And, poor baby, he'd just have to suffer through the lesson.

She knew when he lifted her. The chair creaked louder than a groaning ghost and his hands swept under her fanny. Her arms were locked around his neck, so she had absolutely no fear of falling. She supposed she should be worried about breaking his back, but all she could seem to worry about was the look in his eyes.

"I love you, Montana," she said fiercely. "I love you so much I can't stand it. And I'm going to try—I really want to—to love you so much that you can't stand it."

He started to respond, but the sound that emerged from his throat came from no known language she'd ever heard. When he settled her on the old leather couch, he followed her down. Her sweater was shrugged and tugged off and she'd accidentally neglected to wear a bra, maybe in some crazy hope that the night would turn out this way. The leather was chill-cold against her back, but the fire in his hands couldn't have warmed her faster. His palms stroked and caressed, sweeping over her flesh with treasuring intimacy.

Her nipples hurt under the soft wash of his tongue. That sweet-sharp ache seemed to echo in every nerve ending in her body. Her hands traveled him like a well-loved road, roaming every side bend, every tough, hard flattop and curve from his ribs to his navel.

The glaring light kept flashing in her eyes . . . and his. Any other time that harsh fluorescent light might have brought out her inhibitions—it was impossible to hide anything under that brazen glare—yet it ignited her emotions instead of quelling them. Romance wasn't just a limo and champagne. Romance was what they were together, what they brought together. This heady, dizzy, wondrous feeling came from the inside, not the outside. It wouldn't have mattered if they were in a cave.

"You're not," he discovered, "wearing any panties."

"I forgot."

"I don't think you forgot. I think you knew exactly what it'd do to me when I found out you had nothing under those jeans."

"Possibly," she murmured demurely.

He laughed. Just for a second, but that sound was so exuberantly rich and male and real. He was happy, she thought fiercely. It was that simple, the happiness they brought each other. And he'd known so little of it in his life.

"You going to help me get your jeans off?"

"No."

"Are you going to help me get my jeans off?"

"No. I just don't have time right now, Will. Maybe if you ask me in a little while...."

It seemed he wasn't willing to wait that little while. He didn't want to wait at all. She could have guessed he'd manage the double jeans removal problem with no sweat. Montana was a creative and competent man. He even managed to remember that he had protection stashed in his wallet—which gave her a thirty-second qualm. But, no, right then she didn't want to think about babies or having babies or whether he'd ever be ready to take that risk.

Love was a risk in itself. And they were both willing to take it, both willing to risk being vulnerable and naked and showing need to each other. It was an honest need, this clawing to have him. It was wicked and lusty and a little frightening, how much she wanted him inside her, claiming her, taking her. But there was also tenderness, so huge and overwhelming that it hurt to express it. And wonder, because she wanted to give him that gift, too, how wondrous he made her feel and how perilously, powerfully vulnerable.

Fire lapped and spun, licking at skin, fueling kisses that were already out of control. The lumpy couch was never meant to be a mattress. The office was never meant to be a private bedroom.

"I love you," he whispered, the words so low she almost didn't hear them. "Love you," he echoed again, then again, as his body drove in, dove in, joining with hers completely.

He'd never said the words before. Laura had always told herself that it didn't matter, because she knew how he treated her, how he was with her, knew there was love in his heart even if the word itself scared him. But it did matter, she discovered. It mattered hugely. Because the love in his voice scored an arrow-sharp hit direct to her heart, and emotions spilled from her in an uncontrolled avalanche.

Whatever scared him before, no longer seemed to exist. He most definitely wasn't scared now. Montana, the unprincipled rogue, was mercilessly determined to drive her right off the edge of sanity. She knew the rhythm, but not the height of this refrain. She knew the song, but not the depth of these soul-soft lyrics.

They fit like a key and a lock, she thought fiercely. With a love this strong, the future would surely take care of itself.

She desperately wanted to believe that.

Chapter Seven

"Will, I couldn't be happier in a month of Sundays. I keep telling you." Laura pushed aside the curtains and checked the driveway for the tenth time. "I'm absolutely thrilled that my sister's okay and on her feet again. And it's been two months since she's seen Archie! I can hardly wait to see them together again."

"I know you're happy for your sister, sweetheart. You just seem a little . . . restless." An understatement, Will thought. She was flying back and forth to that window, edgier than a cat in a storm. And he noticed she hadn't let the baby out of her arms in the past two hours.

"I'm not restless! I'm just anxious to see her!"

"I understand," Will said soothingly, and let it drop. All day he'd had a dark feeling of premonition, an uneasiness he couldn't shake—but maybe Laura was as happy about parting from Archie as she claimed.

He pushed his fingers at the ache spot in his lower back and glanced at the debris in the hall. Crib, playpen, diapers, clothes, and the laundry basket full of baby toys were all packed, waiting for Deb's arrival. Nothing left to carry or arrange, except for the few last-minute items that the baby might still need.

Will had arranged more than that over the last few weeks. Laura's sister was no longer living in a women's shelter, but set up in a duplex in St. Louis, with a new computer and the start-up kitty to establish an accounting business from home. The final papers on her divorce were being hustled through. Although a restraining order had been placed against her ex, Will figured it wouldn't hurt to have a watchdog on Deb's tail to make sure the jerk behaved for a few months.

Money solved a lot of problems, and a lot of money made those problems solve dizzyingly fast. Will just wasn't sure money could begin to fix the problem Laura was going to have about being separated from the baby.

Of course, she kept claiming there was no problem. Vociferously. For almost a whole month she'd blithely passed over any mention of babies or families, as if they'd never been on her Christmas wish list.

"She's here!" Laura crowed, and sprang at a gallop from the living room front window to the door.

Deb burst in, and for the next twenty minutes neither woman would probably have noticed a fire. Talk about a female talk fest. Will took her coat, interjected a couple of words that no one paid any attention to, and watched the sisters hug and laugh and exuberantly interrupt each other, talking no sense at all.

Deb, not surprisingly, didn't waste a millisecond before scooping the baby into her arms. Will noted the reunion, but was more interested in checking her out, brotherly fashion. He could only judge from the one time he'd met her before—she was still damn skinny—

but her skin had some healthy color, her shoulders were no longer sagging, and there was life in her eyes. At least for the immediate present, he didn't need to worry about Laura's sister.

Once Deb took the baby, Laura never spared Archie another glance. Naturally she was busy talking ten for a dozen with her sister, but Will felt another shot of uneasiness skid down his spine. For two and a half months she hadn't taken her eyes off the doofus any second the tyke was awake. Suddenly it was as if he didn't exist.

Across the room, from the protective nest of his mom's arms, Archie let out a squawk.

Will sighed. "How about if you two enjoy a cup of coffee with your feet up, and I'll do the honors?"

"The honors?" Deb asked him blankly.

If she didn't know what that squawk meant, Archie wouldn't leave her in the dark for long. Will hiked over to pick up the little monster. "Not to worry. The kid and I are old pros at this changing business. We'll be right back. You two just keep talking while you can."

Deb still looked surprised. "Are you sure he's wet?"

Did it snow in the Arctic? "I think it's a fair guess," Will said blandly.

The back room almost looked like a normal den again, but neither adult had been so insane as to pack up every single thing. Will unsnapped the sleeper like a pro, scrapped the old diaper, and had all the necessary supplies assembled in less than thirty seconds—including a covering over the urchin's shooter.

"You realize this is the last time I have to do this?"
The instant the kid was naked, he curled up and tried to
stick a toe in his mouth—but Will was long, long onto
that trick. "You're getting too fat to do that anymore.
And way too big—why, I'll be darned. You're starting
to grow some hair!"

Diverted momentarily, Will examined the crown of
the baby's head. "Well, there's only about three. I don't
think your mama needs to invest in hairbrushes yet, but
at least there's some hope for your looks. Who'd have
guessed?"

The baby was cleaned up, powdered, diapered, re-
snapped. It took about a second and a half. Will rocked
back on his heels, looking at him. "You won't have me
to kick around anymore, sport. You never did like me,
did you? I figured you always knew I had no experience in that Dad business. Believe me, I had some mixed
feelings about you, too. In fact, if you think I'm gonna
miss you for even a minute..."

He was. But Will didn't know how badly until that
instant. He'd been thinking about Laura's feelings, not
his own. Archie blew him a bubble-gum-size bubble.
The baby had almost cost him to lose Laura, thrown
both of their lives in turmoil, confused the best relationship he'd ever had, nearly destroyed his love life,
cried every damn time an adult was even *trying* to
think....

He scooped up the kid with a lump in his throat. "All
right. So I'm going to miss you a little. But you're
tough, like me. And think about how much your mom

needs you. The wrong kind of guy comes calling, and who could scare off those turkeys better than you? You hear me? You just let 'em know up-front how much trouble you are."

Will refused to think it was the last lecture he'd have the chance to give the kid, but Archie's mom called out from the other room. The next few minutes were predictably mass confusion. The whole crew scurried to pack up Deb's car and see her off. She was having dinner and spending the evening with their dad, but she couldn't be convinced to stay longer than that. Driving at night, while Archie was sleeping, was obviously the easiest way to handle the long ride back to St. Louis.

Laura loaded her down with Christmas presents before she left—sweaters, clothes, purses, stuff. Neither woman seemed to notice that it was two months since Christmas, or to remember that they'd both exchanged gifts by mail at the time. Will couldn't see reminding them of something that was obviously irrelevant, and eventually, finally, the stuffed blue Chevy was backing out of the drive.

Evening was falling by then, that hushed time of day when the sky was a pallet of muted pastels and the air impossibly crisp. Laura turned to him, her face still wreathed in a smile as she snuggled an arm around his waist. "She looked good."

"Yeah, she did."

"It's not right yet, Will. But it's going to be. I could see it in her face. She's really putting her life back together."

"I thought so, too."

She was still hugging him close as they went back inside. "You did so much. For her. For us."

"Yeah, well . . . I never met anyone who didn't need a little help sometimes. And seeing her look so much better was one helluva reward."

Laura chuckled suddenly. "She could hardly keep her hands off our darling. Her eyes just lit up like sparklers when she saw him. They needed to be back together. I think it'll even give my sister more momentum to develop strength. She didn't like being separated from Archie, no way."

Not a word, Will noted, about her own feelings. And the soft happiness in her face was as real as the sunset. "I don't know if you noticed, but you had a really long day. Something tells me you might like to relax in a good, long soaker?"

"Well . . . that does sound kind of good."

It sounded good to him, too, since he wanted Laura out of the way for a few minutes. He'd planned a slight diversion for the evening, something to focus her attention away from the sudden absence of the baby. Once she closed the door to the bath, he sprinted straight for her bedroom.

After pulling down the comforter and blankets, he laid a thick, body-size velour towel on the sheets. The almond massage oil, he'd hidden in his jacket pocket. The deep red Burgundy was already open and breathing in the kitchen and just needed pouring into two glasses. It took some messing around before he had everything right. The lighting needed fixing, too. He flicked off the overhead and switched on the softer lamp on her night table.

Then he straightened and surveyed the scene he'd laid out. Ready, he thought, and released a lazy sigh of pure masculine satisfaction.

Almost to the instant, he heard the thick, harsh, muffled sound of her crying.

Laura had a wet washcloth pressed tight to her eyes when she felt the sudden cool draft of the door opening. Through a blur of tears, she saw a huge scarlet towel aiming straight for her. For a second she couldn't even see Will over the top.

"I'm okay," she said swiftly.

"Yeah? How 'bout if you come out of there and we'll talk about it."

"*Really*, I'm okay." Her voice warbled like a dizzy bird. And warbled worse when she kept trying to talk. "I'm happy. I'm perfectly happy."

"Sure you are. Stand up, sweet pea."

She lifted a hand, spraying a sluice of water in every direction. It was downright impossible to deny the tears streaming from her eyes when he was looking right at them. And Will, damn him, never looked at her so...soft. "I don't know what's the matter with me. This is so stupid. I was just relaxing, taking a bath, leaning my head back, everything hunky dory, not a single thing wrong. Only..."

"Tell me," he prompted her.

"Only then I remembered. . . ." She was only halfway up when Will wrapped the thick velour towel around her. Steam was wisping around the bathroom like mist in a fairy tale, but she suddenly couldn't stop shivering. "I remembered that I forgot to tell Deb about thumping him. You know, you can't just pat him, you have to really thunk, or he *won't* bring up a burp." She lost her voice again. Her throat was just so clogged up, her head thicker than oatmeal, and damn, if she could stop those tears. "If he goes to sleep while he's still got a burp, he'll wake up crying. And she won't know."

Will tossed down the towel and started hooking her arms into a robe. Not the pretty ivory robe she usually wore around him, but the ratty, old, threadbare terrycloth relic from the back of her closet that he was never supposed to see. "I think Deb's smart enough to figure that out, sweet pea. What's killing me is that you didn't figure out how badly you were going to miss him."

"I don't miss him!"

"Okay."

"I'd have to be the world's most selfish jerk to miss him!"

"You're the least selfish human being I've ever met," he mentioned, but she wasn't exactly listening.

"It's my sister's baby, for Pete's sake. She's his *mom*. And you don't know Deb as well as I do, but she's *wonderful* with children. I don't think anybody on earth could make a better mom than her, and being separated from Archie had to half kill her. In fact, that's *exactly* why I'm so happy they're back together."

"I'm glad you're so happy." He pushed the lapels of her robe closed and swept her up, as if he thought she was completely incapable of walking. En route out of the bathroom, he bent down so she could pick up a box of tissues. And en route toward the living room, he pressed a kiss, harder than a brand, on her still damp forehead. "You were a total dimwit to let yourself think you were never gonna miss him."

"Don't insult me *now*, Montana."

"Okay."

"And I don't miss him! I want him to be with his mom!"

"Okay." He edged back into the cherrywood rocker. There were times he'd felt like a sissy, a grown man rocking a kid, but he didn't feel like a sissy holding her. Two people didn't exactly fit; he had to drape her arms over the side and get her adjusted just right in his lap. Then he pushed her cheek into his shoulder so she could hide, because, damn it, she was still crying pretty hard.

"I'm afraid I *am* selfish," she confessed.

"Now don't start talking outright ridiculous, or I'll have to get tough with you. You're *not* selfish. You couldn't even find selfish on a map with an atlas right in front of you." His chin anchored the top of her head. She smelled like peach soap and pure, damp, warm female. His female.

"But I am. I mean it, Will. Because the real truth is that I've been scared."

"Scared of what?"

"Scared of losing you. I'm happy for my sister and relieved she's gotten her life back together and I'll be there for her, again, anytime. But I was also glad this was over. Our lives can finally go back to normal. I *want* our lives to go back to the way they were."

He stroked her hair. He didn't have to prompt her to keep talking that time, because she kept right on going.

"I mean that, Will. You've been patient and wonderful and terrific... but it's been weeks since we had any time alone. Every single time we tried to do something, the baby interrupted our plans. You had to resent that. And I did, too. I'm so glad to have you back to myself. I just want things the way they used to be."

It was just for a bitty moment that he stopped rocking. Laura was winding down, exhausted from all that heavy-weight crying and lulled by the rhythmic motion of the rocker. He heard her sigh, felt her face nuzzling into the corner of his neck. She'd fall asleep in minutes, he guessed. She was too worn out from this whole traumatic day to do otherwise.

So he pushed the rocker back into motion almost immediately. It was just for that millisecond that he stopped. When reality hit him with the subtlety of a blasting blowtorch.

Neither of them could go back to the way it used to be. The stocking stuffer left on their doorstep Christmas Eve had changed everything. Her. Him. *Them.*

There was no going back. For either of them.

* * *

Will was due any second. Laura tilted her head to screw in an earring at the same time she pushed her feet into black suede heels. High-heels. High enough to break her neck as she sprinted across the room for her hairbrush.

Will had always been the one to come up with the romantic ideas. Tonight it was her turn. She'd chosen slinky, silky underwear that would challenge him to get her out of them. "Red" for perfume. Stockings with seams. And a long-sleeved black sheath with a dramatic dip right to her pushed-up cleavage. He'd never know what hit him, she mused wickedly. Which was the general idea.

Will had been too quiet this past week. Much too quiet. She always knew how much their two-against-the-world relationship mattered to him. He valued the freedom of impulsive lovemaking, their ability to take off on any whim. The baby had turned their whole world topsy-turvy.

It had turned *her* topsy-turvy, as well. Laura yanked a hairbrush through her hair. She'd been his *lover.* Then Archie had shot into their lives, and she'd been a witch, a cranky, ornery crab and a frazzled crybaby... hardly the relaxed, carefree woman he'd fallen in love with. Hardly the woman he understood—much less the lover he needed.

Well, he was about to get his lover back, she thought determinedly. Right on the penny, she heard the doorbell ring.

She couldn't gallop to the door in her killer high-heels, but she reached the door at near derby speed and pulled it open.

"Hi, there," Will said. His hair looked rumpled, as if he'd been running in the wind, and he bent to kiss her with a mouth colder than the Wisconsin night and something strange in his eyes.

She gulped quick. Okay, so he hadn't picked up her clue about a "special dinner." So she was dressed a tad formally compared to his old cords, scuffed boots, and salt-and-pepper sweater. No big deal. But that look in his eyes—she'd seen a similar distracted expression when he was so absorbed in working that he forgot to eat or sleep. And he hiked past her as if his mind were in entirely another universe.

"Will? You okay?"

He turned faster than the spin of a dime. "Sure." She saw his smile, but it made her uneasy. He really didn't seem to notice that she was decked out to seduce a monk. He didn't even seem to notice that her hair was behaving—truly a world-renowned and rare event. He noticed her perfume, though, because he came back and ducked his head for another kiss... and a tickling nip on her neck. "You're asking for trouble with that scent," he murmured.

True. She was. And though Will was certainly more accomplished at pulling off extravagant romantic gestures than she, she'd honestly felt quite secure at the scene she'd put together. Only nothing went quite like she planned.

Will tossed his jacket on the hall tree and abandoned his shoes. From that point on, he just seemed to be one step ahead of her.

She had a serious, quality wine chilling in a real-life icer, but he filched a beer before she could mention it. In the living room she'd set up soft lighting and fragrant candles, but he switched on lights the minute he walked in. Everything in the kitchen was technically done—she'd sort of envisioned serving him like a sultan, to match the dozen romantic dinners he'd set up for her. But Will was the one who checked the oven, forked the coq au vin to make sure it was done, and spooned her fancy wild rice—not in her mother's antique crystal bowl—but into one of the plain old everyday ones.

And then he didn't eat. Nor could she, by then. There was no specific reason to suddenly feel this looming sensation of something terribly wrong. Will was helping out, the way he'd always helped out. If he'd failed to notice all the fussing she'd gone to, he had never been an inconsiderate man. He was entitled to be distracted, entitled to an off mood. It was just . . . all week, she'd been afraid that he no longer felt the same about her, afraid she was losing him. And the mountainous lump in her throat kept building until she couldn't even pretend to swallow anything.

Will finally put his fork down, too. "Do you want to take a walk?"

"'A walk,'" she echoed. Truthfully, her original plan had been cuddling up with him after dinner. The option of a walk had never entered her mind. They never took a walk. And certainly not on a night that was pitch black and colder than a well digger's ankle.

"Neither of us seem to be particularly hungry. And there's something I'd like to talk to you about."

"Well...sure. A walk sounds great," she agreed, but as they both rose from the table, her heart was suddenly ticking like a metronome. A sick metronome. She'd guessed something was on his mind, but God knew if she had the courage to hear it—and then there was the small, practical problem of freezing to death in her fancy clothes.

Possibly Will *had* noticed her dipping-low neckline, because he came back from the bedroom with a sweatshirt to put on over her dress. She pulled it on, but the effect had to be downright silly, and even more so when he bundled her up in a ski jacket. Her skirt hung down, and since there was no conceivable way to walk in slushy weather with heels—much less suede high-heels—she pushed those off and peeled on boots.

Will brushed a kiss on her cheek—apparently to reward her for looking like a certified bag lady—but outside, thankfully, there were no neighbors around to notice her attire. The streets were deserted. Everyone sane was holed up by their nice, warm, cozy lamps in their nice, warm, cozy houses...except for them. Stars peppered the ebony sky. The night was burning cold but still, with no hint of wind except for the ghost-white puff of their breaths.

They walked halfway around the block, with Will setting a racehorse pace that was definitely exhilarating but certainly inhibited any chance of conversation. But then he suddenly slowed down and gently, surely, grabbed her gloved hand. He squeezed.

"I need your help with something."

"For heaven's sake, Will. You've got it."

He met her eyes, but it was so damn blasted dark that she couldn't clearly see his expression. "There's something I want to say, Laura. Something I want to ask you. But I'm afraid—like I can never even remember being afraid—of doing it wrong."

"Montana, this is just *me*. There's nothing wrong you could say to me. I thought you knew that."

"Well, this is a little different, love." He took a breath, and then dug a hand into his left jacket pocket. His closed fist emerged, and when he opened it, palm flat, she saw a small, black-velvet box. "I'm hoping you'll want this. As much as I want to give it to you," he said quietly.

She yanked off a glove and pried the box lid open. He'd given her jewelry—all kinds of jewelry—before. But nothing like this. There were no extravagant gems inside. In fact, there were no gems at all. Nested in velvet was an incomparably plain, incomparably simple, gold band. And the look of the ring made her heart spin faster than a manic carousel. She lifted her face.

"I was royally ticked off when you accused me of trying to buy your affection," he said awkwardly. "But I think you were right, Laura. I felt I had to give you things to win you. When I was a kid, nobody ever wanted me around unless I was useful to them. For a long time, I just think I came to associate security with money. Money doesn't have a damn thing to do with the kind of security that counts, now does it?''

"No," she whispered.

"I didn't figure you would believe I'd really changed...unless I showed you. It bit like a whip, I have to admit, to give you a plain gold band. If it were my choice, I'd have spirited you off for a weekend in Tahiti, warm sands and moonlight and a luxurious dinner—with a little devil rum—before I'd risk asking you this question. Only, this way, I hoped you'd believe me. This way, you'd know. I'm not trying to hide or pretend that I have anything to offer you but myself."

That did it. She twisted around and threw her arms around his neck. "That's who I fell in love with. You. Not the gifts, Montana. Never the *things.*"

"Yeah, well, it seemed to take me a hell of a long time to believe that. Too long. For a blue moon I'd just accepted that I wasn't a family man, not cut out for marriage and kids. Both my parents were the restless type. And I've been restless since the day I was born. I didn't want to do that to a woman, or a family—have them find out that I was incapable of settling down." Will cleared his throat. "Archie threw me for a loop."

"I know. He threw us both for a loop."

"But you were wonderful with him. *Me,* he threw up on. From the very start, I was scared to death of him. I figured there was no way I could relate to a baby. No way I could be an adequate dad. No way I could turn into a pinned-down homebody. Laura?''

"Hmm?" So many things were pouring out of him. She understood he needed to talk. She just wasn't sure if he understood that he was also talking with his eyes, with his hands sweeping over her shoulders, with the bucketful of husky, vulnerable love in his voice.

"About that being a homebody—I never found peace like the two months when that monster was in our lives, coming home to you, living out what a real family would be like with you. The night Archie left, when you said you wanted us to go back to the way things were . . . you scared me. Because I want more, Laura. I want it all. And I want it with you."

She touched his cheek. "I wasn't exactly telling you the whole truth. But I was trying to tell you how much I love you, Will, how much you mean to me. And right then, I was pretty sure Archie had scared you off babies forever."

"He might have . . . if I hadn't started thinking that our own kids would probably be more of a handful than him. In fact, our kids could be worse, much worse."

"You've got that *dead* right. It boggles the mind, even thinking about raising urchins with your drive and brain power and all that exhausting energy—"

"And they could have your pride, your ornery stubbornness—"

"Me, ornery? You insulting me, Montana?"

"Only because it turns you on."

"Yeah," she murmured. "It does. Because those insults always reassure me that you *know* me, Will. You know who I am, flaws and all." The last she noticed, her ski parka had been zipped to the throat, but Montana had always been sneaky and clever about such things. Somehow that zipper had traveled its way down. His hands seemed to have found a permanent home under her jacket and were busy, very busy, keeping her warm. But he was still talking.

"What both of us know, first-hand, is how challenging it is to pull off a romantic evening with a baby on board. In fact, I think it's fair to say that we endured a trial by fire. We know exactly what we'll be letting ourselves in for."

"Montana, I'm having the most outlandish, craziest feeling that you're suggesting we make a baby."

"I'm suggesting a houseful."

"Holy kamoly." His mouth was only a heartbeat away from hers. Neither an avalanche nor an earthquake could have made that kiss wait any longer. Her lips touched his, softer than spring. And then sealed tight, in a different kind of kiss, one singing with promises and the deep, sweet richness of love. She let him up for air. But only when she was good and ready, "Get that ring on my finger, Montana. And take me home."

* * * * *

Look for ARIZONA HEAT *by Jennifer Greene—out now!—only from Silhouette Desire.*

This is not a recipe you can eat, but it's something I've made every year with my children since they were little. It's easy and fun and makes the whole house smell like Christmas! We call it

CINNAMON ART

10 tbsp cinnamon
4-6 tbsp plain applesauce

Add the applesauce to the cinnamon in a small bowl; blend together until it forms a dough. Sprinkle a little extra cinnamon on a cutting board and roll it out just the way you would for cookies—about ¼" thick. (Thin is best.) Use cookie cutters to cut out Christmas shapes. If you want to hang these later, poke a hole in the top with a straw or a toothpick.

Put your "cinnamon art" on ungreased cookie sheets in a warm oven—150° F (or as low as you can set your oven). You're *not* trying to bake these decorations, just to *dry* them, so it takes no real heat, just time. They're "done" when they're firm, which takes about 3 hours.

That's it! You can either hang them from the Christmas tree or tie them to packages. If that wonderful fragrance starts to fade, you can add a drop of cinnamon oil to the back side. (They won't spoil—in fact, you can save them from year to year if you pack them in tissue paper.)

I hope you enjoy this as much as we have—and Merry Christmas!

—Jennifer Greene

COMFORT AND JOY
Patricia Gardner Evans

Merry Christmas Therma,
Terri and Petrita,
and many more years of pie

Christmas at Patricia Gardner Evans's house:

As at many houses, the Christmas season at mine starts in the kitchen. Food is a major part of every holiday celebrated this season, and everyone has recipes they dig out only in December. When my daughter gets home—she reversed a three-generation trend of westward migration—we find a tree at the flea market, make "Toys for Tots" and shelter deliveries, half freeze and sing Spanish carols at *unas osadas*, decorate and, of course, cook. On Christmas Eve we light our luminarias, go to Christmas Eve services, and then my daughter locks herself in the den with *The Pink Panther* to wrap her presents.

The holiday traditions she and I have established are a mix of family, New Mexico and us, none more exceptional than anyone else's, but they are special to us, naturally, because they are ours. The past few years we have learned to resist the mad rush that can all too easily overtake us at this time of year and spend time just enjoying being together and remembering what we're truly celebrating.

May you find true comfort and joy this season.

Patricia Gardner Evans

Chapter One

"Next!"

The line squeezed forward, and Claire Ezrin shuffled a half step closer to her goal. The day had not gone well. Her alarm clock had chosen to retire on the morning the new dean of the medical school was holding his first staff meeting, and things had gone downhill from there. A glance in the bathroom mirror, during which she grabbed the tube of zinc oxide instead of the toothpaste, had shown it was a bad hair day. After a brushing and rinsing frenzy that got rid of most of the horrible taste in her mouth, she had rubbed the sample of cuticle remover she'd picked up at the drugstore all over her face instead of the moisturizer sample. On the bright side, it might remove a few wrinkles, she had decided, deciding also that it was wiser to forgo any more makeup than the usual two swipes of mascara.

The red suit that had been going to help her make a good first impression had stayed in the closet because all her panty hose were still in the dryer—wet; it had died overnight. She did have knee-highs in one of the boxes she'd yet to unpack, but, after a glance at the clock, she'd opted for her razor instead and a fast defuzzing just past the hemline of her longest skirt. It hadn't surprised her, however, when the skirt dropped neatly into the toilet—fortunately flushed—as she took it off the hanger. An old pair of gray flannel slacks was all that would go with the sweater she couldn't pull off because the last of the hairspray had gone into what she optimistically called a French knot, although *not* was closer to the truth. It was then that she'd decided to sit in the middle of the last row at the staff meeting and slouch.

The line suddenly leaped forward almost three feet as two more windows opened and a third became free, and Claire saw she would be next. With no time for breakfast, the kitchen had been oddly anticlimactic after the bathroom. All she'd done there was pour the leftover soup she had been going to take for lunch into the cat's dish instead of her own. After that, her car had started right up, the drive into Albuquerque hadn't included even a bad pothole, the new dean was refreshingly short-winded and even announced that he would delay his departmental "tours"—read, inspections—until after the holidays. That was especially good news for the medical technology department, short staffed and in the midst of finals at the moment. By the time the dean got around to inspecting them, classes would be back to normal and, with luck, Sylvia, the department chairman, would have found two more medical technologists who wanted to trade the lab for the classroom. Foolishly, Claire had dared to think that her luck had turned around.

It hadn't. It had only been a lull in the action, so she could appreciate the grand finale that much more. As the urinalysis lab students had been turning in their exams, the lab assistant had tripped with the tray of specimens. Not a single one of them missed Claire's open briefcase. During the ensuing mopping, rinsing, disinfecting and apologizing, she had found the property tax bill for her new home—delinquent as of the day after tomorrow. Which was why she was now standing in line at the Bernalillo county treasurer's office instead of grading final exams. Why wait until tomorrow to get her bad luck over with?

"Next!"

Claire jumped at the deep, sharp male voice, then stepped forward, slightly damp tax bill in hand.

Mid-November of every year, by law, the county treasurer—tax collector, in the local vernacular—sent out property tax bills. Not surprisingly, the citizens of Albuquerque did not appreciate their early Christmas presents, and it was not exaggerating to say that the tax collector was the most hated man in town for the next thirty days.

He was especially hated this year, Jack Herrod thought sourly, as the tax increase passed by those same citizens back in February and then promptly forgotten went into effect. When he had taken office in January, he'd joked that he wouldn't mind the hostility the tax collector always faced because he was a lawyer and used to abuse, but he was feeling more than a little hostile himself today. The computer system kept going down, his chief clerk had announced this morning that Friday would be her last day, and he'd been called "King Herrod" one time too many. Christmas might be only two weeks away, but there was a distinct lack of holiday spirit in the people waving their tax bills in his face, and in him, too. He saw the next taxpayer approaching, glanced at her left hand and unconsciously straightened. Maybe the day was taking a turn for the better.

Slapping a smile on her face, Claire handed over the tax bill, praying he wouldn't notice that it was damp—albeit thoroughly disinfected—or, worse, ask why. She felt her smile dying as he took the bill, glanced at it and his nice—very nice—smile abruptly became a frown.

"Good afternoon, Mrs. Swearingen." It was absolutely asinine, Jack told himself, to be so disappointed at seeing a man's name alongside hers on the bill.

Her smile revived at the providential distraction. "The Swearingens were the previous owners," Claire said quickly. "I bought the property just after the tax bills were sent out. My name is Claire Ezrin." He typed something into his computer, his eyes on the monitor, then turned back to her, and she blinked, as if a spotlight had suddenly turned on her, as his smile returned.

"How do you do, Miss Ezrin?" Jack said. The updated tax file showed a head-of-household deduction, which confirmed her ringless left hand and the "I" she had used instead of "we." Bobby would no doubt laugh at his formality, but he didn't care for the instant first-name familiarity the whole world seemed to favor nowadays—mister, missus and miss were still perfectly good words, he'd told his staff. Besides, any advice about women from a man who'd had three wives in as many decades was suspect.

He was about to introduce himself when she responded, "How do you do, Mr. Herrod?" There was just a touch of shyness under the forthrightness.

It was also asinine, Jack reminded himself derisively, to be so stupidly pleased that she recognized him. Of course, with all the airtime he'd been getting on the local news lately, half the state of New Mexico recognized him. He hit a couple of keys to print out her new tax bill. The computer had been barely crawling along all day, so naturally now, when he wanted it to go slow, it sped up to a gallop. The printer spat out the form, giving him no choice but to give it to her. "Here's the total, but you only have to pay half, of course. The rest won't be due until next April." He held his breath as she looked the bill over. Because a sale automatically generated a new tax appraisal, her bill was higher than the former owners'.

"Oh! That's not as much as I thought it would be." Claire concentrated on watching herself pull her checkbook from her purse. She noticed men, of course; she wasn't dead. She just didn't generally notice them quite so... *hard*.

"That's the first time I've heard that," Jack said dryly. She laughed as she crossed out the printed address and phone number on her check and neatly printed her new ones. Reading the phone number upside down, he quickly scribbled it on a scrap of paper and slipped it into his pocket.

Claire tore out the check and handed it over, along with the coupon for the first half of the taxes. "I have to say, I'm impressed that you're working the counter."

"I couldn't let my staff have all the fun," he said with a wry grimace as the man at the next window stomped away, muttering not quite softly enough under his breath.

His willingness to work in the trenches wasn't all that had made an impression on her. On television he was nice-looking, but in person... He was bigger than she'd thought, over six feet, and, although he was at an age when many men started to grow horizontally, he certainly hadn't; his stomach was as flat as his shoulders were broad. Muscular forearms showed under his rolled-up white sleeves, and the neck inside his loosened collar and tie was strong and firm. His face was too rugged to be called handsome, but his jaw and mouth indicated a strength of character and the crinkles around his blue eyes a good sense of humor. His hair wasn't pepper and salt but sugar and cinnamon, thick and cut close to his head. She really didn't like short hair, but on him, it didn't look so bad. Not bad at all. His eyebrows were still dark, an auburn close to chocolate, like his long, flirty eyelashes.

"Thank you," Jack said briskly, clipping her check and coupon together. He loved her hair. It was light brown, so pale it was silvery, and she didn't have it all hacked off but up in a little bun, with enough soft wisps escaping to tell him it was a little curly. The rest of her wasn't shabby, either. The slacks and sweater she was wearing were a little loose but hinted at nice curves; she clearly wasn't one of those women who were forever on a diet, afraid to eat a decent meal. Her sweater was a thick gray turtleneck with flecks of other colors, most of which were in her hazel eyes, too—blue, green, brown, rust. She was tallish and didn't plaster on the makeup, either. While not a great beauty, her face had something he'd discovered over the years was better— humor, intelligence and honest friendliness, all with a brightness that made him want to grin for no particular reason.

He typed in the necessary information for a receipt, gave the print command, and, for the first time all day, the electronic brain did what he wanted—it went into a coma. "Computer's down again," he told her with patently false apology, "but it'll be back up in a couple minutes." He had those few minutes to help increase his chance of success when he called her later. Leaning over the counter a little, he caught a whiff of something refreshingly light and sweet. "Do you live near Frost Road?" Her address listed Tijeras, a village a few miles out of Albuquerque in the long canyon that ran between the two mountain ranges on the eastern edge of town, but the fact that she owned six acres along with the house meant she was outside the village limits.

She shook her head. "No, I'm just off the interstate, in a little valley in the middle of the canyon." Actually, she decided, "rugged" and "handsome" weren't really mutually exclusive.

He looked at her, surprised. "Not the one across from Zuzax?"

It was Claire's turn to be surprised. "Yes, that's the one. You must have grown up here." Zuzax was the name of an old trading post tourist trap—*"See live rattlesnakes! Genuine turquoise rings, 99¢!"*—that had been torn down years ago, and only someone who'd grown up in Albuquerque would even remember the name, much less its location. Why it pleased her that he was a native like she was, and not one of the recent transplants who now outnumbered the natives several times over, she didn't know.

He nodded. "I was born in the Indian hospital. My dad was in the Public Health Service." Jack paused for a moment, just to enjoy her smile. "It must be hard to move during the holidays."

Claire grimaced wryly. "I wasn't planning on it. I'd made an offer contingent on selling my town house, and it sold three days later. It hasn't really turned out to be a problem, though. My daughter isn't able to come home for Christmas, so I don't have to worry about getting everything unpacked and put away right now," she added brightly.

Jack saw a momentary bleakness in her eyes that he understood only too well. "My son's not—"

The printer started as the computer revived. At the same time his chief clerk, Donna Luna, hurried up behind him. "Jack, I've got a problem here I think you should deal with."

Jack turned in the direction Donna was looking, toward his office, where she had been handling the out-of-the-ordinary problems. Fortunately, there hadn't been many, but, from the look on her face, this one was making up for the earlier lack. Standing in the door of his office was an elderly lady.

Claire couldn't help but look, too. "Mamie?" she said, startled.

"Do you know Mrs. Bonnett, ma'am?"

Not aware that she had spoken until the woman beside Jack Herrod addressed her, Claire answered distractedly. "Yes, I've known her for years... now she's my neighbor." Mamie was eighty-one but had never looked even fifteen years within that age—until now. Now her tall spare body seemed to have shrunk half a foot, her face looked like crumpled tissue paper, and her eyes had the vacant, lost look of senility.

Seeing the chance for a clean getaway, Donna acted immediately. "Good, she should have someone with her. You can go on back." The printer had stopped, and Donna ripped the receipt free, then held it out like a carrot on a stick to get Claire moving in the right direction. "And, Jack," she offered graciously, nudging her boss aside, "I'll take over here so you can go back to your office." Once he was headed in the right direction, too, she folded her hands on the counter and looked out at the long, surly line happily. "Next, please!"

* * *

Jack ushered the two women into his office, then shut the door. "I'm Jack Herrod, the county treasurer, Mrs. Bonnett," he introduced himself as his hand on her elbow gently guided her into the chair in front of his desk. He turned to pull up a chair for Claire Ezrin and found she'd already taken care of it herself. As he sat behind his desk, she took one of Mamie Bonnett's hands between her own.

Claire studied the older woman worriedly. Mamie was no senile old lady. They had first met over twenty years ago while Claire was working on her medical technology degree and supporting herself by doing the early-morning blood draws at the university hospital. She had taken great pride in the fact that she could successfully "stick" anyone—until she was assigned to the pediatric ward. Within fifteen minutes she was on the verge of crying as hard as her little victims. She couldn't even handle the pinpricks for the tests needing a drop or two of blood, much less the vein sticks for those requiring a whole test tube! At that point the head nurse, Mamie Bonnett, had walked in and matter-of-factly, without any humiliating condescension, shared her bag of tricks—a couple of silly distracting songs, a joke-telling stuffed monkey named Goober and several gentle escape-proof holds. The next morning Claire had made her rounds with Eddie Bisgetti, a hot pink stand-up-comic boa constrictor, and forgotten about switching her major to basket weaving. Taking a job in the same hospital after graduation, Claire had seen Mamie regularly until she left to teach, but through the med school grapevine, she knew Mamie had transferred to the preemie nursery—retirement being, in Mamie's opinion, the dirtiest word in the English language—and that her husband had died. Claire had sent a card and made a donation to the suggested charity in lieu of flowers. Discovering a few weeks ago that Mamie would be her neighbor had been a delightful surprise. "Mamie," she said gently, "what's the matter?"

Mamie shook her head with a weary sigh. "Oh, Claire, I've gotten myself in such a mess, and now I'm going to lose my house."

Instinctively—although why it should be instinctive, she didn't know—Claire looked at Jack Herrod. His concern, she saw, matched her own. "What happened, Mrs. Bonnett?" he asked quietly, with no hint of the patronizing humoring practiced by those to whom age was synonymous with senility.

Mamie answered without hesitation, although the sudden tight grip on her hand told Claire it wasn't easy for the older woman. "When my husband died, I discovered he had liquidated all of our retirement investments and put the money into this sure-thing scheme of one of his buddies." She shook her head ruefully. "I loved Leo dearly, but he was an absolute idiot about money. A month later, the sure thing went bankrupt, and that's when I found out the papers Leo had signed made the investors personally responsible for the loss. His buddy declared bankruptcy to protect himself, and I guess I should have, too, but after a lifetime of good credit, I wasn't about to lose it, so—" she took a deep breath "—I took out a mortgage on my house, cashed in my pension and paid back the money."

"And your lawyer approved of this?" Jack asked evenly.

Mamie gave him another rueful look. "No, but I had worked it all out and knew I would be all right financially, and I was—until—" she sighed disgustedly "—I broke my hip."

"You broke your hip? When?" Claire interrupted. In all this appalling news, somehow this last was the worst. And Mamie had never mentioned it, of course.

Turning to her, Mamie patted her hand, comforting *her*. "Four years ago, dear. I'm fine, now." She looked at the man across the desk. "With Social Security and Leo's pension, I was able to handle the mortgage, but I couldn't pay the property taxes that year. I didn't get back to work as soon as I thought, and then only one day a week at first, so I didn't pay the next year, either. I finally was able to start putting aside some money every month, but every time it looked like I might catch up, some emergency would come up—a new roof, the car dying, the well needing redrilling." Her thin shoulders shrugged in exasperation. "And I'd be right back to zero again. When I began working four days a week last month—I still hope to get back to five—I knew I would be able to pay the back taxes and penalties and finally be current by this time next year. The county never seemed too worried about the money. I'd get a letter once a year or so, reminding me about being in arrears, but that was all, so I figured I had the time. Then, yesterday, I got your letter."

Mamie disengaged her hand from Claire's and pulled the letter from her purse. Before she could hand it across the desk, Claire reached for it and, after a slight hesitation, Mamie handed it over.

By the end of Mamie Bonnett's matter-of-fact recounting of her disastrous four years, Jack knew his temper was past the ignition point. Years past the usual retirement age, she should have been taking life easy, not hoping she could work five days a week instead of four. Clearly she wasn't ready for a rocking chair, but she should have had that option, at least. Whoever her lawyer was should be horsewhipped for allowing her to sign away her house and pension. It would have been a royal fight, he conceded—Mamie Bonnett was one formidable old lady, and what she'd survived the past four years without self-pity or defeat proved that—but her lawyer still should have stopped her, and certainly no judge should have approved the settlement. And where the hell was her family in all of this? That thought cooled him down a little. She hadn't said, but he was somehow certain she had no children, and the stark truth was she had likely outlived any brothers or sisters. Well, no matter. Between the two of them, he and Claire would get the mess straightened out. He didn't notice that he had already turned them into a couple, or that she was now Claire, not Miss Ezrin.

He smiled at her as she read the letter. He would have helped Mrs. Bonnett whether Claire was with her or not, naturally, but it wasn't going to hurt his case any that she was here to see him do it, he thought with more than a trace of smugness. His smile froze as she finished reading and raised her head.

"You sent this?"

Her tone was calm, but he wasn't fooled; she was furious. Wordlessly, he held his hand out for the letter. He read it, feeling sicker with every line. A few months ago the head secretary had shown him samples of the various form letters the treasurer's office sent out, and the one sent to those seriously arrears in their taxes hadn't been strong enough so he'd told her to punch it up. What he'd had in mind had been a hard right jab, not a knockout. "Immediate forfeiture... eviction within thirty days... possible additional civil charges..." In other words, pay up or else. The letter made him sound like the villain in an old-time melodrama, except that he wasn't funny. He might not have written the form letter, but the fault was still his, because he hadn't checked it before allowing it to be sent. "Yes, I sent it," he said expressionlessly.

Before he could add that he shouldn't have, she shot to her feet. "We've had some pretty low people in office, but never one as low as you!" What her voice lacked in volume, she more than made up for in scorn.

Standing up, he held out a placating hand, trying to ignore the certainty that whatever he said would be too little, too late. "Miss Ezrin, Mrs. Bonnett should never have received that letter. Please let me ex—"

She wasn't paying any attention. "Come on, Mamie, let's go." She hustled the older woman to her feet. "There's no point wasting any more time on *him*." She threw him a look that had him wincing as if she'd thrown a solid punch to his midsection instead.

Mamie Bonnett tried the placating hand trick, too, with as much success. "He was only doing his job, Claire. I think—"

"Ha! It isn't his job to throw poor elderly widows— no offense, Mamie—out of their homes, and at Christmas, no less! This is the county treasurer's office, not a branch of Grinch, Scrooge and Legree."

"No offense taken, dear," Mamie murmured, looking slightly dazed. As if realizing that she was dealing with an unstoppable force of nature, she let Claire rush her out the door. Just before it slammed soundly behind them, Mamie sent Jack a look of helpless sympathy.

Feeling a little dazed himself, Jack started to sit down. Then the door flew open again, just long enough for Claire to land one more punch. "I must say, you certainly live down to your name, Mr. *Herrod*."

He sank into his chair. At least she hadn't called him King.

Chapter Two

"I'll have pecan pie and a café mocha." Claire closed her menu.

The waiter's pencil hovered over his pad. "Do you want whipped cream on the café mocha?"

"Please." The waiter collected the menus and left.

Claire looked over to Marty Cherpelis. "How's your diet going, Marty?" They always got any talk of diets out of the way immediately so they could eat guilt-free.

"Well, last week I finally lost the last ten pounds and made my goal. This week I've gained two of them back. I should have done what you did years ago and ignored those last ten pounds. Life is too short for salads."

Claire joined in the sympathetic laughter and groans. Nine years before, all four of them had worked in the blood lab at the university hospital, earning the nickname "the vampire ladies." They'd only worked together for a year before three of them left for other jobs, with the usual promises to keep in touch. What was unusual was that they had, meeting every afternoon of the second Thursday of the month for pie. It wasn't always convenient, yet it was rare that all four of them didn't make it.

Their annual argument about whether *bizcochitos*, the traditional New Mexico Christmas cookie, should be made with lard or butter, milk or brandy, and should the anise seed go directly into the dough or just flavor the milk or brandy was over, and they were packing away the small Christmas gifts they had brought for each other when the waiter returned with their order. Claire passed the sugar and sweetener packets. "Do any of you know Mamie Bonnett?"

She wasn't really surprised to find out they all did. "Why?" asked Jeanne Minzner.

"She's about to lose her house for unpaid taxes."

With one voice they demanded to know how such an awful thing had come about. Claire told them.

When she finished, Delia Lopez glared around the table. "That doozel! How could he send a letter like that?"

Claire had come up with "doozel" the year they had worked together to describe an assistant hospital administrator who succeeded in being both a weasel and a doofus, and the term had never seemed more appropriate. Yet by the time Jeanne and Marty had added their less-than-complimentary opinions, she was suddenly dumbfounded to hear herself defending the doozel. "Well, we did elect him to straighten out the mess in the treasurer's office and make all the deadbeats his predecessor had let slide pay up. I suspect a secretary did the letter and he didn't even know what it said."

"Well, he certainly should have!" Delia said.

"Yes, he certainly should," Claire agreed stoutly, to make up for her previous wishy-washiness.

After a few more grumbles and growls in Jack Herrod's direction, the conversation turned to Christmas plans. All four of Jeanne's children and Marty's two, as well as their children, would be back for Christmas. Delia's two, though grown, still lived at home, a fact she mentioned more and more often with less and less humor. Claire was the only one with only one child, the only one whose child wasn't— Ruthlessly, she cut off the thought.

Jeanne provided her with something else to think about anyway. "How did your date with Dr. Swett go, Claire?"

"How did you know—" Claire didn't bother finishing. Jeanne had been retired for three years yet still knew everything about everybody in Albuquerque's hospital community. Delia said she'd missed her calling in the CIA. "Anyway, there wasn't a date. I turned him down."

"Why?" Marty asked, surprised. Marty, Jeanne and Delia were still happily married to their first husbands and, like all the happily married, thought she should be, too.

Claire gave her a patient look. "Because he's thirty-two years old going on twelve, that's why. I've already raised one child. I don't want to raise another one."

Jeanne looked at her, aghast. "You didn't tell him how old you are, did you?" Jeanne had just celebrated her sixtieth birthday—for the third time.

"I tell anyone who asks that I'm closer to forty than thirty," Delia advised. "Of course, I don't mention that I'm even closer to fifty."

"And I'm even closer." Claire laughed ruefully.

"How about Dr. Cooter?" Marty got them back on track. "He's older but not over the hill."

Delia snorted. "No, but he's got a darn good view of the other side."

"I know!" Jeanne announced triumphantly. "Dr. Richwine. He's a little rough around the edges, but you could fix him up, Claire."

That suggestion was met with universal boos and hisses. "Good grief, Jeanne," groaned Delia. "He still wears his bell-bottoms from the seventies."

"A husband is not supposed to be another home improvement project," Marty said severely.

"Besides," Claire added, "I make it a point never to go out with a man whose jeans size is smaller than mine." The good doctor had played Ichabod Crane in a local theater group's production of *The Legend of Sleepy Hollow*, a rare instance of perfect typecasting.

"Well, there's always Bobby Loftis," Jeanne said slyly, avenging herself. "He'll probably be at the med tech Christmas party tonight, and I'm sure he'd ask you out if you gave him the slightest encouragement."

"And even if she didn't," Delia murmured dryly.

"Just remember the surgeon general's warning," Jeanne advised.

"You think I'm going to get lucky on the first date?" Claire asked her with a startled laugh. Actually, she probably could, Claire thought with another laugh, a silent one this time. The thrice-married Dr. Loftis was rumored to be looking for wife number four.

"Speaking of the Christmas party," she said, glancing at her watch, "I'd better finish up and get going. It starts in less than an hour."

"I'm sure we can come up with the right man," Marty said, refusing to give up. "Let's see, what qualifications do we want?"

Amused, Claire listened as the three designed the right man for her.

"He has to be honest and sincere and faithful, of course."

"And have a good sense of humor."

"Good-natured and hardworking, too."

"And he should be financially secure."

"Any kids he has should be grown and on their own." This, not surprisingly, from Delia.

"How about good-looking?" Jeanne put in.

"Um . . ." Marty waggled her hand.

"But he should have a full head of hair," pronounced Delia. Her husband was mourning loud and long the loss of his.

"And a fully charged battery," added Marty seriously.

"He has to sign a prenuptial agreement, too," Jeanne declared. "Claire has to protect her assets."

"I don't know." She frowned. "I have mixed feelings about prenuptial agreements. On the one hand, I understand the need for one, but on the other, it's as if you're saying you don't expect the marriage to last before you even say 'I do.' And frankly, I'd be less interested in finances than getting in writing that he agrees to paint the house, do yard work and bring a dowry of power tools.''

When they stopped laughing, she added, ''Well, when you find this paragon of manhood, do let me know. Just once before I die, I'd like to have a wild affair, with sex so hot, the bed's in danger of a meltdown,'' she joked with an unconscious wistfulness. A possibility presented himself to her clearly overactive and seriously disturbed imagination. She didn't need the surgeon general, she decided; she needed a psychiatrist.

Jack closed the door of his gym locker. ''Where are you and Carole going skiing over Christmas?''

Bobby Loftis slammed his locker shut. ''We're not.''

Jack looked at his oldest and best friend in surprise. ''What happened? I thought you two were getting serious.''

Bobby shrugged as he stuffed his handball glove into his sports bag. ''I don't know. Lately, it's been sort of touch and go for me with women.''

''You touch them and they go?'' Jack asked dryly.

Bobby looked up with a disgusted grin. ''Yeah.'' Zipping the bag, he picked it up and started for the locker room door, shaking his head. ''I don't know, Jack. Women say they want a guy who's good-looking, exciting and smart, when what they really want is one who'll love them, respect them and look after them."

Jack pushed open the gym door. "A lot of times it's the same guy," he pointed out.

"Yeah," Bobby said glumly, then brightened considerably. "But, you know, Jack, I'm sticking to my guns. Sooner or later, women will want selfish, crude, macho pigs again."

Slapping the other man on the shoulder, Jack laughed. "You just keep thinking that, Bobby."

Ruefully, Bobby laughed with him. "What about you? What have you got planned for Christmas?"

"I'm going to my sister's in Gallup."

Bobby slanted him a look. "You and Marcia Teakle aren't doing anything?"

"We went out a few times." Jack shrugged as he unlocked his pickup. "Nothing happened."

Bobby looked at him in disbelief. "But she's cute, nice, built, always looks perfect—"

"That's just it. She doesn't look like you could mess her up any." Bobby leered. "Not just that, Bobby," he said patiently. "She looks like she'd never get her hands dirty, much less the rest of her. No camping, no hiking, no working in the yard—no washing the car, even. She might sweat."

"Cripes, Jack. How picky can you get?"

"I'm not that picky," he said righteously. "I just want a woman who doesn't mind getting dirty once in a while." He thought for a moment. "And one who uses something in a kitchen besides the microwave."

"Now who's the macho pig?" Laughing, Bobby glanced at his watch. "Well, I've got a party to go to." Suddenly he looked Jack up and down thoughtfully. "You're not doing anything tonight, are you?"

Jack looked at him warily. "Why?"

"I just need a favor. Half an hour, tops." A lie for a good cause wasn't a lie, Bobby rationalized.

"I can't believe I let you talk me into this." Jack fought the urge to sneeze unsuccessfully.

"You sound like a broken record," Bobby muttered as he daubed on glue. "And hold still, damn it." He pressed on a shaggy white eyebrow, then tugged to make sure it was secure.

"Ow! What the hell are you trying to do, rip off half my face? And what is that stuff, anyway?" One eye glared at Bobby suspiciously. "It comes right off, right? I'm not going to be wearing this damn beard for the next six months, am I?"

"Really, Herrod, I never realized what a whiner you are." Bobby shook his head in disgust as he stuck on the other eyebrow, then picked up the red hat with attached white wig. "Hold still!" he ordered again as he tried to place the hat and Jack squirmed, trying to relieve a sudden itch.

Another itch assailed him in a new location. "I can't. Not only does this damn suit stink, it has fleas, too," he announced with perverse satisfaction.

"It doesn't have fleas, it just smells like mothballs. Now hold still," Bobby muttered absently. Ignoring the steady stream of curses muffled by the white beard, he fiddled with the hat until it was centered, then fluffed out the long white curls before finally stepping back. "There. That's the best I can do." His tone implied he could have done more if he'd had a better model to work with.

Heaving himself out of the chair, Jack waddled to the tiny mirror hung over the mop sink. Grabbing the hat, he jerked it to the left, then the right.

"Quit that! You'll mess up your hair!" Bobby grabbed at his hand. Jack commented on his friend's ancestry, and the other man grinned. "Shame on you, Jack," he chided. "Santa doesn't use words like that." Santa was added to Bobby's family tree, and Bobby laughed.

"I still don't understand why *you* couldn't be Santa," Jack growled as he shuffled toward the storeroom door.

"I told you. I always do the hot dogs. There's an art to good hot dogs, and I'm sorry, Jack, but you just don't have it," Bobby explained again kindly.

A mop harpooned his bloated belly; Jack wrestled it away, flinging it at his former best friend.

"You know, you really do need that third pillow," Bobby said, ducking. A snarl followed the mop. "Well, okay," he said regretfully, trying to smother another giggle, "if you don't care how you look."

Claire looked across the decorated staff room at the line of children waiting to climb up on Santa's lap. Dr. Daniel Minzner, Jeanne's husband and a wonderful teddy bear of a man, had been playing Santa Claus at their Christmas parties for almost twenty years. Claire's daughter, Emma, had loved to sit on Dr. Dan's lap, even when she no longer believed in Santa and came to the parties only for the stocking full of candy and cheap toys, and the hot dogs. Even grown-ups sat on his lap—female grown-ups only, of course. She did, every year. It had started the first year Dr. Dan had played Santa when a couple of children, to prove how mature they were, had told all the others that there was no Santa Claus. With all the kids upset and a few even crying, they'd needed a remedy fast. Someone had had the idea that if some of the adults sat on Santa's knee, the children would see that even grown-ups believed in him and everyone would calm down. None of the men would, but she and some of the other women did, and it had gradually evolved into a traditional part of their annual Christmas party. Dr. Minzner was genuinely concerned about them and used the party as a sort of annual checkup to make sure their lives were going well and to try to help—even if only with moral support—if they weren't. It was probably silly, and an ardent feminist would be appalled, but she didn't care. There was something oddly sweet and comforting about it, like being a child again, when life was no more complicated than whispering your heart's desire to a man in a red suit, knowing with absolute certainty that whatever you wanted would be under the tree Christmas morning.

Despite the pie and whipped cream earlier, she decided she had room for two hot dogs. Whatever else could be said about him, Bobby Loftis had a way with hot dogs. She found a seat at a table, and a few seconds later Suzi Komadina, her office mate, joined her. "Hi, Suzi," she said around a mouthful of hot dog.

"Claire." Suzi stuffed an onion- and relish-laden hot dog in her mouth.

The last child was climbing off Santa's lap as Claire polished off her last hot dog. Not embarrassed to take her turn but not particularly wanting to be the first adult, she waited for somebody else to step forward. When no one else seemed inclined to, she stood up. "I guess I'll go see Santa, Suzi." Giving her a surprised look, Suzi mumbled something, but since she had a mouthful of hot dog, Claire didn't understand her. "I'll be back in a minute," she told her.

Jack decided to give it another minute or two, to make sure that all the kids who wanted to talk to him had. He would never admit it to Bobby, naturally, but he'd enjoyed playing Santa. He turned his head away to hide an un-Santalike sneeze. Except for the damn beard.

"Bless you."

As his head snapped around, Claire Ezrin sat down on his knee.

He'd seen her the second she'd come in, and after dispatching a little boy to tell the hot dog man that Santa wanted to talk to him, *now*, Bobby had confirmed that she was part of the med tech school, one of the senior staff, in fact. The glances she'd sent his way had been surprisingly benign, giving him the cautious hope that she was no longer angry, but he'd never expected her to plunk herself down on his knee like one of the kids. Bobby had mentioned that quite a few of the women talked to Santa, too, and he'd wondered just what kind of game the good doctor was playing. However, Bobby had assured him that the usual Santa was like a favorite uncle, not a funny one, and that he would pass the word to make sure they all knew about the substitution.

So what was Claire doing here? Deciding it would be wise to remain silent rather than risk antagonizing her again, he waited for her to tell him. Besides, he had a more immediate problem. Something had happened when she sat down that hadn't happened since he was sixteen, a spontaneous reaction that he'd frankly thought he might never get the chance to experience again. He was more than a little happy to be proven wrong while at the same time wondering if he shouldn't have taken that third pillow, after all.

"Jeanne told me about your laryngitis, and I was afraid you weren't going to be able to make it, Dr. Dan. The party just wouldn't be the same without you." Claire gave him a one-arm squeeze around the shoulder. He must be working out, she thought absently; he'd lost most, if not all, of his teddy-bear softness. Funny, Jeanne hadn't mentioned it. "Did the kids wear you out?" she asked sympathetically.

He shook his head, murmuring . . . something. She only caught two words, and she wasn't sure of them—

"joke," maybe, and "hair"? "Oh, you know one of them always makes a joke about your hair," she said, patting his knee. He shook slightly again, like he had when she'd hugged him. Stifling another sneeze, she knew; the beard always made him sneeze.

He started to speak again, and she gently overrode him. "I'll do the talking so you can give your voice a rest. I've bought a new house. I'll show you pictures the next time you come over to lecture. Emma can't come home for Christmas, but she's coming next month." She laughed. "Maybe by then I'll finally have all the boxes unpacked."

He soaked up her sunny laughter. Maybe it was best she hadn't understood him. He had a hunch that if he told her now, she would jump up, hissing and spitting like a scalded cat, and the kids would wonder why the lady was so mad at Santa. She would probably find out pretty quick that she'd been talking to a substitute Santa and be embarrassed, but fortunately Bobby had promised not to mention his name, so she wouldn't be nearly as embarrassed—or mad—as she could be. He would have to tell her eventually, but he would work out how and when later.

"Let's see—what do you always ask me?" Claire thought for a few seconds as she absently tugged down her skirt and Santa had another sneezing attack. "No, I haven't found the right man. I haven't even found Mr. Right Now."

Oh, Lord, if she did find out now, he would pay big-time, yet he couldn't deny that he was pleased as hell to know she wasn't seeing anyone.

Claire sighed. "It isn't that the men I know don't try to make romantic gestures, but I can buy my own flowers and dinner." She smiled wistfully. "You know what would really be a romantic gesture? Putting the new switch in my dryer." He made a sound, and she laughed ruefully. "I know. It's my fault, not the men's. I'd just like someone to work around the house with, go to the mountains with, sit on the porch with—you know, someone to hang out with." She gave him a wry look. "I'm just not romance material, I guess."

Claire took a closer look and suddenly felt guilty. Poor Dr. Dan was so tired that his head was drooping; she couldn't even see his eyes. His arms were hanging limp at his sides, and no wonder. He'd lifted so many children up and down and given every one a big hug in between. Even his leg was cramped with exhaustion, the muscle tight and hard.

"Well, I've got to get home and unpack boxes," she said briskly. "You should go home, too, and let Mrs. Claus make you a hot toddy and put you to bed." Leaning over, she kissed the little bare patch of cheek above his beard. "Merry Christmas, San—" For that brief second she was close enough to see his eyelashes, not short stubby gray Dr. Dan lashes, but long, flirty, chocolate lashes....

"You!" With a furious half whisper she jumped up.

A definitely untired arm whipped around her waist before she'd even cleared his knee and clamped her in place. "Do you want to explain to two dozen children why you're jumping up and yelling at Santa?" he growled.

"I wasn't going to yell," she growled back with as much dignity as she could muster. "Just what are you—"

"Dr. Minzner is still sick, and Bobby Loftis asked me to fill in at the last minute," he explained rapidly in an undertone. "I had no way of knowing you would be here and want to talk to Santa."

"Bobby Loftis? I might have known you two would know each other," she whispered caustically. There were flecks of green in his blue eyes. Disgusted with herself for even noticing—but only because she was virtually nose to nose with him, she told herself—she strained away immediately. His arm loosened enough to let her move back, but not enough for her to stand up. "Why didn't you tell me right away who you were?"

"I tried, twice, if you remember, and you told me to be quiet. At that point I was afraid if I did tell you, you'd do exactly what you just tried to do so I decided to keep my mouth shut, hoping that, with any luck at all, you wouldn't realize it was me."

"Well, your luck just ran out, buster. Now get your Santa paws off me, you—doozel!"

He complied immediately, and she was up and away just as fast. She was, Jack thought with reluctant admiration, a last-word woman. And what in hell was a doozel?

Chapter Three

Claire watched the white bar of soap in her hands turn black. Cleaning chimneys was not as hard as she'd thought it would be, but it was every bit as dirty.

When she finally turned the kitchen faucet off, she realized someone was ringing the doorbell and probably had been for some time. Wiping her hands on a paper towel, she hurried through the house.

She opened the door to see Mamie just turning to leave. "Mamie, hi. You must have come over because you saw me on the roof, dressed so chic, and you wanted to know where I buy my clothes." Her hair under her ball cap had adopted the Medusa look, and her old corduroy jeans and sweatshirt were doing their best shar-pei impression.

After a startled stare, Mamie burst out laughing. Over the older woman's shoulder Claire saw a big silver four-wheel-drive pickup parked in front of Mamie's house. "Whose truck?"

"Mine." Jack Herrod answered her question as he came around the corner of the house. "When you didn't answer the door, I went around back to try," he explained.

It was on the tip of her tongue to ask him—nastily, of course—if he had come out to see what the county was about to get its grubby hands on when she noticed him watching her warily, as if he was expecting exactly that. Mamie was looking at her anxiously, too, and Claire felt guilty for adding in any way to her worries. "Oh," she said instead.

He was dressed as she was, in typical Saturday clothes—old jeans, a blue plaid flannel shirt, running shoes and a ball cap, though his clothes were clean and fit better—her eyes tracked down on their own—much better. Suddenly she was excruciatingly self-conscious, but if he'd noticed what a mess she was or heard her idiotic comment when she opened the door, he gave no sign of it. His face was impassive, although there had been that suspicious twitch at the corner of his mouth a few seconds ago. She watched closely, but it didn't return.

Mamie visibly relaxed, and he did, too, a little. "Claire, Jack's come to tell me what he thinks I should do about my tax situation." With peculiar reluctance, Claire switched her gaze to Mamie. "I thought you might want to hear what he has to say, too."

So it was "Jack" now, was it? "I certainly do," she said, with another, unsmiling look at him.

A minute later they were trudging across the five acre meadow that separated the two houses, Mamie between them. Claire noticed his unobtrusive hand on Mamie's elbow as they crossed the dry creeklet that bisected the meadow and that was now a jumble of small boulders and dead wood after a flash flood the past fall. Hanging back a little at the door of the log cabin Ma-

mie and Leo had built the year they were married,
Claire brushed the soot off her jeans furiously. His
baseball cap came off and went into his back pocket the
second he stepped in the house, she noted with less-
than-willing approval. That was a courtesy most men
forgot now that they seemed to regard ball caps as a
natural extension of their heads. She suspected some of
them even wore them to bed.

Mamie ushered them into the living room, then went
into the kitchen for the coffee she'd made. Trying to
avoid any eye contact and, she hoped, conversation,
Claire looked busily around as if she hadn't seen the
room several times already in the past month. Her eyes
slowed as this time she saw what she should have seen
before. The room was spotlessly clean, but there was far
less furniture than one would expect for a room this
size. She glanced toward the stepped-up dining room
and saw the small table and four chairs more suited to
a breakfast nook; they looked even smaller with no
other furniture to accompany them.

"It looks like there was a china hutch there."

At his murmur, Claire glanced over quickly to see
that he was looking at the same darker square on the
dining room wall that she was. "That or a sideboard,"
she agreed quietly. "There are quite a few pieces gone."
They both inventoried the nearly dozen shadows that
now-missing furniture had left on the walls or hard-
wood floor. The stark emptiness of the rooms was made
even worse somehow by the Christmas decorations.
Hearing Mamie still bustling in the kitchen, she stood

up and crossed the room to swiftly peek into the hall-way leading to the bedrooms. "In the hall and at least the first bedroom, too," she told him in a low voice on the way back to her seat.

Mamie came in with a tray, passed it around, then sat down beside Claire on the worn sofa. Deciding that the subject of the missing furniture was too personal un-less Mamie brought it up herself, Claire didn't mention it, but Jack Herrod had no such compunctions. "What happened to the rest of your furniture, Mamie?"

"I sold it after I broke my hip and couldn't get back to work right away. Most of it was antique, and I got a good price for it," she said matter-of-factly.

Claire saw his mouth tighten into a thin straight line and felt a small shock. She'd thought of him as a rug-gedly good-looking man, but he was, she realized now, a ruggedly good-looking *tough* man. He felt as bad about Mamie having to sell her furniture as she did and was even more angry.

Mamie drained her cup and set it on the cheap table between the sofas. "All right. No point putting it off any longer, Jack. Give me the bad news." Gone was the frightened, quavery old woman Claire had seen in his office; Mamie was once again a strong, vital woman, prepared to handle whatever he said.

He set down his cup, too. "Given the extenuating circumstances, there won't be any forfeiture action, of course, and the accrued interest and penalties have been removed. You just owe the accumulated basic taxes, and we will grant you an extension—"

"Not 'we,' you," Mamie interrupted. "This is how your predecessor got in trouble, Jack," she told him severely. "But even if it is more than just technically legal, I won't let you do it. I won't accept charity. I owe the tax, I'll pay it, penalties and interest included."

"Mamie," Claire began, "it's not char—"

Mamie's upraised hand cut her off. "I know what got me into this mess, Claire. It was stubborn, foolish pride, but I'm too old to change now." She turned to Jack. "But I will take you up on one part of your offer. If you'll hold off on the foreclosure—" she took a deep breath "—I can sell my house myself."

Claire exchanged a frustrated look with Jack. Oh, now he's "Jack," to you, too, is he? a small voice mocked.

"That would solve your problem," he said. "You'd realize enough from the sale to pay off your mortgage and taxes." Claire stared at him in disbelief, longing to give him a good kick in the shins. She was opening her mouth to argue when he flashed her a look. It wasn't an angry look or a warning; it was almost as if he was asking her to trust him. She had reason not to—she reminded herself of the Santa fiasco—but she closed her mouth.

"If you sell your house, though," he continued, "you have another problem. You still need a place to live."

"I'll get a place in town, an apartment. I should have gotten rid of this place years ago anyway." Her hand dismissed her home of nearly forty years as casually as her tone, but Claire saw the slight shaking.

"I understand." His tone was sympathy itself. "Gotten to be too much for you to take care of, has it? Too big to clean, too much yard to keep up with?"

"Yes, it—no, damn it, it hasn't!" Mamie looked at both of them in complete frustration. "But what else can I do?"

Claire felt tears burning at the back of her nose. He darned well better be going somewhere with all this—and soon.

"You can do a reverse mortgage. Have you heard of them?"

Mamie nodded slowly. "Claire gave me a pamphlet on them last night. Someone, usually a charity, buys your house, but lets you stay in it, paying you mortgage payments every month like an annuity. But I already have a mortgage, and it didn't sound like I could get enough with a reverse mortgage to pay it and the taxes anyway."

"I've talked to two possible lenders, and you can. You won't get a monthly annuity, of course, since you have to pay off the old mortgage, but there will be enough for that and the taxes." And she wouldn't be paying the penalties and interest, whether she liked it or not. "The charity will pay the taxes each year and take care of any major repairs."

Claire and Mamie looked at each other. After all the worry and upset, could it really be that easy? Suddenly Mamie's face split in a huge grin as she flung her arms around Claire in an amazingly strong hug. "Oh, Claire, I won't lose my house!"

With a discreet sniffle, Claire hugged her back. "No, you won't, Mamie." She still felt a little stunned, but Mamie apparently didn't. She bounced up like a twenty-year-old and grabbed Jack in a stranglehold hug before he could stand up.

"Thank you, Jack." She planted a smacking kiss on his cheek. "This is the best Christmas present I've ever gotten." Mamie squeezed him again; Jack's eyes met Claire's over Mamie's head, and she returned his smile hesitantly. An hour ago, she'd known exactly what she thought of him, but now... Now she didn't know what she thought.

Finally Mamie drew away from him, allowing him to stand up. "I don't know how to tell you how much this means to me, Jack," she told him soberly, "or how to thank you."

Gently, he took her hands in his. "I'll tell you how. If you ever get in a financial bind again, the first thing you do is call me. Promise?" he said sternly.

Mamie looked at him solemnly. "I promise, Jack."

He freed her hands, and, her joy bubbling up again, she danced around the table, and Claire felt herself enveloped in another hug. "Oh, Claire," the older woman murmured happily, giving her an extra squeeze before releasing her. "Well!" Mamie clapped her hands together briskly. "I'm hungry. Who wants lunch?"

Jack accepted with alacrity.

"Thanks, but I need to go home and clean up," Claire said, looking down at herself. She'd forgotten what a mess she was. When she looked up again, it was straight into amused blue eyes.

"Are you sure?" Mamie paused on her way to the kitchen.

"I'm sure," she said dourly, finally tearing her eyes away and starting for the door.

"I'll take a look at your car while you're getting lunch ready, see if I can figure out why it's hard to start," she heard him call to Mamie behind her.

By the time she had taken two more steps, he was almost beside her; then he stopped. "What are these?"

From his quiet tone, she knew he was talking to her, not Mamie. She pretended not to have heard; then, deciding that was childish—and, of course, she would never be childish—she turned around to see what he was asking about.

"Oh, those are the old bond certificates Mamie inherited from a bachelor uncle." She laughed briefly. "His estate consisted of these and a souvenir spoon from the 1904 World's Fair in St. Louis. The county issued the bonds while New Mexico was still a territory, so they're worthless, of course, but—" she reached out a finger to touch the frame surrounding the parchment with its exquisite Spencerian script and elegant seals "—they're so beautiful, she framed them."

Claire was reaching for a paper towel when the doorbell rang. She hoped it was Mamie, come over to tell her any more details Jack Herrod had given her about the plan to save her house. Opening the front door, she saw not Mamie, but the man himself—holding out a can of extra large, fancy grade, pitted black olives.

"The store was out of olive branches."

Claire stared at the can and the large hand holding it. If she was honest—finally—her behavior of the past few days had been less than stellar. She'd overreacted, even been juvenile, and having him on her doorstep was a fitting punishment for her chickenheartedness in planning to write him a note of apology so she wouldn't have to face him. She accepted the can with a small wry smile. "I probably should pay for half."

Jack made no effort to leave. She rolled the can between her palms, indicating she was a little nervous, but whether that was a good sign, he didn't know.

"I was about to make some tea. Would you like some?"

He hated tea, but this was no time to be picky. "Thanks, I would."

As he stepped inside, the first thing he saw was a copper bowl of bright flowers sitting on the old washstand in the entryway—real flowers, not fake. Hanging over the washstand on a length of red ribbon strung like a clothesline was an impressive number of Christmas cards. The tiled entry opened directly into the living room, while a long hall on the right led to the bedrooms and the shorter one on the left, he discovered as he followed her, to the kitchen.

"You didn't have to bring the olives. What you did for Mamie was more than enough." He couldn't see her face, but he thought he could hear a tiny smile.

"That was for Mamie. The olives are for us."

For us. There was no *us*, but an odd little shiver curled through her anyway. "Are you sure tea's all right? I can get you something else." When she turned around, Claire saw that the ball cap was back in his hip pocket. She caught herself wondering again if his short hair would feel stiff, like a brush, or soft, like fur, and gave herself an impatient mental shake.

"Tea's fine." He leaned against the counter, out of her way. Fine. That was how he was feeling—just fine. The kitchen was bright and roomy, not like in so many new houses, where you took a step and tripped over yourself. She had it decorated for Christmas, with red bows on the antique oak sideboard and the big plant hanging in the bay window, and a goofy-looking snowman made out of a starfish dangling from a cabinet door.

Claire filled a pan with water and set it on the stove. "My teakettle must be in one of the boxes I haven't unpacked yet. If I'm lucky, I'll find it by Christmas," she said with a wry laugh as she took two mugs from a cupboard. He shifted a little to give her room, and she caught the old-fashioned scent of Old Spice and a few clinks. There was a tool belt around his lean hips, from fixing Mamie's car, she supposed. He had a cordless power drill in one of the holsters, like the kind she'd begun lusting after since she'd starting putting up mini-blinds and curtain rods and tripping over the extension cord of her drill.

"You could use the microwave, put the water in the mugs to boil," he suggested.

She glanced at the microwave as if surprised to see it on the counter. "You're right. That would be faster. I guess I don't use it often enough." She said it as though she thought she should apologize.

Claire transferred the water from the pan to the mugs, punched in the time on the microwave, then turned around. His smile, as if he'd just won a big prize, made her momentarily forget what she'd been going to say. His expression sobered, and she shook her head slightly. "You didn't write that letter to Mamie, did you?"

He shook his head. "But my name was on it. I should have known what it said."

Claire nodded. Neither in his office nor now had he tried to put the blame on anyone else or even make an excuse. "I imagine it scared a few deadbeats into paying up, though," she said dryly.

His laugh was just as dry. "Almost three hundred of them."

The microwave beeped, and Claire turned to pull out the mugs and open the tea canister, taking out two bags. After dropping a bag in each mug, she handed one to him. "Were you ever going to tell me that it was you playing Santa?"

He answered without hesitation. "As soon as I had a way to help Mamie. I figured I'd need some points in my favor, although," he added evenly, "that's not why I helped her."

"I didn't think so," Claire murmured, fighting the urge to laugh. She'd expected him to be honest, just not...*so* honest. "Didn't you think somebody would tell me about the substitution in the meantime?"

He grimaced wryly. "I was counting on it. But nobody knew it was me, so I was hoping that by the time I told you, the initial shock would have worn off, so you wouldn't be nearly as annoyed."

His brash matter-of-factness surprised a laugh out of her this time. "You certainly had it all worked out."

He gave her a sardonic look. "For what it was worth."

Amusement vied with annoyance, and amusement won. She laughed again, helplessly, giving up. After taking out her tea bag, she reached for a couple of spoons from the silver drawer. She added a spoonful of sugar to her tea before sliding the other spoon and the sugar bowl down the counter to him. "I have milk, if you want it."

He suppressed a shudder. "No, thanks, sugar's enough." Reaching for the stoneware sugar bowl, he breathed a silent sigh of relief. With Mamie's letter and his Santa masquerade dealt with—and she'd been a better sport about both than he'd had any right to expect—he could get on with his plan. She stretched to drop her tea bag in the sink, the loose sweatshirt pulling tight across her chest and the old jeans tighter over her hips, and he felt a surge of heat and a twist in his gut that had nothing to do with his dislike of tea. Slowly, he reminded himself, slowly.

Following her lead, he deposited his tea bag in the sink, too, saw what else was in it and grinned to himself. "I see you're a sinkie."

Claire glanced at the sink automatically and noted the evidence that supported his conclusion—the small pan with a spoon in it, and the crumpled paper towel that she'd used as a napkin right there on the counter. There was no way she could deny she'd eaten right from the pan while standing over the sink. "I actually do eat off a plate at a table occasionally, but what with trying to get the house organized and everything put away, I've been sinkie-ing," she admitted with a sheepish laugh. "It saves cleanup time, and then there's all the exercise I get standing instead of sitting." He laughed, a bass rumble that seemed somehow to blend with the strong sunlight shining through the window and warming the kitchen. "Are you a sinkie, too?" People who wolfed down their dinner over the kitchen sink were generally single. He wore no ring, but that didn't mean anything. Not that his marital status was of any importance to her. She was just...wondering.

He looked down his interestingly bent nose at her as he dumped two heaping spoonfuls of sugar in his mug. "I'm a fridgee—I have class. I dine by the soft glow of the open refrigerator."

Her giggle was worthy of a twenty-year-old. She wasn't twenty, thank God, but neither did she look close to as old as Bobby said she was.

So he was single, she thought...unless his wife traveled a lot. His eyes drifted downward over the rim of his mug as he raised it, and Claire suddenly remembered that when she'd come home she'd cleaned up the old shed out back but not herself. She'd no doubt established a new personal low in grunge. Raising her own mug, she patted her head casually. Her clothes were hopeless, but surely she could do something about her hair, at least. A few touches destroyed that illusion. After discarding her baseball cap when she'd come home, she'd pulled her hair more or less into a ponytail. It was now definitely less. His eyes were following her hand, a faint, unfocused smile on his face. *Probably wondering when they're coming to take me back to the Home,* Claire thought, deciding a distraction was in order. "Would you like to see the rest of the house?"

He'd about decided he was going to have to ask. Trying not to appear too eager, Jack swallowed another sip, managing not to gag, but it was close. "Sure."

Chapter Four

Unlike Mamie's log cabin box, her house was an adobe that rambled off in interesting directions. Every room had a great view of the little valley. The valley would have been a "holler" in Tennessee and Kentucky, and only the two houses occupied it. With mountains all around and the sense of seclusion, it was hard to believe half a million people lived less than twenty minutes away. Tall pines guarded the rim of the valley, with piñon and juniper thicketing the sides and cottonwoods following the seasonal creek that meandered down the far side of the floor. Aside from the cottonwoods, the only other trees on the valley floor were hers—a few neglected fruit trees, another massive cottonwood that shaded the back of her house and a magnificent blue spruce that stood watch at the front. The interstate crossed the foot of the valley, but the roadbed excavation had created sight- and soundproofing so that no traffic noise polluted the little canyon's serenity, and only an occasional flash of sunlight reflected off the windshield of a semi. The road that provided access left the interstate a mile west and wound back around the mountain, growing narrower as it branched off to other little settlements until it was only a one-lane track, hardly noticeable by the time it entered the valley. He'd seen deer tracks crossing it as he'd driven in.

The furnishings she'd chosen were interesting, too, not androgynous, but not so blatantly feminine that a man felt uncomfortable, either. The living room was a place of warm wood and solid comfort. The colors—dark blue-gray, old gold and tan, with touches of orange and purple—invited you in. The deep couch said "come sit by me." "Do you use the wood stove?" he asked, nodding toward the stone hearth and the black iron and brass stove. She looked in that direction, and he tipped his mug of tea quickly over the potted plant behind him.

"Every night," Claire confirmed. "It's been so mild that's usually enough heat. The furnace hardly ever comes on." The house was actually quite warm now, even without the stove.

Her bedroom was more feminine, but not lace and frills. Forcing himself to look away from the queen-size bed and the teenage fantasies it was giving him—although when he'd been a teenager he hadn't had nearly this much imagination—he focused on the fireplace in the corner, the only jarring note he'd seen so far in the house. It was a kind that had been popular back in the sixties, a freestanding black metal hood with exposed chimney pipe. The pipe was streaked with rust, indicating that it hadn't been installed properly to keep out the rain, and sooty rain spatters stained the white wall behind it.

Claire looked at the fireplace, too, making a face. "That's the only thing in the house I don't like. I don't know what to do with it. I'd like to have a fireplace, just not that one." It would be nice for that affair she'd told Marty, Jeanne and Delia she wanted.

Jack studied the existing fireplace and the space it occupied. Oh, yes, he'd like to have a fireplace, too, so he could lie in bed at night, cozy and lazy after making love, watching the flames.... "Well—" he cleared his throat "—it wouldn't take much to fix the chimney pipe so it wouldn't leak. It was probably just installed upside down. You could replace the fireplace with a small wood stove, a gas log or—" he walked over, automatically pulling the tape measure from his tool belt "—you could put in a kiva-style corner fireplace." Bending, he measured distances. "You can buy a kit. It's easy to install, then you just frame around it and plaster."

Claire looked at him curiously. "You sound like you've done it."

"A few times." He straightened and slid the tape measure back in his belt. "I started buying fixer-uppers about a dozen years ago. I'd worked construction to get through college and law school, so I knew enough to handle basic repair and remodeling. My son and I would move in, fix the house up, sell it and start all over again." He laughed ruefully. "I think that's half the reason he went away to school, then joined the Navy, so he wouldn't have to live in the middle of a construction zone."

His *son* and he would move... no one else. "It must be hard to do the work these days, living by yourself," she said, in a blatant attempt to find out if he did live alone now; he could have married or acquired a live-in. And why she wondered so much, she didn't want to think.

"I can always get a buddy or two to come over and help," he said as he followed her out of her bedroom.

"Are you fixing up a house now?"

"I just finished one, but I don't know when I'll put it on the market."

She smiled over her shoulder as she pushed open the almost-closed door of the spare bedroom. "You've decided this one is too nice to sell?"

That smile could take prisoners for life. "No, I've finally gotten tired of living in a construction zone, too, and the financial incentive isn't there anymore." His gaze swept down the skylit hallway to the living room. "I won't sell until I find the house I want to spend the rest of my life in."

As the door swung open, an orange and white striped cat woke up and jumped out of the pool of sunshine on the futon that was the sole piece of furniture in the room. Jack started to stand aside to let the cat leave, but the animal began winding its long, wiry body around his ankles instead, revving up to a loud purr.

"Tamale!" Claire tried to shoo the cat away. Most men, in her experience, weren't too fond of cats. "Stop making a nuisance of yourself."

"Tamale? Did you buy tamales from that guy, too?"

Hearing the delighted laughter in his voice, Claire abandoned her efforts to discourage the cat, which weren't working anyway, and looked at him. "You don't mean the man who sold tamales at lunchtime on the plaza between the courthouse and the hospital about twenty, twenty-five years ago?" Her tone made it clear that she expected a negative answer.

"Yeah, the one who did a booming business until people started noticing that all the stray cats downtown had mysteriously disappeared."

He grinned as Claire nodded. "You know, I've never admitted it to anyone—" So why was she admitting to him? "—but whatever they really were, those were the best tamales I've ever eaten."

He threw back his head and laughed, and Claire stared at his strong throat until she realized what she was doing. "They were good. I was kind of sorry he went out of business." At her look of horror, he laughed again as he bent to scratch the cat's ears. "Was he a stray, too?"

Claire nodded, watching the cat butt his head against the long, blunt fingers, his eyes closed in ridiculous rapture. "He moved in the day after I did. I opened the door, and he just walked in."

"Well, Tamale," Jack addressed the cat, "I hope you know how lucky you are." *Really* lucky, he thought as he stood up.

"I think he thinks I'm the lucky one," Claire said dryly.

They backtracked toward the kitchen, and Claire looked at Jack questioningly as he paused in the middle of the entry and looked around. "You know, most houses are like the one I'm living in now, just walls and a roof. But a few of them, like yours, have a personality, almost like they're alive. Did it take you long to find it?"

She shook her head with a still-disbelieving laugh. "I wasn't even looking for it. I saw the for-sale sign down by the interstate, and the next thing I knew, I'd sold my town house and was putting boxes in my car." How could she explain that something inexplicable—fate, the real-estate gods, her subconscious—had decided she and the house were meant for each other? He smiled at her, and she saw that somehow he understood. She smiled back, experiencing one of those moments of perfect communication without words, the kind that were supposed to occur between two people who knew each other intimately, not two near-strangers.

She followed him into the kitchen, frowning absently as she passed the split-leaf philodendron sitting on the step leading down to the living room. She could have sworn it needed watering half an hour ago, yet now the soil was wet.

Jack set his empty mug in the kitchen sink before reaching for the photograph sitting on the windowsill above it. "This is your daughter?" He'd seen pictures of the same young woman, her hair darkening from white blond to dark gold as she grew older, scattered throughout the house.

She nodded, her smile proud and unconsciously wistful as she looked at the photograph. "That's Emma."

"She's very pretty, although she looks more like your sister than your daughter."

"Thank you." He'd stated it as a casual fact instead of with the earnest flattery most men used that automatically made any compliment sound insincere.

He set the pewter frame on the windowsill. "But she's not coming home for Christmas?"

For a second Claire wondered how he knew, then she remembered telling him while he'd been figuring her tax bill. "No. She doesn't have enough seniority yet to get any time off at Christmas, so she decided to come in February, when we could spend more time together. She's having Christmas dinner with friends." She forced a bright smile. "I went back to Maryland for Thanksgiving, and we had a wonderful visit, so not spending Christmas together doesn't really matter."

Her stubbornly cheerful tone and smile said it really *did*. "My son's not going to make it, either. Is this the first time you and your daughter won't spend Christmas together?"

"Yes." Claire was disgusted and appalled to feel the sudden stinging at the backs of her eyes. Fiercely, she concentrated on the yellow mini-blind over the sink, reaching up to fiddle with the small valance strip that refused to lie flat. "I can't seem to get this darn thing right," she muttered.

A large square hand appeared beside hers, two long fingers pressed, there was a small click, and the valance snapped exactly into place. He grinned as she looked at him. "There's a trick to it."

"So I see. Thanks." They lowered their arms at the same time, and for a moment she had the crazy idea that he was going to put his arm around her. What was even crazier was that she wanted him to—but only for a moment.

Abruptly, she turned away from the counter. "All that's left to see is the utility room."

She showed him the narrow utility room that doubled as a mudroom, opened the doors that led to the double garage, backyard and pantry, and the tour was over. Instead of following her to the kitchen, though, he stopped at the dryer and picked up the object lying on top. "Is this the new switch for your dryer?"

"Yes, I'm going to install it tom—" He already had his power drill in his hand and the first screw on the front panel loose, and suddenly Claire remembered with perfect and humiliating clarity what she had said while sitting on Santa's knee. It took every drop of willpower to keep from burying her face in her hands and groaning. If he was trying to embarrass her, he was succeeding beyond his wildest expectations. She watched him narrowly, but there was no gloating glance, no secret smirk, no overly innocent look. In fact, he didn't look at her at all.

Then another possibility occurred to her, and a tiny groan did escape her. He glanced up, and she gave him a sickly smile. "That's a nice drill."

He gave it an absent glance as he went back to work. "Yeah, DeWalt makes good power tools. I have a fair number of them."

Claire shifted to give him room as he removed the panel and set it aside. Was he making a serious romantic gesture? If he was, he certainly wasn't making a big production of it. No more production than when, during the "tour," he had whipped out his pliers to do something with the float so the toilet in the smaller bathroom stopped running continuously, or when he'd fiddled with a hinge on the linen closet door with a screwdriver to make it close tight. He'd just seen a problem, had the necessary tool at hand and fixed it, same as now. No big deal . . . and no romantic gesture, thank goodness. What a relief.

"Do you have any electrical tape? I'm out."

"I think so." She found a roll in the kitchen junk drawer, and he tore off a strip, rapidly binding the switch wires together and taping them in place.

And it *was* a relief. Certainly not a disappointment. How could it be a disappointment when, not two hours ago, she would have cheerfully run over him? Well, his foot, anyway. Mentally, she rolled her eyes in disgust. This wasn't a symptom mentioned in any of the menopause books.

Jack picked up the panel and began screwing it in place. "I'm surprised you didn't call a repairman."

From the instruction manual sitting on top of the dryer, the switch carefully highlighted in the electrical diagram, he knew appliance repair wasn't a regular habit.

She laughed ruefully. "I'm genetically incapable of paying ten times more to install a part than the part cost. The switch was five dollars, and the repair company wanted fifty dollars for the service call."

"Ouch." His respect for her grew; most women would have paid the fifty dollars. He tightened the last screw, slid his screwdriver in his tool belt and, with a polite nod, stepped around her to go into the kitchen and wash his hands.

With the narrowness of the space, his shoulder brushed hers as he passed by, and for one crazy moment she wondered how he had absorbed the two hundred and twenty volts of the dryer. As the tingle eased into an all-over lingering warmth, she decided the only other explanation for the jolt she'd felt, that his body and hers had generated some kind of charge between them, was even crazier.

By the time she followed him into the kitchen, he was through washing his hands and was looking around for the trash can to throw away the paper towel he'd used to dry them. She gestured toward the tall cabinet by the light switch. It had taken him eight minutes to do what would have taken her at least an hour and several words she normally didn't think, much less use, but, true to his no-big-deal attitude, he wasn't waiting expectantly for her gushing gratitude. She wasn't going to gush, but she was grateful. "Thanks, and thanks for fixing the other things, too."

He shrugged off her thanks. "It was nothing."

"Were you able to do anything with Mamie's car?"

"The choke was just stuck, but—" rubbing the back of his neck, he sighed "—she needs a new car."

She looked at him soberly. "The reverse mortgage will buy her some time, but it won't solve the problem, will it?"

He shook his head, his mouth grim. "I'm going to set up an investment program for her to build up at least a little nest egg, but she has damn little she can spare to invest."

Claire nodded. Despite the seriousness of the situation, she felt peculiarly confident that he would find a way to secure Mamie's financial future. After all, she rationalized, he had already made back all the money the county investments had lost under his predecessor.

With a covert look at his watch, Jack decided reluctantly that it was time to leave. She'd decided that his romantic gesture wasn't, but if he stayed much longer, the words "hang out" were going to come to mind, and she would guess the truth, which would ruin his personal investment program. After two losses, he'd just made a tidy profit, but it never paid to be greedy—or overconfident. "Well, I'm going to get going."

Opening the front door, he paused. "Thanks for the tour and the tea."

Feeling suddenly and oddly flat, despite his electric grin, Claire forced a smile. ''Thanks again for your help... and the olives.''

''Don't mention it.'' He took a step, then turned around, and she felt herself holding her breath. ''You know you never said—where do you buy your clothes?''

Jack strolled across the meadow, whistling softly between his teeth. He wasn't a bad last-word man, he decided.

Chapter Five

Claire settled at the end of the pew and looked around, then wished she hadn't. This had gone beyond ridiculous, she scolded herself. In the five days since she'd last seen Jack Herrod, she'd spotted him numerous times—at the grocery store, in the mall and at least half a dozen other places. When she'd looked again, she hadn't seen him, of course; it would only be a man with a similar build and height or maybe a roughly similar face, and once the same sugar and cinnamon hair. Now she thought she'd seen him here.

It was his fault, she decided as she stood to let a family pass to the middle of the pew. It would have been easier to sit in the middle, but she'd found that sitting at the end meant getting squashed on only one side, because the symphony orchestra and chorus Christmas concerts were always sellouts. She sat down again. Although she hadn't seen him, he'd left evidence of his visits to her house while she was off running errands. Apparently he'd come back once with the parts to work on Mamie's car some more, and another time to weather-strip her doors and caulk some of the window frames. The first time she'd come home to find the piñon she'd gotten at the flea market snug in the Christmas tree stand, ready to be carried into the house.

Having more room for a tree this year, she'd gotten a little carried away and, when she'd gotten home, discovered it was going to take extra ingenuity to make it fit into the stand, not to mention stand up straight. Waiting for inspiration to strike, she'd left the tree in a bucket of water outside, the stand beside it. Inspiration came easier to him, she guessed. She and Mamie had keys to each other's houses, and later Mamie had said he would have taken the tree inside if he'd known where she wanted it. The implication was clear that she should tell Mamie where and he would do it the next time he came out. She'd carried the tree in herself, instead. It wasn't that she would mind him being in her house when she wasn't there, which was a surprising and somewhat disturbing discovery; it was the principle behind it, that she would, in however small and brief a way, be dependent on him.

The second time she'd come home to see that the gate to the small patio off her bedroom no longer sagged and the faucet beside the back door no longer dripped. He couldn't have seen that they needed repairs the day she'd showed him the house; he must have come back and looked later. That was surprising, and somewhat disturbing, too. If it wasn't that he was doing everything when she wasn't home and making no effort to garner her appreciation later, she would have worried about that idiotic "romantic gesture" comment a great deal more. It did explain why she kept thinking she saw him, though. She was watching for him so closely at home—and wasn't disappointed not to see him, she assured herself firmly—to tell him that while his efforts were appreciated, they weren't necessary, that her vigilance was carrying over wherever she went.

The orchestra took their seats on the raised altar and began tuning up. She unbuttoned her coat as the influx of warm bodies began to heat up the large church. It was simply decorated with pine garlands, and she breathed in the forest scent with a small sigh. This was one of Emma's and her favorite parts of the Christmas season. It was the first time she had ever come alone, without anyone to share the beautiful music with.

The lights dimmed to warn the chatterers dawdling in the narthex. People hurried down the aisle beside her, and she sensed one stopping. Automatically, she stood before even turning to see the person waiting for a seat.

"Jack!" After her thoughts of the past few minutes,, she started to reach out to touch him, to make sure he was real. At the last second, she realized what she was doing and snatched her hand back.

"Hi, Claire," he said prosaically. "I thought I recognized you. Is there room for one more?"

She stood staring at him for a long moment before she roused herself and stepped out of the way. "Of course. Certainly. Please sit down."

As he sat down, the concertmaster lifted his baton, and there was no chance for conversation. With the addition of one more person, the pew was crowded; Old Spice mingled with the scent of the pine garlands, not an unpleasant combination, she discovered. His arm and hip and thigh by necessity were snug against hers, but there was no repeat of that wild charge she'd felt a few days ago when they'd brushed. Just the heat. Unobtrusively, she eased her coat open as much as she could.

The first piece on the program was Bach's *Magnificat,* performed by the orchestra, several soloists and a small section of the choir. His attention seemed totally focused on the music, so rapt he only moved once, his thigh shifting so that even through their several layers of clothes she felt the strength of the muscle in the leg pressed against hers. As aware as she was of him, she would have expected the music to fade into insignificance, yet, oddly, her awareness of him seemed to increase her awareness of it, too. She heard the mighty glory and jubilation and understood, better than she ever had from any sermon, the enormous significance of one baby's birth.

When the music ended, he got to his feet without hesitation to join in the standing ovation. Afterward, people began to move around, to take advantage of the intermission to ease a few kinks or find friends, and they both stepped aside to let people out of the pew.

"Do you want to take off your coat?" Jack asked politely.

"No, thanks." Now that he wasn't sitting next to her, she was chilly. He wasn't wearing a coat, just a suit, but the way he radiated heat, she wasn't surprised. "Do you come to the Christmas program every year?"

He grinned a little ruefully. "I've never come before, and I wouldn't have come tonight, but somebody in the office was selling an extra ticket and I didn't have anything else to do, so I thought, why not? I'm glad I came, though. The music is tremendous." He would have to give Estelle a raise, not just for the opportunity to experience something he would likely never have realized he would enjoy so much, but for the unexpected opportunity to see Claire, too. He'd been planning to ask her out, but this was better, a chance meeting that he should be able to parlay into a couple more hours, at least.

He heard someone call his name and looked around to see a client waving an arm. He was maintaining his practice while he was in office, but since the man wasn't someone he was particularly fond of on a personal level, he decided to go to him so he would be the one who decided how long the conversation lasted.

Getting away wasn't as easy as he'd hoped, and the lights were dimming again when he finally got back to his seat. She stepped aside for him again, instead of scooting over, and he was irrationally pleased. This way she was only sitting next to him; it was as if she was his alone, somehow.

The second half of the program was the full chorus with no orchestra accompaniment. The male half of the chorus took their places and sang what turned out to be a very short medley of shepherds' carols. As they left, he had to admire them for being such good sports about dressing up in black tie for what must have been no more than a five-minute performance. The lights dimmed further, leaving only the stagelike altar lit by what seemed to be muted rays of light, as if from a powerful star. Women began singing in the distance, then gradually came nearer as the female members of the chorus began passing slowly down the side aisles, still not singing loudly, yet somehow filling the large church with their voices. The hair on the back of his neck rose. The women, all dressed in traditional concert black, moved with a slow stateliness through the dim light, singing, and he felt he'd gone back in time and was watching medieval nuns filing through their cloister into an ancient stone chapel. When the women reached the altar, a harpist joined them, the strings of her instrument becoming another of the sweet, strong voices soaring up to the vaulted ceiling as the soft rays of light illuminated them. The program had listed this part as a selection of medieval carols. He didn't recognize any of them, couldn't understand the words, yet he sensed there was something more powerful in this music than in the much more complicated and flamboyant pieces he had heard earlier.

Claire sat motionless, only listening . . . and feeling. As dramatic and effective as the staging was, it was the music, the women's voices and the harp, that captured her. She didn't know the carols, didn't understand the words, but she knew instinctively what they meant. The women weren't singing of the birth of a king of kings, a son of God; they were singing of something much simpler but just as powerful—a mother celebrating the birth of her precious, precious baby. She understood the mother's pride and joy and almost overwhelming love.

The chorus ended their performance as they had begun. Turning to watch them file past, Jack saw the bright glitter in Claire's eyes. His immediate impulse was to take her in his arms or at least put his arm around her, but it was his own need he would be acting on, not hers, he thought sardonically. There was no sadness, no pain, no unhappiness, in her soft expression; if anything, she looked as if she was reliving an especially good memory, and he contented himself with a light touch on her coat sleeve that he was sure she didn't feel.

By unspoken agreement, the audience held their applause until the last notes of the music had faded into silence and the lights came on, and a few minutes later they were walking out the main doors of the church. "I didn't have time for dinner before the concert. Want to keep me company while I grab something at Buddy's?" he asked easily.

He'd phrased his invitation to sound casual, but if she refused she would look mean and selfish, condemning him to eat all by himself, poor lonely soul. But the joke was on him, Claire thought, because she'd already decided she would stop off at Buddy's before she went home. "Sure. Why not?"

Since driving would take longer than walking, they joined the small crowd on the corner waiting for the light to change. Across Albuquerque's main drag from the church and the university campus, Buddy's was a city institution. Beginning as a funky hole-in-the-wall diner thirty years before, it had gradually absorbed the rest of the businesses on the block. Still funky and with the same good, cheap food and space available twenty-four hours a day, it was the university students' favored study hall, although the next booth was just as likely to be occupied by a family or an older couple or professionals tired of coffee bars.

The door swung open, and they were enveloped in a steamy incense of green chile, baking tortillas, hamburger grease and coffee, plus just a touch of disinfectant. Ordering was do-it-yourself, and she stepped up to the only empty spot at the counter. Without bothering to consult the menu painted overhead, Claire gave her order to the clerk who, in true Buddy's tradition, was young, efficient and hideously hairnetted. "I'll have a large coffee and a cinnamon roll." As big as salad plates and dripping with butter, Buddy's cinnamon rolls were a cardiologist's nightmare and at least as good as chocolate.

"Her order is with mine."

The clerk took his word for it, looking past her expectantly, waiting for his order. Claire slowly turned around, her wallet still half out of her purse. Like his tone, his expression was mild as his eyes met hers, his eyebrows slightly raised in bland question, but she wasn't fooled. That toughness she'd seen before was there, lying low, just waiting for her to argue. She wasn't afraid of an argument—in fact, arguing with him might be rather fun—but the price of a cup of coffee and a cinnamon roll wasn't worth arguing about. And accepting his offer didn't make this a date. "Thank you," she said politely.

They found a booth in the third dining room, and Claire set down her coffee and the silverware she had picked up for both of them. "Thanks for putting the tree in the stand and fixing the gate and the faucet. That was a nice gesture," she added casually.

Keeping his head down, Jack divided up the napkins he had grabbed. She was sharp, and sneaky. When he was sure he could keep a straight face, he looked up. "I had a couple of extra minutes. That's a nice tree."

"I got it at the flea market." Same no-big-deal reaction. So now could she stop worrying about his motives and just accept that he was a nice guy? she demanded derisively of herself. "I noticed Mamie's old bond certificates were gone, and she said she gave them to you, that you wanted them for your office." She'd thought that rather odd, but maybe he'd thought that by letting Mamie give him something, she would be less stubborn about accepting his help.

There was a question in her voice, and he would have to be careful how he answered it. "The county didn't keep any of the bonds after redemption. I thought it would be nice to have a couple on display, just as a historical curiosity." Opportunely, the voice on the loudspeaker rattled off a string of numbers, and he stood up quickly. "There's our order. Anything else we need while I'm up?"

When he set the tray on the table a minute later, Claire couldn't imagine anything else they could need, except maybe another person to help eat all the food he'd ordered. Besides the huevos rancheros with beans, red chile and a dinner-plate-size flour tortilla, there was a side order of hash browns topped with cheese and green chile, a bowl of green chile stew with another tortilla and, for dessert, a fried pie. It was hard to believe a man could eat like that and stay in such good shape, but apparently he could.

She picked up her fork and cut off a piece of her cinnamon roll, then closed her eyes to fully appreciate the first wonderful bite. "Mmm." Opening her eyes, she said dreamily, "I love these things."

"I can see that," he murmured. She smiled, and he felt the heat and ache he was becoming resigned to.

"My daughter does, too. I'm sending her some for Christmas."

"Were you surprised when she went back East to work?" He had been wondering about that; from the photos he'd seen in her house and her obvious disappointment that her daughter wasn't coming home for Christmas, he'd thought they must be very close, but maybe not.

She shook her head as she cut off another bite. "Emma went to college in Maryland, and I knew the first time she left for school that she wouldn't come back, not permanently. She never liked New Mexico. She hates brown and actually likes humidity." She grinned wryly. "I wanted to raise a child who was self-confident and strong, who didn't feel she had to live somewhere just because her mother lived there, and I did. Darn it."

"It must be hard, then, that she's not coming home for Christmas," he said quietly.

She made a face. "Yes, but—" she sighed philosophically "—I knew it would happen eventually." Claire blinked at the table in front him. The huevos, one tortilla and the hash browns were gone, and he was halfway through the green chile stew. "Is this the first time your son's not coming home?"

"He didn't last year, but his ship was in port, so I flew out to San Diego. He's out in the middle of the Pacific this year, so there's no way to get together."

There was nothing in his voice to indicate how he felt about that, but a shadow had passed through his eyes. "You and he must be close to have worked on all those houses together," she said lightly. What had happened to his wife? It wasn't common now for a father to get custody, and it had been even less so ten or fifteen years ago.

"We are, but it took a while." Jack noted the empty plate in front of her with approval. She'd eaten all of it, no worrying about counting calories or gaining an ounce. Discreetly, she sucked the fork to get the last drop of the butter sauce. Only a damned fool, he told himself, would be jealous of a piece of silverware.

Claire watched him clean his stew bowl with his last piece of tortilla. "What happened?"

"My wife was an alcoholic," he said matter-of-factly. He took a bite of fried pie and washed it down with a swallow of coffee. "I tried residential treatment programs, hospitalization, counseling, AA, a separation—everything I could think of. Nothing worked. I'd come home and find her passed out in her own vomit or, worse, Gary would. She'd open charge accounts and go on spending binges. She'd disappear for days. She had an affair with her psychiatrist. I'd been working full-time and taking care of Gary for years and," he added dryly, "gaining great respect for single mothers. I didn't know what it was like not to feel tired. Finally, there was nothing more I could do but divorce her."

Claire listened in silence, unable to think of anything to say that wouldn't sound shallow and meaningless.

"I had no trouble getting custody of Gary, but he was twelve and convinced it was his responsibility to take care of his mother, since I had deserted her. Like most addicts, she was extremely manipulative. Whenever I took him with me, he ran away, back to her. I'd given her the house, to make sure she had a safe place to live and somewhere Gary could visit her, so I let him go back to live with her." Sighing, he shook his head. "I didn't really have much choice. Short of handcuffing him to his bed, I couldn't make him stay with me. I knew my old neighbors would let me know how he was doing and—" he grimaced wryly "—they did. His mother was incapable of controlling him, of course, and he started running pretty wild. The morning he went to school with his hair dyed green, three people called to tell me before he'd gone two blocks."

He took another bite of his pie and a drink of his coffee, and Claire waited until he swallowed. "How did you get him back?"

He laughed shortly. "With the first fixer-upper. Between the treatment costs and the spending sprees, I was bankrupt, so I was living in a cheap one-bedroom apartment until I saved enough for the down payment on a government repossession. Fortunately one became available at about half-price because it had been trashed inside. It was about half a mile from my old house, so Gary would come by occasionally to see how it was coming along, and before long, he was working on it, too. He started staying overnight, then two or three nights, until gradually he just moved in. The house was something we could do together without any conflict, and—" he smiled faintly "—ripping Sheetrock off a wall can be very therapeutic. And the time away from his mother let him see her more clearly, too. He realized that no matter how much he loved her, no matter how hard he tried, he couldn't help her."

The same lesson his father had had to learn, Claire thought, as his eyes seemed to focus on something she couldn't see.

"I was dreading Christmas that year, and after so many miserable ones, I think Gary was, too. We were still basically camping out in the house. We had turkey TV dinners and the sorriest-looking tree you ever saw, with less than a handful of presents under it." She saw the glimmer of a smile. "Gary said it was the best Christmas he'd ever had."

After a few seconds of silence, Claire asked softly, "What happened to your ex-wife?"

His eyes snapped to her. "Her parents talked her into moving back to her hometown in Michigan a few years ago. Gary hears from her every once in a while. He says nothing has changed."

She would have spoken, but something in that final statement said he wasn't finished.

"Love doesn't end with the marriage, I discovered," he said slowly, almost reflectively. "It changes. You're not in love anymore, but you still care for the person, still care about what becomes of her." Grinning at her wryly, he shook his head.

"I know," Claire agreed softly. She watched him finish the rest of the fried pie and his coffee. It hadn't been the kind of compulsive gut-spilling some divorced men and women indulged in out of expiation or revenge, or maybe a desire for sympathy or just plain attention. He had been very straightforward, but she'd sensed that, like most men, he didn't generally discuss personal problems, even past ones, and especially not emotionally painful ones, with such frank openness. It was a serious violation of the male code of invincibility, she thought with a dry, silent laugh. Why he had chosen to tell her, displaying a trust she'd done nothing to earn, she didn't know, and she shied away from speculating. Yet she was, oddly, very touched that he had, and pleased, too, because it helped satisfy a curiosity she wouldn't admit.

In fact, he had been so straightforward and matter-of-fact, almost cold, in discussing his former wife that she'd thought he couldn't care less what became of her, but now she understood that he'd told the story much the way he did favors, with no fanfare, no bid for sympathy any more than he sought appreciation or attention. Some people, deservedly so, didn't rate one second's concern from their ex-spouses, but his wife hadn't been that kind. Claire believed that divorce should be expensive and painful, both emotionally and financially; otherwise, the entire concept of marriage was trivialized, but the price he had paid was much higher than most. A lot of men would be bitter or suffering some kind of mistaken guilt, but he wasn't. He had learned what was probably the hardest lesson in life—to accept what couldn't be changed. He was at peace with what had happened; he didn't feel sorry for himself. He had simply gotten on with his life and helped his son get on with his. She could feel sorrow for him, though, as well as admiration. Maybe she hadn't known him long, but it was long enough to see how much love and affection he had to give. It wasn't right that he had no one to treasure the gift—or the giver.

Jack glanced around and almost laughed out loud. Behind them, two small children who were tired and should have been in bed hours ago were loudly whining that they didn't want to go home and go to bed; at the next table sat two street people, one impersonating a gaucho and the other some kind of shaman in a feather cape, while a busboy threw dishes in his tub a couple of booths away. Just the place to tell your life story. He certainly hadn't planned to, and why he had, he wasn't sure, but he wasn't sorry, he decided. Everybody their age had baggage in tow; it was time she knew what his was. Setting down his empty cup, he looked at her with a slight smile. "So, what's your war story?"

She grinned crookedly as she set down her own cup. "Compared to yours, mine was a skirmish. When I married Emma's father, he was a big kid. Ten years later, he was still a big kid, but I had a little kid by then and needed an adult, not another kid. We divorced before things got to the point that the good memories I had were tainted by lousy ones. He moved to Denver, and Emma and I stayed here."

It hadn't been that easy, he was sure. From what he'd seen of her already, she was stubbornly loyal and fiercely protective of those she cared about, but he didn't detect any lingering sadness or sour disappointment. She knew—from birth, he suspected—something that had taken him years of conscious effort to learn—that happiness was a choice, not a natural condition. Dwelling on past happiness or holding out for future happiness was a cop-out for not making any effort to be happy in the present. She worked to be happy with herself and her life, and she'd succeeded very well.

He was about to ask her what she was doing Friday night when the gaucho and the shaman stood up to leave. "Let's go hang out at the Double Rainbow, man," one of them said as they passed by, and he cursed under his breath as she glanced at him as if in embarrassment, her relaxed expression tightening. It was the "hang out" that had done it, reminding her of what she'd said on "Santa's" knee. If he ever got his hands on that Santa suit again, he promised himself, he was going to burn the damned thing. She started to gather her coat around her, and he cursed again. There was no point asking a question he already knew he wouldn't like the answer to.

"Ready to go?" he asked pleasantly, ignoring the look of relief on her face as he stood up. Controlling his impatience with an effort, he reminded himself that he could wait. After all, he hadn't been waiting for her forever—it only seemed that way.

Chapter Six

Jack studied the menu posted in the café window. The food, he remembered, was mediocre, and there was a line stretching to the door for tables. At one point he'd planned on making reservations someplace decent, but now, just for himself, it didn't matter. He turned away, walked up the block and crossed the street. The Plaza Bakery didn't have a line, but what few tables there were were taken, and nobody looked like they were going to be leaving anytime soon. He glanced across the street at the plaza to see if there were any empty benches. He couldn't even see a bench because half the city of Santa Fe suddenly seemed to have converged on the area. Looking back, he considered the dime store a few doors up. While not known for its cuisine, it did have good frito pies.

He walked up the crowded sidewalk and peered through the big plate glass window to see if there were any tables free, or maybe a seat at the counter. He did a double take, then a slow smile spread across his face.

Claire looked up idly, and suddenly she forgot to chew. She hadn't told anyone she was coming here, including Mamie, so how had Jack known where to find her? She sighed resignedly. He hadn't known; this was just another coincidence . . . or another punishment for being chicken.

While she'd been out Tuesday, he'd stopped by Mamie's to replace a broken windowpane and gone over to her house, too, of course. He'd fixed the ripped screen on the bathroom window and also left a note saying the propane man had come by and, despite the note *he'd* left, she did not need a new propane tank, and did she want to go to dinner in Santa Fe Friday? Since Mamie had said he would be back the next day, she'd been able to leave a note instead of calling either of the phone numbers he'd left. She'd thanked him for fixing the screen, warning her about the propane man and the dinner invitation, but she had plans. She'd also left a five dollar bill to pay for the screening. She came home to find he'd put the remaining screws in the cat door she'd installed for Tamale, the one that had come with half the screws missing. He hadn't left another note, but the five dollar bill was still there, the thumbtack pushed in with what she'd thought was unnecessary force.

He turned away from the counter with his order and raised his tray questioningly, and she waved him over, ignoring the little voice that told her she wasn't doing it out of politeness. She remembered she still had a mouthful of frito pie as he slid into the other side of the booth, and she swallowed hastily. "Is this where you were going to take me to dinner?"

He nodded agreeably as he stirred up one of his two bowls of corn chips, chile and Cheddar. "Here or Lota Burger. After just a cinnamon roll and coffee the other night, I realized you were every man's dream—a cheap date."

She gave him a superior look. "I wouldn't have settled for anything less than the Burrito Bucket." Had he really considered the trip to Buddy's a date?

He nodded in rueful resignation as he loaded his spoon. "Good thing you turned me down, then."

The sly glance that followed pointed out that, despite that turndown, she was having dinner with him, wasn't she?

"Have you come to a *las Posadas* here before?" she asked. It hadn't escaped her that, although he'd followed through on his plans, he hadn't asked anyone else to join him. He was wearing old jeans and an equally old flannel-lined denim jacket with a navy sweater that made his blue eyes even bluer and contrasted nicely with his cinnamon and sugar hair.

His mouth full, he shook his head. After swallowing, he added, "I've gone to a couple in Albuquerque."

Through the window they could see the crowd growing and, by tacit agreement, didn't waste any more time talking. *Las Posadas,* —"the inns," in English—was a Christmas tradition that had begun in the Middle Ages in Spain, coming to New Mexico with the first Spanish settlers four hundred years before. It was the reenactment of Mary and Joseph's search for lodgings in Bethlehem. One of the Catholic congregations in Santa Fe organized it, recruiting a couple with a new baby to play Joseph and Mary, but anyone could join the chorus or audience.

Promptly at seven, two men with lit torches started leading the procession slowly around the plaza. Mary, seated sideways on a burro, and Joseph followed them, with the chorus bringing up the rear, singing *"Vamos Todos a Belén"* and other centuries-old carols. Claire didn't know how he managed it, but Jack worked them through the crowd until she was standing on the edge of the street. He was behind her, the press of bodies around them snugging them together like spoons. The warmth she felt wasn't all from the thermal tights she was wearing under her jeans, she knew.

Joseph stopped and begged lodging for his wife and himself, but at each "inn" he was turned away with songs and shouts, while the devil, dressed in red with the traditional forked tail, horns, goatee and pitchfork, ran along the second-story balconies, egging on the innkeepers and threatening Joseph and Mary. Everything happened in Spanish, but it wasn't necessary to know a word of the language to follow the action. The onlookers lining both sides of the street loudly hissed and booed the nasty innkeepers and the devil, lending moral support to the couple until they knocked at the last door and were admitted. Everybody cheered and trooped in after them.

The "stable" was really the courtyard of the Palace of the Governors, which had served as its name implied for over three hundred years, then become the state historical museum. Its three-foot-thick adobe walls had witnessed almost four hundred *las Posadas,* to-night's performance essentially unchanged from the first except for the chorus's modern dress and the flashlights they carried instead of candles to light their way. The centuries of tradition behind the peasants' play and the carols, the cold crisp night, even the raucous audience, reinforced the importance of what had happened two thousand years ago in another adobe stable on a similar cold, starry night.

Burning stacks of pitch pine lit the courtyard, the fragrant oily smoke rising straight up in the still air. Mary and Joseph took their places, flanked by the burro and several sheep who, oblivious to the crowd, munched on Mary's hay bale seat. The couple's baby joined them, well-swaddled against the cold, in a rough pine manger, completing the living nativity scene.

Bizcochitos and hot cider were available, and Claire smiled her gratitude as Jack put a warm foam cup in her cold hands. He shared his fistful of cookies, and they munched and sipped in companionable silence until a guitarist took a seat on a hay bale near Joseph and strummed the opening bars of "Joy to the World"—or *"Paz en la Tierra,"* according to the little songbooks that suddenly began circulating through the audience.

The songbooks were in Spanish, but the tunes were familiar, so, their breath forming wreathes in the cold air, everybody sang. Spark stars flew up into the darkness from the burning pine as the crowd's voices soared toward the real stars in the natural cathedral overhead.

Jack smiled to himself as the guitarist ended "Silent Night" with a flourish. Claire sang just a tad off-key. She turned and laughed up at him for no more reason than that she was happy, and, laughing back, he put his arm around her without thinking and hugged her to him, tight. Reluctantly, he loosened his hold almost as fast, but she didn't make any attempt to pull away, so he left his arm loosely around her. She was just cold, he thought wryly, seriously considering taking off his jacket, since cold definitely wasn't his problem. Since he couldn't wrap both arms around her and pull her hard against him the way he wanted, he contented himself with kissing her hair, the lightest of kisses that she wouldn't feel. Closing his eyes, he slowly inhaled the clean sweetness. She was friendly, open, cheerful, funny, smart, pretty, and probably every man who'd ever met her had fallen a little bit in love with her. He had, far more than a little bit.

Opening his eyes, he smiled down on the top of her head. The idea didn't come as a shock any more now than it had when he'd first realized it a couple of weeks ago. The fall had probably started with her first beautiful smile, continuing with that ineffable something that had made falling in love with her as much a certainty as one and one adding up to two. He laughed in silent ruefulness. Her addition apparently wasn't as fast as his. It had been twenty-seven years, more than half his lifetime, since the last time he'd fallen in love, and never had he fallen so hard and so deep. As impatient—as *horny*, he admitted sardonically—as he was, there was a part of him that wasn't in any hurry, that wanted to savor the feeling, the wonder, the marvel of it.

The last carol in the songbook sung, Joseph and Mary and their son departed with solemn dignity, and the crowd in the courtyard began to disperse. As the arm around her shoulders fell away, Claire suppressed a sigh. She could pretend she was sorry he'd removed his arm because she was cold, but the truth was she was sorry because it had felt so good.

"Let's get some coffee before we drive back," he said, tucking his hands in the pockets of his jean jacket. "You are driving back tonight and not staying over?"

Claire tucked her hands in the pockets of her down jacket. "I'm driving back tonight."

He headed away from the plaza. Ahead of them walked a young couple, each with a small child dead to the world in their arms. "Sometimes I wish I had a little child to hold again," she murmured.

He laughed softly. "I know what you mean. I'm looking forward to grandchildren."

She smiled at him. "Me, too."

He felt his smile lingering after she looked at the street to watch where she was going. Her hair was down tonight, a cloud of curls to frame her wonderful smile. Her cheeks were pink from the cold, her eyes silvery in the soft light of the streetlamps. He lagged a step for a discreet once-over. Her jacket was short enough and her jeans tight enough to allow him to appreciate her trim bottom and long legs. All in all, she looked good enough to eat, but they were only having coffee, he reminded himself. "Not all women look forward to grandchildren."

Claire understood what he hadn't said. "Because they think grandchildren are a sign of old age? Some do," she agreed, then shrugged. "I don't think about my age much. Turning thirty didn't bother me, and I don't think I even noticed forty." She was silent a moment. "Fifty-one is going to bother me, though. It's good I still have a few years to get used to it."

He gave her an amused look. "Why fifty-one? Why not fifty?"

"Oh—" her laugh was half-embarrassed "—I decided a long time ago I was going to live to be a hundred, and when I turn fifty-one, I'll finally have to admit that my life is half over."

Jack laughed as he swung open the heavy carved door of their destination. She was a pure delight.

Claire glanced around after he seated her at the table for two the hostess had shown them to, right by the fireplace. This was a far cry from the dime store, she thought wryly. Innocuously labeled a "grill" on the small sign outside, the place was the upper-scale restaurant of one of the large, expensive hotels that had discovered Santa Fe. Fortunately the decorator hadn't fallen prey to howling coyotes and other Santa Fe style kitsch, but had chosen the true New Mexican style of Navajo blankets, whitewashed adobe, carved pine and good art. Anyplace else and they would have been grossly underdressed, but this was Santa Fe, where jeans and T-shirts were opera attire.

Since he'd only had two bowls of frito pie for dinner, she wasn't surprised to see a plate of quesadillas arrive with their coffee. In keeping with the tone of the "grill," the quesadillas weren't the usual Cheddar or Monterey Jack cheese baked between two flour tortillas but smoked duck and three exotic cheeses, one of whose name she couldn't even pronounce. The accompaniments were traditional, though, and not some nonsense like guava salsa.

"What are you doing for Christmas?" he asked as he expertly scooped guacamole and salsa onto a triangle of quesadilla.

"I'm having dinner with a friend and her family." She loaded her wedge with salsa and sour cream. "What are you doing?" What would Marty say if she arrived with him in tow? More important, what would *she* say?

"I'm going over to my sister and brother-in-law's in Gallup for Christmas Eve tomorrow and coming back the next night." It was probably just as well she had other plans, Jack thought wryly. Carla would faint dead away if he showed up for Christmas dinner with a woman. He remembered that she'd told him her parents still lived in Albuquerque after he'd mentioned that his had retired to Tucson. "You're not going to your folks, then?"

"They're going on a Caribbean cruise with my brother and his wife." She edged the bowl of sour cream closer. He didn't appear to like it, and it shouldn't be allowed to go to waste, she decided virtuously. "My sister invited me to spend a few days with her family in San Diego, but—" she wrinkled her nose "—palm trees aren't my idea of Christmas trees. Besides, I like Christmas at home."

"Me, too," he murmured absently as she licked a dab of sour cream off her finger, then grinned unrepentantly when she realized she'd been caught. He glanced wistfully toward the hotel lobby. There wasn't, he was certain, the slightest chance of talking her into forgetting about driving home tonight and getting a room here instead.

Minutes later, Claire sat back to sip her coffee. With the warmth of the fire, a chair that was getting more comfortable by the second and the lazy jazz drifting in from the hotel bar, she was reluctant to even think about leaving, much less actually do it. Unconsciously she returned the smile across the table. Another possibility occurred to her, and she started to choke on her last sip of coffee. Managing to get herself under control, she sat up straight and drained her cup. Taking that as a sign that she wanted to leave, he took out his wallet and dropped a twenty on the tray with the bill. "I'll leave the tip," she said firmly and reached for her wallet, which she'd tucked in a pocket of her jacket. One of those deceptively mild looks had her leaving it there.

Once outside, she zipped her jacket against the sharp drop in temperature. "A storm's coming," she said as a sudden breeze made it feel even colder.

Jack sniffed the air. "Snow by morning. Where did you park?"

"Just down the block." The cold breeze hurried them along, and Claire unlocked her car scant minutes later. The breeze funneled through the open parking garage, making her shiver as she turned to say goodbye.

Jack reached out to pull the collar of her jacket up around her ears, then let his hands rest lightly on her shoulders. "Are you going home the back way?"

Claire nodded. The breeze seemed to be getting warmer. "It's faster than going down the interstate."

He tightened his hands, drawing her closer. "I'll follow you home. It's on my way."

The breeze seemed to have died down altogether now. "It's about ten miles out of your way," she said wryly. Of their own accord, her hands rose to his chest.

"More like fifteen," he murmured, closing the remaining distance between them.

He kissed her with great seriousness, with a concentration and intensity no man had ever offered her before. His arms closed around her, bringing her body tight into his, and automatically her hands slid up around his neck to make the embrace even tighter. His mouth made no attempt to conquer hers; it invited mutual surrender instead, and she accepted the terms immediately. Her tongue traced the seam of his lips delicately, and it parted as long fingers slid up the nape of her neck, grazing her skull as they buried themselves in her hair, sending a long, erotic shiver through her. They traded tastes and textures, and dimly Claire had a sense of being absorbed. It wasn't a frightening sensation or an unpleasant one, but rather an utterly gratifying and enormously exciting one.

Gradually a noise penetrated his awareness. His fogged brain finally identified it as a car alarm somewhere behind them. It cut off abruptly in midsqueal. Or maybe it was his own alarm, warning him that another few seconds and forget a hotel room, he would have her in the back seat of her own car. He'd been hoping for a warm reaction, if he was lucky; he'd never even dreamed of a meltdown. Summoning up willpower he hadn't known he had, he eased out of the kiss. She let him go with a reluctance that very nearly vaporized every molecule of his damned willpower. "Claire," he whispered.

Her eyes opened slowly, and she stared at him with a hazy smile that had him groaning inside.

"Be careful driving." He kissed her quickly before reaching around to open the car door.

Her eyes huge, she nodded solemnly, then got into the car and shut the door.

As her taillights disappeared, he started walking briskly toward his truck. He'd only gone two and a half blocks before he remembered he'd parked four spaces up from her.

Chapter Seven

"Do you think we're going to be snowed in?" Claire stared out at the fat snowflakes drifting past her kitchen window. True to Jack's and her predictions, the storm had started just before dawn as a furious blizzard that had left a two foot drift by her back door and bare ground outside her front door. The wind had blown itself out before noon, leaving the snow, which had been falling for the past few hours at a slow, steady rate, already covering the bare brown spots with several inches of white.

Mamie gave her a wry look. "I hate to tell you, but we're already snowed in. Neither of us has a car that can handle our road right now."

Claire nodded glumly as her worst suspicions were confirmed. "I was thinking the other day that I should trade in my car on a four-wheel drive." Since it was Christmas Eve, they were guaranteed a rare white Christmas, but she couldn't summon up any excitement over it.

She trailed after Mamie as the older woman headed for the front door. "I'm sorry I wasn't any help, Mamie." Mamie had come over to use the phone, since the storm had knocked hers out; that was when Claire had discovered hers wasn't working, either.

"Don't worry about it. We'll be back in service in a day or two." She paused to examine the split-leaf philodendron on the living room step. "This plant really looks good, Claire."

Claire frowned absently at the philodendron. "I know. It looked like it was dying, then two weeks ago it suddenly perked up for some reason."

After pulling up the hood of her parka, Mamie opened the front door.

"Are you sure you don't want to stay for supper, Mamie? I made a big pot of vegetable beef soup." Claire winced at the near-whine she heard in her voice.

"No, thanks, dear. I left two mincemeat pies in the oven, and they'll be done in a few minutes."

Mamie strode briskly toward her cabin, pausing after she'd gone about twenty-five yards to call back, "Your luminarias look great!"

Claire thanked her with a listless wave. After debating all day, she'd finally decided to take her chances with the weather and set out the six dozen brown paper sacks, weighted by sand and a candle, just before dusk. The softly glowing lights outlined her driveway and the lower half of the road between her house and Mamie's cabin, and they did look nice, she decided, though without taking any pleasure in the sight. When Mamie was safely inside her cabin, Claire turned, absently brushed the snow off the Indian corn and dried red chile wreath on the front door, and stepped inside.

In the kitchen, she lifted the lid of the soup pot, examined the contents without any particular interest and no appetite, replaced the lid and turned off the burner.

A glance into her refrigerator revealed no space for anything bigger than an anorexic pickle, but several minutes of shifting and stacking finally made room, and in went the soup.

Afterward she wandered aimlessly through the house, finding herself on the living room sofa, staring at the lit and decorated Christmas tree, tears running down her face. Try as she might, she couldn't ignore it any longer. It was Christmas Eve, and she was alone.

Tamale jumped on the sofa and curled up on her lap, as if to offer silent sympathy, and the tears came faster. As if moving and work weren't enough to keep her busy, she'd spent the month going to Christmas fairs and stuffing herself with latkes and blintzes at Hanukkah festivals, run the Christmas food drive at work, wrapped toys for tots, made every Christmas recipe in her file—all to fill the cold, empty spot of impending loneliness inside her. Tonight she had planned to go to a Christmas Eve service, then on to the luminaria tour downtown. By staying so busy she wasn't supposed to notice how much she missed Emma. It hadn't worked, of course.

Giving her a disgusted look, Tamale leaped off her lap, stalked to the hassock in front of the wood stove and settled down to rub away the wet spot on his head. Claire grabbed a sofa pillow and hugged it to her tightly, just in case it had any ideas of deserting her, too.

Finally she began to run out of tears, slowing to sniffles punctuated by the occasional hiccup. Releasing the squashed pillow, she took a deep breath and wiped her wet cheeks with the heels of her hands. She should have let herself cry weeks ago and gotten it over with, she thought as she pushed herself off the couch and headed for the bathroom. Instead, every time her eyes had started to fill at the thought of Emma not coming home, she had distracted herself with yet another Christmas project. In between running around and turning the kitchen into a food factory, she'd been making pilgrimages to all the Christmas events she and Emma had most enjoyed together, just the way someone who'd lost a beloved spouse would return to the places they'd been happiest together. How pathetic.

After turning on the bathroom faucet, she doused a washcloth with frigid water, then slapped it on her face. Emma hadn't died, for heaven's sake. She hadn't deserted her, either. She just wasn't coming home for Christmas this year. Claire wasn't happy about it, but neither was it a tragedy, despite how hard she'd tried to turn it into one. It was inevitable that they would be apart sooner or later, and she'd been lucky that it was later. They'd had twenty-four Christmases together, and they would have more—just not this one.

Claire removed the cloth and looked in the mirror over the sink, making a face at her red-eyed reflection. She certainly hoped Emma was behaving with more maturity than her mother. A few more applications of the cold cloth and she actually began to look halfway normal again. Hanging up the cloth, she glanced down to see Tamale watching her warily from the doorway. "Well, cat, let's go see what's for dinner," she said with more lightness—and appetite—than she would have thought possible half an hour before. Now that she'd regained the ability to think straight, she had another, bigger problem to consider, but she wasn't going to tackle it on an empty stomach.

She and Tamale were perusing the contents of the packed refrigerator when it suddenly went dark. It wasn't, Claire realized, a burned-out bulb; the power was out. Mamie had warned her that when a storm knocked out phone service, the power usually went, too.

With the storm, there was no moonlight or even starlight shining into the house, and the kitchen was pitch-black. "Ouch," she muttered as she found the table with her hipbone. Her knee discovering a door-jamb told her that she was going in the right direction, and, inching along, she patted the darkness until her hand encountered the dryer. Feeling around it to the other side, she ran her hand over the wall beyond until a stubbed finger located the rechargeable flashlight plugged into the outlet.

Armed with light, she retrieved the spare box of luminaria candles from the garage. The votive-size candles fit perfectly in jelly glasses, she discovered, and soon she had a dozen lined up on the kitchen counter. Lighting two, she switched off the flashlight and smiled as soft yellow glow replaced harsh white glare.

She distributed the indoor luminarias around the house, one on the washstand in the entry, one in the first bathroom and four in the living room. The candles were good for ten hours, and she had two dozen of them, so she could afford the extravagance, she decided, enjoying the way the combined firelight through the glass window of the wood stove and the candle glow made the ornaments and tinsel on the Christmas tree sparkle and shimmer.

The wood stove was going to be doing more than providing sparkle and shimmer. No electricity meant no heat from the furnace, but luckily, not believing the forecast for clear weather for the next week, she had stacked several wheelbarrow loads of firewood in the garage to be sure she had a dry supply. As long as she kept the sturdy little stove going, the house should stay reasonably warm. But Mamie's wouldn't, she remembered suddenly. Although the cabin had a fireplace, Mamie didn't have any firewood, one of the too many economies she'd had to make the past few years.

Five minutes later she was following her flashlight along the snow-covered road to Mamie's. Thinking about Mamie led to thinking about her financial situation, which automatically led to that problem she'd been going to think about after supper. She was almost fifty years old, for heaven's sake! If—*if*—she had a relationship with a man, she expected it to be placid, comfortable, fond, nothing too exciting or emotional...a *mature* relationship. She certainly hadn't expected to discover she was just as capable of passion, excitement, loving and making a fool of herself as she had been at twenty.

Loving? Even more capable, she thought ruefully; at twenty she'd been too young to know what love really was. And she'd never at twenty had one of those kisses that made you forget where you were; she hadn't had one until last night. Hard as it was to imagine, she'd forgotten she was standing in a dark, frigid, wind-blasted parking garage; in fact, she had no memory of leaving the parking garage or driving the first ten miles home. Just because of a kiss...a two-hundred-proof, mind-dazzling, bone-dissolving kiss.

She probably wouldn't have remembered the rest of the trip home, either, except that she'd recognized the truck behind the headlights in her rearview mirror. He'd followed her all the way to her exit, and she had a suspicion that he had parked on the shoulder until the lights in her house had come on.

All right, she loved him! she yelled silently, giving up. The thought had sneaked in, and she'd tried to pretend it hadn't, but she couldn't deny it any longer. Defying all that was sensible, she had fallen in love with him. Madly. Claire waited for the silent shriek of horror...the hair curling of terror.... A little disgust, at least? Instead she could feel a big idiot grin on her face. She wasn't horrified, terrified or disgusted with herself; she was *thrilled*.

She turned into Mamie's driveway as the dour voice of common sense—or self-preservation—got several words in edgewise. The first reminded her about Suzi, her officemate, who had recently married the first man who'd paid serious attention to her after her divorce last year. She'd admitted frankly that she had married a man she didn't love because she was certain that, given her age—two years less than Claire's own—the odds were that she wouldn't get another offer and she hated the idea of being single the rest of her life. Claire considered the example irrelevant—mostly. Suzi's husband had left for a younger woman, which hadn't happened to Claire, and she had been in her mid-thirties, not mid-forties, when she was divorced. More than one man had paid serious attention to her since, as well; she just hadn't paid any back—until now. There was the possibility that her subconscious was thinking Jack Herrod might be the last man and she'd better grab him. With Emma not coming home for the first time for Christmas, she finally had to face the fact that her daughter had grown up and left home for good, she wasn't just away temporarily. They would always be extremely close, but their lives were growing apart. As they should, Claire thought with bittersweetness, but that didn't mean there wasn't going to be a large hole in hers, at least for a while. Was Jack supposed to fill it?

As if that weren't enough, the heartless voice dug up old family history. Her great-aunt Rose had never married, never shown any sign she wanted to, choosing instead to build a very successful business from nothing, a radical idea for the time. At exactly her own age, Aunt Rose—confirmed old maid, her business flourishing and financially fixed for life—had married a man she'd known for six weeks. It was "the change," she remembered her grandmother and mother saying, giving each other significant looks that she hadn't understood for years. Was Jack her change-of-life romance, a hormonal last hurrah, a pathetic attempt to prove she was still a woman?

If she hadn't been so busy thinking about not thinking about Emma's absence, she might have realized sooner how deep she was getting in with Jack and wondered why it was happening so fast. At her age, weren't these things supposed to happen more slowly, more—she grimaced as she blinked away a snowflake—*sedately?* Instead she had instantly liked him, immediately felt intensely attracted to him, which probably explained why she'd been just as instantly furious with him. She hadn't been angry just for Mamie; she'd been angry for herself because she was so disappointed.

She blinked at another snowflake, then rubbed at it impatiently when it didn't cooperate. If he had suggested going back to the hotel last night instead of going home...what? She would have liked to think she would have said no, emphatically, but the truth was that she couldn't swear she would have. She'd suddenly discovered a desperate need to touch and be touched. She had to figure out what she was doing before she did something she would regret the rest of her life. She didn't do affairs well, and she was certain she would be a disaster at a lightning-quick affair.

But she didn't have time to decide anything now, Claire thought with guilty relief, stepping onto Mamie's porch.

The door opened almost as Claire knocked on it. "I want you to come stay with me until the power is back on, Mamie, and I won't take no for an answer," she said without preamble.

"And you won't get one," Mamie answered immediately. "Come on, let's go." She finally noticed that Mamie already had her boots and parka on and realized the older woman had been at the point of coming over to her house.

They followed her tracks toward her house. "Isn't it beautiful?" Mamie said in a hushed voice that still sounded loud.

"Yes, it is," Claire murmured, seeing what she'd been too preoccupied to see before. The air was utterly still, not even a breath of breeze disturbing it, the only sound the muffled tramp of their boots. She aimed the flashlight over their heads for a moment to watch the large flakes caught in the beam float soundlessly toward them out of the darkness. The temperature was below freezing, but with no wind, it didn't feel particularly cold. Even the occasional icy kiss of a snowflake on her bare cheek felt only cool. The flashlight's long reach occasionally touched the valley slope, revealing piñons and junipers in thick ermine coats.

Mamie laughed softly. "Your luminarias look like an arrow pointing right to your house."

Glancing ahead, Claire laughed, too. Because of the way space between objects narrowed at a distance, the luminarias outlining the road looked like the arrow shaft, those lining the wider drive the head and the few leading to the front patio gate the tip. Amazingly, none of them had gone out in the snow; it wasn't falling fast enough, she guessed.

They stamped and brushed off at the back door, then went inside. The house felt almost too warm after being outside, but Claire threw another log in the wood stove anyway. Despite the darkness, it was only a little after six-thirty, and the temperature outside was only going to get colder, especially if the clouds cleared.

"I was watching the news when the power went off. The state police have closed the canyon," Mamie told her.

The news that the portion of the interstate that ran through Tijeras Canyon—the canyon their little canyon emptied into—was closed didn't surprise her. Neither did the fact that they were temporarily isolated concern her. "Did they say how much longer the storm will last?"

"The weatherman's dart landed on tomorrow," Mamie said sardonically.

Claire's laugh covered the discreet rumble of her stomach. It hadn't forgotten dinner, she thought wryly. "Did you have dinner yet? I'm going to—"

Bright light flashed through the sidelights in the entry. Headlights, Claire realized a second later as she heard the rumble of a vehicle. By the time it stopped outside, she was at the front door.

To conserve heat, she didn't open it until the driver was on the porch. She'd seen who it was through the peephole, but there was still surprise in her voice. "I thought you were going to Gallup, to your sister's, today."

Jack stepped through the door, and she closed it behind him. "I'll go in the morning." He saw Mamie standing in the living room. "You two all right? Both your phones are out."

"We're fine," Mamie answered him. "How did you talk the police into letting you into the canyon?"

"I told them I had family here, and since I have four-wheel drive, they let me through."

Claire saw a shrug, but the look he flashed her reminded her once again of the dryer voltage. The only way he could have known their phones were out was because he had called to see that they were all right, and when he couldn't get through, he had delayed going to his family in Gallup to check on his "family" here. The white lie had just been an expedient, she knew, yet it gave her a warm glow. Like that glance a few seconds ago. "Have you eaten? I was just about—"

Once again the sound of a vehicle interrupted her.

"I thought I saw lights somewhere behind me," Jack muttered as he opened the door. Peeking around him, Claire saw a small motor home stopping beside his truck.

Moments later, the older couple who climbed out of it were introducing themselves in the entry. "We're the Shepherds, Wally and Stella," said the husband. It was true that people grew to look alike the longer they lived together, Claire thought, hiding a smile. They were both tall, spare and slightly stooped, with wire-rim glasses and hair the same color gray. They were even dressed alike in khaki pants and navy pea coats.

"I'm Jack Herrod, and this is Claire," Jack said, his hand resting lightly on her shoulder. "And this is Mamie Bonnett." He nodded toward Mamie as she climbed the living room step to the entry. "Mamie lives next door."

The men shook hands, while the women contented themselves with smiles and murmurs. "Boy, were we glad to see your lights. We hadn't seen a one for miles, and then there they were, pointing like an arrow, right at your house.''

Wally Shepherd aimed his smile at both of them, and Claire realized that he thought Jack was her husband and the house theirs. Not a hard mistake to make, since Jack had made the introductions, neglecting to mention her last name, she thought dryly.

She slanted him a thoughtful look as Mamie laughed at the arrow comment, then said, ''We thought the canyon was closed. Have the police opened it up again?''

Stella Shepherd answered in a voice amazingly similar to her husband's. ''I think somebody got their wires crossed,'' she said with a grimace. ''We were at the roadblock on the east end, getting ready to turn around and go back to Moriarty to try to find a room, when the police got a message that conditions had improved, so they started letting people through.'' She shuddered slightly. ''They hadn't.''

''The road's mostly black ice,'' her husband elaborated. ''Do you mind if we park in your drive until tomorrow morning? The road should be open by then.''

''Of course not,'' Claire said. ''You don't have to stay in your motor home, though. We can make up beds for you in here.'' *We?* Now *she* was doing it.

Stella and Wally shook their heads in unison, and Claire only knew it was Wally speaking because she was looking at them. ''We don't mind staying in the camper. It has a heater, but we'd appreciate access to a real bathroom.''

"Certainly. Won't you come in and stay for a while?" She suspected her smile took a sappy turn as Jack's hand, still on her shoulder, gave it a little squeeze before dropping away.

"Thanks," said Wally, helping his wife off with her coat. "You may have some more company," he added. "I think someone else turned off right behind me."

On cue, there was the sound of a third vehicle approaching. Mamie showed the Shepherds into the living room, while Claire and Jack remained in the entry. As soon as they'd heard the car, he'd put his hand on the doorknob, meaning he would again be the one who opened the door. To make sure whoever was out there was safe, she understood now. It was her house, and she was perfectly capable of taking care of herself, yet she didn't resent his macho presumption because it *wasn't* presumption—it was protection. She supposed some people would consider that macho presumption, too, but she didn't. She was glad some men still considered it their responsibility to protect women.

The new arrivals were another couple, young this time, although it was obvious there would soon be three of them. "Geez, were we glad to see your lights," the dark-haired young man told them as he helped his wife up the small step into the house. "I thought we were going to end up stuck in a ditch for the night for sure, but then I saw that arrow." He looked at them wonderingly. "Wow."

Jack caught her eyes for a moment before he again handled the introductions—with her last-nameless again—and she saw that he was trying not to laugh just as much as she was. The young man introduced himself and his wife as Joel and Marion Duda, and Claire ushered them toward the living room.

As she started to follow them, Jack's hand held her back. He glanced from the couple, now being introduced to the Shepherds by Mamie, back to her. "Hmm. Joel and Marion...sort of like Joseph and Mary. I hope they have a Lamaze manual with them."

"I know," she said in the same undertone with a hushed laugh. "At least we have Mamie."

Passing behind them with the newcomers' coats, Mamie shook her head vigorously. "I diaper, I do not deliver."

They stared after her, then at each other, and burst into suppressed giggles.

Taking a deep breath, Jack got himself under control. "How are we fixed for wood? Should I bring some in from outside and start drying it out?"

Swallowing the last giggle, Claire shook her head. "I've got plenty stored in the garage."

"Good girl." He gave her shoulder a pat. "Then I think I'll bring in some now and stack it by the stove so I don't have to traipse back and forth all night."

Bemused, Claire stared at him. Whoever objected to men as protectors would undoubtedly object to that "good girl," as well, and would certainly object to feeling a ridiculous pleasure at his casual praise. And probably to the quick pat that had turned into a lingering caress that was turning her shoulder muscles into mush. Then there was the even more casual assumption that he was staying the night. With a houseful of people, he had to know there wasn't a chance of sharing her bed, so she knew that wasn't why he was staying. They hadn't discussed it, of course. But she wasn't going to object to that, either, she thought, giving herself a quick mental shake—not that there'd been time to. As seemed to be the case lately, there hadn't even been time to think about it. "Good," she said. "You do that, and I'll figure out how to make some tea or cocoa or something."

They were halfway down the hall to the kitchen and garage when a now-familiar sound stopped them, and they looked at each other. "We have shepherds and Joseph and Mary," he muttered as he started to the front door. "All we need now is a band of angels."

"Is it a band of angels?" she asked jokingly, right behind him as he opened the door.

"Not exactly," he said, an odd note in his voice.

She looked at him, puzzled. "What do you mean, 'not exactly'?"

Wordlessly, he opened the door wider so she could see. No, it wasn't exactly a band of angels, she thought, hardly believing her eyes as the vehicle's front doors opened, illuminating the interior. It was a minivan. Then the side door slid open, and six mini-angels, complete with wings and halos, jumped out.

Chapter Eight

"We were supposed to do a Christmas program at the Veterans' Hospital," Ruth Mora, the driver of the minivan, told the living room at large. Jack watched the six little girls sitting on the carpet at her feet nod glumly in agreement. Ruth Mora had already told them she was the teacher of the second-grade Sunday school class at a Moriarty church. Half of the class had been in her van. The other half had been ahead of them and had apparently gotten through okay.

He looked across the living room, and as if he'd called her name, Claire turned her head. Her nod told him she was thinking the same thing he was.

"You know," she told Mrs. Mora and the angels, "I missed going to a Christmas Eve program because of the snow. And I bet nobody else here got to go, either." She paused, and the Shepherds, the Dudas, Mamie and Jack murmured agreement on cue. "Maybe you could do your program for us."

The little girls looked eagerly at their teacher until the one with one wing askew—Michelle, Jack thought—put a damper on the idea. "Except we don't have everybody. The boys were the shepherds, and the two fourthgraders were Joseph and Mary." Nodding, the angels went back to being glum.

"Well, our name is Shepherd," said Wally. "We'll be the shepherds."

"And our names are almost the same as Joseph and Mary, and we're expecting a baby, so we'll be them," said Marion Duda, and her husband, Joel, nodded in agreement.

Five of the angels went back to looking eager, but not Michelle. "And who will you and Mr. Herrod be, Mrs. Herrod?" she demanded.

The kid had the makings of a good lawyer, Jack decided as Claire shot him a narrow-eyed glance but didn't correct the little girl. He honestly didn't think he had ignored her last name on purpose; he had introduced her only by her first name because, from the first, she had been simply "Claire." He had to admit, though, that "Claire Herrod" had a ring to it. Hiding a grin, he answered for both of them. "We'll be the owners of the stable where Mary and Joseph stay."

"And I'll be the shepherds' sheep," Mamie added, straight-faced.

Apparently those roles satisfied seven-year-old logic, and Michelle nodded soberly.

"Sleep in heavenly peace."

As the angels' voices faded, Claire saw the soft, warm smiles on the faces of the adults around the room. The Christmas program had been very simple—the Christmas story from the Book of Luke interspersed with old, familiar carols. She had attended a number of Christmas Eve services over the years, most of them elaborate, with candelabra and special lighting, large choirs, soloists, musicians and special sermons. None of them had been more meaningful than tonight's, with only candles in jelly glasses, carols sung by untrained voices and simple Bible verses. She felt a light touch from the man beside her and looked up to see the softest, warmest smile.

The angels took off their wings and halos and became little girls again—hungry little girls, judging from the whispering she overheard. Excusing herself, she went into the kitchen. They might not have power or phones at the moment, but food was no problem, she thought wryly.

As she was assembling paper plates and napkins on the counter, she heard someone come into the kitchen. She knew who it was before she turned around.

"Can you scrape together enough for fourteen people?" he asked as he began loading up with plates and napkins.

For an answer, she began opening the various tins stacked on the counter, tins he had assumed were a collection. She had at least half a dozen kinds of cookies, muffins, miniature carrot cakes and pecan pies, and some kind of fancy bread. Then she opened the refrigerator. "Good Lord," he said blankly.

"Emma isn't coming home," Claire mumbled by way of explanation.

"I understand," he said with a tender smile that said, impossibly, he did.

Hours later she was back in the kitchen, straightening up and blowing out the candles. With cocoa made on the wood stove, the fourteen of them had tried their best to empty the tins and the refrigerator. Marion Duda had proved she was eating for two, while her husband must be expecting triplets. Claire laughed to herself. Now almost everybody was asleep, the Shepherds in their motor home, the Dudas in her bed, Mamie in Emma's, Ruth Mora on one of the sofas, and the girls in makeshift bedrolls on the living room floor. She and Jack were going to have to flip for the futon in the spare room, she thought with a yawn.

She met him in the entryway as he was coming out of the living room after checking on the wood stove one last time. As the girls were bedding down, he had loaded it with logs, then dampered it to produce heat all night. One more reason she was glad he was here, Claire thought; she hadn't mastered the idiosyncrasies of the stove yet.

Tamale had finally put in an appearance, too. She'd realized he must have had experience with children when he had vanished at the first sound of a high-pitched voice. Now that it was safe, he was back, investigating the sleeping strangers in the living room with an air of feline disapproval.

He leaped up on the hassock by the stove, the bells she had tied to his collar jingling brightly.

One of little girls stirred and murmured sleepily, "Santa Claus?"

Jack laughed softly. "Too bad we don't have some little presents to leave for them."

"I know," she murmured. Then suddenly she grabbed his hand and pulled him into the short hall.

"But we could leave stockings," she whispered excitedly. "I've got some old socks, and I think I've got enough candy and stuff to fill them."

A few minutes later they were sitting at the kitchen table with half a dozen candles, a pile of old socks from the box where she kept her shoe polish, the leftover Halloween candy she'd stashed in the freezer and a bag of apples. He picked up a fuzzy, hot pink and purple knee sock with a small hole in the heel. "Emma's?" he asked.

"Mine," she said with dignity, then grinned. Holding up its mate, she stared at it thoughtfully. "You know, it would be fun to do stockings for the adults, too."

"We don't have enough stuff," he said pointedly. She nodded disappointedly, but then he added slowly, "I've got a sack of peanuts in my truck, though, and I can probably find some odds and ends in my toolbox."

She looked at him, her eyes shining like a kid's, and he had to remind himself that it was too soon to be thinking about when he could move in.

"And I bet I've got stuff in the pantry that would work," she said.

A short while later they spread their loot on the table. Claire held up one of his contributions. "Nuts and bolts?" she asked doubtfully.

"People always need nuts and bolts," Jack said firmly, then held up one of her contributions. "How come you have three extra toothbrushes?" he asked evenly.

"The dentist always gives me one, and I don't like her kind but—" she shrugged "—I don't like to just throw them away, either." It was several seconds before she understood his sudden grin, and she gave his now downcast head a startled look that slowly turned into a smile. He'd thought she kept a few extras for sleep overs?

"We'd better do one for ourselves so the kids won't be suspicious." He picked up a navy blue crew sock. "What do you want?"

"Um . . . an orange, a couple of your bandages, one of those little bars of hotel soap, some peanuts and some of the Halloween bubble gum." She picked up one of her pink-and-purple knee socks. "What do you want?"

"Another sock," he muttered, and she laughed. "An orange, a toothbrush, a few of those hand wipes, peanuts and a couple of Tootsie pops—but not grape. I don't like grape."

Nodding solemnly, she filled his stocking. "If we're going to do this right, we ought to wrap at least some of the things." She left the kitchen and returned in a few minutes with a roll of wrapping paper, tape, scissors and a spool of ribbon. She'd assumed she would be doing the wrapping, since how to wrap a present and make it pretty was not a skill men were taught, until she watched him wrap a small hotel shampoo bottle, his big blunt fingers fashioning a better bow than hers. He had learned, no doubt, for his son.

It was almost two in the morning when they set the stockings, each tagged with a name, under the Christmas tree in the living room, using the soft glow from the stove to pick their way across the crowded floor. He watched her bend over each sleeping child, pulling up blankets, tucking them tighter. She was the mother his son should have had. It was too late for that, but she could be—would be—the grandmother his son's children would have.

After side trips to the bathrooms, they met again in the spare room. Claire stared at the futon with its two flat pillows and the one skimpy blanket that was left after supplying everyone else. They would have to sleep close to keep warm, especially being the farthest from the stove, but they weren't teenagers on hormonal highs, and they would be sleeping in their clothes like everyone else—she in leggings and a tunic top, he in jeans and a sweater. There was no reason they couldn't share the futon like the mature adults they were and just *sleep*. She put a sudden sharp pang of disappointment down to exhaustion.

He flipped back the blanket, sat down on the futon to pull off his boots, then glanced at her. "Do you want the right or the left?" he asked politely.

It took her a minute to realize he meant the right or left side of the futon. "Oh! The . . . right, I guess."

The left side was up against the wall, so he climbed across the bed, lay down on his back, pulled up the blanket and closed his eyes. "Don't forget to blow out the candle," he said, already sounding half-asleep.

"No—no, I won't," she said, wondering if she sounded as idiotic as she felt.

Jack worked to keep his face sober. The look on her face was priceless. If it hadn't been for that kiss last night, he might have worried that it was prompted by unhappiness over sharing the bed, but it wasn't unhappiness; it was a mixture of desire and nerves and being asleep on her feet. He knew, because he felt the same. He was certain they could overcome being tired with little more effort than a few kisses, but the first time they made love wasn't going to be with a houseful of strangers who would be getting up in just a few hours. He wanted privacy, at least twenty-four uninterrupted hours—though forty-eight would be better—and he wanted her to be sure, because he sensed that she wasn't, yet. He could wait—especially, he admitted as the room went dark, followed by the futon sinking beside him and a wash of her warm, sweet scent, since he was now just about asleep.

Claire pulled the blanket up to her chin and lay absolutely still, willing herself to relax. Suddenly he rolled over onto his side, reached out and rolled her onto hers, gathered her in and kissed her until even her toenails were relaxed. Then he tucked her against him with a long sigh. "Good night," he mumbled, and he was asleep.

It was true, she thought sadly as she drifted immediately into sleep, too. They were mature, so mature that their sex drives had aged and withered to the point that they chose sleep over making love.

* * *

Claire woke slowly out of a lovely dream about an octopus. As she woke a little more, she remembered that octopuses were usually the stuff of nightmares. This one did have her wrapped up tight, but he was warm and so comfortable, his body long and lean, and he smelled faintly of Old Spice. And his name was—she came awake the rest of the way in a rush—Jack Herrod.

"Did you know you snore?" he whispered in her ear.

She rolled over inside his arms to glare at him. "I do not!"

"Uh-huh, you do." He kissed her nose. "It's very soft—" his lips teased hers apart "—and sexy." His mouth took hers lazily, and she returned the favor, slipping her arms around his neck. His hands kneaded her back, while one leg hooked behind hers, locking their hips together tight, and she smiled against his mouth. What nonsense had she been thinking last night about withering? *Nothing* about him was withered.

Sliding her hands up, she did something she'd been wanting to do since the first time she met him. Rubbing slowly, she relished the silky rough tickle of his hair on her palms and between her fingers. One of his hands skimmed up the front of her tunic and closed gently over her breast. His fingers flexed, then his palm circled, burnishing the tight peak underneath, and every muscle in her body loosened.

"Santa came! Look, Santa came!"

The little girls' voices drifted down the hall, and with a mutual groan, they pulled apart. Pressing his forehead against hers, Jack sucked in a deep breath, then let it out as they both began to laugh helplessly. "Merry Christmas," he whispered between chuckles.

"Merry Christmas," she whispered back.

He gave her a quick kiss before he released her. "I love you, Claire."

Chapter Nine

The air was so crisp he could almost hear it crackle. He filled his lungs, inhaling the cedar scent of the juniper crackling and popping on the bonfire in the middle of the Indian pueblo plaza. He tugged on the hand inside his, and she followed, their boots crunching the thin, powdery snow, making it squeak. Before them, the four-hundred-year-old adobe church rose dark against the dawn sky, its wooden cross a benediction over the pueblo below.

At the corner of a house that had been centuries old when Columbus sailed into the Caribbean, a red glowing oil drum radiated heat. Stopping within the circle of warmth, he drew her back against his chest, wrapping his arms loosely across the front of her shoulders. He stood quietly, absorbing the drum's heat—and hers.

She was quiet, too, had been quiet ever since he'd picked her up an hour ago. He wouldn't have been surprised if she had refused to come with him this morning. His timing yesterday morning could have been better, Jack conceded. It had been too soon, of course, and he'd known it, but the words had just naturally slipped out. From her stunned look, they'd been anything but natural to her. She hadn't said anything, but fortunately he'd been in the process of getting up, so he was able to stand up and walk away. As if, he thought wryly, easing fractionally closer, he'd said nothing more than good morning.

Claire watched the crowd gathering around the edge of the plaza. It had been about this same time yesterday morning that the power and phone service had been restored while everyone was busy emptying their stockings. She smiled faintly. Wally Shepherd had been especially happy with the nut and bolt he'd found at the bottom of his, planning to use them to replace the one missing in their license plate holder. The highway department had cleared the interstate, and after doing their best to eat the leftovers from the night before, the strandees had been on their way, with the Dudas promising to send a birth announcement. Jack had been on his way, too. By the time Emma and Claire had opened their presents together over the phone, her road had melted enough for her car, and she had gone to Marty's, dropping Mamie off at her Christmas dinner engagement on the way. When she had come home there had been a message from Jack, telling her to be ready early in the morning, because they would be going to the Christmas dances at a nearby Indian pueblo. After his casual announcement—to which she had made no response, casual or otherwise—she had considered saying no, but when he'd left yesterday morning, she had felt a loneliness, different from but as sharp as the one she felt over Emma's absence. She still had no response, though.

From a distance the tinkling of small bells and the steady, deep beat of a drum announced the first dance.

The music grew louder as the dancers wound their way through the narrow twisting streets until a single long line entered the plaza. The first dance was to be the Turtle Dance, she saw. Bright headdresses of parrot and macaw feathers caught the first rays of the sun, while turtle shell clappers counterpointed the rhythm of the singers and the dancers' feet as they circled the bonfire. She knew the meaning of the dance. As the turtle hibernated all winter, staying inside its shell, awaiting spring, so humans stayed inside during winter, keeping the fire burning, awaiting spring's awakening to new life and new beginnings.

As Claire watched the dancers double back around the bonfire, she came to a sudden understanding. She was like the turtle. With Emma grown up, she had become free to concentrate on herself, her life, yet, like the turtle, she had remained in a kind of hibernation, awaiting the spring that would awaken her to new beginnings and a new life. Spring...in the form of a man, bringing with him a possible new beginning, a new life? A man in whose strong arms a woman could find both comfort and joy? Jack Herrod had told her that he loved her, with no hearts and flowers, no practiced fancy words, no grand gestures. He'd said it with the same naturalness that he used when he fixed gates or wrapped presents. He'd dealt with the problems—and he'd had more than his share—that life delivered with the same sure-handed competence backed by a character like warm granite. She hadn't known him long, but she was old enough to recognize spring; there was no reason to wait for the sake of appearances.

As the rising sun turned the top stories of the ancient pueblo to gold, the dancers began to retreat from the plaza. She turned to look up at him and smiled. "I love you, Jack."

As she watched him walk toward her across her bedroom, his intent clear in his eyes, Claire began reconsidering certain of those appearances, namely her own. Perhaps she should have given that flyer on the staff bulletin board advertising the body-sculpting exercise class a closer read. She had no air-brushed perfection. But she had an excess of nerves to make up for it, she thought ruefully. "Ah...I'm a little out of practice with this." A *little?*

His look was tender. "I know."

He knew? It was that obvious? "Maybe—"

Whatever she had been going to say she forgot as his hands gently framed her face and he kissed her the same way he had the first time—with total concentration and appreciation. Minutes later their clothes had scattered like fallen leaves.

"I'm as clumsy as a damned kid," Jack muttered. When he most wanted finesse, desire was making his every move awkward and rough.

Clumsy! If this was clumsy, she would never survive smooth, Claire thought hazily.

Then finesse and clumsiness became unimportant as instinct and love took over, and bodies and souls fused.

The aftershocks gradually calmed to gentle spasms, but Claire kept her eyes closed, savoring his weight and heat and the wonderful feel of his body against hers. She felt her mouth curve in a smile. Sometimes Santa even brought grown-ups what they asked for.

Poleaxed was the word, Jack decided. Just trying to breathe took all the effort his poor exhausted, abused, ecstatic body could muster. Finally he managed to shift position, to her murmured protest. Propping himself up on an elbow, he grinned at her. "So, would you like to hang out together for the next fifty or sixty years?"

She should have seen it coming, Claire thought, trying desperately not to either close her eyes and groan in embarrassment or laugh in delight. She considered him. "Will you keep on with the romantic gestures?"

He nodded soberly. "I've got tools you haven't even seen yet."

She slanted him a sly leer. "I kind of like the tools I've seen so far."

Laughing, he scooped her into his arms. Lying back, he draped her over his chest. "I've even got a romantic gesture for Mamie."

She looked at him curiously. "What?"

He ran a hand down her back to her hip. "You remember those old bond certificates she had?" She nodded. "When I first saw them, I didn't see any redemption dates, so I did a little checking. It turns out the county had issued those bonds on a call basis, meaning they would call them back in when they had the money to redeem them, paying interest in the meantime. Local governments did that sometimes back around the turn of the century, putting an expiration date on them so that they couldn't collect interest indefinitely in case the owner didn't redeem them when they were called in.''

Claire frowned at him. "But you didn't find any date?" He shook his head, and astonishment began to replace her frown. "You mean..."

He nodded solemnly, his eyes dancing. "The bonds have been compounding interest for almost a hundred years. Instead of the county taking her property, she could take a chunk of the county's."

Claire stared at him for a second, then flung her arms around his neck, strangling him joyously. "Oh, Jack! That's fantastic! Have you told her yet?"

Gently he disengaged her arms enough to answer. "Tomorrow. I thought we could tell her together."

Laughing delightedly, she gave him a huge smile. "What a wonderful Christmas present." He nodded in agreement, but didn't say anything more, and Claire realized what she'd forgotten in the excitement over Mamie's unexpected fortune. Her smile softened as she brushed a kiss over his mouth. "Almost as good as mine." She kissed him again, longer. "I'd love to hang out with you for the next fifty or sixty years," she whispered.

He nodded calmly, then suddenly flipped them over so that she was under him. "I just need to know one thing." He nuzzled her throat as his hands began a leisurely exploration. "What the hell is a doozel?"

* * * * *

These cookies have a number of aliases: butterballs, Russian tea cakes, almond crescents, cocoons, etc. In New Mexico they are *polvorones*—"dust balls" in Spanish. Not a particularly appetizing name but visually descriptive and no doubt given by someone who keeps house like I do. Since the name sounds much nicer and more exotic in Spanish, your family and friends never need know that they're eating dust.

POLVORONES (pole-voe-ROE-ness)

1 cup butter
1/2 cup powdered sugar
1/2 tsp salt
1 cup finely chopped almonds or pecans
1 tbsp vanilla extract
2 cups flour

Cream butter, then cream in sugar and salt until light and fluffy. Add nuts and vanilla, blend in flour gradually and mix thoroughly. Shape into balls or crescents, using a walnut-size lump of dough for each. Bake on ungreased cookie sheet at 325° F for 15-20 minutes, until bottom is just beginning to brown. Cool slightly, then roll in more powdered sugar. Makes about 2 dozen.

—Patricia Gardner Evans

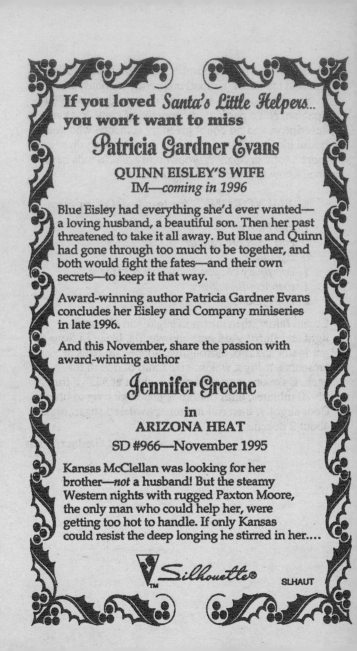

If you loved *Santa's Little Helpers*...
you won't want to miss

Patricia Gardner Evans

QUINN EISLEY'S WIFE
IM—*coming in 1996*

Blue Eisley had everything she'd ever wanted—
a loving husband, a beautiful son. Then her past
threatened to take it all away. But Blue and Quinn
had gone through too much to be together, and
both would fight the fates—and their own
secrets—to keep it that way.

Award-winning author Patricia Gardner Evans
concludes her Eisley and Company miniseries
in late 1996.

And this November, share the passion with
award-winning author

Jennifer Greene

in
ARIZONA HEAT
SD #966—November 1995

Kansas McClellan was looking for her
brother—*not* a husband! But the steamy
Western nights with rugged Paxton Moore,
the only man who could help her, were
getting too hot to handle. If only Kansas
could resist the deep longing he stirred in her....

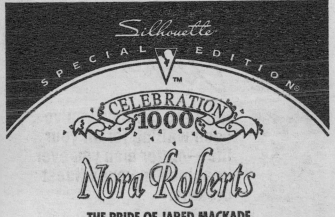

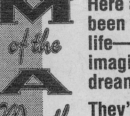

SILHOUETTE® Desire®

ANGELS AND ELVES
by Joan Elliott Pickart

Joan Elliott Pickart brings you her special brand of humor tales of the MacAllister men. For these carefree bachelors, predicting the particulars of the MacAllister babies is much easier than predicting when wedding bells will sound!

In November, Silhouette Desire's *Man of the Month*, Forrest MacAllister, is the reigning Baby Bet Champion and a confirmed "uncle." Until his very pregnant, matchmaking sister introduced him to Jillian Jones-Jenkins, he never would have thought that the next baby he bets on might be his own!

Experience all the laughter and love as a new MacAllister baby is born, and the most unpredictable MacAllister becomes a husband—and father in *Angels and Elves,* book one of THE BABY BET.

In February 1996, Silhouette Special Edition celebrates the most romantic month of the year with FRIENDS, LOVERS...AND BABIES! book two of THE BABY BET.

HEARTBREAKERS

We've got more of the men you love to love in the Heartbreakers lineup this winter. Among them are Linda Howard's Zane Mackenzie, a member of her immensely popular Mackenzie family, and Jack Ramsey, an *Extra*-special hero.

In December—HIDE IN PLAIN SIGHT, by Sara Orwig: Detective Jake Delancy was used to dissecting the criminal mind, not analyzing his own troubled heart. But Rebecca Bolen and her two cuddly kids had become so much more than a routine assignment....

In January—TIME AND AGAIN, by Kathryn Jensen, *Intimate Moments Extra:* Jack Ramsey had broken the boundaries of time to seek Kate Fenwick's help. Only this woman could change the course of their destinies—and enable them both to love.

In February—MACKENZIE'S PLEASURE, by Linda Howard: Barrie Lovejoy needed a savior, and out of the darkness Zane Mackenzie emerged. He'd brought her to safety, loved her desperately, yet danger was never more than a heartbeat away— even as Barrie felt the stirrings of new life growing within her....

INTIMATE MOMENTS®
™ *Silhouette®*

HRTBRK4